BLOODLINE

BY JAMES ROLLINS

BLOODLINE

A Σ SIGMA FORCE NOVEL

JAMES ROLLINS

WILLIAM MORROW

An Imprint of HarperCollinsPublishers

HarperCollins books may be purchased for educational, business, or sales promotional use. For information please write: Special Markets Department, HarperCollins Publishers, 10 East 53rd Street, New York, NY 10022.

FIRST EDITION

Map and interior artwork provided and drawn by Steve Prey. All rights reserved. Used by permission of Steve Prey.

Triple helix drawing by Trish Cramblet. www.lottreps.com.

Library of Congress Cataloging-in-Publication Data has been applied for.

ISBN 978-0-06-178479-8 (hardcover)
ISBN 978-0-06-220305-2 (international edition)

12 13 14 15 16 DIX/RRD 10 9 8 7 6 5 4 3 2 1

To three brothers and three sisters,

Cheryl, Doug, Laurie, Chuck, Billy, and Carrie.

After being in the trenches this past year, it seemed

fitting for us to be together here, too. Love you all.

ACKNOWLEDGMENTS

They say too many cooks in the kitchen is a bad thing. That may apply to the culinary arts, but certainly not the literary arts. Each person mentioned below has made this book better. The first group I hate to lump together, but you all came that way, so what's a guy to do? They are my first readers, my first editors, and some of my best friends: Sally Barnes, Chris Crowe, Lee Garrett, Jane O'Riva, Denny Grayson, Leonard Little, Scott Smith, Penny Hill, Judy Prey, Dave Murray, Will Murray, Caroline Williams, John Keese, Christian Riley, and Amy Rogers. And, as always, a special thanks to Steve Prey for the additional handsome maps and artwork . . . and to Cherei McCarter for all the fodder for great stories! To Scott Brown, M.D., for the medical help (so see, you are in the novel), and Mihir Wanchoo for being there from the beginning. To Carolyn McCray, who finally gets to let her own star shine . . . and David Sylvian for picking up all the pieces and making my digital presence shine. To everyone at HarperCollins for always having my back: Michael Morrison, Liate Stehlik, Seale Ballenger, Danielle Bartlett, Josh Marwell, Lynn Grady, Adrienne di Pietro, Richard Aquan, Tom Egner, Shawn Nicholls, Ana Maria Allessi, Olga Gardner, and Wendy Lee (I'll miss you). Lastly, of course, a special acknowledgment to the four people instrumental to all levels of production: my editor, Lyssa Keusch, and her colleague Amanda Bergeron; and my agents, Russ Galen and Danny Baror. And, as always, I must stress that any and all errors of fact or detail in this book fall squarely on my own shoulders.

Horn of Africa

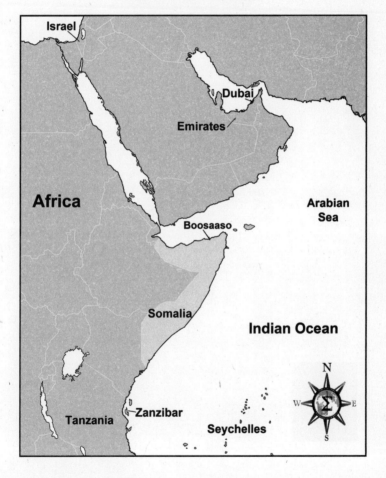

WORDS FROM ASSASSINATED PRESIDENTS

On the existence and threat of modern-day secret societies:

We are opposed around the world by a monolithic and ruthless conspiracy that relies primarily on covert means for expanding its sphere of influence . . . building a tightly knit, highly efficient machine that combines military, diplomatic, intelligence, economic, scientific and political operations.

—JOHN F. KENNEDY, FROM A SPEECH GIVEN AT THE WALDORF-ASTORIA HOTEL ON APRIL 27, 1961

On life and death:

Surely God would not have created such a being as man, with an ability to grasp the infinite, to exist only for a day! No, no, man was made for immortality.

—ABRAHAM LINCOLN

NOTES FROM THE HISTORICAL RECORD

Throughout history, conspiracy theories abound. It is only human nature. We are forever looking for patterns amid chaos, for signs of the invisible puppeteer manipulating the grand scheme of lives, governments, and the path of mankind. Some of these shadowy plotters are cast as villains; others as great benefactors. Some of these secret cabals are based on historical facts; others are mere fanciful fictions; and yet even more are a Gordian knot of the two, woven so inexplicably together that the line between fact and fiction becomes a tangled tapestry of false history.

And for no other organization in history has this stood truer than the infamous Knights Templar.

In the early twelfth century, the order began as a group of nine knights, who swore to protect pilgrims on their way to and from the Holy Lands. From those humble beginnings, a great order would eventually grow in both wealth and power and spread across Europe until even popes and kings feared them. Then, on October 13, 1307, the king of France and the current pope conspired to arrest and disband the order, claiming great atrocities had been committed by the knights, including heresy. In the aftermath of that purge, legends and myths blurred the true fate of the order: stories of lost treasures abounded; tales spread of knights escaping persecution to arrive on the shores of the New World; and some reports even claim that the order still exists today, in secret and under guard, protecting a power that could reshape the world.

But let's set aside such speculations and mythologies and go back to those original *nine* knights. What many do not know is that those nine founding members were all related by blood or marriage, arising from a single family. Eight of them are recorded by name in historical documents. The ninth remains a mystery and a source of much speculation today by historians. Who was this mysterious founding member of an order that would grow in such prominence in history and legend? Why was this last knight never named as plainly as the others?

The answer to that mystery is the beginning of a great adventure.

NOTES FROM THE SCIENTIFIC RECORD

On February 21, 2011, the cover of *Time* magazine declared: *2045, The Year Man Becomes Immortal.* At face value, that might seem a wild claim, but other scientists have made similar statements. Dr. Ronald Klatz, in his book *Advances in Anti-Age Medicine,* wrote:

> Within the next fifty years or so, assuming an individual can avoid becoming the victim of major trauma or homicide, it is entirely possible that he or she will be able to live virtually forever.

We are living in an exciting time when advances in medicine, genetics, technology, and a myriad of other disciplines are opening the newest frontier for mankind: *eternity.*

How will that manifest, what form will it take? Within these pages, you'll discover that answer. The concepts raised in this novel are based on facts, on exhaustive research, going back to studies done by Soviet scientists during the Cold War. But before you turn to that first page, I must make one correction concerning the startling statements made above. They are, in fact, far too *conservative* in their estimates.

For not only is immortality within our reach—*it is already here.*

PROLOGUE

Summer 1134
Holy Lands

They once called her a witch and a whore.

But no longer.

She sat astride a gray destrier as the black-armored warhorse stepped gingerly through the carnage of battle. Bodies littered the fields ahead, Muslim and Christian alike. Her passage stirred the feasting crows and ravens, chasing them up into great black clouds in her wake. Other scavengers—those on two legs—picked through the dead, pulling off boots, yanking out arrows for their points and feathers. A few faces lifted to stare, then quickly turned away again.

She knew what they saw, another knight among the many who fought here. Her breasts were hidden under a padded habergeon and a hauberk of mail. Her dark hair, cropped to her shoulders, shorter than most men's, lay under a conical helmet; her fine features further obscured by a nasal bar. Strapped to the side of her saddle, a double-edged broadsword bumped against her left knee, ringing off the mail chausses that protected her long legs.

Only a few knew she was not a man—and *none* knew she held secrets far darker than her hidden gender.

Her squire waited for her at the edge of a rutted road. The path wound steeply up to an isolated stone keep. The hulking structure, hidden deep within the Naphtali Mountains of Galilee, had no name and looked as if it had been carved out of the hill itself. Beyond its battlements, the red sun sat low on the horizon, obscured by the smoke from campfires and torched fields.

The young squire dropped to a knee as she drew her horse to a halt beside him.

"Is he still there?" she asked.

A nod. Frightened. "Lord Godefroy awaits you ahead."

Her squire refused to look in the direction of the stone-crowned keep. She had no such reluctance. She tilted her helmet up to get a better view.

At long last . . .

She had spent sixteen years—going back to when her uncle founded the Order of the Poor Knights of the Temple of Jerusalem—searching for the impossible. Even her uncle did not understand her request to join the Templars, but her side of the family would not be refused. So she had been given the white mantle of the order and folded in among the original nine, hidden away, as faceless as the helmet she wore, while the order grew around her both in number and prominence.

Others of her family, of her bloodline, continued to manipulate the knightly order from within and without: gathering wealth and knowledge, searching for powerful relics from lost crypts and ancient crèches across Egypt and the Holy Lands. Despite their best planning, they'd certainly had their failures. Just a year ago, they'd missed acquiring the bones of the magi—the relics of the three biblical kings, said to hold the secrets to lost alchemies.

She would not let today mark another failure.

With a snap of the reins, she urged her horse up the rocky path. With each passing step, the number of dead grew as the guardians of the keep put up a final and futile struggle to withstand the assault. Reaching the summit of the hill, she found the gates to the keep broken and splintered, battered apart by a massive steel-shod ram.

A pair of knights guarded the way forward. Both nodded to her. The younger of the two, fresh to the order, had sewn a crimson cross over his heart. Other Templars had begun to take up the same habit, a symbol to mark their willingness to shed their own blood for the cause. The grizzled and pocked older warrior simply wore the traditional white surcoat over his armor, like herself. The only decoration upon their mantles was the crimson blood of the slain.

"Godefroy awaits you in the crypt," the older knight said and pointed beyond the gates to the inner citadel.

She led her destrier through the ruins of the gate and quickly dismounted with a flourish of her mantle. She left her broadsword with her mount, knowing she had no fear of being ambushed by some lone surviving protector of the keep. Lord Godefroy, for all his troubles, was thorough. As testament to his diligence, all across the open courtyard, wooden pikes bore the heads of the last defenders. Their decapitated remains piled like so much firewood along a back wall.

The battle was over.

Only the spoils remained.

She reached a door that opened to shadows. A narrow stair, rough-hewn and cut from the stone of the mountain, led down beneath the keep. The distant orange-red flicker of a torch marked the end of the steps far below. She descended, her footfalls hurrying only at the last.

Could it be true? After so many years . . .

She burst into a long chamber, lined to either side by stone sarcophagi, well over a score of them. Sweeping through, she barely noted the Egyptian writing, lines of symbols hinting at dark mysteries going back before Christ. Ahead, two figures stood bathed in torchlight at the rear of the chamber: one standing, the other on his knees, leaning on a staff to hold himself upright.

She crossed toward them, noting that the last sarcophagus had been pried open, its stone lid cracked on the floor beside it. It seemed somebody had already begun looking for the treasure hidden here. But the violated crypt held nothing but ash and what appeared to be bits of dried leaf and stem.

The disappointment showed on Lord Godefroy's face as she approached the pair. "So you come at last," he said with false cheer.

She ignored the knight. He stood a head taller than she did, though he shared the same black hair and aquiline nose, marking their common ancestry out of southern France, their families distantly related.

She dropped to her knees and stared into the face of the prisoner. His features were tanned to a burnished shade, his skin smooth as supple leather. From under a fall of dark hair, black eyes stared back at her, reflecting the torchlight. Though on his knees, he showed no fear, only a deep welling of sadness that made her want to slap him.

Godefroy drew down beside her, intending to interfere, to try to ingratiate himself into what he must have sensed was of great importance. And though he was one of the few who knew her true identity, he knew nothing of her deeper secrets.

"My lady . . ." he started.

The eyes of the prisoner narrowed at the revelation, fixing her with a harder stare. All trace of sadness drained away, leaving behind a flicker of fear—but it quickly vanished.

Curious . . . does he know of our bloodline, our secrets?

Godefroy interrupted her reverie and continued, "Upon your instructions, we've spent many lives and spilled much blood to find this place hidden by rumor and guarded as much by curses as by infidels—all to find this man and the treasure he guards. Who is he? I have earned such knowledge upon the point of my sword."

She did not waste words on fools. She spoke instead to the prisoner, using an ancient dialect of Arabic. "When were you born?"

Those eyes bore into her, even pushing her back by the sheer force of his will, a buffeting wind of inner strength. He seemed to be judging whether to offer her a lie, but from whatever he found in her face, he recognized the futility of it.

When he spoke, his words were soft but came from a place of great weight. "I was born in Muharram in the Hijri year five-and-ninety."

Godefroy understood enough Arabic to scoff. "The year ninety-five? That would make him over a thousand years old."

"No," she said, more to herself than him, calculating in her head. "His people use a different accounting of years than we do, starting when their prophet Muhammad arrived in Mecca."

"So the man here is not a thousand years old?"

"Not at all," she said, finishing the conversion in her head. "He's only lived *five hundred and twenty* years."

From the corner of her eye, she noted Godefroy turn toward her, aghast.

"Impossible," he said with a tremulous quaver that betrayed the shallow depth of his disbelief.

She never broke from the prisoner's gaze. Within those eyes, she sensed an unfathomable, frightening knowledge. She tried to picture all he had witnessed over the centuries: mighty empires rising and falling, cities thrusting out of the sands only to be worn back down by the ages. How much could he reveal of ancient mysteries and lost histories?

But she was not here to press questions upon him.

And she doubted he would answer them anyway.

Not this man—if he could still be called a *man*.

When next he spoke, it came with a warning, his fingers tightening on his staff. "The world is not ready for what you seek. It is forbidden."

She refused to back down. "That is not for you to decide. If a man is fierce enough to grasp it, then it is his right to claim and possess it."

He stared back at her, his gaze drifting to her chest, to what was hidden beneath hard armor. "So Eve herself believed in the Garden of Eden when she listened to the snake and stole from the Tree of Knowledge."

"Ah," she sighed, leaning closer. "You mistake me. I am not Eve. And it is not the Tree of *Knowledge* I seek—but the Tree of *Life*."

Slipping a dagger from her belt, she quickly stood and drove the blade to its hilt under the prisoner's jaw, lifting him off his knees with her strength of will. In that single thrust, the endless march of centuries came to a bloody halt—along with the danger he posed.

Godefroy gasped, stepping back. "But is this not the man you came so far to find?"

She yanked free the dagger, spraying blood, and kicked the body away. She caught the staff before it fell free from the prisoner's slack fingers.

"It was not the man I sought," she said, "but what he carried."

Godefroy stared at the length of olive wood in her hand. Fresh blood flowed in rivulets down its surface, revealing a faint carving along its length: an intricate weave of serpents and vines, curling around and around the shaft.

"What is it?" the knight asked, his eyes wide.

She faced him fully for the first time—and drove her blade into his left eye. He had seen too much to live. As he fell to his knees, his body wracking itself to death in ghastly heaves upon her dagger's point, she answered his last question, her fingers firm on the ancient wooden rod.

"Behold the Bachal Isu," she whispered to the centuries to come. "Wielded by Moses, carried by David, and borne by the King of Kings, here is the staff of Jesus Christ."

The assassin stared through the rifle's scope and lowered the crosshairs to the profile of President James T. Gant. He double-checked his range—seven hundred yards—and fixed the main targeting chevron of the USMC M40A3 sniper rifle upon the occipital bone behind the man's left ear, knowing a shot there would do the most damage. Festive music and bright laughter from the holiday picnic filtered through his earpiece. He let it all fade into the background as he concentrated on his target, on his mission.

In U.S. history, three presidents had died on the exact same day, on July 4, on the birthday of this country. It seemed beyond mere chance.

Thomas Jefferson, John Adams, and James Monroe.

Today would mark the fourth.

Steadying his breath, Commander Gray Pierce pulled the trigger.

FIRST

PRESENT DAY

1

Gray Pierce pulled into the driveway with a coughing growl of the 1960 Thunderbird's V-8 engine.

He felt like growling himself.

"I thought the plan was to sell this place?" Kenny asked.

Gray's younger brother sat in the passenger seat, his head half out the window, staring up at the craftsman bungalow with the wraparound wooden porch and overhanging gable. It was their family home.

"Not any longer," Gray answered. "And don't mention any of that to Dad. His dementia makes him paranoid enough."

"How is that different from any other day . . . ?" Kenny mumbled sourly under his breath.

Gray glowered at his brother. He'd picked Kenny up at Dulles after a cross-country flight from Northern California. His brother's eyes were red-rimmed from jet lag—or maybe from too many small bottles of gin in first class. At this moment, Kenny reminded Gray of their father, especially with the pall of alcohol on his breath.

He caught his own reflection in the rearview mirror as he pulled the vintage Thunderbird into the family garage. While the two brothers both shared the same ruddy Welsh complexion and dark hair as their father, Gray kept his hair cropped short; Kenny had his tied in a short ponytail that looked too young even for someone still in his late twenties. To make matters worse, he also wore cargo shorts and a loose T-shirt with the logo of a surfing company. Kenny was a software engineer for a company in Palo Alto, and apparently this was his version of business attire.

Gray climbed out of the car, trying his best to push back his irritation with his brother. On the ride here, Kenny had spent the entire time on his cell phone, dealing with business on the other coast. He'd barely shared a word, relegating Gray to the role of chauffeur.

It's not like I don't have my own business to attend, too.

For the past month, Gray had put his life on hold, dealing with the aftermath of the death of their mother and the continuing mental decline of their father. Kenny had come out for the funeral, promising to spend a week helping to get their affairs in order, but after two days, a business emergency drew him back across the country, and everything got dumped back on Gray's shoulders. In some ways, it would have been easier if Kenny had not bothered coming out at all. In his wake, he'd left a disheveled mess of insurance forms and probate paperwork for Gray to clean up.

That changed today.

After a long, heated call, Kenny had agreed to come out at this critical juncture. With their father suffering from advancing Alzheimer's, the sudden death of his wife sent him into a downward spiral. He'd spent the past three weeks in a memory-care unit, but he'd come home last night. And during this transition, Gray needed an extra pair of hands. Kenny had accumulated enough vacation time to be able to come out for a full two weeks. Gray intended to hold him to it this time.

Gray had taken a month off from work himself and was due back at Sigma headquarters in a week. Before that, he needed a few days of downtime to get his own house in order. That's where Kenny came in.

His brother hauled his luggage out of the convertible's trunk, slammed the lid, but kept his palm on the chrome bumper. "And what about Dad's car? We might as well sell it. It's not like he can drive it."

Gray pocketed the keys. The classic Thunderbird—raven black with a red leather interior—was his father's pride and joy. The man had gone to painstaking ends to restore it: tricking it out with a new Holly carburetor, a flame-thrower coil, and an electric choke.

"It stays," he said. "According to Dad's neurologist, it's important to keep his environment as stable and consistent as possible, to maintain a familiar routine. Besides, even if he can't drive it, it'll give him something to tinker with."

Before Kenny could figure out what else to sell of his father's belongings, Gray headed toward the door. He didn't bother to offer to carry his brother's luggage. He'd had enough baggage to deal with lately.

But Kenny wasn't done. "If we're supposed to keep everything the same—to pretend nothing's changed—then what am I doing here?"

Gray swung toward him, balling a fist and tempted to use it. "Because you're still his son—and it's high time you acted like it."

Kenny stared him down. Anger burned in his brother's eyes, further reminding Gray of their father. He'd seen that fury all too often in his dad, especially of late, a belligerence born of dementia and fear. Not that such anger was new. His father had always been a hard man, a former oil worker out of Texas until an industrial accident took most of his left leg and all of his pride, turning an oilman into a housewife. Raising two boys while his spouse went to work had been hard on him. To compensate, he had run the household like a boot camp. And Gray, as stubborn as his father, had always pushed the envelope, a born rebel. Until at last, at eighteen years of age, he had simply packed his bags and joined the army.

It was his mother who finally drew them all back together, the proverbial glue of the family.

And now she was gone.

What were they to do without her?

Kenny finally hauled up his bag, shouldered past Gray, and mumbled words he knew would cut like rusted barbed wire: "At least I didn't get Mom killed."

A month ago, that gut-punch would have dropped Gray to his knees. But after mandatory psychiatric sessions—not that he hadn't missed a few—his brother's accusation only left him iron-hard, momentarily rooted in place. A booby trap meant for Gray had taken out his mother. *Collateral damage* was the phrase the psychiatrist had used, seeking to blunt the guilt.

But the funeral had been a closed casket.

Even now, he could not face that pain head-on. The only thing that kept him putting one foot in front of the other was the determination to expose and destroy the shadowy organization behind that cold-blooded murder.

And that's what he did: he turned and took one step, then another.

It was all he could do for now.

10:58 P.M. SCT
Off the Seychelles archipelago

Something woke her in the night aboard the anchored yacht.

Instinctively, Amanda slid a hand over her swollen belly, taking immediate personal inventory. Had it been a cramp? In her third trimester, that was always her first worry, a maternal reflex to protect her unborn child. But she felt nothing painful in her abdomen, just the usual pressure on her bladder.

Still, after two miscarriages, the panicky flutter in her heart refused to calm. She tried to reassure herself that the other two babies—a boy and a girl—had been lost during her *first* trimester.

I'm crossing my thirty-sixth week. Everything is fine.

She lifted up an elbow. Her husband snored softly beside her on the queen-size bed in the yacht's main stateroom, his dark skin so stark against the white satin pillow. She took comfort in Mack's muscular presence, in the masculine bruise of black stubble across his cheek and chin. He was her Michelangelo *David* chiseled out of black granite. Yet, she could not escape the twinge of unease as her finger hovered over his bare shoulder, hesitant to wake him but wanting those strong arms around her.

Her parents—whose aristocratic family went back generations in the Old South—had only approved the marriage with the strained graciousness of modern sensibilities. But in the end, the union served the family. She was blond and blue-eyed, raised in the world of cotillions and privilege; he was black-haired and dark of skin and eye, hardened by a rough childhood on the streets of Atlanta. The unlikely couple became a poster for familial tolerance, trotted out when needed. But that poster of a happy family was missing one key element: a child.

After a year of failing to conceive—due to an issue with her husband's fertility—they'd resorted to in vitro fertilization with donor sperm. On the third try, after two miscarriages, they'd finally had success.

Her palm found her belly again, protective.

A boy.

And that's when the trouble had begun. A week ago, she had received a cryptic note, warning her to flee, not to tell anyone in her family. The letter hinted at *why,* but offered only a few details, yet it was enough to convince her to run.

A loud thump echoed down from the deck overhead. She sat upright, ears straining.

Her husband rolled onto his back, rubbing an eye blearily. "What is it, babe?"

She shook her head and held up a palm to quiet him. They'd taken such precautions, covering every step. They'd chartered a series of private aircraft under a chain of falsified papers and itineraries, landing a week ago on the other side of the world, at an airstrip on the tiny island of Assumption, part of the archipelago of the Seychelles. Hours after landing, they'd immediately set out in a private yacht, sailing amid the chain of islands that spread out in an emerald arc across the azure seas. She had wanted to be isolated, far from prying eyes—yet close enough to the Seychelles' capital city of Victoria in case there was any trouble with the pregnancy.

Since arriving, only the captain and his two crew members had ever seen their faces, and none of them knew their true names.

It seemed the perfect plan.

Muffled voices reached her. She could not make out any words, but heard the harsh threat—then a gunshot, as bright and loud as the strike of a cymbal.

It set her heart to pounding.

Not now. Not when we're this close.

Mack burst out of the sheets, wearing only his boxers. "Amanda, stay here!" He pulled open the top drawer of the bedside table and hauled out a large black automatic pistol, his service weapon from his years as a Charleston police officer. He pointed to the rear of the stateroom. "Hide in the bathroom."

Amanda gained her feet, bloodless and weak with terror, wobbling under the weight of her gravid belly.

Mack dashed to the door, checked the peephole. Satisfied, he opened the door enough to slip out and closed it silently behind him—but not before giving one last command. "Lock it."

Amanda obeyed, then searched the room for any weapon at all. She settled for a small knife used to carve the fresh fruit placed in their cabin each morning. The handle was still sticky from papaya juice. With blade in hand, she retreated to the bathroom but stopped at the threshold. She could not go inside. She refused to be trapped inside such a tight space. The tiny stateroom's head could not contain the enormity of her fear.

More gun blasts rang out—amid shouts and curses.

She sank to her knees, clutching the knife with one hand, supporting her belly with the other. Her anxiety reached the child inside. She felt a small kick.

"I won't let them hurt you," she whispered to her boy.

Overhead, footsteps pounded back and forth.

She stared upward, trying to pierce through the floors to the starlit deck. What was happening? How many were up there?

Then a furtive scrabbling sounded at her door—followed by a faint knock.

She hurried forward and placed an eye to the peephole. Mack nodded back at her, then glanced quickly back up the passageway. Had he found a way off the yacht—or out of desperation simply come back to defend her?

With numb fingers, she fumbled the lock open and began to pull the door, only to have it kicked wide. She stumbled back in shock. A tall, bare-chested black man stalked into the room—but it wasn't Mack.

He held Mack's head in his right hand, gripping it by the throat.

Shiny blood poured down his forearm from the severed neck. In his other hand, he clutched an equally bloody machete. He smiled widely, showing white teeth like a shark, plainly amused by his joke.

She retreated in horror, forgetting her tiny blade.

Another figure stepped around the monster. A pale man in a perfectly tailored white suit. The only color to him was his black hair and a thin mustache above even thinner lips. He was tall enough that he had to bow himself into the room. He also smiled, but apologetically, as if embarrassed by the exuberance of his companion.

He spoke a few sharp words in some African dialect, clearly chastising his companion.

With a shrug, the other tossed her husband's head upon the bed.

"It's time to go," the suited man ordered her in a genteel British accent, as if inviting her to a party.

She refused to move—couldn't move.

The Brit sighed and motioned to his companion.

He came forward, roughly grabbed her elbow, and dragged her out the door. The Brit followed them across the short passageway and up the ladder to the stern deck.

There, she found only more horror and chaos.

The captain and his two crewmates, along with a pair of the assailants, lay sprawled in pools of blood. The attackers had been shot; the yacht's crew hacked, dismembered by the sheer force of the brutality.

The surviving assailants gathered atop the deck or off in a scarred boat tied to the starboard rail. A handful scoured the yacht, hauling out cases of wine, bagfuls of supplies, stripping anything of value. They were all black-skinned, some bearing tribal scarring, many no older than boys. Weapons bristled among them: rusty machetes, antique-looking automatic rifles, and countless pistols.

Pirates.

Under the moonlight, freshened by the evening's southeasterly trade winds, her mind cleared enough to allow despair and bitter guilt to creep in. Out here in the Seychelles, she had thought they were far enough away from the Horn of Africa to be safe from the modern-day pirates who hunted those waters.

A dreadful mistake.

She was shoved toward the moored boat, accompanied by the Brit. She had read somewhere in her father's briefings about how a few European expatriates had taken to aiding and financing the profitable new industry of piracy.

She stared at the British man, wondering how he had managed to avoid getting a single drop of blood on his pristine suit amid all this carnage.

He must have noted her attention and turned to her as they reached the starboard rail.

"What do you want with me?" she asked, fixing him with a hard stare, suddenly glad that all the papers aboard hid her true identity. "I'm nobody."

The Brit's gaze lowered from her steely resolve—but not out of shame or remorse. "It is not *you* we want." He stared at her belly. "It's your baby."

7:00 P.M. EST
Takoma Park, Maryland

Balancing a bag of groceries on his hip, Gray pulled open the screened back door to his family's home. The smell of a baking pie, rich in cinnamon, struck him first. On his way back from the gym, he got a text from Kenny to fetch some French vanilla ice cream and a few other odds and ends needed for tonight's dinner—the first family dinner since the tragic loss of their mother.

A glance at the stove revealed a large pot of bubbling Bolognese sauce; by the sink, a drying bowl of spaghetti in a strainer. A hissing pop drew his gaze back to the pot. Only now did he note the vigorous boil to the sauce. Unattended and forgotten, red sauce roiled over the lip, dribbled down the sides, and sizzled into the gas burner.

Something was wrong.

That was confirmed when a loud bellow erupted from the next room: *"WHERE'S MY KEYS!"*

Gray dropped the groceries on the counter, turned off the stovetop, and headed to the living room.

"SOMEONE'S STEALING MY CAR!"

Passing through the dining room, Gray joined the fracas in the living room. Overstuffed furniture was positioned around a central stone hearth, cold and dark at the moment. His father looked skeletal in the recliner by the picture window. He'd once filled that same seat, commanding the room. Now he was a frail shadow of his former self.

Still, he remained strong. He attempted to push out of the chair, but Kenny held down his shoulders. He was assisted by a petite woman with a brownish-gray bob, dressed in blue scrubs. Down on one knee, she held his father's hand and urged him to be calm.

Mary Benning was an R.N. at the hospital's memory-care unit. During his stay there, his father had taken a shine to her. Gray was able to hire her away, to serve as a night nurse here at the house, to be on hand when his father had the most trouble. The plan had been for Kenny to keep an eye on Dad during the day, until Gray and Mary could interview and hire a day nurse to cover a full twenty-four-hour shift. It would be expensive, but Director Crowe had arranged adequate compensation, a death benefit, to help cover the costs and keep Gray's father in his own house.

"Harriet! Let me go!" His father yanked his hand free of Mary's, coming close to elbowing Kenny in the nose.

The nurse kept a hand on his knee and gave it a squeeze of reassurance. "Jack, it's me. Mary."

His eyes found hers, a confused look passed over his face, then he sagged as memory washed back over him.

Mary glanced at Gray. "Your father caught you pulling up with the groceries. Saw the Thunderbird. Just got a little panicked and confused. He'll be fine."

Kenny straightened, a stricken look on his face. He'd not really seen Dad get like this before. Shook up, he stumbled away.

The motion drew his father's attention. His eyes got huge. "Kenny, what're you doing here?"

Kenny didn't know what to say, still stunned by the Swiss cheese that was his father's memory.

Mary covered for him, not hiding the truth, only patting his knee. "Jack, he's been here all day."

His father searched their faces, then leaned back in his chair. "Oh, yeah, that's right . . . I remember . . ."

But did he? Or was he only acquiescing in an attempt to feign normalcy?

Kenny shared a glance with Gray, glassy with shock.

Welcome to my world.

"I'd better get back to finishing your dinner," Mary said, standing and dusting off her knee.

"And I'd better finish unpacking," Kenny said, seeking a hasty retreat.

"Good idea and wash up," his father ordered with an echo of his former bluster. "Your room's up—"

"I haven't forgotten where it is," Kenny cut him off, blind to the callousness of such a remark to someone suffering from Alzheimer's.

But his dad merely nodded, satisfied.

As Kenny stepped away, his father finally seemed to notice Gray standing there. The confusion on his face faded, but a stab of old anger took its place. It had taken his father almost two weeks to finally acknowledge and ultimately remember the death of his wife, so, to his mind, the wound was still raw. He also knew the source of that loss. *That* he always remembered. There had been many bad days in the intervening weeks, but what could either of them do? No words could bring her back.

A knock at the door startled them all. Gray tensed, expecting the worst.

Kenny, already headed to the front stairs, opened the door.

A lithe figure stood out on the porch, dressed in black leather and a loose motorcycle jacket over a maroon blouse. She carried a helmet under one arm.

The gloominess of the day lifted at the sight of her as Gray headed to the door. "Seichan, what are you doing here?"

His father interrupted. "Don't leave the lady standing on the stoop, Kenny!" He waved the visitor inside. He might be losing his memory, but he knew a handsome woman when one landed on his doorstep.

"Thank you, Mr. Pierce." Seichan entered, slipping inside, moving with the leonine grace of a jungle cat, all sinew, muscles, and long curves. She cast an appraising glance toward Kenny as she stepped past him—whatever she saw there, she found lacking.

Her eyes found Gray's face next and visibly hardened—not in anger, more like protection. They'd barely spoken since they'd shared a kiss and a promise three weeks ago. The pledge was not a romantic one, only the assurance that she'd work alongside him to expose those who had a hand in his mother's murder.

Still, Gray remembered the softening of those lips.

Was there more to that promise, something yet unspoken?

Before he could dwell on it further, his father pointed to the table. "We're just about to sit down to dinner. Why don't you join us?"

"That's very kind," Seichan said stiffly, "but I won't be staying long. I just need a word with your son."

Those almond-shaped eyes—marking her Eurasian heritage—fixed on Gray with plain intent.

Something was up.

Seichan was a former assassin for the same shadowy group responsible for his mother's death, an international criminal organization called the Guild. Its real identity and purpose remained unknown, even to its own agents. The organization operated through individual cells around the world, each running independently, none having the complete picture. Seichan had eventually turned against it, recruited by Director Crowe to serve as a double agent until her subterfuge was exposed. Now—hunted both by her former employers and by foreign intelligence agencies for her past crimes—she was Gray's partner and his responsibility.

And maybe something more.

Gray stepped close to her. "What's up?"

She kept her voice low. "I got a call from Director Crowe. Came straight here. There's been a kidnapping off the Seychelles by Somali pirates. A high-value American target. Painter wanted to know if you were up for a mission."

Gray frowned. Why was Sigma involved with a simple kidnapping? There were plenty of policing and maritime agencies that could attend to such a crime. Sigma Force—made up of Special Forces soldiers who had been retrained in various scientific disciplines—was a covert wing for DARPA, the Defense Advanced Research Projects Agency. Sigma teams were sent out into the world to protect against global threats, not to address the kidnapping of a single American.

Seichan must have read the suspicion in his face. Her eyes bore into his. She plainly knew more but was unable to speak freely in front of the others. Something big was happening. The realization set his heart to beating harder.

"The matter is time sensitive," she added. "If you're coming, there's a jet already fueling, and Kowalski is on his way to pick us up. We can swing by your apartment on the way out. Otherwise, we'll be briefed en route."

Gray glanced at the chair by the cold hearth. His father overheard their talk, his gaze fixed to his son's face.

"Go," his father said. "Do your job. I've got enough help here."

Gray took comfort in that gruff permission, praying it represented some small measure of forgiveness by his father. But his next words, spoken with a harsh bitterness, dashed such hope.

"Besides, the less I see of your face right now . . . the better."

Gray backed a step. Seichan took his elbow, as if ready to catch him. But it was the heat of her palm, more than anything, that steadied him, the reassurance of human contact—like that kiss weeks ago.

Mary had stepped into the room, drying her hands on a towel. She'd also heard those harsh words and gave Gray a sympathetic look. "I've got things covered here. You take some time for yourself."

He silently thanked her and allowed Seichan to guide him toward the door. Gray felt the need to share some parting farewell with his father. The desire burned painfully in his chest, but he had no words to voice it.

Before he knew it, he found himself out on the front porch. He halted at the top step and took in a deep, shuddering breath.

"Are you okay?" Seichan asked.

He ran his fingers through his hair. "I'll have to be."

Still, she continued to search his face, as if seeking a truer answer.

Before she could find it, the squeal of rubber on the pavement announced the arrival of his transportation. They both turned as a black SUV came to a hard stop. The window rolled down, allowing a pall of cigar smoke to waft out. The shaved head of a gorilla followed, chewing on a stump of a stogie.

"You coming or what?" Kowalski called hoarsely.

As much as the man aggravated him, Gray had never been happier to see his brutish teammate. He headed down the steps, only to have Kenny come rushing out after him, blocking his way.

"You can't leave now. What am I supposed to do?"

Gray pointed back at the house. "It's your turn. What do you think I've been doing all this time?"

He shoved past his sputtering brother and crossed toward the waiting SUV and Seichan's parked motorcycle.

She kept beside him, slipping on her helmet.

"Who else has been assigned to us?" he asked.

"We've been ordered to pick up another two teammates, local assets already in the region, with unique skills to help us on this mission."

"Who are they?"

She offered a ghost of a smile as she snapped down her helmet's visor. Her words echoed out from inside, darkly amused.

"I hope you've had your rabies shots."

2

The low growl warned him.

Already on edge, Tucker Wayne flattened against the brick wall of the narrow street and slid into the deeper shadows of a doorway. An hour ago, he noticed someone following him, watching from afar. He had managed to lose the tail quickly in the labyrinth of alleyways and crooked streets that made up this crumbling section of Zanzibar.

Who had found him?

He pressed his back against a carved wooden door. He intended to stay lost, undiscoverable. He had been adrift in the world for the past three years, now one year shy of his thirtieth birthday. Two weeks ago, he had reached the archipelago of Zanzibar, a string of sun-baked islands off the eastern coast of Africa. The name alone—*Zanzibar*—conjured up another time, a land of mystery and mythology. It was a place to disappear, to live unseen, and where few questions were asked.

People knew better than to be curious.

Still, he often drew second glances here, not because he was white. The ancient port of Zanzibar remained the crossroads for people of every race and color. And after a full year traveling through Africa, his skin was burned as dark as that of any of the local merchants hawking wares in the spice markets of old Stone Town. And he certainly struck a tall figure, muscular—more quarterback than linebacker—though there remained a hardness to his eyes that made any curious glance toward him skirt quickly away.

Instead, what attracted the most attention to him was something else, someone else. Kane brushed up against his thigh—silent now, with hackles still raised. Tucker rested a hand on his dog's side, not to calm him but ready to signal his partner if necessary. And that's what they were. *Partners*. Kane was an extension of himself, a disembodied limb.

While the dog looked like a hard-bodied, compact German shepherd, he was actually a Belgian shepherd dog, called a Malinois. His fur was black and tan, but mostly black, a match to his dark eyes. Under his palm, Tucker felt Kane's muscles tense.

Half a block away, a thin shape burst around the next corner, careening in a panic. In his haste, he collided off the far wall and rebounded down the street, glancing frequently over his shoulder. Tucker sized him up in a breath and weighed any danger.

Early twenties, maybe late teens, a mix of Asian and Indian, his eyes wide with terror, his limbs and face sickly gaunt—from addiction, from malnourishment?

The runner clutched his right side, failing to stanch a crimson bloom from seeping through his white shift. The scent of fresh blood must have alerted Kane, along with the panicked tread of those bare feet.

Tucker prepared to step out of the shadowed doorway, to go to the young man's aid—but the pressure against his legs increased, pinning him in place.

A heartbeat later, the reason became clear. Around the same corner stalked a trio of large men, African, with tribal tattoos across their faces. They carried machetes and spread to either side of the empty street with the clear skill of experienced hunters.

Their target also noted their arrival—igniting his already frightened flight into a full rout—but blood loss and exhaustion had taken their toll. Within a few steps, the victim tripped and sprawled headlong across the street. Though he struck the cobbles hard, he didn't make a sound, not a whimper or a cry, simply defeated.

That, more than anything, drew Tucker out of hiding.

That, and something his grandfather had drilled into him: *In the face of inhumanity, a good man* reacts—*but a great one* acts.

Tucker tapped three fingers against his dog's side, the signal plain.

Defend.

Kane leaped over the prone body of the young man and landed in a crouch on the far side, tail high, teeth bared, growling. The shepherd's sudden appearance caused all three attackers to stop in shock, as if some demon djinn had materialized before them.

Tucker used the distraction to fold out of the shadows and close upon the nearest of the three men. In a swift capture of wrist, followed by an elbow strike to the chin, the machete ended up in Tucker's grip. He flat-handed the man away as the second assailant wielded his blade in a round-house swing. Rather than leaping clear, Tucker lunged forward, entering the man's guard. He caught the deadly arm under his own and snaked his hand fully around the limb and immobilized it. With his other arm, he slammed the butt-end of the steel machete into the man's nose.

Bone cracked; blood spurted.

The man went limp, but Tucker held him upright by his trapped arm.

From the corner of his eye, he saw the third and largest opponent back away two steps and free a pistol. Tucker swung around, using his captured assailant's body as a shield as shots rang out. It proved a meager defense at such close range. One of the rounds blasted through his captive's neck, grazing Tucker's shoulder.

Then a scream bellowed.

Tucker shoved the body aside and saw Kane latched onto the shooter's wrist, the dog's fangs digging deep. The pistol clattered to the street. The man's eyes were round with panic as he tried to shake the shepherd loose. Blood and slather flew.

Only then did the huge African remember the machete in his other hand. He lifted it high, ready to hack at the dog.

"Release!" Tucker cried out.

The command was barely off his lips when Kane obeyed, letting go and dropping back on the street. But the man continued his downward swing at the dog's neck with a savage bellow. Kane could not get out of the way in time.

Tucker was already moving.

Heart pounding, he dove for the abandoned pistol and scooped it up. He shoulder-rolled to bring the weapon up—but he was too slow.

The machete flashed in the sunlight.

A gunshot *cracked* loudly.

The man crumpled backward, half his skull shattering away. The blade flew away harmlessly. Tucker stared at his pistol. The shot had *not* come from his weapon.

Up the street, a new trio appeared. Two men and a woman. Though dressed in street clothes, they all had the stamp of military about them. The leader in the center held a smoking SIG Sauer.

"See to him." He pointed to the bleeding young man on the ground. His voice had a slight Texas accent. "Get him to a local hospital and we'll rendezvous back at the evac point."

Despite the concern about the injured man, the leader's gaze never unlocked from Tucker's eyes. From the hard contours of his face, the close-cropped black hair that had gone a bit lanky, and the stony edge to his storm-gray eyes, he was definitely military.

Likely *ex*-military.

Not good.

The leader crossed over to him, ignoring Kane's wary growl. He offered a hand to help Tucker up.

"You're a difficult man to find, Captain Wayne."

Tucker bit back any surprise and ignored the offered hand. He stood on his own. "You were the ones following me. Earlier this morning."

"And you lost us." A hard twinkle of amusement brightened the man's eyes. "Not an easy thing to do. That alone proves you're the man we need."

"Not interested."

He turned, but the man stepped in front of him and blocked the way. A finger pointed at his chest, which only managed to irritate him further.

"Listen for one minute," the man said, "then you're free to go."

Tucker stared down at the finger. The only reason he didn't reach out and break it was that the man had saved Kane's life a moment ago. He owed him that much—and perhaps even a minute of his time.

"Who are you?" he asked.

The offending finger turned into an open palm, inviting a handshake. "Commander Gray Pierce. I work for an organization called Sigma."

Tucker scowled. "Never heard of it. That makes you what? Defense contractors, mercenaries?" He made his disdain for that last word plain.

That dark twinkle grew brighter as the other lowered his arm. "No. We work under the auspices of DARPA."

Tucker frowned, but curiosity kept him listening. DARPA was the Defense Department's research-and-development administration. What the hell was going on here?

"Perhaps we can discuss this in a quieter location," the commander said.

By now, the man's partners had gathered up the wounded young man, shouldered him between them, and were headed down the street. Faces had begun to peer out of windows or to peek from behind cracked-open doors. Other figures hovered at the corners. Zanzibar often turned a blind eye to most offenses, but the gunfire and bloodshed would not be ignored for long. As soon as they left, the bodies would be looted of anything of value, and any inquiries would be met with blank stares.

"I know a place," Tucker said and led the way.

6:44 P.M.

Gray sipped a hot tea spiced with cardamom. He sat with Tucker Wayne on a rooftop deck overlooking the Indian Ocean. Across the waters, the triangular sails of old wooden dhows mixed with cargo ships and a smattering of tourist yachts. For the moment, they had the hotel's tiny restaurant to themselves.

At the foot of the building, a small spice market rang and bustled, wafting up with a mélange of nutmeg, cinnamon, vanilla, cloves, and countless other spices that had once lured sultans to this island and had fueled an active slave-trading industry. The island had exchanged hands many times, which was evident in its unique blend of Moorish, Middle Eastern, Indian, and African traditions. Around every corner, the city changed faces and remained impossible to categorize.

The same could be said for the stranger who was seated across the narrow table from him. Gray placed his cup of tea onto a cracked saucer. A heavy-bodied fly, drawn by the sweet tea, came lumbering down and landed on the table. It crawled toward his cup.

Gray swatted at it—but before his palm could strike the table, fingers caught his wrist, stopping him.

"Don't," Tucker said, then gently waved the fly off before returning to his thousand-yard stare out to sea.

Gray rubbed his wrist and watched the fly, oblivious to its salvation, buzz lazily away.

Tucker finally cleared his throat. "What do you want with me?"

Gray focused back on the matter at hand. He had read the former army ranger's dossier en route to the Horn of Africa. Tucker was a superb dog handler, testing through the roof in regards to emotional empathy, which helped him bond with his subjects, sometimes too deeply. A psych evaluation attributed such a response to early-childhood trauma. Raised in North Dakota, he had been orphaned when his parents had been killed by a drunk driver when he was a toddler, leaving him in the care of his grandfather, who had a heart attack when Tucker was thirteen. From there, he'd been dumped into foster care until he petitioned for early emancipation at seventeen and joined the armed services. With such a chaotic, unstable upbringing, he seemed to have developed an affinity for animals more than humans.

Still, Gray sensed there was more to the man than just psychiatric evaluations and test scores. At his core, he remained a mystery. Like *why* he had abruptly left the service, disappearing immediately after being discharged, leaving behind a uniform full of medals, including a Purple Heart, earned after one of the nastiest firefights in Afghanistan—Operation Anaconda at Takur Ghar.

Gray cut to the chase as time was running out. "Captain Wayne, during your military career, your expertise was extraction and rescue. Your commanding officer claimed there was none better."

The man shrugged.

"You and your dog—"

"Kane," Tucker interrupted. "His name's Kane."

A furry left ear pricked at his master's voice. The small shepherd lay sprawled on the floor, looking drowsy, inattentive, but Gray knew better. His muzzle rested against the toe of Tucker's boot, ready for any signal from his partner. Gray had read Kane's dossier, too. The military war dog had a vocabulary of a thousand words, along with the knowledge of a hundred hand gestures. The two were bound together more intimately than any husband and wife—and together, with the dog's heightened senses and ability to maneuver in places where men could not, the two were frighteningly efficient in the field.

Gray needed that expertise.

"There's a mission," he said. "You would be well paid."

"Sorry. There's not enough gold in Fort Knox."

Gray had prepared for this attitude, readied for this eventuality. "Perhaps not, but when you left the service, you stole government property."

Tucker faced him, his eyes going diamond-hard. In that gaze, Gray read the necessity to speak warily, to play the one card he had with great care.

Gray continued, "It costs hundreds of thousands of dollars and countless man-hours to train a war-service dog." He dared not even glance toward Kane; he kept his gaze fixed on Tucker.

"Those were *my* man-hours," Tucker answered darkly. "I trained both Kane and Abel. And look what happened to Abel. This time around, it wasn't Kane who killed Abel."

Gray had read the brutal details in the files and avoided that minefield. "Still, Kane is government property, military hardware, a skilled combat tracker. Complete this mission and he is yours to keep, free and clear."

Disgust curled a corner of Tucker's lip. "No one owns Kane, commander. Not the U.S. government. Not Special Forces. Not even me."

"Understood, but that's our offer."

Tucker glared at him for a long breath—then abruptly leaned back, crossing his arms, his posture plain. He was not agreeing, only willing to listen. "Again. What do you need me for?"

"An extraction. A rescue."

"Where?"

"In Somalia."

"Who?"

Gray sized up his opponent. The detail he was about to reveal was known only to a handful of people high in the government. It had shocked him when he'd first learned the truth. If word should somehow reach her captors—

"Who?" Tucker pressed.

Kane must have sensed his partner's growing agitation and let out a low rumble, voicing his own complaint.

Gray answered them both. "We need your help in rescuing the president's daughter."

3

Now the real work could start.

On the lowest level of the West Wing, Director Painter Crowe waited for the Situation Room to clear. The whole process was a carefully orchestrated dance of power: who left first, who acknowledged whom, who exited together or alone.

It made his head spin.

Painter had spent the entire three-hour-long strategy session seated outside the inner circle of the White House. The top-tier officials took posts in the upholstered leather chairs clustered around the main conference table; that included the White House chief of staff, the national security advisor, the head of Homeland Security, the secretary of defense, along with a handful of others. It was a closed meeting: no assistants, no deputies, no secretaries, only the top brass. Not even the Situation Room's around-the-clock watch team was allowed admittance.

The secrets discussed here were restricted to as few ears as possible.

At the start of the meeting, Painter had been introduced as a representative of DARPA, which raised a few eyebrows, especially the gray ones of the defense secretary. Dressed in a conservative suit, Painter was a decade younger than anyone here, his dark hair blemished only by a single lock of white hair, tucked like a feather behind one ear, heightening his mixed Native American heritage.

No one questioned why the president had summoned Painter to this closed-door meeting. Few of them even knew about Sigma's existence, let alone its involvement here.

And that was the way the president wanted it.

So, Painter had sat silently in one of the lower-tier chairs away from the main table, observing, taking a few notes, both mental and typed into his laptop.

President James T. Gant had called everyone into the morning's briefing to get an update on the status of his kidnapped twenty-five-year-old daughter, Amanda Gant-Bennett. It had been twenty hours since the midnight attack on her yacht. The boat's captain had managed to get out an S.O.S. on his marine radio, even disabled the engines, before the raiders boarded the boat, slaying all on board, including the woman's husband. Gruesome pictures of the aftermath had been shown on several of the video panels on the walls.

Painter had studied the president's expressions as those images flashed past: the pained pinch at the corners of his eyes, the hardening of his jaw muscles, the pale cast to his face. It all seemed genuine, marking the terror of a father for a lost child.

But certain details made no sense.

Like *why* his daughter had been traveling under a fake passport.

That mystery alone cost them critical hours in the search for the missing girl. Responding to the S.O.S., the Seychelles Coast Guard had immediately reported the pirate attack, detailing that American citizens had been involved, but it was only after fingerprints had been lifted from the yacht's stateroom that a red flag had been raised in the States, identifying the victims as the president's daughter and her husband.

They'd lost precious hours because of the confusion.

And it could cost the girl her life.

James Gant stood at the door to the Situation Room and shook the hand of the last man to leave. It was a two-handed shake, as intimate as a hug. "Thanks, Bobby, for twisting the NRO's arm to get that satellite moved so fast."

Bobby was the secretary of state, Robert Lee Gant, the president's older brother. He was clean-shaven, white-haired, with hazel-green eyes, a distinguished elder statesman, sixty-six years of age. No one questioned that he'd properly earned his position—even pundits from the other party wouldn't raise the charge of nepotism for this cabinet-post assignment. Robert Gant had served three administrations, on both sides of the political divide. He'd been an ambassador to Laos in the late eighties and was considered instrumental in reopening diplomatic ties with both Cambodia and Vietnam in the nineties.

And now he served his younger brother with equal aplomb.

"Don't worry, Jimmy. The NRO will have a satellite in geosynchronous orbit above the Somali coastline within the hour. I'll make sure no stone is left unturned. We'll find her."

The president nodded, but he seemed unconvinced by his brother's promise.

As the secretary of state exited, Painter found himself alone with the leader of the free world. The president ran a hand through his salt-and-pepper hair, then rubbed the palm over the rough stubble on his chin. The man hadn't slept since word had reached him. He still wore the same clothes, only shedding the jacket and rolling up the sleeves of his shirt. He stood for a moment, straight-backed, lost in his own thoughts—then he finally sagged and pointed to another door.

"Let's get out of this damned woodshed," he said, using the nickname for the Situation Room. With the departure of his executive team, his Carolina drawl grew thicker. "My briefing room's right next door."

Painter followed him into a more intimate chamber. Another conference table filled the room, but it was smaller, abutting against a wall with two video screens.

The president dropped into one of the seats with a heavy sigh, as if the weight of the entire world rested on his shoulders. And, Painter imagined, sometimes it did. Only this day was worse.

"Take a seat, director."

"Thank you, Mr. President."

"Call me Jimmy. All my friends do. And as of this moment, you're my *best* friend, because you have the *best* chance of finding my girl and grandson."

Painter sat down, slowly, warily, feeling some of that weight of the world settle on his own shoulders. That was the other concern. Amanda was pregnant, in her third trimester.

So what was she doing in the Seychelles, traveling under false papers?

The president's ice-blue eyes bore into him. The force of his charisma was like a stiff wind in the face. "In the past, Sigma saved my life."

And they had. It was one of the reasons Painter had been summoned by the president to participate in this search.

"I need another miracle, director."

At least the man understood the gravity of the situation. For now, the Somali pirates had no idea whom they'd kidnapped. As far as they knew, Amanda was just another American hostage. But if they should ever learn her true identity, they could panic and kill her, dump her body in the closest crocodile-infested river, and wash their hands of the situation. Or they'd hide her so well, bury her in some godforsaken hole, that any hope of rescue would be impossible until their demands were met—and even then she might be murdered. The head of Homeland had offered a third, chilling possibility this morning: that she'd be sold to some hostile government, used as a pawn to leverage some concession from the U.S. government.

So, the goal was clear: *Find Amanda before the kidnappers learned the truth.*

"What's your take on this morning's briefing?" the president asked.

"Your team has the larger picture covered. I wouldn't do anything differently. Move a fast-response team into the region, be ready to strike at a moment's notice. Coordinate with CIA assets across the Horn of Africa. But until we get a new satellite feed of the Somali coast, we're operating blind."

In cross-referencing the time of the attack with the logs of satellites passing over the Indian Ocean, they'd managed to download a fleeting view of the actual kidnapping. The resolution had been poor, but they could make out the yacht and the raiding vessel. It had fled east after the attack, heading for the African coast. But unfortunately, within an hour, the ship had passed out of satellite range, so the exact location where it made landfall was unknown. It could be anywhere along the East Africa coast, but Somalia—notorious for its rampant piracy—was the most probable base of operations. A new National Reconnaissance Office satellite was being commandeered and shifted to help search for the missing ship along that rocky coastline.

But that wasn't their best hope.

Painter continued, "Sir, we need boots on the ground there. Our highest probability for a success lies in a surgical extraction, to drop in a small search-and-rescue team under the radar."

"Got it. If we go in all shock-and-awe on their asses, they'll know their captive is important."

"And they'll bury her." Painter regretted his choice of words as soon as they passed his lips.

James Gant's face went ashen, but as a mark of the man's fortitude, he waved for Painter to go on.

"The team I told you about is already in the area. I'll continue to coordinate with NSA, NRO, and my superiors at DARPA. If the pirates' location is discovered, my team is under strict instructions to attempt a rescue only if success is guaranteed. Otherwise, we'll pass on the coordinates and summon in the navy's fast-response SEAL team for extraction."

A worried nod acknowledged his plan.

Painter continued, "The kidnappers will move your daughter somewhere safe, then interrogate her. They'll need to obtain a phone number, a contact here in the States where they can forward a ransom demand. If your daughter is smart—"

"She is."

"Then she'll keep her identity a secret. Hopefully she'll give them some number outside the presidential circle. Perhaps a relative or a close friend. We have to be ready for that. Make sure that recipient stays quiet, doesn't go to the police or the press."

"I'll pass the word."

Painter asked a pointed question: "Can you trust all of your relatives to remain silent?"

"They won't say a word. The Gant clan knows how to keep secrets."

That's certainly true.

For the past month, Painter had been conducting a quiet investigation into the Gant family. Information had come to light during a recent Sigma mission that cast suspicions upon the family. Not that there weren't already rumors surrounding such a high-profile dynasty. They were nicknamed the Kennedys of the South, with generational ties going back to the founding of America. And as America grew, so did this family, rooting and entwining into multiple industries, corporations, the halls of statehouses, and now a second-term presidency.

But last month, a disturbing bit of information about this Southern dynasty had come to light. Documented centuries ago, this same clan appeared to be connected to a shadowy cabal of old aristocratic families. They went by many names: the Guild, Echelon, *les familles de l'étoile*, the star families. All that was truly known about this group was that they moved throughout history, manipulating events, gathering power, wealth, and knowledge, often achieving this by enfolding themselves within a series of secret organizations, brotherhoods, and fraternal lodges.

They were said to be the secret within *all* secret societies.

But the passing centuries had not been kind to them, winnowing the lineage down to a single bloodline: the Gant clan.

Still, that did not mean the president—or his immediate kin—had any knowledge of this organization. The Gant family tree had roots and branches that spread far and wide, on this shore and others. It was impossible to say which family members were involved with the modern-day incarnation of this criminal organization—that is, if *any* of them were involved.

All of it might end up being a wild-goose chase as the true leaders of the Guild—for lack of a better name for them—remained as elusive as ever. But what was known for sure was that the group was deadly, resourceful, and responsible for countless acts of terrorism, global atrocities, and an inestimable number of international crimes. To consider that the president—this man seated across from him, heartsick and terrified for his daughter—was a part of that same organization seemed impossible.

The lack of solid proof was one of the reasons Painter kept his suspicions about the Gant family to himself, trusting no one with this information, not even his fellow Sigma operatives. Especially Commander Gray Pierce, whose mother had been killed recently by a rogue Guild agent. If the man learned the president had any hand in that cold-blooded murder, there was no telling what he would do. As angry as he was, he'd shoot first and ask questions later.

So the questions were left for Painter to ask. He stared back at James Gant. "Not to be indelicate," he started, "but I still don't understand what your pregnant daughter was doing out among the outer islands of the Seychelles. Why was she traveling under false papers?"

There was something *wrong* about this whole situation.

Painter pressed, knowing this matter might offer his best chance to wheedle more information about the family—and, more specifically, about the *First Family*. "Is there anything you're not telling me, Mr. President? Anything you're holding back? Any detail could make a difference between success or failure."

This time, he purposefully avoided saying *life or death*.

James Gant stared down at his hands, as if trying to find meaning in the lines of his palms. "Amanda was always a wild child." He offered Painter a wan, wistful smile. "Much like her father. She was nineteen when I first stepped into the White House, even younger when I was running for my first term. She hated the limelight, chafed against being a president's daughter."

"I remember she once punched a Secret Service agent."

Gant laughed, leaning back and half covering his mouth as if surprised he could still laugh. "That was Amanda. During my second run for office, she was twenty-three, fresh out of college, and off on her own. She flourished out of my shadow, I have to say. Then she met Mack Bennett, a

Charleston police officer. After they married, I thought that would settle her down."

Painter gently directed him back to the mystery at hand. "And this trip out to the Seychelles."

Gant lifted his empty hands and shook his head. "Not even the Secret Service knew about this unscheduled trip. Damned if she didn't slip out from under all our noses. My only guess is she wanted some time alone with her husband, away from the paparazzi and tabloids, before the birth of my grandson. After that, the two would be lucky for a moment's privacy."

Painter studied the president's face, looking for any micro-expression that would indicate deceit. But all he found was a man dissolving into grief and fear.

"If that's all . . ." Gant said.

Painter stood up. "I've got what I need. My team should be flying into Somalia as we speak, and I must get back to Sigma command."

"Very good." Gant pushed out of his seat. Ever the Southern gentleman. "Let me walk you out."

The pair left the president's personal briefing room, pausing only long enough for Painter to retrieve his BlackBerry from a lead-lined box outside the Situation Room. As he straightened and pocketed his phone, a familiar figure appeared at the end of the hall, flanked by Secret Service.

She was dressed in a sapphire-blue twill dress, over which she tied a lace cardigan tightly around her belly. Painter noted her balled fists, the scared cast to her eyes as she found her husband.

The First Lady, Teresa Gant, hurried toward him, balanced between attempting to maintain a professional decorum and raw panic. "Jimmy . . . I heard from your secretary that the meeting was over. I waited for as long as I—"

"Terry, I'm sorry." The president caught his wife, hugged her, and brushed a few loose blond hairs from her cheek. "I had a few more details to attend to. I was going to you next."

She stared up at his face, searching for any news there, plainly afraid to question him in front of her bodyguards. No one could know about Amanda's plight.

"Come, let's return to the residence." The president looked ready to scoop her into his arms and carry her to safety. "I'll tell you everything there."

Gant glanced at Painter.

He understood. Teresa needed her husband. At this moment, they were not the First Lady and the president. They were simply two parents terrified for their child, seeking comfort in each other's arms.

Painter left them to their grief, more determined than ever to find their daughter. But as he headed down the hall, he could not escape the feeling that the events in the Horn of Africa were masking something far greater—and far more dangerous.

He checked his watch. Gray and his team would be landing in Somalia in the next hour. If anyone could ferret out the true intent behind the kidnapping of the young woman, it was Commander Pierce. Still, Painter felt a stab of misgiving for having sent Gray in blind, for failing to mention his suspicions about the president's family.

He prayed that silence didn't cost lives.

Especially the president's daughter and her unborn child.

4

The truck continued its slow crawl through the mist-shrouded forest.

Amanda Gant-Bennett rode in the back of the older-model Land Rover. Modified with an open top, it must have once served as a safari-touring vehicle. A massive grille protected the front end, and four large driving lights were mounted on the roof rack. She'd also noted the two winches—front and back—along with a shovel and ax secured to the fender, ready to help free the vehicle if it became bogged down or stuck.

From the terrain they traveled, she understood the necessity for such modifications. The road was little more than a muddy track through the dark jungle. Somalia suffered from an arid climate, but the rainy season—called *gu,* she'd overheard—had just ended. These highlands, bordering the Gulf of Aden, received most of that rain. And what didn't fall here as precipitation remained as thick fog.

A jarring bump threw her high. Only her seat belt kept her from flying out of the truck. She had initially thought of doing just that, of leaping free and taking her chances out in the dark jungle. But seated beside her was a heavyset guard, armed and sweating, chewing *khat,* a local stimulant used by nearly everyone. A second, larger truck followed at their heels, making any chance of escape impossible.

And she ultimately knew that any attempt would put more than her own life at risk.

She pushed the lap strap of the seat belt lower, below the bulge of her belly and above her hip bones. She had to protect her child. The baby boy growing in her womb was more important than her own well-being. He was the reason she and her husband had risked this flight halfway around the world.

To keep you safe . . .

And now her baby had fallen into another set of hands, becoming a tool to generate a larger ransom by the pirates. She remembered the Brit's hungry eyes on her belly as she was taken off the yacht. Here, life was a commodity to buy and sell, even the new life growing in her belly.

Oh, Mack, I need you.

She closed her eyes, her heart constricting with the last memory of her husband, the fear and love shining in Mack's eyes. She shied away from the horror that followed, his severed head tossed upon the bed where they'd made such careful love only hours earlier. But she had no time to grieve for her husband.

She drew a long, steadying breath, taking in the damp and redolent smell of junipers and wild lavender of the dense forest. Though numb with grief and terror, she had to stay strong. In the South, it was unseemly to be caught sweating in public. On the campaign trail with her father, she had learned to maintain a placid and friendly exterior—even when screaming on the inside. Instead, it was all smiles, handshakes, and warm pats on the back. Even with your enemies . . . *especially* with your enemies.

So, she continued to cooperate with her captors. Jumping when they said jump, remaining always pliant and obedient. Still, all the while she watched. It was another lesson from her father, his words echoing in her head, explaining the best way to gain the upper hand.

Keep your eyes open and your mouth shut.

And that's what she intended to do. So far, the pirates gave no indication they knew she was the president's daughter. They'd not even questioned her yet. In fact, they'd barely said a word. A grunt here or there, a pantomimed instruction, a few terse orders. Mostly about drinking water.

We don't want anything to happen to your baby.

The warning had come from the man seated in the passenger seat up front, the Brit with his thin mustache and impeccable attire. He remained the only consistent presence around her—though he'd ignored her most of the day, bent over a laptop computer attached to a satellite phone and GPS navigation unit.

She studied the back of his head, trying to figure him out, searching for a weakness. He tapped at his laptop and the screen changed to a topographic map. She feigned a kink in her back to stretch forward, trying to peek at the screen, to discern some idea of where she was and where they were going. But her guard yanked her back, his hand lingering over her left breast, which was tender and swollen. She slapped his fingers away, which only earned her a lascivious leer.

Defeated, she stared sullenly out at the misty forest.

Exhaustion and fear had stretched the day's journey into a blur. At dawn, they'd made landfall at a small coastal town, a booming shantytown of bars, hotels, restaurants, and whorehouses, all serving the pirate trade. And from the number of expensive cars lining newly paved streets and half-constructed villas along the coast, it was plainly a lucrative and thriving business. To protect that industry, militiamen swerved through the streets in Mercedes SUVs, weapons bristling from rolled-down windows, making sure no one attempted to rescue any of their hostages.

And there must have been others like her.

As their boat had entered into port, she'd spotted numerous captured vessels: fishing trawlers, sailboats, a sleek yacht, and, anchored out in the deeper waters, an oil tanker. They'd only remained in town for less than an hour. There, she was handed over to another pirate gang and put on a hot, poorly ventilated Volkswagen bus out of town.

They drove half a day through lands hammered dry and flat by the merciless sun, the featureless landscape only broken by the occasional village of dry huts. They'd stopped only long enough for her to urinate, which was often, and humiliating each time. In the distance, mountains had loomed, seeming to grow higher with each passing mile.

Soon it became clear that the broken spine of rocky peaks was their destination. Upon reaching a village nestled in the scrubby foothills, the gang changed yet again, but not before a heated argument ensued, accompanied by a machismo display of shaken weapons and hurled threats. Finally, the Brit had facilitated the exchange of additional funds, bills banded in thick bundles, and Amanda found herself transferred into this old safari vehicle headed into the misty highlands.

A metallic snap drew her attention forward as the Brit closed his laptop with an air of finality. The reason became clear. A fiery glow appeared in the forest ahead, turning the wisps of fog into crimson trails threaded through the dark-green jungle. She smelled roasting meat and woodsmoke.

With a final haul of fifty yards, the Land Rover broke into an open glade in the jungle. Overhead, camouflage netting masked the camp below, giving the space a cavernous feel. A trio of small bonfires illuminated the hidden glade, along with a few electric lamps on poles.

The Land Rover pulled to the side and parked beside a handful of other vehicles. Additionally, a trio of camels, settled for the night, raised their heads to study the newcomers.

Likewise, Amanda, her eyes huge, tried to make sense of the camp. A neat circle of military-style tents surrounded a larger structure that looked like a picturesque gabled house, raised on pilings a yard off the ground. Across the front, a quaint wooden porch held a pair of deck chairs draped with mosquito netting. It looked like the jungle home of some African missionary. Furthering that impression, a large bloodred cross decorated one side of the building.

But as the Land Rover drew to a halt, the charming illusion evaporated. The house was actually a makeshift tent-cabin, with white tarpaulin stretched over a wooden pole-frame. And the crimson cross was less religious in appearance and more medical, like something borrowed from the American Red Cross. Only this cross had strange markings along its lengths, a twisting and coiling pattern that looked vaguely familiar.

Before she could understand what nagged her, the Brit pulled open her door and held out his hand to assist her.

"Home sweet home," he said without any sarcasm in his voice.

She climbed out, unsteady, supporting her belly, and searched around. The steady chug of a diesel generator mocked the wild beating of her heart.

Men and women climbed out of tents to eye the new arrivals. Most of those faces were black, African, but they didn't have the starved and desperate look of the pirates. Even the weapons in view looked modern and well-kept.

What is going on here?

The other faces matched the Brit's: white, European, professional. This last assessment came from the number of them wearing blue scrubs, like they'd freshly stepped out of a modern hospital for a smoke break.

The Brit led her through the circle of tents and toward the makeshift cabin, trailed by her guard. She climbed the steps to the small porch.

A spring-loaded door opened as they reached the cabin. A tall woman joined them, her blond hair trimmed into a short, athletic bob. She was young and fresh-faced, as if she just slipped out of a swimsuit ad and into surgical scrubs. Belying that image was the severity of her expression, especially her narrowed eyes. She took in everyone with a single steel-blue glance, barely noting Amanda. Her gaze settled on the Brit.

"Everything is ready, Dr. Blake."

Amanda swung toward the Brit, surprised.

Doctor . . . ?

The man noted her consternation. "I'm sorry. I never did properly introduce myself." He held out his hand. "Dr. Edward Blake. Ob/gyn."

She didn't take his hand. Instead, she stared beyond the blonde's shoulder and into the cabin. A hospital bed rested against the far wall. Beside it stood an IV pole and a bank of monitoring equipment. On the other side, a technician lubricated the transvaginal probe of an ultrasound unit.

Dr. Blake seemed to take no offense that Amanda had refused his hand. Instead, he rubbed his palms together.

"Okay, then, Mrs. Gant-Bennett. Why don't we step inside?"

Amanda bit back her shock at the mention of her name.

He knows who I am . . .

Dr. Blake motioned with his arm. "We should check on how your baby boy is doing after the long journey. We can't let anything happen to him, can we? He's much too important."

Amanda backed away in horror, her worst nightmare coming true.

Not only did they know *who* she was, they knew *what* she carried.

"No . . ."

Hands gripped her shoulders from behind and shoved her toward the open door.

Please, she prayed. *Please someone help me.*

5

"They'll take good care of her," Amur Mahdi promised. "At least for now."

"Why do you say that?" Gray asked.

Seichan looked equally doubtful. She was dressed handsomely in jeans and a local *guntiino,* a bright length of crimson cloth, knotted at the shoulder and draped to the waist. The look must have worked, because Amur kept casting sidelong glances in her direction.

Next to her, Kowalski, outfitted in regular street clothes, simply swirled his tea, looking inattentive.

The four of them shared a table at a seaside restaurant overlooking the Somali port of Boosaaso. The open-air patio looked out onto the Gulf of Aden, the moonlit harbor crowded with massive ships bearing flags of various Arab states, along with the triangular sails of hundreds of smaller, wooden-keeled dhows.

Gray's team had arrived at the Bender Qassim International Airport outside of Boosaaso forty minutes ago, traveling under the cover of UNHCR, the United Nations refugee agency. The relief group maintained a presence here in Puntland, the northeastern state of Somalia, where most of the country's lawless pirates operated. Boosaaso was the main crossroads for this region and the best base of operations to begin gathering intelligence.

This introductory meeting was with Amur Mahdi—a former pirate turned CIA asset. He was an older man dressed in regional attire, which included loose trousers and a sarong-like kilt, known as a *macawiis*. He also wore a traditional embroidered cap atop his grizzled hair. The man had lost one leg at the knee several years back, an injury that sidelined him from his former profession as a pirate.

The sight of the prosthetic limb reminded Gray of his father, who'd been similarly disabled. A twinge of guilt flared at being half a world away from him, but he fought it down and concentrated on the conversation.

The meeting had been arranged by Director Crowe, channeled through various intelligence agencies. The goal of this meeting was to evaluate the current situation in Somalia. While word was still pending on the search for the raiders' ship via satellite, Painter wanted eyes on the ground.

Meanwhile, a pair of Black Hawks idled at a U.S. base to the north, in the neighboring tiny East African nation of Djibouti. SEAL Team Six, under the operational orders of Joint Special Operations Command, waited to be summoned once Amanda's location was determined.

But where was the First Daughter?

Amur explained his lack of concern for the hostage's safety. He didn't know about the victim being the president's daughter, only that she was an American woman. "For the most part, Somali pirates make decent hosts. Beatings are rare, but they do occur. Otherwise, they keep their guests protected and well-fed. It does no one any good if a hostage dies. In fact, the feeding and housing of captured crews help maintain the economy of Puntland."

Gray knew how lucrative the piracy trade was. Last year alone, Somali pirates collected $160 million in ransom. And that was only the tip of the true cost of piracy in the region. The shipping industry and governments spent $7 billion during that same time, accruing additional expenses from insurance premiums, from heightened security, even rescue missions, like the recent one that secured the safe return of an American and a Danish citizen.

"And what about the Somali government?" Seichan asked. "What are they doing about the rampant piracy?"

Amur leaned back in his chair and lifted his arms hopelessly in the air. "What Somali government? The central government fell back in 1991,

throwing the country into chaos. Without anyone patrolling our territorial waters, the tuna-rich seas around here were plundered and stripped
by foreign fishing fleets, stealing the food and livelihood from our local
people. Is it any wonder our fishermen armed themselves, becoming their
own militia, and confronted the illegal boats and crews?"

Gray had read the briefings on the flight out here. "And those confron-
tations eventually led to the fishermen confiscating ships and personnel
and demanding ransoms—"

"More like a toll," Amur corrected, earning a scoffing grunt from
Kowalski. Their informant's face reddened, his back stiffening with pride.
Though the man had turned informant, Gray was reminded of the old
adage: *Once a pirate, always a pirate.* Or maybe Amur's justifications were
merely a reflection of national pride.

"We deserved some compensation for our plundered seas," he continued. "Who else is looking after us? Look at the port here." He nodded to
the bustling harbor. "This place used to be a hellhole, with no infrastruc-
ture, no hope, everything crumbling apart."

Kowalski raised a skeptical eyebrow toward the dusty city, seeming to
think the description of *hellhole* still fit it.

"After the government fell," Amur continued, "we took care of each
other. A local businessman started our phone system. Teachers worked for
free. The police are all volunteers, too. Now we're one of the busiest ports
in the region. A boomtown, as you say. We export tens of thousands of
goats, sheep, and camels across the Arab world."

Kowalski's skeptical eyebrow refused to lower. Gray understood as he
looked out at all the new construction going on across the nighttime city,
at the palatial mansions rising behind high walls. He suspected not all of
that largesse came from Boosaaso's import/export industry.

Gray had read how this city was still ranked as one of the most likely
places to get kidnapped. Not exactly a high honor. Though the local government was attempting to change that. Its jails were full of pirates—but
how much was that for international show? Piracy continued to be the
main industry running the Puntland economy.

How were they going to make any headway in finding the president's daughter against those economic odds? Money could free tongues—as it had with Amur Mahdi—but it also bought silence.

"And now the fishes return to our waters," Amur said with a note of vindication and finality. "With the foreign fleets afraid to come near, our seas once again teem with tuna and our people are no longer hungry."

Gray had to admit that much was true. Somali piracy had a positive impact on reversing the overfishing of its territorial waters. But at what price?

Amur stood up. "The night grows late. I will see what I can discover about this missing American woman. But as you know, rescue attempts over the past year have resulted in pirate deaths. It will not be easy getting information."

Gray stood and shook the man's hand. He read between the lines. To break that silence would require additional funds. But Gray feared if too much money was thrown into the search, it could raise the suspicions of Amanda's captors. A delicate balance had to be struck here—but for now they had no choice.

"I understand. Do what you must," Gray said. He shook the man's hand and wished him good night, using his native tongue, which earned an appreciative smile from Amur. *"Haben wanaagsan."*

Gray waited for Amur to leave the restaurant before motioning the others up. "We should get back to the hotel."

They headed out as a group. Even at this hour, the streets were clogged with trucks, people, and carts. Sizzling food stands, tiny tea stalls, and makeshift shops packed both sides of the street. All around, Boosaaso bustled, hammered, rang, and shouted.

They kept to a tight knot as they traversed the crowded streets on their way toward their hotel.

Seichan spoke at his ear, her breath hot on his cheek. "You were right. We've picked up a tail."

Gray stopped at a fruit stand, studying the exotic fare while searching the street behind them. He noted two figures in street clothes who ducked out of sight as he had stopped. "Two of them?"

"Three," Seichan corrected. "The woman in the green sarong by the door of that Internet café."

Gray didn't notice anything out of the ordinary in her appearance, but he trusted Seichan's assessment.

Kowalski remained oblivious. He picked up a banana and sniffed at it. "Are we buying something or not?"

Gray headed away, continuing toward their hotel, drawing the tail in his wake.

"So Amur is not as loyal as the CIA claimed," Seichan whispered.

She leaned toward him like a lover. Physical contact between men and women was frowned upon in this country, but there was a strange, heightened intimacy in being this close without touching.

"Painter suspected as much," Gray mumbled.

The director had reviewed the various potential contacts here and selected Amur specifically because of discrepancies in his behavior in the past. It seemed the man was not above playing one side against the other, especially with big money involved.

Once a pirate, always a pirate.

Gray sauntered down the road with his teammates, not bothering to try to shake the tail. He *wanted* the others following his team. Amur was playing a dangerous game, but one that suited their purpose.

Because *two* could play that same game.

9:01 P.M.

Tucker Wayne maintained a safe distance behind Amur Mahdi, keeping a city block between them.

The radio embedded in his ear buzzed. "Do you have him?"

It was Commander Pierce. Tucker touched his throat mike and subvocalized his answer. "Affirmative."

To blend in with the locals, he had pulled a loose plaid *macawiis* tunic over a thin Kevlar jacket and donned a regional turban to hide his hair and further shadow his features. Not that there weren't white faces here.

It seemed the city drew opportunists from around the globe. He heard German, Spanish, and French spoken alongside the continuous dialects of African languages.

Still, he kept almost entirely out of sight of his target, trusting another's eyes more than his own.

Several meters ahead, Kane kept to the shadows, ghosting along, sticking to the crumbling wall of a palatial estate, gliding around and over obstacles. Few eyes glanced at the shepherd's passage. Plenty of dogs—half-starved waifs, showing ribs and bony legs—roamed the streets.

A block away, Amur turned a corner and angled away from the busier zone of newer hotels and larger estates. He moved with determination into a bulldozed section of the city, occupied by cranes, piles of rubble, and metal trailers, all in readiness for the expansion of the neighboring business district.

Tucker radioed the change in direction. "He's heading out of New Boosaaso, aiming for a rougher part of town. Definitely not going home."

Tucker had memorized everything he could about his target, mapping out the man's life in his head: where he lived, where he met friends for drinks, where his mistress was holed up. Amur wasn't heading toward any of his usual haunts.

"Keep following, but maintain your distance," Gray warned. "We don't want him spooked."

I know how to do my job, Tucker thought sourly as he reached the corner. *This is what you hired me for—or, rather, hired us.*

Kane had already stopped at the corner and glanced back. Tucker signaled an open palm.

Stay.

Tucker surveyed the terrain ahead. Tall security fencing, screened by barrier fabric, lined both sides of the road, keeping pedestrians out of the construction zones. At this hour, no one else was in view. He had no choice but to wait.

If I follow, I'll be immediately spotted, my cover blown.

For now, they had a small advantage. Gray had gone to painstaking ends to keep knowledge of Tucker's involvement in this mission secret. They'd even traveled from Tanzania to Somalia by different planes. Gray wanted all eyes diverted and focused on his team and away from Tucker, freeing him to move independently.

At the end of the street, Amur stopped at a locked gate in the security fencing. A lounging guard with an AK-47 greeted him. They leaned their heads together, then the guard nodded and unlatched the gate. Amur vanished inside, drawing the guard with him.

What is he up to?

Tucker headed down a few meters until he discovered a gap between the fence and the sandy ground. A tall metal Dumpster helped hide the spot. He drew Kane there, then pointed to the gap, circled a finger, and touched his nose.

Crawl through, search for the target's scent.

Tucker knew this was a task Kane could handle. Humans had 6 million olfactory receptors in their nose; hunting dogs had 300 million, which heightened their sense of smell a thousandfold, allowing them to scent a target from two football fields away.

At the end of the instructions, Tucker lowered his palm facedown, signaling Kane to stay hidden if the target was found.

Finished, Tucker slipped a hand to the shepherd's flank, running his fingers over the black jacket that blended perfectly with his fur. It was a K9 Storm tactical vest, waterproof and Kevlar-reinforced. He checked Kane's earpiece, which allowed them to communicate in the field—then flipped up an eraser-size lens of a night-vision video camera secured near the collar and positioned it between the dog's pricked ears.

The team needed eyes and ears in there.

Tucker pulled out a cell phone, tapped in a code, and a grainy, dog's-eye view of himself appeared on the small screen. He leaned down and gave his partner's nape a fast ruffle. He also shook the vest to make sure nothing rattled to betray Kane's position in the field.

Satisfied, he knelt and cradled the dog's head in his palms. A muscular tremble betrayed Kane's excitement. His tongue lolled as he silently panted. Dark eyes met Tucker's. It was one of the unique features of domesticated dogs—*they studied us as much as we studied them.*

"Who's a good boy?" he whispered to his friend, a ritual of theirs.

Kane's nose shoved forward, touching his, acknowledging their bond. Tucker finally stood and flicked his wrist toward the gap in the fence. *Go.*

Kane swung and lunged smoothly through the hole, his tail vanishing away in seconds. Tucker checked his phone. A juggling view of parked bulldozers and piles of rebar-ribbed broken slabs of concrete appeared on the small screen. The image bobbled and swung like some badly directed horror movie.

Tucker touched his throat mike. "Video's up, commander. In case you want to watch the show."

As he waited for a response, Tucker slipped a Bluetooth earbud into his free ear. Through it, he heard the soft whisper of Kane's panting breath.

In his other ear, Gray responded, "Got it. Let's see what our friend Amur is up to."

Tucker kept to the shadows of the Dumpster and watched his partner's progress. Fear prickled over his skin.

Be careful out there, buddy.

Kane races low to the ground, senses stretching outward, hunting for his prey. Around him, night brightens into shades of gray, frosted by muted hues. Piles of stone grow high on either side, offering sheltered pathways forward. The stir of a breeze shifts a crumpled paper cup, the movement twitching for attention but ultimately ignored.

When sight fails him, scent fills in, layer upon layer, marking time backward and forward, building a framework of old trails around him.

Bitter musk of spoor . . .

Acrid sting of a urine marker . . .

Burned oil from silent machines . . .

He moves through the maze, taking in more smells, drawing them upon his moist tongue, deep into the back of his throat and si-

nuses. His ears swivel at every hushed whisper of sand: from breezes, from the pad of his paws.

On . . . always onward . . .

He holds his nose high at a turn, tracking.

Then . . . familiar sweat, spicy and pungent, drifts to him, basking outward in the wake of the prey.

His legs slow.

He lowers his body, keeping to the shadowed trails.

He forces his panting to grow quiet.

Ahead, the prey approaches others. They are out of sight, but their musk betrays them. They are hidden behind a pile of metal, smelling of rust and burrowed through with the scent of scurrying things. The odor of man wafts past it all, impossible to ignore, stinking and strong.

His prey walks forward, trailed by another with a gun.

Kane knows guns—by scent, sight, and sound, he knows guns.

The hidden others show themselves at last, stepping into the open. The prey falls back, the scent of his fear spiking sharper—then it quickly fades, snuffing out again.

Among the four, lips are pulled back, showing teeth, but not in threat. They speak, making noise.

Kane creeps closer, finding a spot to watch unseen. He lies still, on his belly, but his haunches remain tense, ready to flee or charge.

For now, he stays.

Staring, obedient.

Because he asked.

Kane continues to draw in the night, ever vigilant, painting the world around him in scents and sounds. He smells his own trail, going back, buried among so many others. But through it all, one trail shines like the sun in the night around him, connecting him to another, both bound together forever by blood and trust.

He knows that name, too.

By scent, by sound, by sight.

He knows that name.

9:12 P.M.

Tucker spied on the meeting between Amur and his trio of compatriots, fellow pirates judging by their tribal scars and harsh manners. They gathered near a rusted stack of old iron H-beams and broken cement bricks. In his ear, he heard their harsh laughter and words spoken in a local Somali dialect. A translation program converted the conversation into a tinny computerized version.

"How long can you draw them out?" one asked.

"How much money can you get?" another added.

"Hassan, Habib, trust me." Amur smiled, lifting his arms. *"There is more going on than they tell me. For that, I can make them dance on a string at my whim."*

"So you say," the third said doubtfully.

As proof of his word, Amur removed a wad of bills and stripped out several for each. *"But first,"* he said, *"I must give these Americans something to chew on, to keep them hanging on my words, yes?"*

The others ignored him, counting their bills and stuffing them away.

"What have you heard about this American woman?" Amur asked, drawing back their attention.

"Only rumors, Amur." These words earned nods among the three.

Another voice spoke in Tucker's other ear: "At this point, I'll take rumors."

That assessment came from Commander Pierce. It seemed the team leader was listening into the feed with as much interest as he was.

"Then what is the word?" Amur pressed.

"A friend of my brother's uncle, up near Eil, he says a white woman came through his village. He says they were moving her into the mountains."

"The Cal Madow mountains?"

A shrug answered him.

"That is much territory to cover," Amur said, but he didn't seem disappointed. He rubbed his chin thoughtfully. *"If she is among those mountains, she will never be found. I can easily give that information to the Americans*

without truly telling them anything. And with Allah shining upon us, I should be able to tease out our relationship for several profitable days."

"And after that?"

"Then I will no longer have a use for the three Americans. It would be unfortunate if something happened to them—unfortunate but not unusual in these treacherous lands, yes?"

Grins followed, shared all around.

"So it seems Amur is not the hospitable host he pretends to be," Gray said in his ear. "I think we'll have to—"

The commander's words were cut off by a low growl.

The view on the small screen shifted as his partner retreated, clearly sensing something.

"What's your dog doing?" Gray asked, also noting the sudden movement.

"Hold on. Something's spooked him."

The grainy image leaped and joggled as the shepherd bounded and circled around a steep pile of concrete debris. It looked like the dog was trying to outflank Amur and his group.

Then the view settled again.

Farther out in the construction zone, a team of six men descended toward Amur's group. They were outfitted in black body armor and wore helmets equipped with night-vision goggles. At their shoulders, they carried assault rifles. These newcomers were no rough pirates; they clearly had military training. Their intent seemed anything but friendly.

Amur's inquiries must have reached the wrong ears.

Not good. Not now.

Tucker watched as hand signals from the squad's leader split the group. They spread out to either side, a pincer move intended to trap Amur's group between them.

Unfortunately, the former pirate was not the only one caught in the trap. Tucker's heart thudded in his throat.

6

"Stay put!" Gray ordered.

Seichan stood at his shoulder; Kowalski at the other. They had stopped at the mouth of an alleyway, a few blocks from their hotel, observing the feed from the shepherd's camera. The armored commando team had swept wide, circling Amur's group, clearly intending to let no one escape.

"Can't do that, commander," Captain Wayne responded. "Not until Kane's out of harm's way."

Gray knew there was nothing he could say to stop Tucker. He had no authority over him, and if the man was spotted—or worse, caught—he'd jeopardize the entire mission.

"Then at least wait until I get there," Gray pressed. "We'll do this together."

A long pause followed, long enough for him to worry that the man had already gone.

Then an answer came. "I'll wait," Tucker said. "For the moment. But no promises."

That was as much concession as Gray would get from him.

"I'm on my way," Gray radioed—then faced the others and pointed down the street. "You two, head to the hotel. Keep the tail chasing after you. Convince them we've retired for the night."

Seichan stepped closer. "You shouldn't be going alone. You barely know the city."

He tapped up a street-view map of Boosaaso on his phone. "I'll manage. Besides, we have no choice. Amur surely has other friends in the city. We need an alibi if he comes to a bad end in that construction yard. We don't want his murder pinned on us."

"What're you going to do?" Seichan asked.

From the corner of an eye, he caught sight of the three-man team sent to tail them. The trio had gathered near a cloth stand, feigning interest in the stacked fabric rolls.

"At the next corner ahead, when we're momentarily out of sight, I'll head down a side street. You two rush to the front of the hotel. Let them see you going inside, cause some commotion. Hopefully they'll believe I've already entered."

From the furrow between Seichan's eyebrows, she had little confidence in his plan.

He reached for her hand and gave her fingers a quick squeeze. It was a reflex move, more intimate than he intended. "I'll be fine," he mumbled.

If nothing else, the brief and surprising contact left her speechless.

"Let's go," Gray said before any further discussion could start.

They headed together down the street, sauntering at a leisurely pace. Once Gray passed around the next corner, he hurried to the mouth of another alleyway ahead. If the map was correct, he should be able to circle back and join up with Captain Wayne.

As he turned away, Seichan's last glance remained unreadable.

Kowalski was more blunt. "Watch your ass out there."

He planned on doing just that. Behind him, Seichan and Kowalski rushed headlong, aiming for the broad steps to Hotel Jubba at the end of the block.

At least they knew how to take orders. He prayed Tucker Wayne would do the same. But with each step, Gray hurried faster, knowing that was not likely. Tucker was as much a creature of instinct as his furry partner. The man would react before thinking.

Especially if his dog was in danger.

Kane huddles in the shadows under a protruding slab of broken concrete. Beyond his hiding place, the night around him is a complex weave of scent trails, echoing sounds, and movement. He stares un-blinking at it all, allowing the landscape to build before him, as much a map of the present as the past.

The whispery crunch of a stone under boot . . .

The leathery tap of a rifle strap on cloth . . .

The heavy pant of excitement of a predator closing in on prey . . .

His original prey remains clustered with his pack, deaf to the danger approaching. Kane tracks the newcomers as they cut through old scent trails, even his own, creating a new one, stinking of man. It fully circles the others now.

Then draws tighter as they move in on their prey.

Kane stays in his hiding place, unmoving, placing his trust in shadows.

And one other.

9:22 P.M.

Tucker crouched outside the fence, hidden behind a Dumpster, his attention fixed to the feed from Kane's camera. Still following his original instructions, the dog remained focused on Amur's group, who continued to discuss where to spend the money in hand, where to eat a late dinner, and how to get more payments out of Commander Pierce.

All the while, a deadly noose tightened around them all.

Even Kane.

Tucker dared not risk calling his partner back to him. The movement would draw the commandos' attention.

As if the dog had heard his silent worry, the view on the screen shifted as Kane glanced backward, over his shoulder. The angle turned enough to reveal a commando in black body armor closing toward Kane's position. The shepherd remained at his post, as Tucker had ordered.

Kane thinks he's hidden well enough, Tucker realized.

But the dog was wrong.

Night-vision goggles hid the approaching commando's eyes. Kane's shadowy shelter offered no protection from such technology. In a moment, the shepherd would easily be spotted, along with the foreign vest—then all hell would break loose.

Tucker glanced up and down the street. Commander Pierce was nowhere in sight, and he had to do something.

Now.

Twisting around, he dove for the fence, to the gap along the bottom where Kane had crawled through. It was too small for him, but coils of razor wire blocked the way over the top. With no other choice, he placed his phone on the ground and dug with both hands into the hard-packed sand.

All the while, he stared at the phone beside him, watching the commando draw closer to Kane. He dug faster, scooping out sand, deepening the hole, bloodying his fingers.

Finally, unable to wait any longer, he squirmed his way through the gap. The loose tunic ripped on the fangs of the fence's lower end, exposing his Kevlar vest beneath.

He reached back and grabbed his phone.

The view of the video feed stopped his heart.

On the screen, the grainy image of the commando jerked to a stop, plainly startled. And the reason was obvious. The soldier shifted his rifle and pointed it directly toward the camera.

Directly at Kane.

9:23 P.M.

Damn that fool . . .

Seichan moved briskly, angrily, into the tiled lobby of the Hotel Jubba.

Kowalski followed at her heels. She hated abandoning Gray and hated that it bothered her so much, but in the end, she also recognized the necessity. The pair had succeeded in drawing their tail to the steps of the building, hopefully leaving them unaware of Gray's disappearance.

Still, she could not relax the tense knot between her shoulder blades. Gray shouldn't have gone out there alone. If they'd taken an extra few moments to plan, some other ruse could have been calculated to fool the ones tailing them. Instead, his action had been unusually rash, even reckless. And not just here. They'd come close to losing Tucker Wayne and his dog back in Zanzibar. Not a mistake Gray would normally make.

And she could guess the cause. A deep current of fury and frustration still flowed through his core. She recognized it in the storm-gray of his eyes, in the hard set to his jaw, in the clipped edge to his conversations. There was a manic edge to Gray that she'd never seen before, and it made her nervous. Not for herself, but for him.

Maybe it was too soon for him to be out in the field.

But they were committed, and there was no retreating from here.

Kowalski slipped out a cigar and set about lighting it. A thick pall of smoke already filled the lobby, making her eyes sting. A soccer match played on a large-screen television in the hotel restaurant, drawing in a boisterous crowd that spilled into the lobby and obstructed the way toward the stairs.

Her partner nodded back toward the hotel's entrance. "Looks like our friends are setting up camp out there. Making sure we don't leave."

Seichan glanced over at the trio who had followed them. They sat at a coffeehouse that offered a view of the hotel's front steps. Clearly Amur intended to protect his investment, ensuring no other informant intruded on his territory.

A loud cheer drew her attention back to the restaurant. The match between Brazil and Germany was heating up. A group of German patrons began singing their national anthem.

"Let's get out of here," she said, intending to return to their rooms.

Kowalski lingered, puffing on his cigar, adding to the pollution in the lobby. His eyes had drifted to the soccer match on the television. His legs drew him toward the machismo camaraderie of the live sportscast.

At least that should keep him out of trouble for the night.

She was wrong.

Within a few steps, he bumped into a harried waiter holding aloft a huge tray full of teacups and pots of steaming water. The tray went flying, crashing into the mass of men crowded at the entrance to the restaurant. Shouts and curses erupted as scalding water splashed over those closest.

Then a push became a shove, and a fist struck a nose. In a matter of seconds, bedlam broke out. The restaurant emptied into the lobby, escalating into a full brawl.

Kowalski backed Seichan in a corner as a bottle flew past his nose and shattered against the wall.

"What did you do?" Seichan scolded.

Kowalski grinned back at her, keeping the stogie crushed between his teeth as he spoke. "There's a rear exit through the kitchen. Let me get this party going full swing, and you can duck back into the streets unseen."

He locked eyes with her. She read the sharp glimmer buried within that dim exterior. So she wasn't the only one worried about their partner.

"Are you ready?" he asked.

She nodded, which made his grin spread wider, a terrifying sight.

With a roar, he turned and leaped into the raucous fray, a veritable bull let loose among the others. In moments, the fighting rolled like a tide toward the hotel's front doors and spilled out into the streets, spreading the commotion and chaos.

Seichan twisted in the opposite direction, slipping out a scarf and wrapping her head and most of her face. Kowalski bellowed behind her— sounding disturbingly happy, finally in his true element.

Now to find Gray.

She had Tucker Wayne's call sign and last position noted on her own phone's navigation system. That's where Gray would be headed.

She burst out the rear door, leaving behind the clatter of pots and pans from the kitchen, and into the dark silence of the back alley.

Before she could take a step, a bright light speared her, blinding her.

A harsh voice with a thick British accent accosted her, punctuated by the cocking of a pistol. "Take another step, and I'll put a bullet through your pretty skull."

7

Standing by the fence, Tucker watched the rifle lower toward Kane. The grainy image on the phone set his heart to pounding. He'd never reach his partner in time.

Reacting instinctively, he yanked out his pistol, a black SIG Sauer, pointed it into the air, and fired two rounds. The gun blasts stung his ears and echoed across the empty construction site.

On the screen, the soldier's aim shifted away as he dropped low, startled by the gunfire.

Tucker was already moving, heading toward Kane's hiding place. On his phone, he pressed a green icon in the shape of a small ear and lifted the phone to his lips. He spoke two commands, transmitting them to the receiver behind Kane's left ear.

"TAKEDOWN! DISARM!"

The image on the screen blurred into chaos.

Tucker continued to sprint, staying low.

I'm coming, buddy.

Kane tastes blood, feels the crack of bone under the power of his jaws. He holds tight as a pained cry pierces the night. Then a booted blow to his ribs finally knocks him loose.

The night spins, but rights itself as he rolls his legs under him.

His prey crouches, holding his limb to his chest, wrist crushed, gun on the ground. Both hunters face each other—but only for a breath.

Kane dives low, snatching cloth at the ankle and throwing his body to the side, yanking the prey's limb from under him. The other falls, head striking broken stone. Goggles knock away, revealing narrowed eyes. Kane smells his fear, still tastes the blood on the back of his tongue.

But the other is a hunter, too.

A flash of a blade in the other hand. It stabs down—but Kane is already gone, spinning away, running low into the night.

But not without a hard-won prize clutched in his jaws.

9:25 P.M.

Gray sprinted along the barrier fencing as fresh gunfire erupted from the construction zone: the chugging coughs of automatic weapons along with the sharper blasts of smaller arms.

A moment ago, as he reached the street, he'd heard the initial pistol cracks.

Two shots.

They had risen from a different part of the site, well away from the current firefight.

Had to be Captain Wayne.

This was confirmed when Gray heard Tucker's radioed command to his partner. There was no sign of the man on the street, so Gray rushed toward a gate at the next corner. He found it unguarded and pushed inside, his gun already in hand.

A bulldozed road led straight toward the fighting.

He spotted bodies on the ground.

Amur's men.

Gray ducked to the side, into the shadows of a pile of broken concrete. A commando stepped into view and kicked one of the bodies. An arm lifted off the ground, a pleading gesture. The soldier's pistol pointed down. A single crack, and the arm fell limply.

They were killing everyone.

As quickly as the firefight had started, it ended. The last few sputters of automatic gunfire died away.

Gray subvocalized into his throat mike. "Tucker, respond?"

The answer didn't come from his radio.

A fresh flurry of gunfire erupted to the left, away from the pile of dead bodies. The commando in view dashed in that direction.

Biting back a curse, Gray rolled around the pile of concrete and headed that way, too. Gunplay spattered out, as Tucker played cat and mouse with the hunters.

Gray struggled through the maze, straining to track the gunfire, while keeping a watch around him. At last, he spotted Tucker. The man, pistol in hand, ran along a row of parked dump trucks at the edge of the rubble field, trying to stay out of sight.

Gray headed toward him—but before he could take more than three steps, a shadowy figure appeared a few yards ahead, his back to Gray, blocking the view. It was the same commando who had been slaughtering the last of Amur's men. The soldier spotted Tucker and fired a flurry of rounds at his target.

Ricochets pinged off the dump truck.

Exposed, Tucker tried to twist away. But a round struck him square in the chest, knocking him against the bed of the dump truck with a loud clang. He fell hard to the ground, his pistol flying from his grip.

Gray raised his own weapon, strode two fast paces, and shot the commando through the back of the neck. The soldier collapsed to his knees, then to his face, gurgling harshly as he died.

Gray stepped past him, kicking the assault rifle away from his fingertips.

Ahead, Tucker struggled to stand up, a palm on his chest.

Damned lucky the man had been wearing a Kevlar vest.

But luck only lasted for so long.

A fresh crack of a pistol came from the right, from out of Gray's field of view. Tucker ducked as a round buzzed his ear and struck the dump truck's huge tire. More shots rang out, blasting sand from between Tucker's legs and by his left hand. Tucker scrabbled away, disappearing from view.

Gray hurried forward, but the shooter was still out of sight.

Where—?

Then the commando burst into the open, running low, heading toward where Tucker had vanished, pistol raised forward. His other arm was clutched to his chest, his wrist held at an impossible angle, dripping blood. Judging by the wild blasts, fury fueled this attack.

Gray struggled to fix the attacker in his sights, but the target was moving too fast and heavily armored. Gray fired anyway, emptying his weapon. But the soldier was so focused he didn't even flinch from the rounds pinging off the truck's side, even at a shot that glanced off his helmet.

Then his target was out of sight again, pursuing Tucker.

Gray ran forward, ejecting his spent magazine and slapping in another. In a few more steps, he spotted the gunman leaning over Tucker. His teammate, one shoulder bloodied, was sprawled on his back by the truck's cab. The armored commando held his pistol at Tucker's face, ready to shoot point-blank.

Gray could not stop him—then a miracle happened.

9:26 P.M.

The smoking barrel of the pistol lowered and pointed between Tucker's eyes. His shoulder burned, but not as much as his blood. He stared past the gun to the eyes of the assassin. He recognized the fury there.

It matched his own.

As the gunman ran up, Tucker had spotted his broken wrist, the ripped bloodied flesh. He recognized Kane's handiwork. This was the commando who had threatened his partner.

In the other's eyes, he read the satisfaction of the kill to come.

It matched his own.

And another's.

A fierce growl erupted from the shadows, drawing the gunman's attention. His pistol jerked in that direction.

Using the distraction, Tucker yanked out the rifle hidden under the truck—the commando's own weapon. He twisted the barrel forward and fired at the gunman's face, blowing him backward.

As his body fell away, Gray appeared behind him, racing forward—then skidding back in surprise. "How . . . where did you get . . . ?"

Tucker, still on his back, turned to the shadows under the dump truck. Kane crouched there, panting, his eyes glowing brightly out of the darkness. As commanded, his partner had not only taken down his opponent but also *disarmed* him. Tucker pictured his partner dragging the rifle by its leather strap in his teeth, ever obedient, obeying down to the word.

"Good boy," Tucker said, staring back into those clever eyes. "Good boy."

9:35 P.M.

Gray headed down the street toward Hotel Jubba. After he found Tucker, the pair had quickly retreated out of the construction area. They found no further resistance. With the mission completed, the remaining commandos—likely hired mercenaries—had pulled out and vanished into the night.

Whoever had employed those assassins plainly wanted Amur silenced. His inquiries must have alerted the pirates involved in Amanda's kidnapping and triggered this swift reaction.

Now Gray and Tucker were back among the street throngs in the new section of the city, stopping only long enough to bandage Tucker's shoulder. Luckily the bullet had only grazed his upper arm.

Tucker finished explaining what happened. "From the video feed, I saw that Kane had retreated somewhere among these dump trucks and went looking for him."

"And you got ambushed."

Tucker scowled and glanced down at the dog at his side. He'd stripped off the dog's vest and held it bundled under his good arm. "I wasn't leaving him in harm's way, commander. And I never will. Kane looks after me with equal diligence. I wouldn't be alive now if it wasn't for him."

And you wouldn't have been in danger if you'd obeyed orders.

But Gray let that lie for now.

Tucker continued. "Once at the trucks, Kane must have tracked me down, keeping hidden, closing in on my scent."

"And he brought you that rifle." Gray could not keep the tinge of respect out of his voice.

"I'd ordered him to disarm his opponent. He'd been trained well."

Gray suspected such coordination went beyond training, that it had more to do with an inexplicable bond between dog and handler, tying them together by something deeper than just hand signals and spoken commands.

Whatever the reason, they'd all made it out with only a few scrapes and scratches. Amur's group might have been killed—silenced by the hired assassination team—but because of Kane's help, they now knew the president's daughter was being held somewhere in the Cal Madow mountains to the west.

Before Gray could formulate a plan of action from here, he noted the tumult outside of Hotel Jubba. Tables were overturned, stalls broken, windows shattered. Men sat in the street, nursing injuries. It looked like the aftermath of a small riot.

"What happened?" Tucker asked.

"I don't know."

Gray hurried to the steps of the hotel. He found the lobby equally ransacked. A televised soccer game played in the neighboring restaurant. A few men stood idly, sipping tea, amid the carnage of tables and chairs, as if nothing had happened.

Gray touched his throat mike and radioed both Kowalski and Seichan. No response.

Tucker shared a worried look with him.

Together they mounted the stairs. Their room—a two-bedroom suite—was on the second floor. Gray led the way down a tiled hallway, softened by a threadbare Persian runner. He kept his tread quiet as he approached the door. From inside, the cheers of an audience echoed out, coming from a television, likely broadcasting the same soccer match.

Gray pulled out his pistol and grabbed the door handle.

Tucker held a palm toward Kane, readying his partner.

Gray burst into the room—only to find Kowalski sprawled in his boxers on the sofa in the suite's common room, a washcloth full of ice held to his right eye.

Kowalski barely acknowledged them, still focused on the game.

Gray searched around the room. Nothing seemed amiss.

"Why didn't you respond to my radio call?" Gray asked.

Kowalski stared sheepishly toward the table. His radio and earpiece rested there. He ran a hand through his wet hair. "I took a shower and forgot to—"

Gray cut him off. "Never mind. What happened downstairs?"

Kowalski heaved his legs to the floor with a pained groan. "You said to cause a commotion when we got here."

"I meant a diversion, not World War Three."

Kowalski shrugged. "So things got a little out of hand. I gotta say, these Muslim guys—no sex, no alcohol—they sure *needed* to blow off some steam."

Gray relaxed, holstering his weapon. "Where's Seichan?"

Kowalski lowered the ice from his face, revealing a swollen bloodred eye. "I thought she was with you guys."

"Us? Why?" Gray's chest tightened painfully. Kowalski's next words only made it worse.

"She left to go find you."

8

Seichan sat in a windowless cement-block basement. A single bare bulb hung above her head. The space stank of bleach and had a drain in the middle of the floor.

Never a good sign.

Her left hand throbbed from where she'd sliced the meat of her thumb on a piece of broken glass when she was forced to drop on her stomach in the back alley. They'd immediately stripped her of all communications equipment and dragged a hood over her head. Forced at gunpoint, she traveled a few blocks by foot, stumbling along—then by open truck, judging by the wind, the sound of the engine, and the jolting of the suspension. She had to cling to the door frame to keep her seat, her cut hand stinging with every bump. The gun shoved in her rib cage discouraged any attempt at escape. They'd gone no more than ten minutes before stopping, so she couldn't be far from the hotel, but in the jumbled maze of the city, they might as well have taken her to another planet.

Once here, the hood had been removed, and she'd been ordered to strip down to bra and panties and been thoroughly searched again. Afterward, her wounded hand had been tended to, though blood still seeped down her fingertips and dripped to the floor. They'd allowed her to slip her clothes back on, but she still felt half-naked.

She tugged at the plastic slip ties that bound her to a metal chair. She tried rocking, but her seat was bolted to the concrete floor.

Resigned, she silently cursed her carelessness—placing an equal amount of the blame on Gray.

If the bastard hadn't gone off so recklessly on his own . . .

But she knew she bore as much guilt. She had acted no less rashly than Gray. And that troubled her, especially since she knew the cause. She remembered that kiss in the hospital, both needing each other but for very different reasons. Her carelessness this night was born out of that kiss. Fear for his safety, worry that she'd lose him, blinded her and made her sloppy.

She should have known better than to run headlong into a back alley. Hadn't their premission briefing warned of the rash of kidnappings in the city? The only balm to her ego was that her captors hadn't been pirates.

The single door to the room finally opened. Two figures stepped inside. One carried a thick file folder; the other, a chair identical to her own. The seat was placed in front of her, and the man who had ambushed her in the alley sat down, resting a file on his knee. He had short sandy-blond hair, balding at the top, ruggedly handsome in his own way.

His companion—a slender Indian woman with mocha skin and smoky eyes—took a post behind the chair, stiff-backed, one hand resting on a holstered sidearm. Like the man, she was dressed in khaki pants and a buttoned blue blouse, all crisply creased, giving the casual clothes the look of a uniform.

Seichan locked eyes with her. "You were one of the three following us this evening, wearing the green sarong."

The woman gave no reaction.

Seichan glanced between the two. She spotted an older photo of her, grainy but unmistakable, clipped to the folder. "Let me guess, you all have nothing to do with Amur Mahdi at all."

The man answered, his British accent polite but firm. "I think I'll be the one asking questions." He flipped open the folder and glanced through the first few pages. "Considering your number of aliases, I don't even know what to call you."

"How about your worst enemy," she said sourly.

This earned the smallest uptick of the woman's lip—not out of amusement, but disdain.

The man ignored her comment. "Your employer committed an act of terrorism on our soil, a few years back at the British Museum, orchestrated by a terrorist named—" He sifted through some papers. "—Cassandra Sanchez. A nasty piece of work, that one."

A chill iced over Seichan. Cassandra had been a Guild operative, like herself, planted beside Painter Crowe before he was director of Sigma. Seichan knew little else about that operation except the woman was dead.

Since her capture, Seichan had been struggling to determine *who* had ambushed her, running various possibilities through her head. She was on the watch list of multiple foreign intelligence services for her past activities with the Guild. From the man's accent, she narrowed down the possibilities. They could be SIS—the British Secret Intelligence Service, sometimes referred to as MI6—but she caught the whiff of military about them.

"You're SRR," Seichan concluded.

The man straightened, staring back at her. "Impressive."

The Special Reconnaissance Regiment was a newer division of the British Special Forces, established recently to engage in covert surveillance operations, specifically to conduct counterterrorism actions. They were also the most selective and most secretive—and the only British Special Forces unit to recruit women.

She stared at the Indian woman.

Few knew anything substantial about SRR activities. But it made sense they'd employ field operatives in Somalia. Pirates had kidnapped several British nationals over the past decade, and the lawless rural areas of this country were the training grounds for a handful of Islamic terrorist factions.

Unfortunately, she must have been swept up by their surveillance net by accident.

The man confirmed this. "We have facial recognition software hacked into the security cameras at the airport here. You were lucky it was us who found you. As I understand, the Mossad have a shoot-on-sight order regarding you."

Seichan continued to put the pieces together in her head. "Your tail on us . . . it had been purposefully sloppy. You wanted us to know we were being followed."

"And we expected you'd try to shake it, escaping out a back door—and right into our hands." The man leaned forward. "But who are you traveling with? The two men? We've identified them both as former U.S. armed forces—but nothing after that. Their records are clean, spotless, suspiciously so. Are they Guild operatives, or merely mercenaries for hire, or were you using them in some manner?"

Seichan hesitated, unsure how to respond. No one knew she'd turned traitor against the Guild and now worked for Sigma. Only a handful of people in the U.S. government even knew about her involvement. Her past crimes precluded her from being officially sanctioned. So if she were ever caught—like now—she would be denied. She was on her own, certain to vanish forever down some black-ops hole.

"If you continue to refuse to cooperate," the man began—when the door exploded behind him, ripped off its hinges.

A silver object bounced into the room.

Seichan closed her eyes, wishing she could cover her ears.

The flash-bang exploded in the confined space, searing through her eyelids and deafening to the point of nausea. She gasped out as it faded, and opened her eyes. Blearily, she saw a small shape dash into the room, running low to the ground. She felt the brush of fur against her bare calf, and the cold nose exploring her bloody fingers.

"About time you got here," she croaked out, deaf to her own words.

Gray and Tucker swept into the room, pistols in hand. The two SRR operatives were down on the floor, in postures of agony, having taken the full brunt of the flash-bang's impact. Still, the female had enough wherewithal to aim her weapon at Seichan. Though sightless at the moment, she kept enough of her senses to free her weapon and blindly shoot in the direction of Seichan's chair.

The muzzle flashed, and the shot sparked off the concrete floor, stinging her toes with stone chips. The shepherd leaped away from her chair, startled.

Gray swung his weapon toward the shooter.

Seichan yelled, "Stop! Don't shoot!"

Tucker, closer, pistol-whipped the woman and dropped her to the floor, then collected her weapon.

"They're British Special Forces!" Seichan shouted, finally beginning to hear her own words as the effect wore off.

Gray pointed to the pair. "Keep them down," he ordered Tucker. "Until we can sort this all out."

He turned next to Seichan, a small military dagger appearing in his hand. He rushed to her side and sliced her bonds free, careful of her bloody hand. As he crouched, he rested his palm on her bare knee, his fingers electric on her inner thigh.

"Are you okay?"

With her ears ringing, she still understood enough to nod. "I'm fine. I cut myself on purpose. Made sure I kept the wound open as I clung to the truck's door frame on the way here. Figured it was time for that damned dog to earn his kibble."

Tucker heard. "Leaving a blood trail for Kane to follow. Smart."

It wasn't *smart*. It was *planning*.

On the flight to Africa, she had studied up on their potential new teammate, ascertaining the dog's strengths and weaknesses, as she would *any* partner in the field. A report she read stated that a trained dog could distinguish a single drop of blood in an Olympic-size swimming pool. She hadn't planned on testing that sensitivity, but she was more than happy to prove it true now.

She gained her feet, still unsteady from the auditory assault, but at least she could hear. "What about the other SRR personnel?"

"We took down one outside the hotel," Gray said with a worried look. "He's still tied up in the back alley, out cold. Kowalski has the other secured upstairs. Took him down like a battering ram when we burst inside, might've broken his leg."

"Definitely broken," a gruff voice answered at the door. Kowalski stepped to the threshold and pointed his thumb toward the stairs leading out of the basement. "Got him gagged and tied up there. So how much trouble are we in for kicking some British soldiers' asses?"

The answer came from the floor. The man had also regained enough of his senses to glare, teary-eyed, at them. "I think your American colloquialism is *a shitload*." He stared at the assemblage in the room. "Who the bloody hell are you all?"

Gray holstered his weapon and offered out an arm to get him back on his feet. "Someone who needs your help."

The man took Gray's hand suspiciously, but he allowed himself to be pulled back to his feet. "This is a fine way to ask for it."

Kowalski offered the only possible explanation. "We're Americans. It's how we do things."

11:34 P.M.

An hour later, Gray had everyone gathered back at their suite at the Hotel Jubba. They sat in the common room. A call to Director Crowe, followed by a flurry of communiqués between the two countries' intelligence agencies, facilitated some candid conversation.

"The kidnapped woman out of the Seychelles," Captain Trevor Alden said, holding a steaming teacup in the palm of his hand. "She's the president's daughter?"

"That's right," Gray said. "Amanda Gant-Bennett."

The two groups sat on opposite couches, Americans on one side, Brits on the other. A tea service tray rested on the table between them. Kane kept near his handler as Tucker balanced on the arm of the sofa, but his nose kept drifting toward a stack of tea biscuits.

Captain Alden's eyes shifted to Seichan, seated next to Gray. "And she works for you chaps now."

Gray simply nodded, not bothering to go into the complicated details of their professional relationship.

Alden leaned back. "Someone could've informed us all of this before you got here. Would've saved Major Patel a great deal of hardship."

Kowalski paced behind the sofa, near the balcony doors, where the smoke from his cigar was less offensive. "Sorry. Maybe I shouldn't have sacked him so hard, but he got in my way." He shrugged, showing little remorse. "But aren't you guys supposed to wear special berets or something?"

"Not on a mission. We're a covert team," Alden explained. "Just the four of us—or three now, I guess."

Patel had been shot up with morphine and was sleeping in the next room, awaiting evacuation due to his broken leg. On the sofa, the captain was flanked by his two other associates: the Indian woman—Major Bela Jain—and a black, wiry soldier, Major Stuart Butler.

Gray redirected the conversation to the problem at hand. "Captain Alden, any local intelligence you can supply us, to help figure out where the president's daughter might have been taken, would be most appreciated."

"No appreciation necessary. We've been ordered to offer our services." Alden winced, then gently placed his teacup on the tray. "My apologies. That came out less sincerely than I intended. I have a young daughter of my own. If she'd been kidnapped . . ."

Alden leaned forward and offered his hand.

Gray took it and found the man's grip firm and dry.

"You have our *full* cooperation," Alden promised.

Gray found himself warming to the man. Once past the stiff British reserve, he seemed likable enough. And he had captured Seichan, not an easy thing to do.

However, from the way Seichan sat with her arms folded over her chest, fingering the tiny silver dragon pendant at her throat with her bandaged hand, she didn't share Gray's opinion of the SRR captain. Likewise, Major Jain barely said a word, her features hard and unreadable, her posture rigid. Gray imagined the woman's head still ached from the effects of the flash-bang, not to mention being pistol-whipped by Tucker.

Not the most opportune way for allies to meet.

Still, they'd all have to find a way to work together.

"Do you have any clues at all to the whereabouts of the young woman?"

Alden asked, getting down to business. "Where she made landfall? Who took her?"

"Not much."

Gray had briefly related their encounter with Amur Mahdi and the attack by an assassination squad in the construction yard. The captain was unaware of any of it, so Gray got him up to speed.

Next, he reached to the table and unfolded a topographic map of the country. Alden leaned closer as Gray ran a finger along the mountain range to the west of the city. It cut clear across northern Somalia.

"All we know," Gray said, "is that she was likely taken somewhere up in these mountains."

"That's a lot of rough territory. Jungles, chasms, caves. You could spend years searching up there and only scour a tenth of those peaks. Do you have any other intel?"

"We're still waiting for an NRO satellite to search the coastline for the raiders' ship."

"Needle in a haystack," Alden pronounced grimly with a shake of his head. "And they move those ships regularly. Even if you found it, that doesn't mean that's where the boat made landfall."

Gray couldn't disagree. He closed his eyes and replayed the conversation between Amur and his men. The man's group had been silenced for a reason. There had to be a clue there, something useful.

Then he remembered and straightened. One line of that conversation played out in his head.

A friend of my brother's uncle, up near Eil, he says a white woman came through his village. He says they were moving her into the mountains.

Gray opened his eyes and stared at the map. "Do you know some town named Eil?"

Alden nodded, studying the coastline. "It's a small place, a tough town, pirate run." He finally tapped the map. "Right here, by this deep-water cove."

"One of Amur's men said they'd heard of a white woman, a hostage, who had been through that village. If we went to that town—"

Alden cut him off. "You'd be shot on sight. And even if you did somehow survive, they'd tell you nothing. Anyone squeals there, and it's an
instant death sentence."

Gray pictured the last of Amur's men being shot.

Still, Alden did not seem despondent. "If they went directly from Eil
to the mountains, that could narrow your search." He ran a finger inland.
"I'd suggest you call your director and ask him to have the NRO give
up the satellite search for the ship and concentrate on this section of the
mountains."

He marked off a box with his fingertip.

"That's still hundreds of square miles," Gray said.

"True."

"What about an infrared sweep?" Tucker offered. "If the satellite can
pick out heat signatures, narrow the search parameters . . . ?"

"Maybe. But as hot as it gets here in summer, those rocky peaks retain
plenty of heat throughout the night." Alden leaned closer to the map. "But
I may have a better idea."

"What?"

Alden smiled and glanced at the closed bedroom door. "I think I just
found a good use for our poor Major Patel."

9

Painter sat in his office, struggling with a puzzle that set his teeth to aching. Since this morning's briefing with the president, he'd been ensconced in his windowless office at Sigma headquarters, buried several floors beneath the Smithsonian Castle, yet steps away from the halls of power and many of the country's best scientific institutions and think tanks.

Earlier, he'd reviewed the video feed from Somalia, listened to the audio recordings. Without a doubt, Amur Mahdi had been executed in order to silence him. The CIA was already squawking about the murder of one of its local assets, even though Amur was clearly playing one side against the other. And in this case, the turncoat had gotten crushed between them.

Still, the assassination of Amur offered further support to the idea that there was more to the kidnapping of Amanda Gant-Bennett than simple piracy.

Painter was sure of it.

But what?

So far, no ransom demand had been made. There continued to be no chatter among the various regional terrorist groups, no one claiming responsibility. If they had the president's daughter, they'd be crowing from the rooftops about it.

So what game were they playing out there?

Painter could not shake the feeling that Amanda's kidnapping was somehow tied to the Guild. Perhaps she was being used as a pawn by a competing criminal organization to put pressure on the Gants—that is, if the Gants were indeed the true puppet masters behind the shadowy Guild.

He had a hard time balancing that with the raw fear he'd seen in the president's eyes, the anguish and grief in the First Lady's embrace of her husband in the hallway. Even Gant's older brother, the secretary of state, had seemed openly sincere about finding Amanda.

But that didn't mean *other* family members were not involved.

He returned his attention to the large LCD monitor on his desk. Using a mouse, he scrolled through the long list of names glowing on the screen, each of them connected by branching and crisscrossing lines marking family ties: marriages and births, even infidelities and children born out of wedlock. It mapped out the genealogy of the Gant family clan, stretching back two centuries. It was less a family tree than an interlacing matrix, so complicated it required being diagrammed out in three dimensions.

Clicking and dragging, he spun the matrix in a slow turn, a spiral galaxy of power and influence going back to before the founding of this country. And it was still incomplete. He had historians and genealogists from around the globe working piecemeal on the puzzle, to keep the project secret, building a picture of the true breadth and extent of this ancient clan. He doubted anyone had ever performed such a comprehensive analysis of the Gant clan.

He also noted lines that crossed into and out of the matrix, distant cousins marrying back into the family—not an unheard-of situation in such a powerful, aristocratic family. It seemed, generation after generation, no one wanted to drift too far from that wellspring of power and wealth.

And what a wellspring it was . . .

Painter had lost count of the number of inventors, scholars, statesmen, and leaders of industry that shone like stars amid the lineage. Not to mention rogues and several persons of ill repute.

But every family had its bad apples.

He frowned at the screen, seeing his faint reflection superimposed over the matrix. Was the truth of the Guild hidden here or was it all a wild-goose chase?

To remind himself of the true nature of his adversaries, Painter clicked on an image file and brought up a symbol onto the screen—or rather a *nested* set of symbols.

It represented the Guild.

At the center stood a tiny crescent moon and star. It was one of the oldest symbols in the world, going back to an esoteric order out of ancient Egypt. Enclosed around that, the more familiar square and compass, representing another secret fraternity: the Freemasons. And at last, circling them all, the shield of the Knights Templar, a medieval order infamous for its hidden mysteries.

" 'The secret in all secret societies,' " he whispered, repeating the dying words of a Guild associate. That was the significance of the nested symbols. It was said to represent the Guild's path, tracing its treacherous footsteps deep into the past.

The same dying man also suspected there were more levels and tiers—other secret societies—beyond those revealed in the old symbol, secrets continuing into modern times, leading at last to what he called the *True Bloodline*, the ultimate masters of the shadowy Guild.

"One family," Painter mumbled, staring at the vast lineage of the Gant clan.

To survive the scrutiny of time, the Guild had hid itself within one secret society after another. Was he staring at the same subterfuge here?

Was the true heart of this shadowy organization buried within the breadth and majesty of this family dynasty?

If so, how many were involved?

He studied the three-dimensional map, sensing he was missing something, that it stared him square in the face. But whatever nagged him refused to come to light.

A knock at his door interrupted him. A tall, auburn-haired woman in dress blues stood at the threshold. Painter tapped his keyboard and wiped the Gant genealogy off the screen.

It was meant for his eyes only.

"Kat," he said and waved the woman inside.

Captain Kathryn Bryant was his second-in-command, specializing in intelligence-gathering services for Sigma.

Painter pulled his attention fully to the present, to the matters in Somalia. "Have the Brits settled down after the mess in Boosaaso?"

"Barely. But the SRR has agreed to keep things under wraps and to offer their assistance out there."

"Very good."

"But that's not the only reason I stopped by," Kat said. "I brought someone to see you."

She stepped aside and a familiar face, draped by blond hair, peered coyly around the corner.

"Lisa!" he said, delight filling his voice. He stood up and crossed around his desk. "I thought you weren't getting back until tonight."

Dr. Lisa Cummings slipped inside, dressed in jeans and a loose pale-blue blouse. She tapped her wrist. "What time do you think it is?"

As usual, he'd let the day escape him—but he wasn't going to do the same with his girlfriend. He pulled her into a warm hug, kissing her cheek, appreciating how *right* this felt.

She sagged into him, expressing a similar thought. "It's good to be home."

They lingered in each other's arms for another breath until finally falling away, leaving only their hands clasped together. Lisa had been gone a week at a medical symposium. He had not realized how much he missed her until this moment.

He guided her to one of the chairs and settled her there before letting go of her hand.

"I heard about the president's daughter," Lisa said dourly. "I remember her from one of those black-tie affairs at the White House several months ago. She had just found out she was pregnant."

"Speaking of which . . ." Kat took the other seat. "Director, you asked me to gather information about Amanda's pregnancy."

Painter leaned back against his desk. He had a full dossier on the president's daughter, but almost nothing regarding the baby she carried. He wanted every base covered. Something was odd about this entire affair—from the false papers to the trip to the Seychelles, and now this kidnapping.

He dared leave no stone unturned.

"First of all, her unborn child is not her husband's," Kat began.

Painter's brows rose in surprise. This was news to him.

Kat explained, "Apparently Mack Bennett had fertility issues that required the use of a sperm donor and in vitro fertilization."

"Interesting." Painter folded this new knowledge into the case, testing various permutations, different possibilities.

Could there be some motive here? A custody issue?

"Where was this done?" he finally asked.

"A fertility clinic in South Carolina, outside of Charleston. I looked it up. Very cutting-edge. Using the latest technology. With a client list from around the world."

"And the donor for the child?"

Kat shook her head. "Confidential."

Painter hated loose ends—they had the tendency to unravel into a mess.

Kat read his expression. "I can make some calls, but without a court order—"

Painter shook his head. "A legal action would raise too many red flags, get others inquiring about Amanda's whereabouts. We can't risk that exposure."

"Not to mention it would be a significant invasion of her privacy," Lisa reminded him.

"And in the end, the child might have nothing to do with this," Kat added.

Painter crossed his arms, unconvinced. "Amanda fled to the Seychelles just a couple of weeks before she was due to deliver. Traveling under false papers, like she was running from someone—or protecting someone."

"You're thinking it's about the baby," Kat said. "But why?"

"I don't know. But some answers might be found at that clinic."

"I could send a team to investigate."

"Or I can go," Lisa offered. "I'm an M.D. Simple professional courtesy could open doors easier than a commando raid."

Painter's lips hardened. Lisa had helped Sigma multiple times in the past. Her medical expertise, especially in regards to Amanda's pregnancy, could prove useful—and likely why Kat had involved her today. And Painter had to admit that Lisa's suggestion made sense, risked less exposure, but he hated to put her in danger.

"I can accompany her," Kat offered. "Possibly posing as a potential new client."

"But you've got a newborn and a toddler at home."

"And I've also got a husband with too much time on his hands," she argued. "Monk can keep an eye on Harriet and Penelope for a couple of days."

Monk Kokkalis, her spouse, was a former Sigma operative who had opted to retire so he could spend more time with his wife and family. He'd also had one too many close calls during prior missions and called it quits.

"I don't think your husband would want you out in the field," Painter warned.

"It's not like I'm traveling halfway around the world. It's barely a day trip."

Kat's face betrayed her. Her eyes danced at the thought of getting her hands dirty again. After two back-to-back pregnancies, she clearly needed some fresh air, to stretch her legs with a little fieldwork. As proficient as she was in her role at Sigma headquarters, she was still a soldier at heart. She had not graduated from the U.S. Naval Academy and gained the rank of captain in order to be stuck in an office all day.

He sometimes forgot that about her.

He nodded. "I can get you a flight out first thing in the morning."

She smiled, glancing over at Lisa, who wore a similar grin.

Painter realized the truth at that moment. The two women had played him from the outset, intending this result all along. Rather than calling them on it, he simply resigned himself to the inevitable.

"We should return to my office," Kat said to Lisa. "Get everything in order before our morning flight."

Lisa stood, gave him a quick peck on the cheek, and headed after Kat—but not before hanging back in the doorway with a smile that held infinite promise. "I'll see you tonight."

Painter watched them head down the hall. It was not an unpleasant sight. As they disappeared around a corner, the worries settled back over his shoulders.

He reached to a file on his desk and slipped out the top photo inside. It was the last picture taken of Amanda, smiling next to her husband, one hand supporting her belly, protective, proud.

Painter stared harder at the picture, noticing for the first time the edge of fear in her eyes, the way she leaned close to her husband, almost sheltering herself. Even the arm clutched around her partner's waist clung a bit too tightly.

What were you so scared of, Amanda?

11:59 P.M. East Africa Time
Cal Madow mountains, Somalia

The needle sank into Amanda's belly, delivering a burning sting of anesthetic. Her fingers dug into the thin sheets of the hospital bed. She watched it all, refusing to look away.

Her hospital gown had been pulled up over her stomach, exposing her swollen belly and protruding navel. A privacy sheet covered her from the waist down—not that they'd spared her from any indignities up to now.

"That should numb her well enough, Dr. Blake," the tall blond woman said, disposing of the used syringe in a red sharps container. She had a slight German accent, maybe Swiss.

"Thank you, Petra."

The British doctor patted Amanda's arm. Like his nurse, he wore scrubs—but rather than the typical blue, his were old-fashioned, solid white. "We'll be done in a few minutes, and you can get some rest for the night. I know it's been a long day."

The pair left to finish final preparations for the procedure.

Amanda had no choice but to wait in the bed. She kneaded her belly, reassuring herself and the child inside. She noted the leather restraints hanging from the rails. It frightened her that they hadn't bothered to tie her down. It demonstrated their unflagging confidence in the security surrounding the cabin.

She stared at the ultrasound's monitor, dark at the moment but waiting to be used in the procedure to come. They'd already performed a scan of her abdomen when she arrived here, recording her baby's position, measuring the dimensions of his skull and approximate body length. She hadn't resisted that first ultrasound. At the time, she had wanted to know the status of her child as fiercely as the doctor had.

In the end, it had brought her great relief to see the flutter of his heartbeat, his tiny curled fists, his small, sleepy movements. After a close examination of the sonogram, the doctor pronounced her boy wonderfully healthy.

But it seemed the medical team was not done with her.

Dr. Blake returned. Petra carried a tray holding a large syringe equipped with a five-inch-long needle. Amanda had already had an amniocentesis when she was eighteen weeks along, so she knew what to expect.

Petra swabbed her stomach with fresh antiseptic, then powered up the ultrasound and handed the lubed probe to Dr. Blake. With an eye on the monitor, the doctor guided the needle deep into her belly. The pain was minimal, like a mild menstrual cramp.

She looked away from the monitor as the tip of the needle approached her sleeping child. It was too disconcerting to watch. One slip and she could only imagine the damage that might be done.

In the end, all went well.

Fluid was drawn skillfully from the amniotic sac around her boy, and the needle withdrawn. She finally let out the breath she had been holding. Tears suddenly blurred her vision.

"Monitor her for fever," the doctor ordered Petra. "Watch for any vaginal bleeding."

Petra nodded.

Dr. Blake turned to Amanda. "There's no need for tears. At least not now. We won't have the genetic test results until the morning."

Her first amniocentesis had been routine, done to rule out various chromosomal abnormalities like Down syndrome or genetic disorders like cystic fibrosis. But she knew that wasn't all the doctors had been searching for—not then, not now.

The note that sent her running from the States had warned of something genetically *different* about her baby, something others wanted to possess. She didn't understand much else, only enough to run before they came for her child.

Blake continued, "If the genetics are stable, your child will live—the very first of his kind. If not . . . well, we'll worry about such matters then, won't we?"

Again that paternal pat on her arm.

Even if the results were *stable,* she knew awful consequences would be in store for her baby boy. And if they weren't, the medical team here would likely perform a late-term abortion.

She turned her head to the side, not knowing which result to hope for in the morning. Tears welled again as her hands found her belly—but she was certain of one thing. With the last breath in her body, she would die defending her baby.

I won't let them harm you.

A bonfire in the outer camp glowed through the canvas wall, high-lighting the crimson cross she'd noted earlier. Again she saw the odd, almost fanciful decorations along its spans, a twisting and coiling pattern that traversed both crosspieces. Only now—after the amniocentesis, af-ter the worries about chromosomal abnormalities—did she recognize the structures.

They were helices of DNA.

Genetic code.

She stared, disbelieving. Coldness crept through her body. Though she'd never seen this cross before, she had heard whispers about this sym-bol, marking an ancient mystery that traced back to the founding of her family, to a secret buried at its heart.

She had thought its existence a myth, a story meant to scare children.

But now she could no longer deny the horrible truth. It was what that cryptic note had warned her about, what had sent her running to the Sey-chelles in terror.

The Bloodline.

They've found me.

10

Gray adjusted the bulky earphones, muffled against the roar of the helicopter's twin engines. He stared out the cabin window as Captain Alden pointed.

"There it is!" the British SRR officer yelled.

The aircraft swept low over a sun-blasted rolling landscape of parched fields, broken red rock, and occasional patches of scraggly trees. Herds of goats scattered from under the pummeling wash of the blades. In the distance, a mountain range thrust into the morning sky, breaking the horizon into jagged lines. But the medical transport chopper would not be flying that far.

Alden pointed to a large camp of tents and huts sprawled at the intersection of two gravel roads. The top of many of the tents bore red crosses. Parked vehicles—civilian cars and United Nations trucks—dotted the surrounding fields, along with many camels.

It was a relief camp run by UNICEF and operated by the French organization Médecins Sans Frontières, known in the States as Doctors Without Borders. It lay sheltered in the foothills, halfway between the mountains and the ocean, acting as a way station for those living both inland and at the coast.

A groan drew Gray's attention back to the rear cabin of the helicopter. Major Patel remained strapped in a stretcher on the floor, his morphine wearing off from the hour-long flight from Boosaaso's airport to this medical enclave. The French doctors here would have no trouble casting his broken tibia and stabilizing him enough for travel back to Europe.

But that was not why they'd really come.

Patel's condition was merely a cover to explain this inland journey.

Alden leaned closer, but used the radio built into the headphones to communicate. "I have a contact who should be waiting for us after we land. If any word of the kidnapped woman passed through the camp, he'll ferret it out."

Gray nodded and glanced over at Tucker and Seichan. Kowalski was up front with Major Butler, who was flying the helicopter.

It wasn't a bad plan. The camp lay within the shadow of the Cal Madow mountains. As the only relief facility for hundreds of miles, the site was the major crossroads for the entire region, as Somalis from all walks of life, travelers, and nomads, came seeking medical help, continually flowing into and out of the place. Because of that, the camp was also a strategic and important clearinghouse for information. It was no wonder the SRR had someone posted on the inside here.

With care, Gray's team might learn something vital about Amanda's whereabouts—or at least, narrow the search parameters. Back in DC, Painter was coordinating a satellite scan of the neighboring mountains. Between boots on the ground and eyes in the skies, the hope was to pinpoint Amanda's location before nightfall.

Sand suddenly swirled beyond the windows, kicked up as the chopper descended. With a final, stomach-lifting drop, the skids finally kissed the ground.

Alden hauled the cabin doors open. Sand and heat pounded inside as the roar of the engines whined away. They all exited the helicopter and were met by a medical team of four, who rushed forward to help offload Major Patel. His stretcher was carried away to an idling Jeep. Major Butler accompanied his injured partner, to make sure he was properly attended to and to spread the cover story that their group were foreign aid workers.

Tucker patted his dog's side, reassuring the shepherd after the long, noisy ride.

Kowalski merely scowled at the grim surroundings. "Once . . . just once . . . why can't we end up at some beach where women are in bikinis and where drinks come in coconuts?"

Seichan ignored him and stood at Gray's shoulder. "What now?"

"This way!" Alden answered, heading off, accompanied by the last member of the British SRR team, Major Bela Jain. The captain pointed toward a cluster of thatched-roof huts.

As a group, they crossed through a parking lot of rusted trucks, skeletal sand-rail buggies, and beat-up motorcycles. Guarding them all stood an older Daimler Ferret Scout car, painted United Nations white and emblazoned with their blue symbol. It looked like a minitank with a fully enclosed armored cabin and mounted with a Belgian L7 machine-gun turret. A United Nations peacekeeper leaned against the vehicle, eyeing them suspiciously as they passed.

Alden noted Gray's attention. "Camps like this need to be protected. Raids are common, for drugs, even for water. Drought has devastated much of this region, contributing to famine and death, driving the people to the coasts or up into the mountains."

They reached the circle of huts to find a French doctor kneeling beside a long line of Somali children. A nurse prepped a syringe and handed it to the doctor, who jabbed it into the bony arm of the first boy in line.

Gray had read how the civil war going on in the southern part of the country had displaced hundreds of thousands of civilians and their children, leading to outbreaks of cholera, dysentery, and hepatitis. But a vaccination program against measles and polio, along with the administration of simple deworming tablets and vitamins, was saving countless young lives.

"Here's the contact I was telling you about," Alden said, pointing to the doctor. "He hears everything going around the camp, misses nothing. He's a great asset."

Gray studied the French M.D., a middle-aged man with bulky glasses and sunburned nose and ears. But Gray was wrong about the focus of attention.

"Baashi!" Alden called out and waved an arm, stepping forward.

The spy at the camp winced as he was injected in the arm. The young dark-skinned boy thanked the doctor in French. *"Merci."*

Pulling his tunic sleeve down, the child headed over. "Ah, Mr. Trevor. You come!"

"This is your contact?" Kowalski mumbled under his breath, plainly not pleased. "What is he, fourteen?"

"Thirteen actually," Major Jain said softly. She stared at her superior with raw admiration. "Captain Alden rescued the boy from a group of Muslim insurgents outside Mogadishu. A child soldier. Only eleven at the time, hyped on bloody amphetamines, brutalized and bearing scars from cigarette burns."

Gray's heart ached at the sight of the boy's mile-wide smile as he rushed forward and hugged Captain Alden, who had dropped to one knee. It seemed impossible to balance such simple joy with the horrors Major Jain described.

Alden hooked an arm around the boy's thin shoulders and led him back to the gathered group.

"Here are the people I wanted you to meet, Baashi."

The boy smiled, staring around, but Gray saw the hint of fear in his eyes, a wariness of strangers. He leaned more tightly against Alden. Here were the cracks that exposed the past trauma.

Tucker's dog squirmed forward, sniffing, wanting to get the scent of the newest addition to their pack.

Baashi's eyes got huge. A small squeal of terror stretched out of him. "Ayiiii . . ."

"Kane, come here," Tucker ordered, at the sound of the boy's distress.

The shepherd returned to his handler's side.

"Down." Tucker reinforced the command with a flat-handed gesture. He sank to a knee next to his dog, but his words were for the boy. "He won't hurt you. I promise. He's a good dog."

Tucker held out a hand, asking the boy to come forward.

Baashi remained frozen at Captain Alden's side.

"Just let the boy be," Seichan warned. "He's clearly afraid of dogs."

Kowalski made a grunt of agreement, even Jain's eyes pinched with concern.

Tucker ignored them all and kept his arm up.

Seichan looked to Gray for help. He simply shook his head, remembering the man's empathy scores. They had been through the roof. Tucker had a preternatural ability to interpret another's emotional core. And maybe it wasn't just with animals.

Clearly bonded to the child, knowing the boy, Alden also seemed to share Tucker's understanding. "It's okay, Baashi. If you want . . ."

The boy stared at the dog for a long breath, cocking his head, perhaps searching inside himself for that lost bond children have for all things furry and warm. Finally, he stepped clear of Alden's legs, trembling a bit.

His gaze never shifted from Kane. "He good dog?" Baashi asked.

Tucker nodded once.

Baashi crept forward, approaching as if toward a perilous cliff.

Kane remained alert, only the tip of his tail twitching with excitement. Baashi reached out the back of his hand toward the dog. Kane stretched his nose, nostrils flaring, snuffling.

Baashi moved an inch closer—it was far enough.

A long pink tongue slipped out and licked the boy's fingertips. The tail twitch turned into a big wag.

"He likes you," Tucker said softly.

Baashi's smile returned, shyly at first, then stronger. He moved near enough to touch Kane on the top of his head. The dog's nose sniffed along the length of his arm.

Baashi giggled and said something in a Somali dialect.

"Tickles," Alden translated.

Moments later, the boy was sitting on the ground, ruffling the dog's fur and trying to avoid an onslaught of licks. Gray stared at them both, remembering Kane's savage attack on the commando yesterday. Likewise, he tried to picture the boy with a rifle at his shoulder. In different ways, the two—boy and dog—were both warriors, and maybe Tucker had recognized that such harshness needed an outlet of innocence and play— and also trust.

Alden joined Gray. "Baashi is slowly coming around. The base here works with such children. They try to rehabilitate them, to bring out the scared child still trapped within the nightmares of those past horrors." He eyed Baashi and the dog—then Tucker. "You've got a good man there."

Gray had to agree.

Tucker stood off to the side, studying the distant mountains. After seeing how the handler and his dog had operated back in Boosaaso, how the shepherd had tracked Seichan's blood trail through the myriad scents and smells of the city, Gray wondered if it wouldn't be better to simply drop the pair into the mountains, let them hunt Amanda down by themselves, and radio back her location.

But that could take days . . . days he felt sure the president's daughter didn't have.

10:34 A.M.
Cal Madow mountains, Somalia

From the shouts and calls beyond the tent-cabin, Amanda knew something was happening. She heard the coughing choke of several truck engines, accompanied by the barking of orders.

One of the African soldiers burst into the cabin, talked to Dr. Blake, then turned on a heel and dashed back out again. Blake crossed the medical ward and disappeared behind a privacy screen that hid another bed. The outline of his nurse shadowed the screen. They bent their heads together, talking softly.

Amanda strained to hear. If she could've slipped quietly out of the bed to eavesdrop, she would have attempted it. But *stealthy* was not a word that best described her current state. Still, another reason also fired that desire. The outline of the other hospital bed clearly showed someone occupied it.

She had no idea who it was. An injured soldier? Another of the medical staff who had fallen ill? Whoever they were, they'd been slipped into the tent in the middle of the night when she'd been sleeping. She woke to find the privacy screen up and the doctor and nurse going back and forth to attend the new patient.

All she knew was that it was a woman, hearing at one point a small cry rising from beyond the screen, definitely feminine. But the new patient had been silent ever since. Likely sedated.

At last, Blake appeared again and headed over to Amanda with a chart in his hands. He must have read her worry. "Nothing to concern yourself with, my dear." He waved an arm toward the commotion going on out-side. "It seems someone has been making inquiries as to your whereabouts. Practically knocking at our doors."

Hope surged in Amanda at his words, stirring the child enough to kick. "Shhh," she whispered, rubbing her belly.

Having traveled under false papers, she feared that no one knew she was the true target of the midnight raid in the Seychelles. She avoided glancing at the cross symbol with the genetic markings, knowing the truth. The high-seas kidnapping had not been random bad luck. It had been purposefully planned and executed.

But now . . . could someone be trying to rescue me?

Icy water quickly doused that momentary hope as Blake continued, "But they'll be dealt with swiftly enough." His eyes settled on hers. "We wouldn't want to be interrupted. Especially with such good news in hand."

She understood, looking at the chart he held. "You got back the am-niocentesis results."

Blake flipped through a couple pages. "Your baby tested perfectly. The genetics remain stable. Better than we hoped." He smiled at her. "You're about to give birth to a miracle."

11:42 A.M.
UNICEF camp, Somalia

Seichan huddled with Gray inside one of the huts at the edge of the hos-pital encampment. Kowalski and Major Jain kept guard outside, making sure no one overheard their conversation—and considering how loud they were arguing, that wouldn't be a problem.

"Because beef is murder!" Jain said. "Hindus believe that God—"

"And if God didn't want us to eat cows, he wouldn't have made them so damn tasty—especially smothered in barbecue sauce!"

"That's not an argument. You'd probably eat your own shoe if it had barbecue sauce poured on it. I mean look at your ass."

"What about my butt?"

"I've seen cows with smaller rear ends."

A sputtering sound followed, then, "Quit looking at my ass!"

Tucker stared toward the door. "Diplomacy at its finest," he mumbled. "Your friend out there sure knows how to mend fences."

Tucker had been included in the meeting inside the hut—not because his expertise was needed. It was because of the skinny black arm around his dog's neck. Baashi had taken a real shine to Kane and what had started as terror now seemed a source of strength.

"No, I tell you again," the boy stressed. "I heard *no* one speak of a white woman in the mountains. Not here. Not at all."

A map had been spread out on the dirt floor.

Captain Alden crouched on the far side of it, next to the boy. "Okay, Baashi." He leaned back and sighed. "I'm sorry, commander. I may have sent you miles out of your way for nothing. Word may have never reached here."

Gray stared at the map. "It was a gamble," he conceded.

Seichan heard the *tick* in Gray's voice. Without even seeing his eyes, she could imagine the gears turning. He wasn't giving up, not yet.

And it wasn't just him.

"I can go out again," Baashi offered. "Into the camp. Ask questions. Not just listen."

"No," Seichan snapped. The vehemence of her response surprised her.

Still, Gray backed her up. "Seichan's right. It's one thing just to eavesdrop and pass on what he's heard, but to actively ask questions will put him in the crosshairs of our enemy. Remember what happened to Amur Mahdi back at Boosaaso."

"And it's not just the *risk* to the boy," Seichan started. "It's more than that."

Gray gave her a concerned look, perhaps hearing the sudden stress in her voice. She gave a small shake of her hand, not wanting to continue, not trusting herself. The boy had already been used and brutalized as a child soldier. How would they be any different if they turned the boy into their spy? It was bad enough that the British SRR was using the kid as an informant.

Seichan stared at her hands and found her fingers tightly bound together. She knew how easy it was to twist such innocence to foul purposes as the strong preyed on the weak, twisting children into monsters, turning them into soldiers or scouts, or even sending them ahead of an advancing army as living mine detectors.

She forced her hands apart. Her fingers found the silver dragon at her neck. She recognized why the boy's situation struck her so deeply, so personally. The realization made her both angry and ashamed.

She remembered little of her own childhood in Vietnam. Bits and pieces, none that included her father. And what she remembered of her mother she wished she could forget: of being ripped from her arms, of her mother being dragged out a door, bloody-faced and screaming, by men in military uniforms. Afterward, Seichan spent her childhood in a series of squalid orphanages across Southeast Asia, half-starved most of the time, maltreated the rest—until finally she'd taken to the streets and back alleys. It was there, when she was little older than Baashi, that the Guild found and recruited her. Over the course of the next year, the trainers stripped away not only her remaining childhood but also much of her humanity, leaving behind only an assassin.

I was this boy, she thought, *abused and tortured into bloody servitude.*

But she also knew there was one distinct difference between them. She pictured Baashi playing with the dog, carefree and happy. Unlike her, he was still young, malleable enough to rediscover his humanity.

She let her fingers drop from the dragon pendant, the memory of her mother dissolving away into faded whispers in the night and soft kisses on her cheek—but even then there had been tears, as if her mother knew she was about to lose her child.

The memory sparked a sudden insight regarding their current mission. "She's a mother, too," Seichan said, drawing Gray's attention. "The president's daughter . . ."

His eyes narrowed on hers—then widened with understanding. His fingers found her hand and squeezed his thanks, then remained there.

She stared down, wanting to feel more, but at this moment, all she felt was loss—for her childhood, her mother, even Gray. How could she ask more of his heart when she wasn't sure what was left of her own?

"Amanda's not only unusual because she's *white*," Gray explained to the others, "but also because she's *pregnant*."

Alden nodded. "Such a condition is rare in a kidnap victim. Someone might have made note of it."

"And hopefully talked about it." Gray turned to Baashi. "Have you heard anything about a pregnant woman being moved into the mountains near here? Someone with a large belly?"

To emphasize, Gray pantomimed a swollen stomach.

Baashi twisted his lips in thought and sat quietly for a moment, then slowly sagged. "No. I hear nothing about a big-belly woman with the pirates."

Seichan studied the boy. He stared too hard at the map, kept his attention diverted away. Even his arm fell from around Kane's neck.

"He knows something," Seichan said. Tucker wasn't the only one capable of reading emotions buried under the surface.

Especially this boy.

I was this boy.

"He wouldn't lie to me," Alden said.

"He's not lying," Seichan agreed, but angrily. "We're just not asking the right question."

Baashi's gaze met hers. Fear shone there—and resistance.

How many times had the same emotions warred inside her?

Tucker came and sat next to the boy. "It's okay, Baashi. Kane and I won't let anyone hurt you."

A silent hand signal followed: a flick of fingers, a digit pointed at the boy's lap. Baashi didn't see it, but Kane obeyed. The dog came forward and rested his muzzle on the boy's knee.

Baashi placed his palm on the dog's shoulders, drawing strength there.

"It's okay to tell us," Alden said softly. "No one's mad."

Baashi glanced sheepishly up at his father figure. "I no lie. I hear *no* stories about big-belly woman."

"I never thought you did, my boy. But what is scaring you? What are you so afraid to tell us?"

He finally broke down. "I hear other stories. Of a demon man in the mountains. He make a place like this." Baashi waved his other arm in a circle.

"Like the hospital here."

Baashi nodded. "But he only look after the big bellies on the woman."

"He takes care of pregnant women?" Alden asked, repeating Gray's pantomime of a swollen stomach.

"Yes, but they say bad things. Mothers go there. Never come back. A *very* bad place."

Tucker patted the boy on the shoulder. "You did good, Baashi."

The boy refused to look up, showing no relief.

Gray shifted to the map. "Do the stories say where in the mountains this doctor works?"

"Yes," Baashi said, but he still wouldn't look at the map.

"Can you show Kane?" Tucker said.

The boy glanced from soldier to dog—then slowly nodded. "I show you. But it's a bad place."

As the boy reached for the map, Kowalski burst into the room. "We've got a chopper inbound."

Alden seemed unconcerned. "They have medical drops all the time. Could be another patient, supplies, or—"

Major Jain shoved past Kowalski and dove inside. "Incoming! Get down!"

Gray rolled Seichan to the floor. Tucker and Alden sheltered the boy, pinning him under their bodies. Baashi clung tightly to Kane.

A sharp whistling screamed across the roof of the hut—followed by a massive explosion that shook thatch from the roof.

Jain returned to the door.

Another sharp scream of a rocket erupted.

She leaped back with even worse news. "This one's coming straight at us!"

11

Painter woke to the ringing of his cell phone, a crescendo of escalating notes that set his heart to thudding hard in his chest. He lay in bed next to Lisa, their naked limbs tangled together, his hand resting on the curve of her backside.

She sat up with him, going instantly alert, trained from years of being on-call at a hospital. The sheets shed from her breasts; her eyes shone in the predawn darkness. She also knew that particular ringtone, set for extreme emergencies.

Painter grabbed his cell phone from the nightstand and answered it.

"Director, we've got a problem." It was Kat Bryant, calling from Sigma headquarters. He glanced at the clock. It was barely after five in the morning.

When he'd left last night with Lisa, Kat had still been in the bunker, running logistics for Gray's operation and coordinating the various intelligence branches. Had she ever left?

"What's happened?" he asked.

"I'm fielding some frantic S.O.S.'s out of that UNICEF camp in Somalia, where Gray was headed. Reports of rocket fire. Some sort of attack."

"Do we have eyes on it?"

"Not yet. I'm already working with NRO. I tried to raise Gray, but so far there's been no response."

Likely a tad busy.

"What about support? We have the Navy SEAL team cooling its heels in neighboring Djibouti."

"I can get them airborne, but it'll still be forty to fifty minutes for them to reach that inland camp."

Painter closed his eyes, his mind racing through various parameters and scenarios. If he called in the SEAL team, it could threaten the entire mission, expose his hand too early. SEAL Team Six had been assigned here specifically to extract the president's daughter—not to play UN peacekeepers.

"Do we have any idea who is attacking?" Painter asked.

"The camp has been raided twice in the last ninety days. Both drug runs. And two months ago, a doctor got kidnapped by one of the local warlords. This attack may have nothing to do with Gray or the search for Amanda."

Painter wasn't buying it. He pictured the assassination of Amur Mahdi. The enemy seemed to know their every move. With all of the various intelligence agencies engaged in this mission—and now the British SRR—something was leaking out.

Painter trusted his own organization, but there were too many cooks in this international kitchen—not to mention the president's family. The leak could be coming from anywhere.

Painter had to make a tough decision. He could not lose focus. He had to preserve the SEAL team and its operational readiness for a possible fast extraction.

"Director?" Kat asked.

He kept his voice firm. "Get me eyes in the field as soon as you can, but for now, Gray's team is on their own."

A short pause followed, then Kat responded, "Understood."

Lisa's hand slipped into his. She didn't say a word, offering only her warmth.

"Should I delay the mission to South Carolina?" Kat asked.

Painter remembered the scheduled investigation into the clinic where Amanda had her in vitro fertilization performed. He could not escape the feeling that Amanda's sudden flight to the Seychelles had something to do with her child. First, the assassination of Amur, and now this new attack on the hospital camp—somebody intended for Amanda never to be found.

"No," he said, glancing at Lisa. "We'll head over to Sigma command right now. I want you both out on that first flight to Charleston."

A longer delay followed. Painter wondered if he'd lost Kat—then she came back on the line. "Director, I've got a few captured still shots of the camp. From a French weather satellite. They're not the best, but I'm sending them to your phone."

Painter pulled the device from his ear and switched to speaker as he waited for the image to fill the small screen. Line by line, the horror of the situation in Somalia revealed itself.

The image offered a high aerial view. Few details were discernible, especially with the thick pall of smoke obscuring most of the camp. Tiny dots represented people and vehicles trying to escape the attack. Overhead, the blurring image of a helicopter hovered above the chaos, like some predatory bird, waiting to pick off the weak.

Kat's small voice emerged over the speaker. "Did you get the sat-photo?"

"Got it."

Lisa peered over his shoulder, covering her mouth with a hand.

Painter struggled to keep to his original plan. It was easier to abandon Gray's team to a bad situation when it wasn't staring him in the face. But no matter how tough or callous, he knew his original decision was the correct one.

With a few final instructions, he signed off with Kat and lowered the phone. He stared out into the darkness.

Someone desperately wanted to stop Amanda from being found.

But who?

12:12 P.M. East Africa Time
Cal Madow mountains, Somalia

Dr. Edward Blake held the radio handset to his ear. He stood in the communications tent, crammed with gear and festooned with satellite dishes. The swelter of the day drew beads of perspiration down his forehead.

But he knew all of that sweat was not from the heat alone.

He even held his white safari hat in his other hand—not because he was indoors, but because of the presence at the other end of the line. Few personages ever intimidated him. He had been raised in an aristocratic family in Leeds, whose lineage included earls and dukes, all distantly related to the royal family. At estate dinners throughout the ages, their home had hosted famous figures of past and present, from the wartime leader General George Patton to entertainers who had been knighted by the queen. In Oxford, his roommate had been a billionaire's son, a prince out of Saudi Arabia, a deadly man who would eventually head a Muslim fundamentalist group until he'd been caught and hung.

Still, none of that affected him or impressed him—not like now.

Edward's fingers tightened on the handset.

The voice on the other end was computerized, masking the identity of the speaker. Edward had no idea to whom he spoke—but he knew the power behind that cloaked voice. It was somehow appropriate the voice was computerized, because he knew he was speaking to a vast machine, a powerhouse that had moved throughout the ages, destroying all in its wake and retooling the chaos to suit its ends.

And Edward wanted to be more than a cog in that vast machine; he intended to drive that massive engine. It had been luck that landed Amanda on his doorstep—his egg-harvesting clinic, one of many in this region, had been chosen to facilitate this matter—but it would take his skill to turn that good fortune into an opportunity to move up the ladder.

To achieve that, he needed success.

"The problem is being addressed," Edward promised. "The Americans will never reach the mountains in time."

"AND THE FETUS?" the voice asked.

"The DNA is stable. As we all hoped."

He dabbed the sweat from his brow with the back of a sleeve. At least that was good news. Plans could move forward—behind schedule, yes, but still salvageable.

Edward continued, "As to that other matter, I can perform the C-section immediately. Get things ready."

"VERY GOOD." Though the voice was flat and affectless, Edward imagined the satisfaction behind those inhuman inflections.

"And what of the mother?" Edward asked, suspecting this was a touchy matter.

The answer came without hesitation. "SHE'S NO LONGER OF USE. HER DEATH WILL SERVE A GREATER PURPOSE."

"Understood."

The voice moved on to exacting detail about how preparations and procedures would continue from here. One last item concerning the mother was addressed.

"BURN HER BODY. IT SHOULD BE UNRECOGNIZABLE."

The sweat down his back went cold. The pure callousness both appalled and excited him. What would it be like to move through the world with such utter disregard for morality—driven only by purpose?

The call finally ended.

Lost in preparations, he vacated the communications tent, strode through the sun-speckled glade of the camp, and up the steps to the makeshift medical ward. He tried his best to wear such a mantle of amoral drive as he stepped through the door and let it clap shut behind him.

Petra glanced up, shifting a fall of blond hair, her face open and questioning.

Edward looked beyond her to the hospital bed at the back of the ward. Amanda stared at him. He must have failed to fully don that cold mantle; something must have still shone in his face. The patient pulled her legs up, an instinctive desire to protect her child.

But it's not your child that needs protecting at the moment . . .

Edward turned to Petra. "Get everything ready. We're doing this now."

12

With the blast still ringing in his head, Tucker pulled the dazed boy to his feet. Kane shook off dust and pieces of thatch. Smoke and sand floated in the air. The air reeked of burned flesh and flaming fuel.

The rocket had hit outside the hut, collapsing a corner of the clay-brick structure. A large blackened crater opened a few yards away. Bodies lay strewn at the edge, tossed and torn like so many rag dolls.

Tucker found his breathing growing heavier, flashing back to prior firefights in Afghanistan. He pulled the boy's face into his chest, not wanting him to see. Baashi didn't resist. Though deafened, he still felt the boy crying in terror, felt his wracking sobs.

Captain Alden groaned and rolled onto his rear end. Blood covered half his face, but it appeared to be only from a scalp wound. He must have caught a piece of the blast debris.

"Get him out of here!" Alden yelled, flopping his arm weakly toward the door.

Others rose out of the smoke, shedding rubble, bearing cuts and abrasions. Gray stumbled forward with Seichan.

Kowalski helped Major Jain to her feet. She wobbled slightly but found her footing. "You okay?" he asked

She shook free of him—teetered sideways, then grabbed his arm again. "Maybe not."

When the Indian woman spotted her captain, she still tried to go to him, concern on her face. Alden waved her off. "Go with them, Jain. Help get them clear."

"What about you?" Gray grabbed the map from the floor and passed it to Baashi. They still needed the boy to pinpoint the secret medical encampment rumored to be up in the mountains. Even rattled, the commander never lost sight of the mission objective. "Captain, you need medical attention."

Alden grinned through the gore. "Then I guess I'm bloody well at the right place, aren't I, commander?" He teetered back to his feet. "Besides, I've got two men here. I'm not leaving them until I know they're safe."

Or dead, Tucker added silently.

Punctuating that dour thought, another blast rocked deeper into the camp. Kane flinched, ducking lower.

Gray grabbed the captain by the upper arm. "You'll do your men no good on your own." He dragged the Brit out the door. "Come with me."

Alden looked ready to argue, but Major Jain backed Gray up.

"Commander Pierce is right, sir."

"Maybe we can argue later!" Kowalski shouted at them by the door. "Chopper's swinging back this way!"

"Out of here! Now!" Gray ordered.

The captain reluctantly followed. They rounded the hut and moved out among the field of parked vehicles.

Tucker guessed where the commander was taking them. He would've done the same, to utilize every resource to survive.

Gray led them straight to the minitank, painted white and emblazoned with the UN world logo. The Daimler Ferret armored car still sat where they'd seen it earlier. The peacekeeper posted beside it had climbed into the turret, manning the machine gun. The weapon smoked from prior shots, but the helicopter was currently beyond range on the other side of the camp, although it wouldn't take long for the chopper to circle back around.

Gray called to the peacekeeper as a handful of refugees fled to either side of them. "You're a sitting duck up there, soldier! You need to get this vehicle moving, help defend the camp."

The man, dark-skinned and helmeted, yelled back in a French accent. He was young, likely not even twenty. Fear frosted his words. "I am alone! I cannot shoot and drive, *monsieur*."

Gray turned to Alden. "*Here* is how you can best help your men. Put this tank in motion. Draw the chopper's attention and take that bastard down."

Alden understood. "I'll do what I can to cover your escape." The captain pointed to a pair of sand-rail buggies fifty yards away. The skeletal dune runners looked perfectly suited for this rough terrain. "If there are no keys, they're easy to hotwire. Just jam something sharp into the ignition and twist to get them started."

The captain's next words were for his fellow soldier. "Stay with them, Jain. Get them all clear, and I'll see what I can do from here."

The major looked exasperated, but she knew how to take orders and nodded.

Gray shook Alden's hand as they parted ways. "Be safe."

"You do the same." The captain stopped long enough to give Baashi a fast hug. "Do what they say!"

"I . . . I will, Mr. Trevor."

The captain nodded and climbed into the armored car.

Gray hurried them forward, ordering them to secure their radio earpieces in place.

Ahead, the sand-rail cars were little more than engines strapped to roll cages with some seats bolted in place. They had no windows, fenders, or doors. But Tucker had played with them back in the dunes near Camp Pendleton. Their advantage was a low center of gravity and high flotation tires perfect for skimming over sand and hopping over obstacles.

Kowalski must have had a similar experience and rubbed his palms together as they reached the vehicles. "Which one's mine?"

Machine-gun fire erupted behind them. They all leaped forward and split on the run, dividing between a smaller two-seater, which Gray and Seichan commandeered, and a larger four-seater with a bench in the rear.

Jain reached the driver's seat first, but Kowalski wasn't having any of it.

"I'll drive!" he yelled.

"Listen, boyo, I've had plenty of tactical driving—"

"And I didn't just get a concussion. So move it, sister!"

She looked ready to bite his head off, but she *was* still wobbly on her feet. She finally relented and abandoned the driver's seat to Kowalski. He discovered a screwdriver already jammed in place in the steering column, serving as a key. Judging by the roar next to them, Gray started his vehicle with no more difficulty.

Jain took the passenger seat up front, leaving the rear bench to Tucker and the boy. Kane crouched between them, panting, flinging a bit of drool in his adrenaline-fired excitement.

"Hang on!" Kowalski yelled, grinning way too big.

The buggy leaped forward like a bee-stung horse—just as an ear-shattering explosion flung a nearby truck into the air.

Another rocket blast.

Tucker twisted around. Behind them, the helicopter roared out of the camp and aimed toward them. An M230 chain-gun on the chopper's undercarriage chewed across the sand—chasing after them.

But they weren't defenseless.

The Ferret armored car raced into view, as fleet-footed on its large tires as its nimble namesake. It crossed into the path of the attack helicopter. From the minitank's turret, the machine gun chattered, firing up at the bird in the sky.

Captain Alden manned the weapon himself, shrouded in gun smoke and swirls of dusty sand. The minitank skidded around to face the diving helicopter head-on. Rounds cracked into the chopper's windshield, driving the bird to the side as the pilot panicked.

The armored car spun a full circle and took off, driving wildly through the parked vehicles. The chopper twisted in midair and took off after them, like a hawk after a fleeing rabbit—or, in this case, a fleeing *ferret*.

Tucker settled back around, looking forward. Kowalski hit a ridge at full speed and jumped the buggy into the air. The driver hollered his joy.

Tucker and Baashi flew into the aluminum half-roof over the bench seat. Tucker managed to get hold of Kane's leather collar as they crashed back down.

The dog growled angrily, ready to bite someone.

Tucker couldn't blame him. He glared at the back of Kowalski's stubbly head, suddenly wishing he were back with the rockets and chain guns. It would be safer than this backseat.

No wonder Gray had fled to the other buggy.

He was no fool.

12:48 P.M.

Maybe this wasn't so smart.

Gray's buggy twisted sideways down a steep hill, made treacherous by loose shale and slippery scree. He broadsided a patch of brittle bushes at the bottom of the slope and crashed through them.

Seichan ducked away as thorns and broken branches exploded through the open roll cage.

Once clear, she yelled at him, "Make for the gravel road we saw from the air!"

"That's what I'm trying to do!"

He had set off overland initially, thinking the road would be too obvious an escape route if the helicopter decided to give chase. He'd already spotted other cars, trucks, even camels fleeing up that road, driven all in the same direction by the attack. He didn't want to be trapped in that traffic jam if there was a firefight.

His original plan was to travel as far as they could, then cut back to the road. But the hilly terrain proved tougher than it looked, broken up into rocky hummocks, sudden cliffs, and thick patches of bushes and trees. Ahead, it looked even worse as the land pushed up toward the mountains.

Risky or not, the road had to be safer than this.

With that in mind, he drove the car up the next rise to get a better view and gain his bearings. In the rearview mirror, he spotted Kowalski following him. And farther behind him, an ominous column of oily black smoke marked the horizon.

Let's hope that's the helicopter.

"There!" Seichan pointed.

He turned his attention forward. A quarter mile away, the road looked little better than a dry riverbed winding across the bitter terrain. It disappeared into the higher hills and scraggly lower forests.

Kowalski skidded up next to him.

Gray touched his throat mike as he nosed his vehicle down the far side of the rise. "Kowalski, we're heading back to the road. We'll make better time there."

"Too bad," his partner responded in his ear. "It was just getting fun."

From the white-knuckled grips of his passengers, Gray doubted they'd describe his driving in such a positive light.

Though the dune runners were made for spinning, jumping, and turning—all necessary skills to traverse this torturous terrain—it still felt like riding a jackhammer on top of a cement mixer. And the last quarter-mile journey back to the road was no gentler on his kidneys.

At last, he fishtailed his buggy onto the gravel, which, after the off-road trek, felt as smooth as a freshly paved highway.

He sped gratefully down the road, which climbed in sweeping switchbacks up into the mountains. Over the next hour, he kept a hard pace, passing the occasional slower truck.

The forest slowly grew thicker and taller as they gained elevation. Rounding a sharp turn, he came close to a head-on collision with a camel. The creature dodged around the buggy with a bleating complaint. Gray noted the empty saddle and the bundle of gear tied to it as the beast continued downhill.

Worried, he slowed his buggy to a stop.

Kowalski flew around the corner with a rumble of his engine and a throaty grind of gears. He came close to rear-ending Gray, but swerved to a halt in time.

Gray cut his engines and signaled Kowalski to do the same.

In the silence, Gray strained—then heard a distinct *pop-pop-pop*.

Rifle fire.

He pictured the empty saddle.

"Ambush," he said.

Seichan immediately understood, too. "Someone set up a roadblock ahead. They're sweeping up after the helicopter."

Gray nodded. Any refugees who attempted to flee into the mountains were being gunned down ahead. But another cold certainty settled in his belly. It had been nagging him since the first rocket blast. He had hoped the air attack had been orchestrated by local insurgents or warlords. Drugs and medical supplies were as good as gold here, especially in the war-torn south. But this ambush on the road into the mountains removed any uncertainty.

This was about Amanda Gant-Bennett.

And worse . . .

"This is too bold a move for pirates," he said. "The chopper attack, now this roadblock. They're not trying to hide their actions any longer. They're pulling out the big guns and making a final stand."

"What are you getting at?" Seichan asked.

"This isn't defense. This is an endgame." He turned to Seichan. "They wouldn't move so openly, so brazenly, unless they saw no further need to keep their mountain enclave secret."

Realization dawned in Seichan's eyes.

"Either they've moved Amanda already—" she started.

Gray finished, "Or she's dead."

1:48 P.M.

Amanda tugged against the padded leather cuffs tying her to the hospital bed. Minutes ago, they'd placed an IV catheter in her right arm and given her an injection that fogged the edges of her mind. A saline bag slowly dripped next to her.

She wanted to panic but couldn't.

More than the drugs, what kept her calm was the steady *beeping* of a fetal heart monitor. The nurse had strapped a sensor belt around her belly. It communicated wirelessly to the bedside device.

My baby's fine . . . my baby's fine . . .

It was her mantra to keep her sanity.

Especially with all the commotion in the room. Blue-smocked medical personnel came and went, busy behind the privacy screen of the other bed. Elsewhere, soldiers hauled out equipment under the direction of Dr. Blake.

Movement to the side drew her muddled attention to Petra. The nurse hauled a portable anesthetic machine to her bedside.

At the sight of the clear mask hanging from the hoses, Amanda fought against her cuffs, but she was already too weak.

Dr. Blake came over and touched her wrist. He raised a syringe filled with a milky fluid. "Don't worry. We won't let any harm come to your baby."

She was unable to stop him as he inserted the syringe needle into her IV line and slowly pushed the plunger.

Petra lowered a mask toward her face.

She twisted her head away. Across the room, she watched one of the medical staff push aside the privacy screen. At long last, she saw who shared the ward with her, who lay in the other bed.

Horror swelled through her.

She screamed as Petra grabbed her head and forced the mask down over her nose and mouth.

"Now, now, it'll be all over in a few seconds," Blake promised her. "Three, two . . ."

Darkness closed around her, narrowing her view of the world to a pinpoint.

"One . . ."

Then it was gone.

13

Gray paced the shoulder of the road while the sun baked the gravel into a shimmering mirage. He and the others kept to the shadows of the neighboring forest. It sang with the buzz of cicadas and the calls of songbirds. Farther up into the highlands, green forests beckoned, draped in mists, like a sliver of Eden. Emphasizing this, the occasional breeze carried down the scent of wild-growing jasmine.

He clutched a satellite phone in his hand and weighed the risks of opening an encrypted communication channel to Sigma command. From the series of attacks—both in Boosaaso and here—intelligence was clearly leaking to the enemy.

And right now, his team had a thin advantage.

No one knows we're still alive.

Gray wanted to keep it that way. But more than that, what would be gained in the end if he reached out to Sigma? What support could they offer? To mobilize an adequate response would risk exposing both their survival and their location. Even SEAL Team Six, awaiting word in neighboring Djibouti, could not be activated. Such an overt force had a limited window to get in and get out safely. It was up to Gray's team to first pin down the whereabouts of the president's daughter.

If Gray attempted to call the States and if word should reach her captors that his team was closing in on her position, the enemy would be more apt to act rashly, to kill her on the spot.

Knowing what he had to do, Gray shoved the satellite phone back into his pack.

We're on our own until we find her.

With that settled, he waved Seichan over to him. She approached with Baashi, a hand resting on his shoulder. Gray noticed how protective she was with the boy. He had never seen her bond so quickly to another person.

Gray knelt in front of Baashi. "Can you show us on the map where the other hospital camp is hidden? The one with the bad doctor?"

The boy looked down at his toes and shook his head. "I no can't."

Baashi looked scared. Gray imagined the gunfire must have spooked him, likely triggering memories of other firefights he had been in as a child soldier. Kane could probably help soothe those rattled nerves, but Tucker knelt with his dog at the edge of the forest, suiting his partner up in a Kevlar vest. The pair readied themselves for a reconnaissance mission, to get some eyes on the ambush ahead and ascertain what sort of force lay between them and the mountains.

Farther away, Kowalski and the SRR woman, Major Jain, had returned to the last switchback, blocked the road with their two buggies, and turned away any vehicles trying to use the road to get into the mountains. Jain knew the native dialects well enough to persuade them to take a different route, though Gray suspected Jain's pistol and Kowalski's rifle did most of the persuading for them.

Gray had to admit the British major was an asset and, considering how she handled Kowalski, matching him toe-to-toe, she was one tough soldier.

They would need that ahead.

Gray returned his attention forward. The best chance for Gray's small team was to slip past that enemy line unseen. They didn't have the manpower for a full frontal assault.

But once past that roadblock, Gray needed to know where to go—and fast. The clock was ticking down for Amanda. He was sure of it.

He leaned closer to Baashi and coaxed those large dark eyes to face him again. "We won't let anyone harm you, I promise."

The boy's face hardened, offended. "I no afraid."

"Of course you're not. I know Captain Alden is very proud of you. So then why don't you show me on the map where the secret camp is located?"

Baashi sagged, crestfallen, and admitted the reason for his reluctance. "I no have the map."

Gray hid his shock, not wanting to scare the boy. He had given Baashi the topographic map back in the hut, so he could study it. "Where is it?"

Baashi's eyes looked wet with pending tears. He waved toward the way they'd come. "I no have it. Blow away."

Gray realized the boy must have lost it during the rough trek here.

"It's not his fault," Seichan said. "If the rattling had gotten any worse, I might've lost a filling or two myself."

She was right, and Gray knew where the true blame lay. He'd not been thinking when he'd trusted the map to the boy. Baashi looked so much older than his few years, aged by his rough treatment. But Gray also knew this wasn't his first mistake during this mission.

The hard glint to Seichan's icy eyes suggested those errors hadn't gone unnoted.

"But I show you," Baashi said, brightening. He tapped a thumb against his skinny breastbone. "No map—but *I* map. I take you there."

Seichan fixed Gray with a resolute stare. "We can't put the boy in such danger. We don't even know what lies ahead."

He nodded and glanced to Tucker and Kane. "We'll wait to see what they discover. We'll only move forward if there's a safe path around this ambush."

2:02 P.M.

Tucker knelt in front of Kane. He pointed into the forest and touched a finger to his lips. From here, they needed the utmost stealth.

He roughed up the fur of the shepherd's neck and stared Kane in the eyes. "Who's a good boy?"

The dog touched his nose to Tucker's.

That's right—you are.

Tucker felt the others' eyes upon him. He didn't care, unabashed by the display of affection.

"Let's go," Tucker commanded and held up five fingers, instructing Kane to keep five meters ahead of him.

Together, they moved into the deeper shadows of the forest. Kane slipped away, vanishing with the barest rustle of leaf. Tucker followed, stepping carefully, letting his dog take the lead, becoming an extension of his senses.

In his earpiece, he heard Kane's quiet breath, along with the whisper of birdsong and creak of branches. He kept one eye on the shielded screen of his phone that gave him a survey of the upcoming terrain from a dog's point of view.

They slowly but steadily paralleled the road through the forest.

Kane's night-vision camera stripped away shadows, making sure they didn't stumble upon any sentries hidden in the forest. But more than the night vision, Tucker trusted his partner's nose.

When Kane slowed, so did Tucker. When the dog circled wide, Tucker kept the same wide berth. Though separated by several yards, they moved in tandem, like a choreographed ballet.

All the while, Tucker radioed soft instructions via Kane's earpiece, keeping the dog following the rough turn of the gravel road.

Through the sensitive microphone on Kane's camera, harsh voices suddenly reached Tucker's ear.

"Slow," he subvocalized to his partner. "Creep. Left."

The view through the camera dropped low; forward movement became a step-by-step approach back to the road.

The trees grew thinner.

Three trucks—all Land Rovers—appeared ahead, blocking a choke point where the roadway had been blasted through a steep ridgeline. Soldiers paced in front; more stood on the hoods. Other men rolled vehicles to the side of the road or dragged bodies, leaving bloody trails.

The entire force wore black vests, helmets, and carried assault rifles.

Same as the crew who had assassinated Amur Mahdi.

Tucker counted at least fifteen men.

"Down," he instructed Kane. "Stay."

He touched his throat mike and reported to Gray. "Commander, do you see this?"

"Affirmative. We aren't getting through that logjam without a major firefight. Can you find another path around them?"

"Do my best."

He left Kane to guard his back, to maintain his post by the road. Earlier, while en route here, he had heard the faint tinkling of water through his dog's microphone. He crept through the woods slowly, heading away from the road, searching for the source. It did not take long to discover a thin stream of water trailing along a sandy gully.

It flowed only a foot wide and a few inches deep, runoff from the highlands, the last vestiges of the rainy season trickling away, so small it would never reach the arid plains below.

Still, he dipped his finger into it, remembering an old adage of his survival-training instructor: *Where there's water, there's a way.*

He headed upstream, hoping for that to be true.

Within fifty yards, the feeble wash reached the steep ridgeline that blocked the way forward. There he bore witness to the power of water, even a flow as anemic as this one. Centuries of wet seasons had slowly eroded a cut through the sandy rock. It was narrow, dropping through a series of short falls, and easily climbable, giving them ready access to the highlands above.

Focused upward, he failed to note the figure kneeling by the pool at the base of the cataracts, filling a canteen, a rifle resting beside him.

Tucker had forgotten his other survival-training instruction.

Never let your guard down.

2:13 P.M.

The heat of the day, even in the shade, wore on Gray. He kept a watch on the phone screen, viewing the feed from Kane's camera. The assault team remained a quarter mile up the road. He watched them mill, heard their harsh laughter. But at any time, they might send a scout or one of the trucks down this way.

They needed to be gone before that happened.

He checked the clock on the corner of the small screen. Tucker had been gone for ten minutes. No word. That was long enough. He raised his fingers to activate the radio mike at his throat.

Before he could speak, a rustle drew his attention back to the woods.

Seichan raised her pistol.

Tucker shoved through some bushes and into the open. His eyes had a wounded, tired look. "Found a way," he said. "Let's go."

Gray quickly gathered the others. He and Seichan flanked Tucker as they hurried into the forest. Kowalski and Jain followed with Baashi between them. The woman had an arm around the boy, intending to keep him safe.

"Any problems?" Gray asked Tucker, sensing something troubled the man.

"Only a small one," he said sourly.

They reached a tiny creek and followed it uphill, moving as quietly as possible. The waterway led to a steep ridge, eroded throughout by a series of cataracts.

"Who is that?" Jain asked, pointing the muzzle of her rifle at a soldier gagged and hog-tied—out cold—sprawled beside a small pond at the base of the falls.

Seichan moved warily closer, searching the remaining woods.

"He's alone," Tucker said dully. "Came for water. But someone could come looking."

"Why didn't you just kill him?" Kowalski asked. "Hide his body?"

Tucker mumbled. "Almost did kill him. Caught me by surprise."

Seichan dropped to a knee and examined the soldier, then glanced at Baashi. Her voice held a sharp edge. "He's only a boy."

Gray got a better look at the soldier's face. He looked even younger than Baashi.

"I jumped him," Tucker said, breathing harder. "I moved fast, barely thinking. Didn't want him to alert the others. Had my arm around his neck, ready to snap it like a twig—only then saw he was a child. Still, I squeezed him until he passed out."

Tucker stared down at his arms in disbelief and shame.

Gray remembered the fly Tucker had spared back in Tanzania, blocking his hand from swatting at it. The man clearly had enough of killing, any killing—unless it was in self-defense or to protect others.

To the side, Baashi stared at the boy on the ground, unblinking.

Did he see himself lying there?

Baashi looked at Tucker—and took a step away, scared.

That fear, more than anything, wounded the man.

"C'mon," Gray said. "He'll be fine. Someone will find him, but we don't want to be anywhere near here when that happens."

Tucker radioed his dog as the others climbed the steplike cataracts through the ravine. Gray waited beside him.

"You had no choice," Gray said.

"We always have a choice," Tucker answered bitterly.

Kane came silently into view, rushing forward, not gleefully but subdued. He sidled next to his handler, rubbing against his legs, as if sensing Tucker's dark mood. Tucker patted him, reassured him.

Gray suspected some of that went both ways.

He had worked with military handlers and their dogs in the past. They had a saying—*It runs down the lead*—describing how the emotions of the pair became shared over time, binding them together as firmly as any leash.

Watching Tucker and Kane, he believed that now.

The two consoled each other, supported each other, found reserves of strength that could only be forged by such a deep connection.

Finally, Tucker stared over at Gray; so did Kane.

He nodded back at the pair.

They were ready.

They were soldiers.

All three of them.

And they had their mission.

14

Painter found himself back in the Situation Room. His boss, the head
of DARPA, General Gregory Metcalf, had summoned him to this early-
morning meeting. The other attendees gathered in the president's private
conference room.

General Metcalf was already seated. He was African-American, a
graduate of West Point, and though in his midfifties, he was as sturdy as a
linebacker. The general leaned his head toward his superior, the secretary
of defense, Warren W. Duncan, who wore a crisp suit and whose stark
gray hair looked oiled and combed into rigid submission.

The three remaining members of this intimate summit were all of one
family. Two were seated opposite the military men. The First Lady, Teresa
Gant, looked like a faded lily in a beige twill dress. Her dark blond hair
had been piled neatly atop her head, but strands had come loose and hung
along the sides of her face, framing eyes that held a haunted look. Next to
her, resting a large hand on hers, was her brother-in-law, the secretary of
state, Robert Gant, sitting stiffly, defensive. His steely gaze upon Painter
hid daggers.

And the greeting from the final member of the group was no friend-
lier.

President James T. Gant stalked the far side of the table. With his
usual crisp directness, honed from his prior years as the CEO of various
Gant family enterprises, he laid into Painter.

"What is this about an attack on some hospital camp in Somalia? Why is this the first I'm hearing about it?"

Painter had suspected this was the reason for this sudden call to the White House. The intelligence communities were already abuzz in regards to this attack, further complicated by the involvement of British Special Forces. Painter had hoped to keep a lid on this smoking powder keg for at least another couple of hours, to keep its connection to Amanda's kidnapping secret.

That wasn't to be.

Warren Duncan put a nail in the coffin. "I heard from the British Special Reconnaissance Regiment. They said they had men in the field there, that they were assisting some covert American team."

James Gant pointed a finger at Painter. "Your team." He swung around, unable to hide his disgust. "Show him, Bobby."

The president's brother tapped a video remote and brought up a live satellite feed from the UNICEF hospital. The camp was a smoky ruin, pocked by mortar craters. Survivors rushed about, seeking to aid the injured, or kneeling over bodies, or trying to put out fires.

President Gant shoved an arm toward the screen. "You said to avoid shock-and-awe, to keep Amanda's kidnappers from knowing they'd acquired a high-value target—*my daughter*!" This last boomed out of his barrel chest, making him sound like a Confederate general rallying his troops to a fight.

And, plainly, this was going to be a brawl.

With Painter as the punching bag.

"That looks like *shock* to me, director," Gant said. "And I'm certainly not *awed* by such a ham-fisted operation as you're running. Not when my daughter and unborn grandson are at risk."

Painter bore the brunt of this tirade without breaking eye contact with the president. The man needed to vent, to lash out. He waited for the fire to die back, enough to let reason slip past the panic of a frightened parent.

"What do you have to say for yourself?" Gant finished, running fingers through his salt-and-pepper hair. His voice cracked on the last couple of words.

That was his opening. He kept his response just as blunt and direct. "Mr. President, the kidnappers *know* they have your daughter. I suspect they've known from the very beginning. For some unknown reason, she had been targeted for abduction."

His statement both deflated the president and flared the fear brighter in his eyes.

"From this attack," Painter continued with a nod to the wall, "and other incidents, it's clear Amanda's kidnappers have forgone hiding their knowledge. The boldness of this assault suggests two things."

He ticked them off on his fingers. "*One.* The enemy must be spooked to act so brazenly, which suggests my men are closing in on her true location. *Two.* Amanda's best hope for recovery lies with that same team."

Support came from a surprising source. Painter's boss cleared his throat. "I agree with the director, Mr. President," Metcalf said. "We have no other assets available. Even the fast-response SEAL team in Djibouti needs a hard target—something we don't have. As much as this operation has blown up in our collective faces, we have no other viable options for securing your daughter."

Okay, it was *lukewarm* support, but Painter would take that from his boss. After bumping heads, the two of them had a professionally respectful but uneasy relationship. And Metcalf was savvy enough in Washington politics not to stick his neck out—at least, not out too far.

"But how do we know your team is still out there?" Gant asked, getting a nod from his brother at the table. "They might all be dead."

Painter shook his head. "They're not."

"How can you be so certain?"

"From this."

Painter stepped forward, took the remote, and tapped in an encrypted code. He'd preestablished the feed with one of the Situation Room's watch team. On the wall-mounted monitor, a grainy video appeared, stuttering, full of digital noise.

"I apologize for the reception. I collected this feed via an ISR plane cruising at thirty-eight thousand feet above Somalia."

Teresa Gant stirred enough to ask, "ISR?"

Her brother-in-law answered, "Intelligence, surveillance, and reconnaissance. Basically, ears in the sky."

"From there, I patched through the NRO satellite in geosynchronous orbit."

Warren Duncan sat straighter. "This is *live*?"

"Maybe a six-second delay. I acquired the feed only half an hour ago."

The president squinted a bit. "What are we seeing?"

The view was low to the ground, racing along a dirt track. Fleeting images of trees and leafy bushes flashed past at the edges.

"From the GPS coordinates transmitted, we're seeing a road through the highland forests of the Cal Madow mountains."

On the screen, the view zoomed up to a pair of legs, then the face of a small black boy. Audio was even worse, cutting in and out.

". . . here . . . over by . . . hurry . . ."

The boy fled from the camera, racing away with the exuberance of youth.

"Who's filming this?" the defense secretary asked.

Painter allowed a moment of self-satisfaction. "One of my newest recruits."

3:08 P.M. East Africa Time
Cal Madow mountains, Somalia

Kane chased after Baashi.

"Come see!" the boy exclaimed and skittered to a stop. His arm pointed toward the jungle, to a rutted track that cut off the main road.

If you could call it a road, Gray thought.

His team had been hiking into the highlands for the past forty-five minutes, leaving the ambush miles behind. They had returned to the gravel road after giving the murderous choke point a wide berth.

Gray kept a continual ear out for the growl of truck engines behind him as he set a hard pace into the heart of the mountains. Slowly over time, the gravel under his boots gave way to dirt, then, once into the misty highlands, to nothing more than tire tracks worn into the sandy silt.

Soon, the arid lowlands were a forgotten world. Here, verdant high meadows rolled down into valleys filled with misty forests of junipers and frankincense trees. And all around them, like broken dragon's teeth, jagged peaks thrust toward the sky.

"That Shimbaris," Baashi said, pointing to the highest peak in that direction. It looked like a toppled skyscraper covered in emerald forest. "They say the bad doctor in Karkoor Valley. That way."

He thrust his arm again toward the rutted track off the main road.

Tucker crouched at the turnoff, picking up clods of freshly turned dirt. "Been recent traffic through here. Mud tires."

"The Land Rovers at the roadblock," Gray said, meeting his eye.

They were on the right path.

Gray turned to the boy. "I want you to stay here, Baashi, off the road, hidden entirely out of sight. You don't come out until you see one of us."

"But I help!" he said.

"You've helped enough. I told Captain Alden I'd protect you."

Seichan pointed a finger at the boy's nose. "And you promised him you'd listen to us, right?"

The two of them sounded like scolding parents—and got the usual sullen teenager response. Baashi sighed heavily, crossed his arms, expressing his disappointment with every fiber of his being.

With the matter settled, the boy went into hiding, out of harm's way, while Gray and the others headed down the shadowy turnoff, a tunnel made by a canopy of woven branches. They'd not taken more than a few steps when Major Jain called from the rear.

"Hold!"

Gray turned; the British soldier still stood at the edge of the main road in the sunlight. She held a hand up, then pointed it toward her ear.

Gray cocked his head, listening. He first heard Kane, rumbling deep in his throat, sensing something, too. Then in the distance, echoing off the surrounding peaks, the deeper groan of truck engines.

"Company coming," Kowalski said.

Jain ducked off the road and into the shadows to join them.

Tucker grimaced. "Must've found the boy I tied up."

"Or they've had enough killing for one day," Kowalski said.

"Or they're looking for more," Jain added.

Kowalski grimaced. "You had to say that, didn't you?"

She shrugged. "No matter how you cut it, boyo, we're bloody screwed."

Gray couldn't argue with her, but they had no choice. They had to forge ahead, find Amanda, and do their best to survive.

"Let's go." Gray pointed his arm forward. "Tucker, I want Kane's eyes and ears ahead of us. I've had enough surprises for one day."

Tucker gave a curt nod and went to his dog.

They hurried down the road, staying at the periphery. The forest to either side offered better protection, but the dense growth would slow their progress, make too much noise.

Right now, he needed to put some distance between them and the approaching trucks.

"We can't do this on our own," Seichan said, striding fast next to him. "A guarded camp ahead of us, mercenary soldiers behind us—not great odds."

Gray had already come to the same conclusion. He had to trust his gut that Amanda was here, that there was a reason for such lethal and overt reaction to their presence in the mountains. He shifted his shoulder pack and removed his satellite phone.

It was time to call in the cavalry.

That meant reaching Washington.

Gray dialed up Sigma command, hoping the quantum encryption built into the phone would keep the call from reaching the wrong ears. After a long moment and a series of passwords, he heard a familiar voice.

"Commander Pierce."

Gray let out a hard breath of relief. "Director, I believe we've found where Amanda was taken. I'm not sure she's still here, but as a precaution, we should mobilize SEAL Team Six to my coordinates, so they're ready when—"

"Already done," Painter said, cutting him off. "I got approval from the defense secretary a few minutes ago. The SEAL team is en route to your position with orders to engage only if the president's daughter is positively identified. They're about forty minutes out."

Forty minutes? That may be too late.

Confirming this, the roar of engines in the distance grew steadily louder. Amanda didn't have forty minutes.

A disconcerting question rose in Gray's mind. "Director, how do you know our position?"

"We've been monitoring your progress for the past half-hour."

How?

Gray searched around him, then saw Tucker send his shepherd running ahead, hugging the forest's edge.

Kane . . .

Tucker must have left his dog's camera running since the roadblock.

"It was Kat's idea," Painter explained.

Of course it was. If anyone had the brains to find them without raising an alarm, it was Kat Bryant. She had proved countless times to be an elusive and crafty spider when it came to the intelligence web.

"Kat set up a passive search algorithm, set to the wireless frequency of the dog's camera. Nothing that would trigger any alarm bells. We could watch over your shoulders without giving away your location."

Gray was grateful for the covert support, but it also made him vaguely uneasy. In the future, he'd have to make sure to circumvent that ability if he wanted total privacy.

"Audio is bad, though," Painter finished. "Cuts in and out, so keep that in mind. We can see you, but not always hear you."

"Got it."

Ahead, Tucker came running back toward him.

That had to mean trouble.

"Have to sign off," Gray said.

Painter's voice went hard. "I can see why. Go. But be—"

Gray cut him off before he could warn him to *be careful.*

It didn't need to be said—shouldn't be said. It was like wishing an actor good luck instead of break a leg.

Tucker came up, breathing hard. "Another Land Rover is blocking the road ahead, counted six men around it. Another handful in the camp." A worried frown creased his face. "Look at this."

Tucker held up his phone, displaying a dog's-eye view of the facility.

A large tent-cabin, raised on pilings, stood in the middle of a cold camp. Around it, ash pits marked old bonfires. Garbage, rusted stakes, oil stains, along with a few collapsed tents, abandoned in haste, were all that was left of a large campsite. A few shreds of camouflage netting still draped from the trees at the forest's edge, but that was it.

"Looks like most of the camp bugged out already," Tucker said. "I'd say no longer than an hour ago."

Gray felt the pit of his stomach opening to despair.

Were they already too late?

"But I did see shadows moving inside that cabin," Tucker offered. "Someone's still there."

Seichan overheard. "Maybe they left their victim here, fearing reprisals, and scattered."

Gray grasped at this thin hope.

Kowalski joined them. "So, what are we doing?"

Jain stood at his shoulder, bearing the same question on her face.

They needed a plan from here.

He ran various scenarios in his head. "We can't risk panicking the remaining soldiers. We also don't want to needlessly expose ourselves to the enemy combatants if Amanda has already been moved. We'll do her no good dead."

"Then what?" Kowalski asked.

Gray turned his focus upon Tucker. "We need to see inside that cabin."

15

Tucker lay on his belly with Kane at the edge of the forest. Forty yards of open space stretched between his position and the cabin. With men milling at the entry road and three more soldiers scavenging the grounds ahead for anything of value, any attempt to cross here would be readily spotted.

Even a dog on the run.

Tucker stared through his rifle's scope, studying the terrain. A lone soldier pushed a dented wheelbarrow past his field of view, stopping occasionally to pick something out of the discarded debris.

The radio scratched in his ear. It was Kowalski, reporting in from his post down the road, acting as rear lookout. "Company has arrived. Trucks—three of 'em—are reaching the turnoff."

Gray responded on all channels. "Kowalski, rally back to our position."

The rest of the team—Gray and the two women—had crept forward through the forest and lay in wait several meters from the lone Land Rover that guarded the ruins of the camp. They all waited for Tucker's signal. If Amanda was in the tent, they'd ambush the vehicle, trusting the element of surprise and the cover of the jungle to overcome the enemy's superior odds. If Amanda wasn't here, they'd all retreat into the woods and regroup.

Gray spoke with a note of urgency. "Tucker, now or never."

"Still, not clear," Tucker whispered under his breath.

Thirty yards away, the man with the wheelbarrow picked up a sleeve-less DVD, judged it, then flung it away with a flip of his wrist.

It seemed everyone was a critic.

Keep moving, asshole.

"Tucker," Gray pressed, "the other trucks are turning and heading this way. You've got two minutes, or we have to start shooting and hope for the best."

Tucker stared at the AK-47 slung over the soldier's shoulder as the man continued sifting through the debris.

I'm not going to send Kane out just to be killed.

Tucker flashed back to that painful moment in Afghanistan. He again felt the *pop* of his ears as the rescue helicopter lifted off, felt the rush of hot air. He had been clinging to Kane, both bloodied by the firefight, by the exploded ordnance. But Tucker had never taken his eyes off Abel, his partner's littermate, who'd knocked them both clear before the buried IED detonated. If Kane had been Tucker's right arm, Abel was his left. He'd trained them both—but he'd never readied himself for this moment.

Abel raced below, limping on three legs, searching for an escape. Taliban forces closed in from all directions. Tucker strained for the door, ready to fling himself out, to go to his friend's aid. But two soldiers pinned him, restraining him.

Tucker yelled for Abel.

He was heard. Abel stopped, staring up, panting, his eyes sharp and bright, seeing him. They shared that last moment, locked together.

Until a flurry of gunfire severed that bond forever.

Tucker's grip tightened on his rifle now, refusing to forget that lesson. He had a small black paw print tattooed on his upper left shoulder, a permanent reminder of Abel, of his sacrifice. He would never waste another life like that, to send another dog to certain slaughter.

"I need a distraction," he radioed back fiercely to Gray. "Something to pull attention away from here. Kane'll get shot before he can get halfway to the cabin."

The answer to his desperate plea came from an unexpected location—from directly behind Tucker.

"I do it," said a squeaky voice with the strain of forced bravery. "No want Kane shot."

Tucker rolled around in time to see Baashi dart away into the forest. Cursing under his breath, he radioed Gray. "Baashi followed us. Heard me. I think he's going to do something stupid."

Kowalski responded, "See him. I'll grab him." Then, seconds later, defeat tinged his voice. "Kid's a friggin' jackrabbit."

A shout cracked across the forest, coming from the direction of the narrow road. *"ISKA WARAN!"* Baashi called out. *"HA RIDIN!"*

Tucker pictured him approaching the Land Rover, hands in the air.

A rapid exchange followed in Somali.

Jain translated via the radio. "He's telling them his mother is sick. He came a long way from his village to see the doctor here."

Tucker's fingers tightened on the stock of his rifle. The three soldiers adrift in the camp moved toward the gate, drawn by the commotion. For better or worse, Tucker got his distraction.

He reached and gave Kane a warm squeeze on his ear. They didn't have time for their usual good-bye ritual.

With a twinge of foreboding, he flicked his wrist, leaving a finger pointing toward the cabin.

Kane took off like a shot, dashing low across the open field.

"DAAWO!" Baashi called out.

"He's asking for medicine," Jain said.

He got something else.

A savage spat of gunfire burst forth.

3:26 P.M.

Seichan watched Baashi dance backward, dirt exploding in front of his toes. Laughter followed from the soldiers gathered in front of the Land Rover, enjoying their sport.

A hard man with a jagged scar splitting his chin and turning his lower lip into a perpetual scowl waved the others to silence and sauntered with the haughtiness of a reigning conqueror. He had his helmet tilted back, his flak jacket open. He rested a palm on a holstered pistol as he approached Baashi, who cowered, half-bowed under the other's gaze.

"Jiifso!" he commanded. *"Maxbuus baad tahay!"*

Major Jain hid on the other side of the road with Kowalski. The British soldier translated, softly subvocalizing into her radio. "He's telling Baashi to lie down, that he's his prisoner."

Baashi obeyed, dropping to one knee, placing a hand on the ground, groveling in submission.

The soldier grinned, made meaner by his scarred lower lip. He pulled his pistol out.

He's going to execute the kid—but not before terrorizing him.

Seichan remembered another man, another weapon. He had held a knife at her naked throat, his breath on her neck, twice her weight, thick with hard muscle. They sent him against her when she was seventeen, a training exercise. A sadist of the darkest ilk, a perverse predator, he wouldn't just kill her; he intended to degrade and savage her before taking her life. To survive, she had to submit, to tolerate his touch—only long enough to secure his knife when he let his guard drop for a hot breath. She had gutted him in the end—but she still remembered the ruin of that day, the utter degradation of the powerful over the weak, and, worst of all, what was destroyed forever in her.

She wouldn't let that happen to another.

Seichan shifted her SIG Sauer pistol toward the soldier. Gray crouched at her side where they hid, meters into the forest, shielded by a thicket of bushes. He touched a finger to her shoulder, warning her not to shoot, not yet.

Metal glinted as Baashi's other hand, half-hidden by his thin body, slipped a military dagger out of the back of his pants. It looked as long as the boy's forearm.

The sight shocked her, proving her earlier assessment. She and the boy were the same.

I was this boy.

But Baashi was going to get himself killed.

Seichan steadied her aim, feeling Gray's fingers tighten on her shoulder, ordering her not to act. She obeyed, but it left her body trembling with rage—and not a small amount of shame.

What is taking Tucker so long?

They needed confirmation from him—or, more precisely, from his partner.

Kane abandons bright sunlight for darkness as he ducks through heavy posts and under the raised wooden structure. It is cooler here. For a breath, he is blind as his pupils dilate and adjust to the darkness. Still, his ears prick, stretching senses deep into the shadows. He takes it all in, to fill the darkness with meaning and substance.

The creak of wood above . . .

The beat of boot heels on planks . . .

The drip-drip-dripping farther back . . .

He tastes the shadows with tongue and nose. Waste and spoor, oil and sludge. Farther back, a sharper taint that sets his hackles to rising. Fetid, with the promise of meat. He follows the trickling sound, sniffs where it falls in fat droplets from above.

Blood.

But that is not why he's come.

He has been given a scent, trapped in a wad of cloth, smelling of sweat, and salt, and oil, and a feminine musk. He was sent on the hunt for it. He lifts his nose toward the planks above, where the blood seeps. He sniffs, drawing in the richness there, expanding trails in all directions, so many.

But through it all, a single thread matches, connecting here to that wad of cloth. He has found what he hunted.

He points his nose to the scent and voices his success—not the howl of wildness buried in his bones. That is not his way. He lets flow a soft whine, deep in his throat, proclaiming his victory.

He hears words in one ear that melt through him. "Good dog."

He breathes in his satisfaction and lowers to his haunches; only now do his eyes fill in the spaces left bare by scent and sound.

Out of the darkness, a pair of red lights shines back at him, tiny and sharp. They come from devices attached to large barrels, reeking of rusted metal and bitter oil.

His hackles shiver, sensing danger.

At the edge of the forest, Tucker lived half in his skin, half in another.

He had heard what Kane heard: *creaking and boot steps.* And he saw what Kane saw: *fluid seeping through the planks from above.* But was it blood, oil, water? He couldn't say for sure.

Then Kane pointed his nose, followed by a soft whine.

Success.

He radioed it to Gray. "Kane found Amanda's scent at the cabin. She was there."

And maybe still is.

"Understood," came the response, tense. "Clear a path and get in there. I'll join you as soon as I can."

As Gray finished, the image on the small screen swung to the side. The gritty night vision of Kane's camera revealed two large barrels, spaced at equal distance in the crawlspace under the tent-cabin. He read the word KEROSENE stenciled on one of them. Worst of all, attached to their sides, two glowing transmitters illuminated explosive charges.

Panicked, he touched his throat mike. "Commander—"

Gunfire cut off the rest of his warning.

3:27 P.M.

Seichan fired, clipping the scarred man in the left knee. He toppled with a scream of surprise. Gray strafed the soldiers gathered on their side of the Land Rover. Kowalski and Jain did the same on the other.

Seichan dashed out of hiding to protect the boy, who had dropped flat as the firefight commenced. She strode to the downed soldier, while firing two rounds at another commando sheltered behind one of the Land Rover's open doors. The scarred monster on the ground swung his pistol at her, but she put a bullet through his throat, collected his weapon, and fired both guns at the truck, pistols now blazing in both fists.

"Get off the road!" she hollered at Baashi.

He leaped like a frightened doe into the sheltering forest.

A commando got behind the wheel of the Land Rover, cranked the engine, and hit the accelerator. The truck barreled toward her.

She stood her ground, aimed both guns, and fired a single round from each.

Left, to shatter the windshield.

Right, to put a round through the driver's eye.

She stepped aside as the truck's momentum carried it toward her, veering drunkenly at the last second and crashing into the woods.

The firefight lasted another ten seconds—and ended as abruptly as it started. Soldiers sprawled, limp and unmoving on the road.

Gray cleared the forest, holding a hand over his left ear, listening, likely to Tucker. He glanced toward the tent-cabin with a grimace of worry. He pointed his other arm down the road.

The loud rumble of trucks drew her attention around. Brakes squealed. Those coming had heard the gunplay.

"Keep them off our backs for as long as possible," he ordered—then took off into the campsite on foot.

Seichan stared down the forested tunnel. Her group had the element of surprise before. That was no longer the case. And the enemy had three times their force, vastly outnumbering and outgunning them.

Kowalski and Jain joined her, sharing concerned but determined looks.

Seichan glanced over her shoulder as Gray disappeared from view. She hoped the president's daughter was still here, still alive. Either way, they were committed now. She waved the others back into hiding.

"You heard Gray," she said. "We hold our ground here."

It had better be worth it.

3:28 P.M.

Tucker dropped the last of the three soldiers in the camp, the one with the wheelbarrow. The kills felt cowardly, but he had no time for delicacy; all he could do was grant them clean head shots.

But he knew there was at least one other enemy, remembering the creak of boards from inside the cabin. Whoever was holed up there had surely heard the attack—but what would they do?

Gray appeared to his left, pistol in hand, running for the lone structure. Tucker had managed to get word to him as the firefight ended, warning of the fiery bomb hidden under the tent.

Tucker took a fast glance at his phone's screen. A bobbling image showed Kane still struggling to yank away the first glowing transceiver from the explosive charge. Tucker had lost precious seconds trying to get his dog to understand, directing Kane via radioed commands. Even as close as they were, there were limits to their communication.

Tucker had to do something. He burst out of hiding and sprinted toward the cabin, too. He was closer, but Gray had a head start. They should reach the door at the same time.

He lifted his phone. On the screen, Kane yanked his head and the bright glow of the transceiver died.

Good boy.

Kane turned to the other charge, shining brightly in the dark. He took a step toward it—when the light began to blink rapidly.

Illuminated digits flared into existence on the device.

00:30

00:29

Cursing, Tucker skidded to a stop. The bastard inside had activated the charge, set to a timer. Rifle blasts drew Tucker's attention from the screen. The last soldier slammed out of the cabin door, weapon at his hip, firing wildly, trying to make a break before those seconds ran out.

Gray dropped flat, sliding on his belly, pistol pointed forward, gripped in both hands. He fired three fast rounds.

The gunman tumbled headlong down the steps from the raised porch. He landed hard, but from the placement of Gray's rounds, all to the face, he was surely dead before he even hit the ground.

Tucker stared at the tiny screen as Kane closed in on the second barrel. 00:23

The dog would never be able to work the transceiver free in time, and with the device activated, any attempt to remove it could set it off prematurely.

"Kane!" he yelled, not bothering with the radio. "To me!"

Gray scrambled to his feet and looked over at him.

Tucker pointed toward the crawlspace between the pilings. "It's set to blow! Twenty seconds."

The two men sped toward the tent.

Kane flew into view, tail high, and ran to Tucker's side. The group reached the porch steps together, pounded up, and shoved through the spring-loaded door.

The makeshift medical ward looked as stripped and vacated as the rest of the camp: upended boxes, stray pieces of hospital gear, a toppled privacy screen. The place had been abandoned in a hurry. They must have suspected time was running out for them.

But the ward had not been entirely emptied.

At the rear, a hospital bed rested against the back wall. It was not vacant. A blond woman lay under a thin blanket, an oxygen mask over her face, her limbs secured with leather straps. The bedding over the mound of her belly was stained red, soaked through. More blood ran from under the blanket and pooled on the plank floor.

Gray rushed forward, yanked away the mask, then ripped back the covers. He exposed what had been so chastely hidden.

Tucker fell to his knees in horror.

They were too late.

16

"NO!"

The anguish in that single word, that long, sustained note of pain and grief, echoed off the walls of the small conference room. The First Lady swung away from the screen, covering her face as if to make the sight go away.

Her husband stood stiff, frozen, staring unblinking at the screen.

No one said a word—Teresa's cry encompassed everything.

The last image remained fixed in Painter's eye, when Gray pulled back the bedsheets. Someone had operated on Amanda, sliced her open from rib to pelvis, exposing the ruins of her empty uterus. They'd performed a C-section, stolen the baby, and left Amanda's dead body behind like an empty husk.

On the screen now, Painter watched Gray swing away, grabbing up Tucker from the floor. The image bobbled wildly as the two men and the dog fled the cabin. He understood their haste. They'd all seen the barrels of kerosene, the glow of the explosive charge, and the timer counting down.

An image of running legs, a distant forest—then a bright blast that sent everyone tumbling forward. A fireball rolled overhead. The second barrel of kerosene rolled off to the side, jettisoned clear by the blast wave, leaving behind a trail of oil before it vanished out of view.

The audio feed frazzled, then went silent.

A moment later, Tucker's face appeared as he checked on his dog. His mouth moved, but there was no sound. In the background, Gray got up on his hands and knees, hurriedly shrugging free his shoulder pack, which was on fire. He threw it aside and rolled in the dirt to put out the smoldering back of his shirt.

They'd live.

Painter should have felt relief—but he was not there yet.

Teresa burst out of her seat and into her husband's arms. It was not to seek comfort. Her fists pummeled his body, sobs shook through her, weakening the effort. Tears flowed down her face.

"This is your fault!" she yelled into his chest as James Gant pulled his wife tight to him. "All our fault . . . they . . . they cut my baby open!"

She sagged in her husband's arms, pressing her face into his chest, still shaking her head, trying to dismiss what she saw.

He held her up, looking over the crown of her head at Painter.

Anger burned through the raw grief in his stony eyes, directed at Painter, at Sigma.

The president's brother stood and gently coaxed the grieving parents toward the door. "Go, Jimmy," Robert urged. "Take care of your wife. We can handle matters from here."

Gant didn't resist. The pair, still wrapped together, bonded by unimaginable grief and horror, slipped out of the room, gathering Secret Service men in their wake.

The defense secretary, Warren Duncan, placed a hand on Robert's shoulder. "Sir, why don't you go, too? Family should be together during times like this."

Robert's normally gentle and even tone turned acerbic. His gaze passed over Painter, scorching him with his bitterness. "Someone in the family should bear witness to the end of this fucked-up mission."

Painter's boss closed his eyes and gave the smallest shake of his head, utterly embarrassed and defeated.

On the screen, the dog's-eye view showed a pair of trucks careening into the campsite, guns silently blazing from their side windows.

Despite the futility of the operation, it wasn't over.

3:34 P.M. East Africa Time
Cal Madow mountains, Somalia

"Go for cover!" Gray hollered.

He ran with Tucker and Kane away from the blasted ruins of the cabin. Black smoke swirled across the camp as flaming debris littered the ground and continued to drift down in flaming bits of tent fabric. The thick pall of smoke offered them enough cover to make a break for the forest as two Land Rovers skidded into the camp from the road.

Automatic fire sprayed from windows, mostly directed back the way they'd come, aiming for the others hidden in the forest. A furious firefight continued back there; likely his team had managed to ambush the third vehicle from the roadblock, but that battle was still far from over.

Before Gray, Tucker, and Kane could reach the shelter of the forest, their retreat was spotted. Gunfire ripped toward them. Kane yelped and sped faster. Tucker gave chase—but not before Gray grabbed the man's rifle out of his fingers.

He swung it toward the Rovers and fired, cracking one of the side windows and forcing the shooter to duck.

"Go!" Gray yelled to Tucker. "Make for the others!"

Gray ran to the side, drawing fire. One of the Rovers fishtailed in the sandy soil and sped back toward the road, intending to go to the aid of the embattled third truck. The last Rover circled the smoking ruins of the cabin, coming around to face Gray head-on.

Then a new noise cut through the peppering blasts.

The gunplay lulled for a breath as the others heard it, too.

The *thump-thump* of a helicopter grew louder.

Gray searched the skies, knowing it was too soon for the SEAL team to arrive—and he was right. A familiar military-gray chopper rushed across the treetops, coming from the direction of the main road. It was the same attack helicopter that had laid waste to the UNICEF base.

It seemed *all* of the hens were returning to roost.

A whistling rocket screamed from the chopper's undercarriage, blazing a trail of fire and smoke. It streaked down and slammed into the hood of the Rover headed toward the forest. The truck flipped end-over-end—then exploded as it landed.

Gray crouched, stunned.

Overhead, gunfire chattered from the open door of the chopper's rear cabin as it rushed past. A familiar figure hung out the door, pointing his weapon below.

Captain Trevor Alden.

Gray remembered his last view of the British soldier, manning the turret of the Ferret armored car, guns blazing. He must have somehow forced the chopper down and commandeered it for the British Special Forces. Then he'd come looking for them.

A decision the captain might still regret.

The second Rover, which had braked to a stop with the arrival of the helicopter, believing them allies, gunned its engine and raced across the camp. The chopper had to swing around, twisting in midair to bring its rockets to bear.

A soldier popped out of the Rover's open sunroof, hauling and balancing the black tube of a grenade launcher on his shoulder. At such close range, the shooter could not miss.

Gray lifted his rifle, but the Rover zigzagged crazily across the fiery camp. He'd never hit the soldier holding the launcher. But he found something that wasn't moving.

The second barrel of kerosene, blasted free by the explosion, lay on its side in a pool of leaking oil. The Rover, its driver focused above, sped toward it—or at least close enough. Gray couldn't trust firing into the barrel itself. Despite what had been portrayed in movies, such shots seldom caused an explosion.

Instead, he needed to light the barrel's wick.

Cocking his eye to the scope, he fired into a neighboring smoking section of floor planking. The wood exploded and rained fiery slivers across the pool of kerosene. Flames flared where they landed and chased across the oil's surface, aiming for the leaking barrel.

The Rover then sped across and blocked his view.

Had he timed it—?

The explosion blew a fireball into the sky and shoved the truck to the side. Flaming oil blasted through the open windows, setting fire to everything.

Screams rang out.

A door fell open, revealing the hell inside.

Then the stockpile of grenades exploded within the cabin, shattering apart the Rover.

Gray ducked.

The helicopter dove away, churning through the smoke.

Straightening back up, Gray realized—after his ears stopped ringing—that all the gunfire had ended. He turned and saw Kowalski and Seichan enter the camp from the road, shouldering the thin form of Jain between them. The trio must have dispatched the last truck on their own, but not without a cost. The major limped on one leg, the other bled fiercely.

"She's shot!" Kowalski bellowed.

Jain frowned up at him. "I'm fine. It's your bloody body odor that might kill me before this little scratch."

Still, Alden must have witnessed the injury to his teammate.

The chopper tilted to the side and sought a safe place to land.

Tucker also returned from the forest with his dog. Gray noted the eye of the camera facing him. His satellite phone was likely melted to slag inside the ruins of his smoldering shoulder pack.

The sting of the burn along his back flared as he searched the debris. He needed to communicate with Painter. This couldn't wait. But the director had warned him that the audio pickup was crap on the dog's video feed. Gray could not let this next message be misconstrued.

He found a piece of tent fabric, burned at the edges, and used the tip of a charred stick to write a short note.

He prayed it reached Painter.

8:44 A.M. EST
Washington, DC

Smoke obscured most of the view of the fiery camp. There was little else to see on the video, especially as the helicopter landed, stirring up a whirlwind of debris.

Painter wasn't the only one to realize the same.

The defense secretary still stood beside Robert Gant with a hand on the man's shoulder. "Go," Duncan said. "This is over, Bobby. Join your family. They need you now more than we do."

Robert continued to stare at the monitor, but Painter suspected he didn't see anything, lost in the depths of the tragedy.

Finally, a rattling sigh escaped him. He stared at Painter, but the fire there had snuffed out in his eyes, leaving only a dull grief. He looked a decade older than his sixty-six years. He simply patted Duncan's side and exited without a word.

But the defense secretary was not done. He pointed at Painter's boss, his voice stone-cold. "I would have a word with you, General Metcalf. In private."

"I understand." Metcalf cast Painter a withering glance.

The two men exited, but not before Duncan poked a finger into Painter's chest. "I want a report on my desk within the hour." He waved to the monitor. "And a copy of this feed. I want a full accounting of this tragedy . . . every detail on how this all went to hell."

The two men exited, leaving Painter alone in the conference room.

On the monitor, the smoke cleared. Gray's face swelled into the camera. His lips moved, but the audio was still down. Then Gray stepped back and lifted a bit of burned fabric into view. He had written something on it.

As Painter read the scribbled words, he stumbled forward in disbelief. He caught himself on the edge of the table.

How could this be?

He stared toward the door, ready to run out, to call the others back.

He even took a step in that direction—then stopped, his mind working furiously, running various permutations through his head.

He covered his mouth with his hand.

There remained too many variables, too much unknown and unexplained. The truth revealed on the screen was too valuable to release without thought. But it was also a cruelty beyond words to remain silent.

Still, he slowly turned to the table, picked up the remote control, and switched off the monitor. He would have to edit away this last bit of video before he handed it off to Warren Duncan.

He stared at the dark monitor, judging if he was capable of doing this. But his job was to make the hard decisions, no matter who got hurt. And this was one of the hardest.

He pictured Teresa dissolving into despair and grief; he heard again her scream of denial, her railing against what could not be true.

In the end, the First Lady had been right.

Though the monitor was off, Gray's last message still burned in his mind's eye.

God, forgive me.

No one must know.

17

Her senses returned like a bright light that slowly pooled outward, watery at the edges. She felt as if she were a swimmer rising from the depths of a black sea. Faces hovered over her. Voices spoke, muffled and indistinct. Her throat hurt, her tongue was dry, which made it hard to swallow.

". . . Coming around," a familiar voice said in a German-Swiss accent.

She made out the severe blond bob, the icy eyes.

Petra.

The horror of her situation swelled through her again, sharpening her senses as she surfaced into the cold, hard reality of the moment.

Another face leaned over her. A bright light flashed into her eyes, stinging, searing into the back of her skull. She shied away, turning her head.

She lay in a shallow box, cushioned all around. She heard the drone of jet engines, felt the vibration of flight.

"Pupillary response is good," Dr. Blake said. "She's tolerating the sedation well. What about the fetus, Petra?"

"Heartbeat and oxygenation continue to remain within normal parameters, doctor. With the wireless transmission from the fetal monitor around her midsection, we'll be able to assess her condition from a distance after we land."

"How long is the flight?"

"Another three hours."

Dr. Blake's face pulled away. "No need to revive her fully, then. For now, keep her lightly sedated with a propofol drip. We can send her deeper once we're in final approach to land."

"We should also allow at least fifteen minutes to secure the royal diplomatic seals around the coffin."

Coffin?

Amanda turned her watery focus to the pillowed sides of the box. Fear spiked through her.

"You're right, Petra. Even with all the palms and wheels greased by our benefactors, we don't want any trouble going through customs with the casket. Luckily everyone now believes she's dead."

Dead?

Blake continued, "So no one will be looking for her. With everyone off our backs, we'll finally have the time to deliver this baby safely. In another couple of hours, it will be good to wash the stink of the jungle off and return to a proper medical lab." Footsteps retreated. "I'm going to the cabin bar. Can I get you a drink?"

"Water, with a sliver of lime."

"Always the professional, Petra," he scolded with an amused tone. "Stop fretting. We'll have the package delivered by nightfall. Then maybe you'll relax."

Petra's face loomed larger, her breath smelling of cinnamon and cigarette smoke. "I'll relax once we have her fetus on the vivisection table at the lab."

"I keep forgetting that's your specialty, my dear. I thought I was skilled with scalpel and forceps . . . but you put me to shame with your ability to tease a body into so many perfect anatomical sections."

"That's the easy part," Petra said, straightening up.

"Of course." A small laugh accompanied his words. "Where you truly shine is how you keep those sections alive."

Alive?

What did they mean? What were they talking about?

Amanda tried not to picture such a horror, but it filled her head anyway. She wanted to clamp her hands over her ears. She had known her baby was under threat—it was why she had fled the States—but she never imagined anything as horrific as this. It went beyond her worst nightmares.

I don't want to hear any more.

Her silent plea was answered.

The creak of hinges rasped to the left. A dark shadow rose and fell heavily over her, shutting out all light and sound. The lid of her coffin had been closed.

Amanda shuddered in the blackness, praying that this casket truly became her coffin, that she'd suffocate before they landed. Better that than allowing her baby boy to suffer the atrocities planned for him.

. . . how you keep those sections alive . . .

Those dismaying words haunted the darkness—along with an all-consuming question.

Where are they taking me?

4:00 P.M.
Cal Madow mountains, Somalia

"She was definitely being held at the camp here," Gray said, holding the satellite phone to his ear, reporting in to Sigma command. "Tucker's dog confirmed Amanda's scent before all hell broke loose."

His choice of words was appropriate. He stared at the smoldering wreck of the cabin, at the fiery remains of the two Rovers. His other teammates were making sure no other enemy combatants remained a threat. Captain Alden's helicopter rested across the way, engine idling, rotors turning slowly. A British medic from Alden's rescue crew worked on Jain's leg.

Kowalski looked on, concerned. Despite the differences in size and gender, the pair were two peas out of the same pod. A scary proposition. A *female* Kowalski.

Gray had retrieved the satellite phone from the big man's pack. He didn't know if Painter had received his frantic handwritten note and wanted to follow up as quickly as possible.

"But why do you want to keep Amanda's survival a secret?" Gray asked, questioning again the need for such a cruel deception. "I understand the fear of an intelligence leak. But to keep the president and his family in the dark . . . it must be killing them."

"It is, but the administration—if they suspect she's still alive—will insist on bringing all forces to bear in finding her. And look how that turned out this time around. For Amanda's sake, we've got to restrict this knowledge to as few ears as possible."

Gray took a deep breath. It was a ballsy move on the director's part, but it made brutal sense, especially in light of his own suspicions. He shared them with Painter. "Director, I'm almost certain that events here were purposefully staged to make it look like Amanda was killed."

"Why do you think that?" Painter asked.

"The woman in the bed. She was blond, the same size and body shape as Amanda. From the distension of the uterus and belly, she was obviously once pregnant, possibly an equal number of weeks along. But more incriminating, when I removed the oxygen mask, I saw her mouth was a bloody ruin. Someone didn't want Amanda's dental records pulled to identify the charred remains."

Painter remained silent, digesting the information.

"Even the rushed C-section suggests the same conclusion," Gray said. "I think they feared any fetal remains might not match those on record from Amanda's prenatal exams."

Painter's voice grew hushed at the horror of it all. "So they cut out the baby."

"Exactly. And disposed of it to cover their tracks. I also smelled an accelerant soaked into the bed. I think that's what the last soldier was doing here, prepping the remains. They wanted to assure the body was burned so thoroughly that no DNA could be extracted. But we caught them off guard before they could complete their task."

"Why would Amanda's kidnappers go through such effort?" Painter asked, but it sounded more like he was pondering the question, thinking out loud.

Still, Gray answered. "They obviously wanted to throw off anyone still looking for her. If the world thinks she's dead, the hunt ends here."

"True. But I fear our enemy is even smarter than that."

"What do you mean?"

"Think about it. They knew you were closing in, forcing their hand. They had to move her, but they turned the situation to their own ends. Staging Amanda's death—but also achieving another goal."

Gray's mind raced alongside the director's line of reasoning. He knew everything that had befallen Painter at the White House. He suddenly understood. "The enemy was able to blame Amanda's death on our operation."

"At least partially."

As Gray considered *who* might have such an end goal, his blood went cold. There was only one organization harboring such a vendetta against Sigma.

"Director, are you suggesting the *Guild* is somehow involved in Amanda's kidnapping?"

Gray felt his vision narrowing, picturing his mother's casket lowering into the cold dirt.

"Commander Pierce, we don't know that for certain. But either way, it gives Sigma a black eye—if not a fatal blow."

Gray knew that had been an ultimate goal of the Guild for years. They had tried multiple times to destroy Sigma, once even leading an assault upon their headquarters.

He closed his eyes.

Have I played right into their hands here, done their work for them this time?

"What are we going to do?" Gray asked.

"Your mission objective remains the same. To find Amanda. That's all that matters at the moment."

Gray choked down the anger that flared inside him. He forced his fingers through his hair, triggering a twinge of complaint from his blistered back. The director was correct. He had to stay on mission, which meant answering one all-important question concerning Amanda.

Where to begin looking for her?

Painter voiced the same question. "Were you able to get any clue from inside the cabin, anything that might point to where they were taking Amanda?"

Gray stared at the smoking pile of debris. "We didn't have any time. She could be anywhere."

Painter let out a long sigh—not in defeat but in renewed determination. "Then we start from scratch. We're not giving up. I'll see what I can do at my end. You and Captain Alden canvass any locals in the area. Someone must know something. In the rush to evacuate, something might have fallen through the cracks."

Gray agreed. The enemy clearly hadn't expected his team to arrive at the camp so quickly—if at all.

"Pierce!" The call came from Tucker.

He turned and found the man waving to him from the road that exited the camp. Tucker stepped aside to allow a small figure to run into view. It was Baashi. Gray had last seen the boy diving into the forest after almost getting shot.

Seichan had gone out to look for him.

She appeared steps behind him, dragging a prisoner with her, clutching him by the shirt collar as he stumbled alongside her.

Gray spoke into the phone. "Director, I'll call you back in a few minutes. We may have caught a break."

Signing off, he strode over to the group. Captain Alden headed over there, too.

Seichan met Gray's eyes as he reached her. "I found Baashi leading this kid back out of the forest, heading our way."

Baashi vigorously nodded. "I tell him you all good."

Tucker looked pale. "It's the same boy I jumped earlier by the creek."

Gray saw he was right. It was the child Tucker had strangled and hog-tied. So the bound boy *had* been discovered by the enemy. No wonder the crew had hightailed it back to camp.

"Kid must've fled during our attack on the third truck," Seichan said. "But Baashi tracked him in the woods and convinced him we were okay."

From his wide, scared eyes, the new boy must be wondering if he'd made the right decision.

"Mr. Trevor!" Baashi burst out brightly and ran to meet the British captain as he joined them. He patted Alden on the chest and spoke to the other boy. "This the man I tell you about."

Seeing the confused look on the captive's face, Baashi repeated what he said in Somali. Then he stepped over like an excited tour guide and patted Kane, too, ending with "He good dog."

Gray sidled next to Alden during all of this. "See if Baashi could ask the boy if he knows where Amanda was taken."

"I'll do my best."

Gray had to wait while a fervid series of exchanges commenced. It involved a lot of back-and-forth and not a few suspicious glances cast his way. Finally, the boy seemed to relent. Pointing this way and that, he spoke briskly in Somali.

Alden eventually straightened and rejoined Gray.

"It seems, like with Baashi, people are willing to speak more openly around a child. He overheard some of the medical staff at the camp talking, making preparations to move the young woman to an airfield used by drug-runners. He says he heard them speak of flying to Dubai. But I don't know if that's just a stopover or a final destination because he also said they're planning to go to heaven."

To go to heaven? What did that mean? Was it some sort of suicide pact?

That didn't sound like the enemy—and certainly not the Guild. Alden must have read his confusion and shrugged. He had no better explanation.

Still, Gray's mood lightened. "At least, Dubai gives us a solid place to start looking. To hopefully pick up her trail again."

Alden stared over at Jain, on a stretcher, one pant leg cut away. "Good luck, commander. I'll see to the boys here." He motioned to Baashi and the other kid. "In the meantime—"

The thumping of a helicopter cut him off, drawing his attention skyward.

"I believe that's your SEAL team," the captain said. "A bit late to the bloody party, but they can help secure the area. I'd suggest you and your team borrow that helo of mine. Clear out before too many questions get asked."

"Before that," Gray started, "about Amanda . . ."

Alden winked at him. "I heard she died here. A real tragedy." So the good captain had already perceived, as Painter had, that Amanda's best chance of survival lay in everyone continuing to believe that lie. "That's what I'll be reporting to my superiors."

"Thank you," Gray said and shook the man's hand, grasping his forearm with the other.

"No thanks needed, mate. If it wasn't for your quick thinking, there would've been more casualties at that UNICEF camp, including possibly my own men."

With matters settled, Gray drew his group together and hurried toward the idling chopper. He wanted to be out of here before the SEALs clamped things down. The SEAL team was under orders to retrieve the charred body, to return the supposed remains of the president's daughter back to the States—not a duty he would wish on anyone.

He called Painter again, reported what he'd learned, and coordinated logistics on their next move.

"We're pulling up stakes here," Gray said. "Any intelligence Kat can gather while we're en route would help us hit the ground running once we're wheels-down in Dubai City."

"Understood. I'll put a team on it. But I've got Kat working another angle."

Gray paused as everyone loaded into the helicopter. Tucker lifted his dog. "What other angle?"

As Painter explained his worry that all of this bloodshed and terror somehow involved Amanda's unborn child, Gray pictured the brutality of the cesarean performed on the anonymous woman, her body charred beyond recognition.

In his gut, Gray knew the director was correct.

This was all about the baby.

As he signed off and strapped into his seat aboard the chopper, another concern nagged him. It also centered on Amanda and her child. Gray couldn't escape the sense that Painter had been withholding something from him. The director's decision to keep Amanda's survival a secret from her own parents never sat right with him. Painter was certainly a master chess player and could be coldhearted and tough when he had his back against the wall—but never *this* callous. His explanation felt forced, like there was something he didn't want to share about Amanda or her family.

But what could it be?

With a roar of its engines, the helicopter slowly rose from the ruins of the camp, stirring smoke and ash, leaving the horrors below.

He might not know what gambit Painter was playing—but he knew one thing for certain.

This was just the beginning.

Much worse was still to come.

11:00 A.M. EST
Washington, DC

Robert Gant stepped through the air lock and entered the Class 1000 clean room, a stark white chamber with glass walls that looked out into the rest of the genomics lab. Staffed only by three researchers, the entire facility lay in an industrial area on the outskirts of Alexandria, Virginia, and was listed as a private DNA test lab.

But that was not its purpose.

Its true function had been etched into one of the glass walls of the clean room: a frosted cross, decorated with spirals of DNA along its cross-pieces.

"Show me," he said, using the deep baritone that served him well in the past as a U.S. ambassador and now as secretary of state.

He allowed some of his irritation to ring out. He'd left Jimmy and Teresa to their grief to attend to private family business, but he wanted to keep this visit as short as possible.

The researcher, Dr. Emmet Fielding—decked out in white coveralls, gloves, boots, and hood—drew him to a laboratory table. A sealed crystal cylinder, about the size and shape of a hockey puck, held a murky aquamarine fluid. Beside it on the table rested a titanium sculpture that looked like a clawless crab supported by six articulated legs. Its flat metal carapace measured a foot across, reminding Robert of the land mines that still peppered Southeast Asia, where he'd spent the bulk of his ambassadorship.

Fielding lifted the cylinder from the table and held it in the palm of his hand. "This is the latest generation," he said proudly. "Half a million neurons harvested from human fetal cortical tissue to form this new brain. And, once implanted, it will communicate via five thousand microelectrodes. A fourfold improvement from the last generation."

And a huge advance from where this all started.

This was Robert's pet project. He had learned of the first tentative steps taken by the University of Reading in England back in 2009. A researcher in neuro-robotics discovered that a handful of neurons, collected from the cortex of lab rats and grown in a culture medium, could be wired into a small wheeled robot, and through electrode stimulation, it could control and operate the tiny vehicle, learning over time as new synapses formed to avoid objects and work through mazes. Shortly thereafter, another scientist, at the University of Florida, upped the ante, wiring twenty-five thousand rat neurons to a flight simulator. Over time that tiny brain learned to fly a jet flawlessly through mountains and thunderstorms.

Years later, utilizing the family's financial and technological resources, Robert had moved that bar much higher. Initially, the research had been folded into a larger project, one going back decades, investigating the fusion of man and machine as a means of extending life—a goal sought by the Bloodline for centuries.

But this research into cyborg technology proved to be a dead end.

It became clear that it would never be a feasible means of sustaining or prolonging life, especially with the more promising advent of stem-cell research. At that point in time, the Bloodline turned its eye in a new direction, forsaking the *macro* world of robotics for the *micro* world of genetics.

But even Robert didn't have full access to that newest venture.

Instead, he'd been left to oversee this older project. Neuro-robotics still showed the potential to be a lucrative new weapons technology for the military. If rat brains could fly jet planes years ago, why not something more ambitious for the battlefield of the future?

"Let me give you a demonstration of the hexapod," Fielding said.

The researcher opened the titanium carapace of the metal crab, exposing the microelectronics inside. He seated the neural cylinder into the electrode base at the heart of the pod and secured everything in place. Next, he carried the device to a neighboring chamber in the clean room. It had been set up as a test maze—but this was no ordinary flat puzzle. This labyrinth filled the entire ten-by-ten chamber, rising through fifteen levels of tunnels, chutes, and spirals.

"I ran the hexapod through this maze once already today. Now watch."

Fielding inserted the crab-like machine through a lower slot, sealed the door, and used a Bluetooth device to activate it.

Tiny green lights flared along a groove that ran around the periphery of the hexapod's carapace. Titanium legs stretched and tapped.

Robert leaned closer, unimpressed. "Why isn't it—?"

The creature shot away, dancing on its six legs, gaining speed until it was a silvery blur. It sped through the maze with unerring accuracy, no doubling back to correct a wrong turn. It had remembered the complex path through the maze perfectly.

"I'm estimating the new brain's neural intelligence is about that of your average canine," Fielding said proudly.

A half-minute later, the hexapod reached the exit platform near the top, skidding to a stop.

Robert grinned. "Impressive."

Fielding matched that expression, thrilled at the rare praise. He reached to the door and unlatched it. Before he could swing it open, the hexapod rammed forward. It burst out and latched its legs onto the researcher's forearm. The sharp-pointed legs dug into his flesh. Blood seeped through his white coveralls.

"Motherf—" Fielding yelled and hit the Bluetooth controller, powering down the hexapod.

Still, he had to return to the table and manually pry each leg out of his arm to get it to release.

"The aggression of this newest generation is also through the roof," Fielding said, wincing and nursing his bloody arm as proof. "I'd say we've engineered the equivalent of a limbic region of the mammalian brain, the lizard intelligence buried beneath the cortex, driven by base needs for survival."

"For a battlefield weapon, that's not an undesirable trait."

"True."

"And speaking of battlefields, you promised a field trial of the latest hexapods. That's why I came all the way down here in person."

"Of course. I have a monitor set up over here with live feed from the Lodge. Everything's ready. They've been waiting for the green light."

Robert followed Fielding to a fifty-two-inch HD monitor. The screen was subdivided into sections, each offering a different bird's-eye view of a remote and isolated patch of woodland hills hundreds of miles away.

The centermost square showed a small concrete bunker sticking out of a meadow, like a giant anthill. A metal door sealed it shut.

"If you're ready?" Fielding said.

"Get on with it," Robert snapped.

Fielding spoke into a cell phone. Moments later, the metal door burst open and a woman was shoved outside. She wore a hospital gown and nothing else. She stumbled to her knees, shielding her eyes against the midday sun. Robert absently wondered how long it had been since the young woman had seen actual sunlight.

From the way she jumped and glanced back to the door, someone must have barked at her.

"They're telling her to run if she wants to live."

Robert frowned, not appreciating the sadism. This was an experiment, not a bloody sport, and should be conducted as such.

The subject took off for the forest at a dead run.

"There!" Fielding pointed to movement through the grasses, a dozen arrows, aiming for the fleeing woman. A pair split off, zipping away faster, intending to flank her. "Look how they're pattern-swarming. I employed a new wireless communications system and linked the individual hexapods to one another, allowing them to function as a group or pack. Look how quickly they're learning."

Robert watched—half-aghast, half-excited.

The woman made it to the edge of the woods, but she must have heard the hunters. She looked over a shoulder, and the horror of what she saw tripped her feet. She fell to her knees, her mouth open in a silent scream.

Then the hunters reached her.

It did not take long.

Fielding held his chin in one hand, appraising the trial. "The new battlefield modifications of the pods seem to be working as engineered. The circular blades, the razored leg flanges . . . all performed flawlessly. I may want to tinker with the digging spades, see if I can get them to burrow better."

"I've seen enough," Robert said, straightening and stepping away.

Fielding followed him. "With your approval, I'd like to move the testing forward into the larger quadruped line."

"That would be fine."

Fielding pressed him. "But I'd need a few more test subjects. Something more challenging."

Robert pictured the macerated remains of the woman on the screen. "I'm sure we can find them somewhere."

SECOND

HEAVEN AND HELL

18

Captain Kathryn Bryant had come to sell her body.

She stepped off the crosstown bus into the steamy swelter of a Charleston summer. Her worn sneakers crunched in the gravel at the shoulder of the road. She pulled on a pair of cheap sunglasses purchased at the airport against the glare of the sun, but they did nothing for the heat.

Ninety degrees with ninety percent humidity.

I thought Washington's summers were bad.

In a feeble attempt to compensate, she'd gathered her long auburn hair into a ponytail and wore a ball cap to shade her face. She also wore a pair of light shorts and a nondescript loose blouse, no bra, finishing her appearance as a down-on-her-luck woman looking for a little extra money.

The bus pulled away with a choking cough of diesel fumes. She followed in its wake.

The North Charleston Fertility Clinic rose two blocks ahead, the complex covered a full city block, set amid a small park of towering oaks and palmettos. The rest of the neighborhood was a mix of commercial businesses and trailer parks. She was not unfamiliar with the area, having spent a few months while in service at the Naval Weapons Station, which hugged the Cooper River three miles away.

As she headed toward the clinic, she slipped out her cell phone to keep a promise. The phone was a disposable, tied to her alias. She connected her call through Sigma to ensure it couldn't be traced. If anyone tried to pull the LUDs, the phone records would only discover a call placed to a local pawnshop.

The line clicked and a gruff voice answered, "So you're still alive?"

Her husband, Monk, did his best to make it sound like a joke, but she heard the undercurrent of tension in his voice. He hadn't been thrilled she'd taken this assignment, but he understood the necessity.

"For the moment," she replied with a smile. "I'm just heading toward the clinic."

"You give them hell."

Her smile widened. "That's the plan."

She pictured Monk at their apartment, balancing one of their babies on his knee. He was not what most women would consider handsome, with his shaved head and stocky but muscular physique, but he still could make her melt with his smile and she'd never met a man with a bigger heart, a heart that only grew larger with each addition to the household.

"Did you give Harriet her second bottle?" she asked.

An exasperated sigh followed. "Yes, dear. And I went to Costco and got the Pampers. You go save the world. I've got things covered here."

She had hoped her call would erase that edge of apprehension hiding behind his jovial banter, but it only seemed to make it worse.

"Monk, I'm almost at the clinic. Give Penny and Harriet a kiss for me."

"Done. And I'll save what I've got for *you* until you get home."

"Ah, always my gallant knight," she said sarcastically—but it was forced. Because he was her knight . . . and always would be.

His voice grew husky. "Just get back here safely."

"I promise."

"You'd better. I'm holding you to it."

After she hung up, the world seemed slightly less bright. A twinge of guilt plagued her as she pocketed her phone.

What am I doing here? I should be at home.

Still, she could not discount the electric thrill that coursed through her as she reached the grounds of the clinic and turned her attention to the task at hand. It happened with every mission. She had a duty, and she was good at what she did. And knowing her family was safe—and always would be with Monk—helped steady her. He was her rock, even hundreds of miles away.

With renewed determination, she crossed along the tall stacked-stone fence of the clinic and stepped through the wrought-iron gates, entering a garden oasis set amidst the surrounding commercial parks. A path led alongside the entry road, winding through manicured hedgerows, small burbling fountains, and perfumed beds of blush-pink roses.

Someone had gone to great expense to make the clinic feel warm and inviting, a veritable Garden of Eden, where dreams of infertile couples could not help but come true. No wonder this place drew celebrity clients and people from around the globe—including the president's daughter.

Then again, the complex was owned by a subsidiary of a Gant family enterprise, one dedicated to biotech and genetic engineering. The clinic, established in the early eighties, was the end result of much of that research, offering the latest innovations to the public. The clinic also employed its own research protocols, drawing reproductive scientists from as far away as Japan. The place continued to be at the forefront of fertility studies and stem-cell research.

Over the past eighteen hours, Kat had investigated the clinic extensively—from its staffing and clientele down to its latest tax filings. She knew everything about the clinic: where they got their bed linens, the average weight of their hazardous waste material per day. The deeper she delved, the more certain she grew that the reason for Amanda's kidnapping lay hidden somewhere within the four buildings that made up this facility.

This conviction came not from anything she uncovered—but from what she didn't. After a full decade gathering global intelligence, she had developed a nose for when something was being hidden from her. During her investigation, she had reached too many dead ends that made no sense, certain matters that didn't balance in her head. Worst of all, she stumbled across an impenetrable corporate firewall at one point, employing encryption algorithms that were military-grade. Even if she could, she feared smashing through it. The act alone could set off too many alarm bells, alerting the powers that be at the clinic that someone was sniffing at their door.

So she opted for a more direct approach.

On foot.

She reached the parking lot and spotted the rental car, a silver Audi A6 sedan. Lisa Cummings had beaten her here, but her friend hadn't had to navigate through two bus transfers from the airport to reach the clinic. They had come separately, each with her own mission.

Kat climbed the steps to a wide porch that fronted the main build-ing. It looked nothing like a medical facility. The façade was typical for Charleston: a Georgian stone mansion with wrought-iron railings, three floors of balconies, and a gambrel roof covered by mossy-fringed slate tiles.

She stepped through the doors into an air-conditioned main lobby, re-freshing after the hot bus ride and short walk. A reception desk beckoned. She approached it, noting out of the corner of her eye that Lisa sat in the waiting area, a space as sumptuously furnished as would be expected from the exterior, decked out in velvets and overstuffed cushions.

Lisa matched the décor in a handsome St. John platinum dress with a drawstring waist. Her blond hair hung loose and shone under the soft lights; her makeup was flawless. She came posing as the private doctor for a select Washingtonian clientele, coming to interview the clinic for pos-sible referrals for her patients. She had an appointment to meet with the head of the facility in a few minutes.

Lisa was conducting this cursory investigation from the top down.

Kat was taking the other extreme.

"How may I help you?" the receptionist asked. She was a small woman with large eyes, made even more prominent by her harsh eye shadow.

Kat moved closer to the desk, pressing against it, leaning a bit too forward as if trying to keep the conversation from being overheard. "I heard . . . someone told me . . . that you all are looking for donors."

The receptionist's brows pinched in irritation.

Kat pushed even closer, glancing surreptitiously over her shoulder, raising an embarrassed blush to her cheeks. "You know. Looking for a woman's eggs. I heard you pay good money."

The receptionist sat straighter, her voice growing hushed, if not a touch condescending, made worse by the patronizing tone of her Carolina accent. "Hon, that's handled elsewhere. This is for patient intake. If you'll stand over there . . ." She waved a manicured hand away from the waiting area, toward a corner. "I'll have one of the staff assistants come fetch you and bring you to the donor facility, if that's all right?"

Kat nodded and slunk back. "Thank you."

The woman made a noncommittal noise and picked up the phone.

As Kat retreated to her corner, she met Lisa's gaze. At the moment they were divided by a cultural and financial gulf. Lisa represented the end buyer; Kat embodied the product to be sold. There continued to be much ethical and moral debate about the sale of human ova. Once a price tag was put upon such a commodity, it became tied to the power of supply and demand—and the inherent abuse.

In much of the Third World, entire villages now sold kidneys or became surrogate mothers, selling rental space in their wombs. It was called the *red market*—the wholesale buying and selling of body parts—and it was a booming business, both legally and illegally. She had read a report of Bolivian murderers who sought out victims to sell their fat to European beauty supply companies. In China, prisons were harvesting the organs of dead inmates, gutting them out, with whispers that some prisoners were being purposefully killed for profit. And in one case in Nepal, a dairy farmer had turned from delivering milk to supplying blood. He captured local hikers, imprisoned them in his barn, and repeatedly drained his new livestock of their blood, keeping them forever at the edge of death.

Worst of all, such a marketplace moved in only one economic direction: from the poor to the rich. It was an unfortunate side effect when a price tag was placed on organs. Inevitably, flesh moved only *up* the social ladder, never *down*.

Movement across the room drew Kat's attention. A mahogany door opened and a rugged-looking man in his midforties stepped into the waiting room. He had jet-black hair, stood six feet tall, and was decked out in a knee-length white lab coat over expensive navy-blue trousers, a crisp white shirt, and a crimson tie. His smile was overly broad as he approached Lisa, who stood to greet him.

"Welcome to NCFC," he said and shook her hand.

It was Dr. Paul Cranston, head of the clinic. Kat knew everything about him, even his social security number and where his passport had last been stamped: New Zealand.

He led Lisa out of the waiting room and into the inner sanctum of the facility. As that door closed, another opened. A man, likely a hospital orderly, stood at the threshold of a doorway neighboring the front desk. He looked like a pit bull in scrubs. The receptionist beckoned to Kat.

She stepped forward.

"If you'll follow me," the man grunted, not bothering with her name.

She hurried forward but stopped at the reception desk to grab a business card. She fumbled and purposefully knocked the holder off the counter and onto the reception desk.

"I'm so sorry," she said, reaching over to help collect the scattered cards.

The receptionist sighed heavily and picked a few cards off the floor by her chair. Kat used the moment to slip the ballpoint pen palmed in her hand into the receptionist's cup. It held a tiny camera that recorded audio and video passively to a micro SD chip. A small antenna allowed burst transmissions of the saved data with the pinged call from a cell phone.

She had four more pens in her purse, with the goal of strategically placing them in key locations throughout the facility—or, at least, where she could reach without raising an alarm. If given the chance, it would be easy for a confused girl to get lost in here and wander where she didn't belong.

But first she had a role to play.

"Just go," the receptionist said and pointed to the side door.

Kat apologized meekly and followed the orderly waiting for her. He led her out of the world of gardens and velvets and into a sterile environment of vinyl floors and stark white walls. Here was the hospital hidden behind the façade: sparse and utilitarian.

They eventually reached and entered a short enclosed walkway that connected the main building to a more drab structure at the back of the grounds. As she marched, she noted each of the four clinic wings was connected in a similar manner. It seemed there was no need to leave the air-conditioned splendor for the summer heat. She also eyed the windowed walls to either side. The glass was thick, appeared bulletproof.

Then again, the clinic's clientele were often celebrities or foreign dignitaries. Maybe the extra protection was necessary.

Still, a chill that had nothing to do with the air-conditioning swept through her. The space felt less protective than it was imprisoning.

They entered the next building, and Kat was taken to a small examination room, one of a long row of them in this wing. The orderly handed her a series of forms to fill out, secured on a clipboard.

"Fill everything out. Someone will be in to talk to you in a few minutes."

He left, looking as bored as when he'd first collected her.

She began to fill out the forms when she heard a small click at the door. Stepping forward, she tested the handle.

Locked.

She frowned, fighting back a flicker of panic. Securing the door might be protocol, to maintain confidentiality. Either way, she was committed. She'd have to keep playing her hand—but something was definitely wrong about this place.

She hoped Lisa was faring better.

12:18 P.M.

"As you can see, we do all of our work in-house," Dr. Paul Cranston said, stopping before a window that looked into a sealed in vitro fertilization lab.

Lisa studied the space with a critical eye. The room was state-of-the-art, with enclosed workstations equipped with laser oocyte scanners and Narishige micromanipulators for egg fertilization. Nothing was substandard, from Makler counting chambers to automatic sperm-analyzers, advanced warming blocks, and cryogenic chambers.

Her guided tour had already included the surgical suite, used for both egg collection and embryo implantation. The clinic's high-tech operating theater would put most hospitals to shame. Even the neighboring recovery rooms were private spaces that could have graced the pages of *Architectural Digest,* with fine linens, subdued lighting, and tasteful decorations.

Clearly this tour was meant to impress.

And it did.

"We are a one-stop shop," Cranston finished, offering a beaming, self-effacing smile. "From sperm and egg collection, to fertilization and implantation. We do all of our own patient monitoring, but we're certainly happy to work in collaboration with a primary care physician."

Lisa nodded. "I'm sure some of my clients would prefer the anonymity of care outside the DC circles."

"Understood."

His eyes lingered a bit too long on her. Plainly, he desired to know more about whom she represented, but he knew better than to inquire directly. Lisa's ironclad cover had been built to draw the personal interest of the clinic's head, and obviously succeeded. She had been given the grand tour, along with the full-court sales press.

"Why don't we return to my office? I can supply you with brochures detailing each level of service, including fact sheets containing our success rates, and, of course, I'll be happy to answer any other questions."

"That would be perfect." She checked her watch in a move to urge him to hurry along. "I won't take up much more of your time."

His office was up a level from the workspaces. It was like walking into a mahogany library, with bookshelf-lined walls, trophies, and framed diplomas, including one from Harvard, his alma mater. Like the rest of the tour, the room was also designed to impress. Huge arched windows overlooked the parklike grounds with views to the other three buildings that made up the complex.

Cranston circled around his desk, where a prepared binder was already waiting for her atop his leather desk blotter. He handed it toward her, but she ignored it, focusing her attention out the window. She also kept a keen eye on his reactions. Besides a medical degree, she had earned a master's in physiology. She understood bodily responses and could read them as accurately as most lie detectors—but unlike those detectors, she also knew how to manipulate those responses for a desired result.

Now to get to work.

"What happens in those other buildings?" she asked.

He lowered the binder and followed her gaze outside. "The wing directly behind this one is for donor evaluation and collection."

Lisa eyed the three-story structure.

That must be where Kat is.

"The other two buildings are strictly for research," he said. "We run reproductive studies for a dozen different universities, including as far away as the University of Tokyo and Oxford."

She turned her back to the window. "I'm assuming that any biological specimens, eggs, or embryos from my patients wouldn't be used for such purposes without their consent."

"Of course not. We have a robust donor program that supplies such material. Let me assure you, Dr. Cummings, our research programs and patient services are completely separate. There is no crossover."

"Very good." Lisa returned to the chair in front of his wide desk and sank into the seat, shifting her purse into her lap. "Now let me be frank with you, Dr. Cranston."

"Please call me Paul."

She smiled, giving him that much. "Paul, I must be honest that I have been considering other facilities. It's come down to here or a clinic outside of Philadelphia."

"Of course."

He kept an even demeanor, but she did not mistake the flicker of desire—to poach another client was even better than merely to win one. That was the bait.

"But I assure you," he continued, "you'll find no other facility with the level of technological advancement, the latest tools, and the professional staff to oversee each stage of the process."

Cranston definitely wanted her imaginary high-profile client list—but how badly?

First to let some slack in the line, intended to unnerve him. "I understand and appreciate that, Paul, but Philadelphia is also much *closer* to DC. I must take that convenience into account. My clients' time is very important."

He looked crestfallen. "I can't argue with that."

Now to dangle hope. "But your clinic has one distinct advantage. Beyond your stellar *medical* reputation, you have an unmatched *social* reputation, an excellent pedigree, if you will."

"How so?"

"Amanda Gant-Bennett."

The edges of his eyelids grew more strained at the mention of Amanda.

"Several of my patients are well acquainted with the First Family," she continued. "They know of the delicate situation regarding the president's daughter and how matters were handled at your clinic. In many ways, Washington is a small town."

She offered him a modest smile.

He echoed it—the desired effect.

"One patient of mine in particular is faced with a similar situation: an infertile husband. She asked me to specifically inquire into your donor program. To put it bluntly, using my patient's words: 'If it's good enough for the president's daughter, it's good enough for me.' "

She rolled her eyes, feigning amused disdain. "In certain Washingtonian circles—whether it's the latest purse or the season's designer fashions—name brands are all that matter. And this even extends to the choice of medical facility and, in this case, even the preference of donor."

He gave her an understanding nod and steepled his fingers under his chin. "There is, of course, no way to divulge who was the male donor in this situation. But I can guarantee you that *each* of our donors must pass the most thorough and exacting background check and evaluation. Each is ranked on several criteria: physical appearance, IQ, medical history, ethnic background, and many others."

"And if someone wanted to pick a donor of, let us say, *equal* criteria as the president's daughter . . . ?"

His smile grew steadier, as he discovered a way to win her over. It was human nature: to almost have something in one's grasp, then suddenly lose it, only made the desire to win it back that much stronger. It was why gambling was so addictive.

"I'm sure that could be arranged," he said. "We'd hate to lose you."

I'm sure you would.

"Wonderful." She rewarded him with a genuine smile of delight. "And would it be possible to obtain a list and description of such donors, something tangible I can present to my client? As they say, the proof is in the pudding."

Cranston swung to his computer. "Certainly. If you can give me a few minutes . . ."

She settled back into her chair. Painter wanted that shortened list of donors, a way to narrow down the number of potential biological fathers for Amanda's unborn child. But he also needed a way to turn the anonymity of those donors into real names.

That meant gaining access to clinic records.

As Cranston worked, Lisa snapped open her purse and pretended to check her phone. She pressed a button on it as instructed by Painter, then slipped the thin device into the seat cushions of her chair, using her purse to hide her actions. The phone had a wireless micro-router built into it, allowing Sigma to link and hack into the clinic's server. Painter had tried to explain it in more detail, but electronic engineering was not her specialty. All she knew was to follow his instructions: wait until Cranston had logged into the computer and used his password, then activate the wireless router and leave it running nearby.

She clicked her purse closed.

Her work here was done.

It seemed too easy, but then again, it was supposed to be.

Painter had described the mission here as a *soft* infiltration. Rather than a full-frontal storming of the gates, Kat and Lisa's only goal was to leave a trail of electronic bread crumbs: listening devices, cameras, wireless taps. Most of the tools had been engineered by Painter, made for easy concealment and minimal signature.

But anything can be detected, given enough time, Painter had warned.

So the second part of this mission was not to loiter.

And she obeyed that now.

In short order, she had everything she needed from Dr. Cranston, including the binder of brochures and information. He walked her back to the lobby, left her with promises to keep in touch, and she soon found herself back under the swelter of the midday sun.

She headed over and climbed into her Audi sedan, a luxurious rental to match her cover. Though her part of the mission was complete, a knot of tension remained in her neck. The plan was for Kat to meet her back at their hotel in downtown Charleston. She would be relieved only when they were rejoined. From there, the electronic devices could do all the spying for them.

She swung her sedan out of the parking lot and onto the street, still worried about Kat, feeling guilty for abandoning her partner.

Her only reassurance: Kat was a pro.

Nothing fazed her.

1:14 P.M.

What the hell is going on here?

Pacing the small exam room, Kat checked the clock on her disposable phone. It had been over an hour since she first walked through the clinic's front door. She should've been in and out by now. She had completed the sheaf of paperwork and handed it to the same orderly who marched her here and locked her in the room.

He'd told her to sit tight, that the initial approval process could take some time. And that it wasn't all paperwork. *A doctor will be in to do a pelvic exam and ultrasound in a few minutes. You will be paid a small stipend now in order to draw your blood and collect a urine sample. Within five business days, you will be informed by phone whether you're selected as a donor.*

This was all related in a bored monotone, as if he'd repeated the same speech a hundred times each day. And maybe he did. Through the walls, she heard other men and women coming and going, doors opening and closing along the long exam hallway.

She had hoped to get a cursory tour of the donation center, to plant another pen camera here, maybe even attempt to reach the other two research buildings. That didn't seem likely unless she was bolder.

She stepped to the secured door. She had a lock pick incorporated into the sole of her right shoe, and a folded combat blade hidden in her left. But her escape out of a locked room would be hard to explain if she was caught later. There was an easier way.

She knocked loudly and raised a plaintive lilt to her call. "Hello! I need to use the bathroom! Can someone help me, please?"

It didn't take long for the door to be unlocked.

She expected to see the same orderly as before—but instead it was a white-smocked doctor, a svelte woman with gray eyes. The orderly hovered behind her, holding a tray with a rack of vacuum tubes for blood collection and an array of syringes.

The only warning of trouble: one of the syringes was *full.*

Before she could react, the doctor stepped forward and jammed a black wand against her stomach. The snap of electricity was loud in the small space. Agony shot through her body, centered on her belly, contracting her abdominal muscles. Her limbs betrayed her, and she toppled to the side, a slim edge away from a full convulsion.

Anticipating this, the doctor caught her and lowered her to the floor. The orderly closed the door and came around her other side, syringe in hand. Even through the electric pain, she felt the needle jab in her neck.

Her vision began to immediately close down.

Kat fought against it, wondering how her cover could have been blown. She'd been so thorough to craft her alias as a shiftless transient with no familial or local ties, nothing that could be easily verified or tracked back to her.

Unfortunately, that proved her undoing.

"She seems in better than average shape," the doctor said to the orderly, examining Kat as if she were a prized pig at a county fair. "Unusual. Feel this muscle tone. I don't see any track marks on her arm or signs of chronic drug use. You're sure she met the standard protocol?"

"Everything checked out, Dr. Marshall. She just moved here. No job. No family. Changed cities three times in the past year before coming here. Gainesville, Atlanta, now Charleston. No one to miss her."

Kat's world folded and closed over her.

Their conversation followed her into oblivion. "Then it's perfect timing. I received a message from the Lodge a short time ago. They're demanding more research subjects."

Kat felt her body lifted by the muscular orderly.

"The Lodge?" he asked. "Do you know what they do up there?"

"Trust me, you don't want to know."

19

Gray stood before the hotel windows and stared out at the jeweled night-scape of Dubai's skyline, an emerald oasis perched between the desert and the blue sea. Towers and cloud-scraping spires blazed with lights, rising from a modern mecca of huge malls, hotels, and trendy residential complexes, all wired and connected by ribbons of flowing neon of every fathomable hue. The panorama looked less like a city and more like a glowing circuit board buzzing with the electricity of the entire region.

It seemed impossible that five hours ago he'd been in a country devastated by war, famine, and drought; a land ruled as much by pirates as any government.

Now he floated above a miracle.

Grown at a blistering pace, Dubai had risen like a mirage out of the desert, with the crown jewel being Burj Khalifa, over two hundred stories high, the tallest skyscraper in the world, appearing like a thin mountain pinnacle at the edge of the sea. Architects from around the world continued to compete to construct the most awe-inspiring designs, seemingly with one common theme: the defiance of nature and its elements. Within the city, one could lounge on a sun-baked beach, and an hour later be snowboarding down the slopes of the world's largest indoor ski resort. And if one wanted the best of both worlds, the newly opened Palazzo Versace hotel had its own refrigerated beach to keep tourists cool while sunbathing.

But the greatest of the nature-defying projects lay beyond the beaches: Dubai's famous man-made islands. Their hotel neighbored Palm Jumeirah, an artificial archipelago in the shape of a palm tree, so large it could be seen from space. Its trunk grew out from the mainland and burst forth with sixteen fronds, all circled by a crescent-shaped breakwater. Another two such islands were being constructed along the coastline, multiplying the amount of Dubai beachfront tenfold.

Gray had read of other projects still in the works for Dubai: a twenty-seven-acre underwater hotel called Hydropolis; a German-designed floating palace made entirely of ice, fancifully named the Blue Crystal; and, even farther out to sea, the partially completed deep-sea island of Utopia, shaped like a starfish and sheltered by a breakwater crescent, intended both as a tourist destination and a corporate enclave, due to its unique isolation.

Here in Dubai, nature held no sway against the lofty dreams of man.

"You gotta try the shower, Pierce." Kowalski came out of the bathroom, a towel wrapped around his waist. "They got jets that hit you in all the right places—and a few wrong ones."

It seemed the dreams of some men weren't as lofty as others'.

Gray turned his back on the cityscape. With his shoulders still blistered and sore, a shower held no appeal at the moment.

Maybe a long bath.

The group shared a two-bedroom suite. Kowalski and Gray had one room; Seichan, the other. Tucker and Kane staked out the couch in the common room, equipped with a pool table, a wet bar, and a flat-screen television. Gray heard a BBC broadcast playing out there.

"I'm going to see if Tucker wants to lose a few bucks playing pool," Kowalski said and headed toward the door, hauling on a robe and letting his wet towel fall to the floor.

Gray stepped toward the bathroom.

There wasn't much else they could do except to continue waiting for an intelligence report from Sigma command.

Painter was gathering data on flights into and out of Somalia, comparing all routes that could bring Amanda and her kidnappers to Dubai. He was also checking passenger manifests, searching custom records, specifically looking for faces that matched Amanda's, in case someone tried to sneak her through with a fake passport. He also had a team scouring security footage from Dubai International Airport.

Gray didn't hold out much hope. His team had already spent an hour at the airport, tracking all the exits and baggage areas, checking to see if Kane could pick up her scent.

Nothing.

Maybe she never came here—or came and left.

But Gray didn't think so and couldn't exactly say why. It was more than a gut feeling—like something that beckoned at the edge of his awareness, something he was missing.

In the bathroom, he turned on the tub's tap, tested the water, and, once satisfied, he slowly peeled off his shirt. Pieces stuck to his shoulders, pasted in place by his blistered skin. With a groan, he tugged the shirt off, stripped out of the rest of his clothes, and climbed into the tub.

It was wonderful agony to sink into the steaming heat.

He left the tap running, letting the waterline climb up his belly. He leaned forward, hugging his knees, carefully stretching the stiffened skin across his shoulders.

"Dear God, Gray . . . your back looks horrible."

He twisted half-around to face the open door. Seichan stood there, her gaze not shying from his nakedness. He was too tired to be self-conscious. They'd both seen each other at their best and worst. What was a little bare skin?

He turned off the flowing tap. "I'm fine. What is it?"

"You're not *fine*. Why didn't you tell someone your burn was this bad? I'm getting the med pack. Here." She stepped forward and passed him the satellite phone. "Call from Sigma."

He took the phone. "Director?"

"Gray, I just wanted to give you an update, while I have a spare moment."

He sat higher in the tub. "Any leads?"

"No, I'm afraid not. We've searched every record and videotape from Dubai International. I can find no evidence that Amanda ever passed through there. I'll keep monitoring the airport and inbound manifests, but I've also expanded the search for flights *out* of the city. We have to take into account that she may have already been moved."

"If that's the case, we're not likely to ever find her."

At least not alive.

"I'll keep looking," Painter said. "But for now, we'll keep your team on-site. Even if she has shipped out, it might not have been far, and I want you and the others close by."

"Understood."

Gray signed off as Seichan returned. She took the phone, set it aside, then tapped the edge of the tub. "Up here. Back to me."

She opened the combat med kit and pulled out a tube of burn cream and Water-Jel tactical dressing.

"I don't need you to—"

"I could get Kowalski to do it. But I don't think either of you would like that."

He sighed heavily, pulled out of the bathwater, and balanced on the lip of the tub. She patted his skin dry with great care. From the corner of his eye, he caught her reflection in the mirror. She rubbed the cream between her palms and placed them against his heated skin.

The balm's cooling agent sank deep into his flesh, outlining each of her fingers. A small moan escaped him.

"Am I hurting you?"

"No," he said, more huskily than he intended.

Her hands spread outward, washing away the worst of his pain. He stretched his back, loosening his shoulders even further. His breathing grew heavier, deeper as she worked. His eyelids drifted closed.

She remained silent. He heard only her breath, sighing in and out. Fingers rode up to his neckline and down his spine. He found himself leaning back into her touch—and not just because of the cooling effect of the balm. In fact, warmth was returning to his skin, but not from the burn. It rose from a fire deeper inside. His body responded, but he didn't bother to hide it, not that he could.

"Gray . . ."

He heard the need in her voice that matched his own.

He reached back and caught one of her hands. He held it, poised between pulling her closer or pushing her away, trapped between heaven and hell. Her fingers, soft and silky, trembled in his palm, like a bird fluttering to escape.

Not this time.

His hand tightened on hers, making a decision at last.

He chose *heaven*.

As he drew her arm around him, twisting to face her, their lips brushing against one another—then he suddenly knew the truth. He froze with shock.

"Gray? What is it?"

He tilted back, his eyes widening as his certainty grew.

"I know where Amanda is."

11:32 P.M.

"You should keep walking," Dr. Blake said, supporting her by the elbow. "It can help the baby get into a better position."

Amanda shambled down a featureless white hallway. She had no idea where she was, nor the time of day. She'd woken in a windowless hospital room four hours ago. The medical team had performed another ultrasound on her, along with a pelvic exam, removing a sponge-like object from inside her.

Dr. Blake had explained, *We inserted a synthetic osmotic dilator while you were sedated, to gently help open your cervix. It's an old-school technique but still effective in preparation for labor.*

It was only then she had learned they were inducing her, forcing her to deliver her baby early. She protested, but the protests fell on deaf ears.

All she got for her trouble was a patronizing reassurance that she was well enough along and that there would be little risk to the baby or herself.

That failed to relieve her. She remembered what she'd overheard during the flight: the plans for her child to be dissected like some lab animal. She had to find a way to stop them.

As she walked, she supported her belly with one hand, as if trying to hold her baby where it was safe, willing her body not to surrender. But ten minutes ago, a prostaglandin gel had been applied vaginally, the first step toward inducing labor.

I won't let them have my baby.

Ahead, she saw a wide window on one side of the hallway, bright with light. She hurried forward, breaking free of Blake's grip.

Maybe there is a way out. Or some sign of where I am.

And deeper down lurked darker thoughts, of throwing herself out a high window, of plummeting to her death rather than letting them torture her baby boy.

She reached the window and fell back in horror. The light did not come from the sun but from the stark halogens of a biological clean lab. She flashed back to a similar facility in Charleston, where her in vitro fertilization had been performed. Like back home, this lab had multiple workstations and microscopes. It was all polished stainless steel or nonporous surfaces.

But what made her weak in the knees was the research project facing her—literally. A disembodied human head hung before her, bolted to a stanchion above a rack as tall as a man. A foot below that horror, a nest of plastic tubing suspended a human heart. A pacemaker-like device had been wired into the dark muscle and sat atop the tissue like a silver spider. The heart contracted every couple of seconds, jumping slightly in its webbing. And below that, a set of pink lungs hung in a glass vat, the disembodied tissue bellowing in and out, hooked to a ventilator. Other body parts loomed in murkier jars farther down, but she shied away from them, fearing what she would find.

Instead, she found her gaze transfixed on the victim's face. His mouth had been taped shut; his eyelids drooped at half-mast. The stump of his neck was sealed in a tight bandage that trailed bloody tubes and tangles of wires, all flowing to a desk-size machine behind the rack.

It was as if someone had stripped the man down to his component parts, separating them each for some macabre study.

She could no longer look and swung away, running into Dr. Blake's chest. He caught her in his arms.

"What is all of this?" she cried.

"We're saving lives," he answered calmly. "Continuing a Russian research program started back in the forties. They were using dogs back then, discovering how long they could keep body parts alive via artificial means. Even seven decades ago, using the crude tools available at the time, the researchers were able to keep the severed heads of their subjects vital for days, animated enough to respond to sound, to attempt to bark, to twitch their ears."

Amanda shook her head, aghast at such a thing.

"Ah, but you see, Amanda, as gruesome as that may sound, those early experiments eventually led to the development of the first ventilator and the first cardiopulmonary bypass machine. A leap forward in technology that saved thousands of lives over the next decades."

"But this . . ." Amanda waved a hand weakly toward the window.

"This is just as important and groundbreaking. The animal model could only take medical science so far. And with the accelerating advances in nanotechnology, microsurgery, neuroscience, cardiopulmonary medicine, and pharmaceutical sciences, there is no limit to what we're on the threshold of accomplishing. What we're doing here—experimenting with longevity studies of major tissues—promises not only to save lives but to *extend* them as well."

She heard the exaltation in his voice. He openly worshipped at the altar of cold science, where morality had no sway. He believed as fervently in the truth of his convictions as any preacher, and, like any devoted disciple, sought to convert the nonbeliever.

But she wasn't about to drink that particular Kool-Aid.

Movement in the lab drew her eye back to the horror show inside. A figure—gowned in a one-piece hooded clean suit—stepped from a rear chamber, carrying a tray of surgical tools. The worker noted the audience at the window and looked over.

Above the white mask, Amanda recognized those cold, watery eyes.

Petra.

At the same time, she remembered Blake's praise for his nurse's ghoulish skills, a talent to be applied to the child in her womb. She stared between Petra's face and the disembodied head. Did they intend to do the same to her boy?

Petra's earlier words rang in her ears.

I'll relax once we have the fetus on the vivisection table at the lab.

Amanda stared at the tray of sharp stainless-steel tools.

Blood drained to her legs, making her swoon.

Why? she cried inside. How could her child be important to these grisly "longevity studies"? What were they looking to find in her baby boy?

Petra crossed and dropped the tray atop a workstation. Steel clanged on steel, as sharp as a gunshot.

The eyelids of the corpse popped open.

Dead pupils stared back at Amanda.

She screamed—letting all the day's horrors crash out of her. She fell to her knees, felt something give way deep in her belly, hot fluid washed down her inner thighs.

Dr. Blake dropped beside her, cradling her under one arm. "Her water's broke!" he called to Petra through the glass, then turned his attention back to Amanda. He patted her leg. "It won't be long now."

Amanda closed her eyes, knowing at last where she was.

I'm in hell.

11:45 P.M.

"She's in heaven," Gray said, speaking to the group gathered in the suite and to Painter back in Washington.

With the satellite phone on speaker, he stepped again to the large window that overlooked the city and beachfront. Far out, near the horizon, a glow shone against the midnight sea, like the reflection of the moon. But it wasn't a reflection *or* the moon, but another celestial body.

Gray fogged the glass with his breath and drew on the window with his finger.

A five-pointed star.

"The new island of Utopia out there is in the shape of a starfish." Gray faced the others, as Painter listened on the line. "The boy back in Somalia said that Amanda was being taken to *heaven*. Maybe he misinterpreted *utopia*, translating the name as best he could as a heavenly place. Or maybe he heard the destination of the kidnappers was shaped like a star, a piece of the heavens."

"Or maybe you're grasping at straws," Kowalski said.

Seichan stood with her arms crossed, similarly unimpressed.

Gray remembered their brief intimate moment in the bathroom. In that fleeting instance, the worries of family and mission responsibilities faded. He existed in the simple purity of touch and possibility. With his mind cleared, the nagging puzzle stuck in his head broke through the muddle of his awareness. The answer burst forth fully formed, shining with the certainty of truth.

But maybe he was the only one convinced.

Even Painter put a noncommittal spin on his revelation. "It's something I can look into. Maybe by morning—"

"We can't wait until morning. Amanda could be moved again or harmed. We need to take advantage of the hours of darkness left to us."

"You're talking about putting a lot of resources to bear on a hunch,"

Painter argued. "You could burn your cover, expose the fact that you know Amanda's still alive, all for nothing."

"I know I'm right," Gray said.

"How can you be so sure?" Seichan said.

Gray returned to the window. "Because of the breakwater around Utopia, the same as can be seen out the window surrounding the palm islands."

He fogged the glass again with a hard breath and filled in the rest of his map of Utopia, drawing in a crescent breakwater around the starfish-shaped island.

"A moon and a star," Gray said, poking at the symbols.

A gasp rose from Seichan.

Kowalski swore.

Tucker shrugged. "I don't get it."

Gray glanced at him, remembering the man knew nothing about the Guild. "It's the root symbol for a shadowy organization, one that's committed acts of terrorism around the world. The director already suspected this group might be behind Amanda's kidnapping."

"Now you tell me," Kowalski grumbled. "If I'd known that, I would've sat this one out."

Tucker still shook his head. "The crescent and the moon. You can find that emblem on most Arab national flags. The Emirates is an Islamic country. The design of the islands might simply be representing that Muslim symbol."

Painter agreed. "He's right, Gray. But you've convinced me enough that the island is worth investigating. I've ordered a team to assemble an intelligence brief on the place. I already pulled a picture off the Web, photos showing the towers under construction on the main island. Impressive. Several are already occupied by businesses, with the remainder of the spaces nailed down by corporations from around the world. From what I'm seeing, security is tight around that island."

"That's why I wanted to head out there tonight. Go in dark."

"No good." It sounded like Painter was reading from a report. "They've got a radar-monitoring system that circles the entire island. They'll know you're approaching from a mile away."

"Then we can get as close as we can and use scuba gear to—"

"I may have a better way," Painter said, letting out a long sigh. "There's someone in the area I can reach out to. His name came up during the initial intelligence sweep of Dubai. A deep-sea salvage operator. He's got a pair of submersibles, possibly something we can use to ferry your team to Utopia. He's been doing survey and engineering work on the seabed for an underwater hotel being constructed offshore."

"Hydropolis," Gray said, remembering the latest addition to the Dubai waterfront.

"That's right."

From the sound of the director's voice, Painter was still not too keen on involving a third party, especially this person.

"Director, if you don't trust this guy . . ."

"It's not that. He can be trusted. He's performed many high-security clearance projects for the government, even for the military."

"Then what's the matter?"

Again that heavy sigh. "He's Lisa's ex-boyfriend."

Kowalski turned away, mumbling under his breath, "Oh, that's not going to be awkward."

20

"And Jack's agreed to help?" Lisa asked.

She stood by the open balcony door on the second floor of Harbour-view Inn, a historic building in the heart of downtown Charleston that overlooked the river and a waterfront park.

"He did," Painter said. "Even agreed to keep this midnight mission a secret from the rest of the crew of the *Deep Fathom.* He'll be taking the sub out personally."

She closed the French doors, returning inside to the air-conditioned luxury. Her room was appointed with a four-poster bed and period pieces, and featured an exposed redbrick wall and working fireplace, a richness of accommodation to help bolster her cover.

She hadn't thought about Jack Kirkland in some time. She had been fresh out of UCLA medical school, working under a National Science Foundation grant to study the physiological effects of deep-sea work on the human body. Jack had been the captain of an eighty-foot salvage ship, the *Deep Fathom,* manned by a team of scientists and treasure hunters. The two had a brief, fiery relationship that burned out as fast as it started. It was all physical, but not from lack of trying—lots of *trying,* multiple times a day. She smiled at the memory. Though almost a decade had passed, it felt like a lifetime ago.

What happened to that bikini-clad, bronze-legged girl?

A pang of melancholia swept through her.

Painter redirected her to the present, stoking the worries that had died down by the distraction of his call. "And Kat's still not back?"

"No." She checked her watch. It was almost five o'clock. She'd been back at the hotel for over two hours and expected Kat to join up with her shortly thereafter. They weren't supposed to communicate with each other until reunited at the hotel, to keep their distance from each other.

"And you've not heard anything from her?" she asked.

"Not a word, but when you called an hour ago, I pinged her recording devices. The pen camera in the reception area is still operational, but offered no clue to her whereabouts. The other devices in her possession were never activated. And the remote hacking device you planted continues to transmit data. So far they've not found it, and we've been gathering reams of data."

"Anything about Amanda?"

"I got the profiles you e-mailed, but we've hit a wall when searching for Amanda's medical file—a *fire*wall. I have a skilled engineer trying to sap a way under that digital barrier, but it's delicate work to keep from raising alarm bells. Still, if Kat had been caught, I doubt our surveillance devices would still be operational. They'd sweep the place clean."

"So then where is she?"

"I don't know. The clinic doctors could be running tests, or maybe she got nabbed by in-house security for trespassing and it's taking extra time to talk her way out. Or maybe it's as simple as traffic. She does have to take the bus back to the city."

Lisa let his words calm her. Due to construction delays, it had taken her an hour to wind her way across town to reach the hotel. And Kat would have to change buses twice to get here.

Maybe Painter's right . . .

Still, she couldn't escape the feeling that something was wrong.

"Wasn't the original plan to rendezvous at the hotel at six o'clock?" Painter asked.

"That's true. But why hasn't she at least reported in to you if she'd left the clinic?"

Painter's reply took too long. "I don't know," he finally admitted. "We'll keep monitoring what we can. We'll give Kat until six o'clock to break silence before we make a move."

Lisa knew that would be an agonizingly long hour for her.

Painter spoke in her ear—not talking to her this time, but to somebody who must have stepped into his office. Though he lowered the receiver away from his face, she still heard his voice sharpen. "Send me everything," he ordered, then returned to Lisa. "Kat activated a second pen camera. Technicians are downloading the camera's SD card and sending the contents to my computer."

A knock on the door drew her attention. "Someone's at the door," she said.

In her ear, Lisa heard a commotion over the phone—then Painter swore brightly. "Lisa, don't answer it! Get out of there!"

Wood splintered as someone kicked the door.

Panic spiked. She twisted away.

Another kick sounded behind her.

The door crashed open.

4:46 P.M.

Kat let her hand drop away, accidentally dragging her purse off a metal table beside her gurney. The contents spilled across the floor, but she was too weak to stop it from happening. It had taken all her effort to lift her arm and groggily reach into her bag, fumble for one of the surveillance pens, and press its disguised clip to activate the camera inside.

No video would be recorded inside her purse, but audio would still be picked up. The same could be said for Kat in her current drugged state. Her vision remained a blurry pinpoint; her stomach churned queasily. But she could hear well enough to know someone came running into the small room, drawn by the clatter of her upended bag.

"Looks like she was going for her cell phone."

A shadowy shape dropped next to her bed and began scooping up the contents of her purse, shoving them back inside. It sounded like the orderly from earlier.

The next voice supported that supposition. Judging by the frosty New England accent, it had to be Dr. Marshall, the woman who cattle-prodded Kat into convulsing submission. "Roy, I thought you said she'd be out for another ten to fifteen minutes."

"From the dosage, her body weight, she should've been. I just stepped out to grab a fresh gown before stripping her for the intake exam."

"Didn't I warn you she was fit, *robust*. She's not like the usual malnourished, strung-out subjects that land here. You should have anticipated that, Roy. She might have injured herself."

"Sorry. It won't happen again."

Judging by the gist of the conversation, they remained unaware of Kat's true identity, blind to her connection to Sigma. But where was she? Her head lolled around, trying to get some bearing as to her location. She innately sensed that not much time had passed. All she could tell was that they'd moved her to another room, likely within the same facility. The space looked sterile. Too many bright surfaces pained her eyes, and the air definitely had the antiseptic smell of a hospital.

Painter's instinct had been correct about the fertility clinic. Something was wrong here. But what? *Why* had they drugged and kidnapped her?

"I'm not ready for her exam yet," Dr. Marshall said. "So you might as well take her to her cell."

Cell?

"Let her shake off the rest of the sedative," the doctor finished. "She'll be easier to work with if she's not as limp as a rag doll. Besides, the sooner she learns to behave the better."

Dr. Marshall still held her cattle prod, tapping it against the gurney, emphasizing who was the boss.

The orderly, Roy, hauled Kat onto the gurney and drew her out of the room and down a poorly lit corridor. Though there were no windows, she sensed she was underground, in a basement level.

Roy stepped to a locked door and used a key card hanging from a lanyard around his neck to open a set of swinging doors. Stepping to the head of the stretcher, he wheeled her through and into a large circular ward, painted a soothing light blue with tables scattered around and a television playing silently in the background. A set of double doors lay directly opposite, painted a warning shade of red. Likely it was locked as securely as the doors into the ward.

The orderly swung her gurney to the side. She noted the living space had bookshelves, a showering facility, and, all along the periphery, small rooms—*cells*—a dozen in all, each sealed by metal-framed glass doors.

A single woman stood framed in one of the doorways, behind glass, dressed in a blue smock, her hair shorn to a crew cut, her face expressing fear and sorrow. She placed a palm against her glass door, either as a sign of solidarity or to warn her off.

But there was nothing Kat could do.

At least not yet.

She leaned her head to the side and studied the red steel doors, only now noting the raised symbol spanning that exit. It was a cross, adorned with stylized representations of helical DNA. She sensed that whatever secrets were hidden at this clinic, the answers lay beyond that threshold.

But right now she had another door to worry about.

Roy reached a vacant cell—there seemed to be many—and used a master key to unlock the door and haul it open. Next, he shouldered Kat up into his arms. Dr. Marshall's descriptive use of the term *rag doll* was appropriate. She couldn't keep her feet under her; her arms felt cast in cement.

The orderly hauled her to the unmade cot in the room and tossed her on top of it. "Stay out of trouble this time."

Kat had enough strength to watch him leave. As he shoved the door shut and wheeled away the stretcher, she spotted her purse atop the gurney. She pictured the surveillance device inside.

Dear God, let someone be listening.

5:02 P.M.
Washington, DC

"We're still not picking up any audio or video," a technician reported.

Another analyst called from across the room. "I've got security feed from Harbourview coming up over here."

Painter pointed to the tech. "Keep monitoring *all* of Kat's surveillance devices." He stepped toward the analyst. "Show me that feed from Lisa's hotel."

Painter crossed Sigma's communications nest, moving the eye of a hurricane with him. He had other intelligence analysts and agents laboring across the banks of computers and monitors that formed a semicircle across the back of the room. To his left, an adjoining windowed office looked into the space.

It was Kat's command center, her nest within the nest. A single monitor glowed in that dark space, illuminating the young face of her chief analyst, Jason Carter, who hunched over a keyboard working on a separate project.

Out here, chaos reigned as Painter sought answers to the fate of Kat and Lisa. He kept one ear fixed on the flow of information in the room while his left hand held a Bluetooth earpiece in place, awaiting any more audio from Kat's surveillance device. A pair of wall monitors displayed the video from the two pens she planted. One showed the reception area of the North Charleston Fertility Clinic. The other was dark, receiving no video.

Painter had heard the initial conversation that was downloaded after the second pen was activated. It sounded like someone had drugged and kidnapped Kat and was now holding her prisoner.

But after that, nothing.

The feed had fallen unnervingly silent for the past twelve minutes.

At the moment, he didn't know if Kat was still at the fertility clinic or taken somewhere else. They tried to track her disposable cell phone but ended up hitting a blank wall. Either reception was being blocked, or her phone's battery had been stripped out.

He was ready to contact the Charleston law enforcement, have them storm the clinic, but to what end? Kat might not be there, and if she was, her captors would likely kill her before warrants could be issued. Such an effort would also lay bare Sigma's continuing investigation into Amanda and the Gant family.

That must not happen.

His mind raced through countless stratagems, while his heart pounded in his throat, fueled by yet another fear, another unknown.

Where are you, Lisa?

When he received Kat's transmission, he'd been on the phone with his girlfriend. When he recognized that Kat was in trouble, his anxiety shifted immediately to encompass Lisa—especially when, seconds later, an analyst burst into his office to inform him that the hack into the clinic's computers had suddenly got severed.

He got a brief warning out to Lisa—then heard the crash of a door in the background and the line went dead.

"I've got the hotel feed now." The agent pointed to a monitor in front of him. A stuttering image flickered, silent, showing three assailants in a hallway, all wearing ski masks.

So they knew about the cameras.

One knocked on the door, shook his head, then another stepped back and kicked the door in. The three rushed inside, vanishing out of view. Without a camera inside the hotel room, there was no telling for sure what transpired after that.

As he watched, Painter found himself holding his breath. He had to force himself to breathe. Panic would not serve either Lisa or Kat.

After Lisa's phone went dead, he had immediately called hotel security and reported the break-in. The head of security called back within five minutes. It had been the longest five minutes of his life.

When he finally heard back, he was relieved with the report but far from settled: *We chased the intruders off, but the hotel room was empty. We found a purse and a cell phone and luggage. No occupant.*

Painter watched the same scenario play out again on the screen. A two-man security detail came racing down the hall, but the three assailants dashed out, one shooting at the approaching guards, forcing them back. The three then took off, disappearing down a stairwell.

A neighboring analyst swung around in his chair. "Director, I have Harbourview security again."

"Patch them through." When he last spoke to the hotel, they were still searching the premises for Lisa.

His earpiece clicked, and a gruff voice could be heard shouting orders, before centering back to Painter. It was the head of security.

"I'm sorry to report, sir, that we've found no sign of your girlfriend anywhere in the hotel. I've interviewed staff and guests. No one saw any woman being manhandled off the property."

Painter felt the smallest flicker of relief. If Lisa wasn't in the room or spotted by the hall cameras or staff, then she must have escaped out the window.

The man on the line came to the same conclusion. "The police are on the scene, but it appears to me that she fled."

"Thank you. If you hear anything or learn anything—"

"You'll be the first I call."

Painter pictured Lisa running scared through the streets—no money, no phone—doing her best to keep ahead of the hunters and not knowing whom to trust. She needed to reach a public area, get access to a phone. Then he could facilitate her rescue. He already had field operatives flying into the area. There'd be boots on the ground in Charleston within the hour.

Hopefully, by that time, he'd have more information on Kat's whereabouts, too. Painter glanced at the technician assigned to monitoring Kat's surveillance equipment. He got a shake of a head in return.

Still no new feed from Kat's second camera.

With an extra moment to think, Painter paced the length of the communications nest. He began putting together the most likely scenarios. Somehow Lisa's cover got blown after the discovery of the wireless router hidden in the head clinician's office. And since Kat's cameras were still functioning, her cover must still be intact.

No one connected them together yet.

It was the only silver lining in this black cloud—but he'd take it.

Still pacing, Painter turned to find his way blocked by Jason Carter. The young man was rail-thin, former navy like Kat, only twenty-two years old. According to Kat, the tow-headed kid was some sort of savant as an intelligence analyst. He also knew his way around computers. He'd been kicked out of the navy for breaking into DoD servers with nothing more than a BlackBerry and a jury-rigged iPad—or so the story went. Still, Kat had snatched him up, in the aftermath, for Sigma.

Jason's face was paler than usual. He blamed himself for accidentally alerting the clinic during his attempt to hack the last firewall, and for exposing Lisa. He was also deathly worried about Kat. The young man worshipped at her feet.

To keep the kid distracted and focused elsewhere, Painter had assigned him to finish the intelligence brief on Utopia.

"Director, there's something you should see." He lifted an arm toward Kat's office.

Painter followed him and closed the door. He could still smell a whiff of jasmine in the air, a ghost of its former occupant.

Jason led him to a large computer monitor. Upon it spun a 3-D rendering of the star-shaped island of Utopia. The surface of the man-made superstructure bristled with towers, clustering up each leg, rising in height from the tip to the center, like the spines of a starfish. And in the middle rose the tallest of the spires, appearing like a molten pyramid whose tip had been stretched taffy-like into the sky to the height of five hundred feet.

"Where did you get this schematic?"

"Made it myself."

"That was fast."

Jason shrugged. "Before all hell broke loose, you had me already doing a search into the various corporations and businesses involved with Utopia. I just pulled the architectural schematics from each building, paired them with their GPS locations on the island, and had it all rendered in 3-D. The hard part was showing the levels of completion of each phase of the various towers. I shaded the completed projects in gray. The other,

ghostlier sections denote floors or phases of construction either unfinished
or still in the planning stages."

"Impressive. Can you forward this schematic to Commander Pierce's
team?"

"No problem, sir, but that's not why I wanted to talk to you." He
waved to the screen. "This was all busywork while I waited for my data to
compile on the various businesses invested or renting space in Utopia. Let
me show you."

He tapped a screen and the grayscale schematic burst forth with tiny
patches of color, in every imaginable hue, filling in office floors and apartment spaces. "Each color represents a different company with vested interest in Utopia," Jason explained. "Two hundred and sixteen in all."

Painter gaped at the view. Gray's team faced a daunting task to hunt
through that corporate maze for Amanda.

But, apparently, Jason was not done. "You also had me search business
records and financial reports to discover the true owners involved."

Painter nodded. He had assigned Jason to strip away the shell and
dummy corporations, to expose the various front and holding companies,
all to discover who was truly investing time and money in Utopia.

To reveal the real peas under all those fake shells.

"That took some work," Jason said with a proud grin and hit a key-
stroke. "Now watch."

On the screen's schematic, the various dots and splashes of colors
began to change, blinking through a cascade of shades, then settling and
blending together—until most of the screen glowed one uniform color, a
deep crimson.

"Once the shell game settled out," Jason said, "I discovered seventy-
four-point-four percent of the island is actually owned by a *single* parent
company."

Painter felt the cold creep of dread in his gut. He could guess the answer. "Gant Corporate Enterprises."

Jason glanced up at him, his eyes surprised. "How did you know?
What does the president's family—?"

Painter cut him off and leaned closer. "Rotate that schematic to get a bird's-eye view of the island."

Jason manipulated a toggle to swerve the view up and over the star-shaped island, to look down upon that crimson corporate tide. The kid whistled appreciatively.

"Amazing," Jason exclaimed. "The pattern forms a perfect cross atop the island."

"A Templar cross," Painter mumbled, picturing the symbol he'd studied only days ago, the mark of the Guild.

Doubt evaporated inside him.

The Gants are *the Guild*.

And Gray's team was sailing blindly toward their newest stronghold.

21

Gray led the others down a long dock that cut through the center of a massive marina. A full moon and the blaze of Dubai's skyline turned night to day here, while jazz music tinkled across the water from an open-air nightclub. A soft breeze blew gently off the sea, cooling the warm night and smelling of ocean salt and diesel fuel.

The tiny harbor lay at the tip of the man-made island of Palm Jumeirah. They were to meet their escort at a berth in a remote section of the marina, where fewer eyes were likely to pry.

To Gray's left, the giant trunk of the artificial palm-shaped island stretched two kilometers to shore, sparkling in the night with hotels and residences, divided by an eight-lane motorway. He hadn't appreciated the sheer magnitude of this archipelago until here on its shores. Each engineered palm frond was a mile long, lined by villas and mansions. And to his right, across the water from the marina, stretched the seven-mile-long breakwater crescent, turned into a playground of hotels and water parks. And two more palm projects were in development, each bigger than the next; the largest would be seven times the size of Palm Jumeirah.

Another of Gray's party was also fixated by the enormousness of everything in Dubai.

"I guess size does matter," Kowalski said, gaping at the mega-yacht docked at the upcoming berth. It had its own helicopter tied down at the stern, and it wasn't even the biggest boat here. "Somebody's compensating for something, if you know what I mean."

Seichan strode alongside him. "We all know what you mean, Kowalski—it's why none of us have commented on those cigars you keep sucking on."

He took out his stogie and frowned at her. "Whatcha talking about?"

She shrugged.

Tucker bent down and unclipped Kane from his leash. The shepherd, freed at last, trotted ahead, nose in the air, tail high. The dog had been confined to a leash while in Dubai, not the most dog-friendly city, but out here in the marina at this late hour, no one was around to complain.

His handler hung behind them, lost in his own thoughts.

Gray followed Kane down the dock. The number of empty berths grew as they neared the end, leaving the opulence and grandiosity of modern Dubai behind. Moonlight shone off the dark water ahead, no longer competing with the reflected dazzle of the city's towers and playgrounds. A slight breeze took the edge off of the warm night. Looking out to sea, with stars twinkling and with the call to prayer echoing hauntingly from the shoreline, it was easy to get transported back to another time, to the medieval era of Ali Baba and lost desert kingdoms. Despite the excesses and extravagances of Dubai, the ancient world still glimmered through the cracks, a shimmering mirage of past glories.

"About time you all got here," a voice called out of the shadows of the next berth. The only evidence of his presence was the smoldering tip of a cigar. The figure stepped into a pool of light cast by a pole lamp. He wore a pair of black Bermuda shorts, flip-flops, and an unbuttoned white shirt.

On edge, Gray searched to make sure the man was alone. Kane seemed to have no such qualms. The dog ran forward and greeted the newcomer warmly, bouncing a bit on his front legs.

"Stay down, Kane," Tucker warned.

"I don't mind him at all." The man leaned over and gave the dog a vigorous rub. "Reminds me of my old dog Elvis. He was a shepherd, too. German, that is. What's this boy?"

"Kane's a *Belgian* shepherd," Tucker said. "A Malinois."

"Hmm. War dog, I'm guessing."

"That's right. Army. Retired."

"If you don't mind me asking, what was Kane's rank?"

"Major."

Kowalski glanced at Tucker. "Wait? *Major* Kane? Your dog out-ranked you?"

Gray knew that wasn't unusual. A military dog always ranked one level higher than its handler, so any abuse was a court-martial offense. Not that Tucker would ever harm his partner.

Straightening, the man thrust a hand toward Gray. "Jack. Jack Kirkland."

Introductions followed all around.

Their escort stood over six feet, with salt-and-pepper hair. From the scarring down one side of his body, he'd seen some action in the past. The man also carried his rugged, ageless masculinity with a boyish grace—even Seichan was struck by it.

Gray had never seen her so enthralled. He heard her giggle at something the man said. Seichan *never* giggled. It slightly pissed him off. A reaction that caught him by surprise. In a matter of minutes, the man had charmed everyone on his team.

Or almost everyone.

Kowalski shook his hand. "What're you smoking?"

Jack glanced at the cigar balanced in his fingers. "Cuban. *El Presidente.*"

"Oh, man . . ." Kowalski stared at his own stogie, disappointed.

"I've got a whole case aboard the *Ghost.*" Jack nodded his chin in the direction of the dark berth. "I'm sure I wouldn't miss one if it happened to grow legs and walk away."

Jack headed off in that direction.

Kowalski stayed put. "That guy really gets me."

Gray shook his head.

Okay, now I've lost everyone.

Seichan sidled up to Gray, brushing his shoulder and leaning closer. "Wow."

That one word pretty much summarized the man.

Gray sighed and followed Jack toward the berth. No wonder Painter was so hesitant to drag this guy back into his life. *If I were Painter, I wouldn't want Jack within a thousand nautical miles of Lisa.*

At least, the man was wearing a wedding ring.

"Here she is," Jack said, stopping ahead. "My new pride and joy. The *Ghost*."

Gray didn't see anything moored in the neighboring berth.

Jack leaped from the dock, as if to plunge into the water, but he landed on a firm surface. Only then did Gray appreciate the docked vessel as it rocked under the man's weight. Even still, it was hard to discern its presence against the dark water.

The submersible's bulk remained below the waterline. Only a conning-tower-like hatch protruded above the surface and a fraction of its upper deck. What made it so hard to discern, what made it blend so well with the water, was that it appeared to be sculpted out of glass.

Jack tapped his toe against the clear surface. "Her shell's made out of a new borosilicate polymer, strong as steel yet with a low refractive index, perfect for underwater viewing. And the deeper you go, the harder the glass becomes. Up to a point, of course. I'm not planning on testing that limit today."

"I see why you call it the *Ghost*," Seichan said.

"She's my new love—comes with all the bells and whistles a guy could want." He ticked them off proudly. "The latest sonar and communications equipment, fly-by-wire joystick, electronic buoyancy controls, expanded air supply. But what really gets me purring is her sexy curves. I designed her after the old X-1 mini-submarines. Sleek, fast, and seductive."

Kowalski snorted at the hyperbole. "Do you need a moment alone with her?"

"Do you still want that cigar?" Jack countered.

Kowalski hung his head a bit. "Sorry, I should know better than to insult another guy's girl. She's sexy. Very, very sexy."

"That's more like it," Jack encouraged with a huge, bawdy grin.

"C'mon aboard. Let's get you all settled. We have a bit of a jaunt to reach Utopia, but then again, whoever said getting into heaven was easy?"

Ignoring the man's joviality, Gray stared toward the horizon, unable to shed his dark mood, knowing Amanda was not having this much fun.

1:30 A.M.

The next contraction wracked her body.

Amanda sobbed, tears streaming down her heated face. Waves of nausea swept through her. Sweat soaked her gown to her skin. The worst of the pain was dulled by the miniepidural they'd given her, but not all of it.

"Dilated eight centimeters," Petra reported from between her legs.

"Right on schedule." Dr. Blake stood at her bedside, evaluating a labor monitor. "That was a good contraction. But I'm pushing another bolus of pit."

Pit was slang for *pitocin,* a labor-inducing drug.

He injected the medicine into her IV line, then turned his attention to Amanda. He took her hand, which was strapped in place to the bed, and gave her fingers a squeeze.

"Would you like some more ice chips?"

Fury cut through her. She dug her nails into the tender flesh of his wrist. "Fuck you," she spat at him. She never swore, but it felt good to do so now. "You goddamned monster."

"I'll get you some ice chips," he said, unfazed by her outburst. He gently but firmly freed his arm, then patted her hand. "Everything's going well. You're doing great."

Other medical staff worked at the periphery, monitoring vitals, trading out dirty linens that she'd soiled, dragging in equipment. A pair off to the side were preparing a radiant warming crib in anticipation of the newborn's arrival.

Blake returned with a tiny paper cup full of crushed ice chips. He lifted it to her lips. But she turned her head away, refusing to cooperate in even this small measure.

She willed her body to resist, too.

I won't let them have my boy.

But nature—fueled by strong drugs—could not be stopped. Minutes later, pressure again rose inside her abdomen, a storm front rising from deep inside her, as relentless as the tide. She squeezed her eyes shut, knowing what was coming.

No . . . please, no . . .

Her plea fell to ashes. The next contraction tore through her. She screamed—not so much in pain as knowing she was losing this last battle.

"Push!" Blake said, but he sounded far away.

She fought against it, but her body was no longer her own, transforming into a primitive machine, one forged in the evolutionary furnace of survival. Willing or not, all her flesh drove toward one function: to procreate, to move her genes forward into the future. She had no will but to obey.

Abdominal muscles contracted in a crushing heave.

Tissue ripped.

Blood flowed.

Pain became purpose.

"The baby's crowning!" Petra called out, her voice ringing in triumph.

Lost deep in the violence of birth, Amanda cried out to the world, surrendering to the inevitable, driven now by the most basic of all maternal needs.

Someone save my baby.

1:44 A.M.

Seated inside the *Ghost,* Gray swiveled his chair to face the curved glass wall of the submersible. A pool of light cast by the sub's headlamps illuminated the dark waters around the vessel as it coasted away from Palm Jumeirah. The sandy seabed flowed a few feet below his toes.

The effect was unnerving. The clear borosilicate shell allowed a full spherical view of the surrounding waters. *Like floating in an air bubble,* he thought, which wasn't far from the truth.

The *Ghost* was little more than a tapered glass cylinder strapped into a hydrogen-cell-battery propulsion drive. Ancillary electrical, mechanical, and engineering systems acted as an exoskeleton around the living quarters.

Curious denizens, drawn by their light, would dart up, stare googly-eyed at the strange sight, then flash back into the blackness.

He could imagine what they saw.

The vessel reminded him of the neon tetras he once raised as a kid. He'd lie on his bed for hours, staring as the tiny fishes darted back and forth inside his aquarium. Tetras were best known for their iridescent blue and red racing stripes, but Gray had always been fascinated by their translucent skin. Their spine, ribs, even their quivering tiny hearts were exposed for the world to see. At the moment, he felt similarly naked, like he'd been swallowed up by a giant version of a glassy tetra.

Still, he had to admit the panorama was stunning.

One passenger was not as impressed.

"This is so wrong," Kowalski said. He was seated across from Gray; the big man had one palm against the glass window, another on the ceiling. He stared between his legs. "How long is this going to take? What if we run out of air?"

Gray recognized the space was cramped, especially for someone of Kowalski's bulk. Jack piloted the craft from a single seat up in the nose. The four chairs in back left little room to maneuver. Even Kane had to balance on Tucker's lap, panting at the view, ears high, trembling all over.

Seichan sat behind Kowalski and reached a reassuring hand to touch his shoulder. "Calm down. We've got plenty of air." She patted his back. "I'd be more worried about us springing a leak."

Kowalski swiveled in his seat, searching around the cabin with wide eyes.

Gray gave her a scolding look. All they needed was a panicked bull in their midst.

"How much farther?" Kowalski moaned.

The answer came from up front. "We have to cross the entire World to reach your destination."

Jack tapped a button on a touch-screen interface. A heads-up display appeared above his controls, glowing against the window. It depicted a map of the surface, showing hundreds of tiny islands forming silhouettes of the seven continents.

Gray recognized it as another of Dubai's projects. The World was one of the city's latest endeavors: three hundred mini-islands off the coast, each offered for sale to private buyers. But financial concerns and problems with sand erosion threatened the development. The islands remained mostly deserted, with the sea reclaiming some.

On the display, a red blip marked their progress as they navigated through this man-made archipelago.

Beyond the window, a dark hummock of one of the tiny islands loomed. As they circled past it, a large ray, disturbed by their passage, shook out of the sand and sailed away from the light and back into the gloom. Other sea life appeared, growing more abundant as they glided through the shallows and wound past the small isles: hermit crabs scuttled along the sandy floor, pink anemone and green sea grass waved, a lone barracuda torpedoed past them, and schools of fish flashed and swirled in shimmering silvers and dazzling colors.

Tucker suddenly swore. Kane barked.

Gray turned to see a shoal of hammerhead sharks come lancing out of the darkness and shoot past overhead. They all inadvertently ducked. There was no real threat, but it was a sobering reminder of the dangers ahead.

After a few more silent minutes, they left the World behind.

The deeper seas beckoned.

The *Ghost* sailed out into the blackness, slowly sinking into the depths as the coastal shelf fell away. As they dove, the watery glow of the moon died overhead. The only lights now were their own.

And even that had to end.

"Going dark," Jack warned. "You'll find your goggles under your chairs."

Before Gray could find his, all the exterior lamps clicked off. Blackness crushed around them. Kowalski gasped. The small lights from the control console were the only illumination inside the submersible, and even those went dim.

Gray's fingers discovered the strap for his night-vision headgear and tugged them free. He pulled the goggles over his head and settled them in place. The world beyond the sub reappeared again, lit now by the infrared LED emitters along the nose of the vessel. The goggles were able to perceive this spectrum of light, turning the world into a grayscale shadow of its former brightness.

"Don't want to ride up to Utopia with our lights blazing," Jack said. "Even with the sub submerged, someone might see us coming. Luckily, we don't need lights. I incorporated this naval IR system to accommodate for night dives. Makes for less of a rude intrusion into the dark world of our deep-sea denizens."

Or when you need stealth, like now.

The plan was to sneak *under* the island's security net. The surface radar defense system was meant to discourage pirate ships, like those in Somalia, from reaching the island's coast undetected. Additionally, armed security guards watched the docks and shorelines, and a small fleet of jet boats patrolled the waters around the island.

Painter and Jack had already worked out an alternate entry point— but first they had to reach it.

The *Ghost* traveled another twenty minutes, soaring swiftly with the quiet burble of its engines. Jack worked his pedals and joystick to glide them along the seabed, riding over teeming reefs and across stretches of open sand.

Positioned ten miles from shore, Utopia had been built in waters eighty meters deep. It was an engineering marvel, the first deep-sea artificial island. The heads-up display continued to track their path away from the coast, mapping a bird's-eye view of their passage. At the top of the screen, the tip of one leg of the star-shaped island poked into view and slowly stretched downward as the *Ghost* closed in on its destination. More of the island appeared, revealing its unique shape.

But its *shape* was the least unique feature of the island.

As they neared the tip of one corner of the star, a massive concrete py-lon appeared out of the darkness, twenty yards wide. A forest of such tow-ers lay farther ahead. This was the secret behind the engineering of Utopia.

It wasn't so much an island as a massive fixed platform with a land-mass sitting on top of it.

Gray had read the history of Utopia. Its engineering was not new or groundbreaking, but based on technologies developed many years ago, patterned after the Hibernia oil platform constructed off the coast of Newfoundland in 1997. The same engineers and construction company had been hired as consultants for this Dubai development.

In many ways, Utopia was an easier project. The Hibernia platform had been built in deeper waters and constructed in seas prone to rogue waves, Atlantic winter storms, and floating icebergs. The waters here were calmer, and the environmental threats less severe. On top of that, this location had been chosen for Utopia because of a natural coastal ridge. The outcropping had been reinforced and built up with boulders and compacted sand to form a protective crescent, stretching four miles wide.

Within those sheltering arms, Utopia was slowly constructed. Like Hibernia and other oil platforms, the *island* was basically a gravity-based structure, meaning the more weight on top, the more stable and secure it became. So, while Hibernia was *taller*, Utopia was *wider*, the equivalent of twenty such platforms connected in a honeycomb cluster to form a star-shaped base. Atop this massive foundation, whose upper surface lay submerged to the depth of five meters, the same engineering techniques that built Palm Jumeirah were employed here: laying down a thick base of massive boulders on top of the platform, then flooding and covering it with dredged sand and compacting it all to the hardness of concrete.

And within five years, a new island had risen out of the sea.

"Now comes the tricky part," Jack said.

He guided the *Ghost* into that Brobdingnagian forest of massive steel-reinforced concrete pylons that supported the island. The columns rose from the seabed, set amid piles of boulders and mountains of ballast. He slowed their pace to a crawl.

Gray craned his neck, staring up through the clear roof. In the distance, he could make out the bottom of the foundation platform. He imagined the crushing weight overhead, pictured the stack of corporate towers topside.

Kowalski groaned.

This time, Seichan didn't tease him.

The sub suddenly rolled, heaving to one side.

Jack swore, fought his controls, and righted them. "Sorry about that," he said. "Currents are tricky under here. In fact, one of the auxiliary power sources for the island is a series of tidal turbines, driven by the daily ebb and flow of the ocean. That same flow makes maneuvering through here a thorny bitch."

They continued on for five more excruciatingly long minutes. The star-shaped island was two miles wide, but they only had to delve a quarter of that distance under its bulk. Still, that journey was nerve-wracking enough.

"Sonar says we're here." Jack pointed up.

Everyone searched in that direction. Far overhead, a tiny star shone in the darkness. Jack aimed for it, spiraling around one of the columns as he headed up.

As they rose, the star grew larger and brighter, revealing itself at last to be a crack in the foundation platform. A handful of such breaks had been engineered into the project, serving as pressure-relieving points. In turn, the city planners had taken advantage of those construction necessities and turned them into various urban design features.

"I'm turning off the IR emitters," Jack said. "You can take off your goggles. You should have plenty of ambient light to see."

Gray pulled his night-vision headgear off. The black-and-white world brightened into shades of aquamarine. The pool of light overhead bathed them in its glow.

Jack set the sub to hovering in one spot. He dumped ballast to adjust their buoyancy, and the *Ghost* floated smoothly upward, rising through the crack in the foundation platform, a six-meter-thick wafer of concrete and steel. Once through, those industrial walls tilted back, sloping into sandy beaches.

The sub slowed its ascent and glided forward until sand once again swirled a few feet under Gray's boots. Jack studied a small monitor on his control console. Spying over his shoulder, Gray caught a glimpse of the world topside as Jack employed a digital periscope.

"Looks clear," the pilot concluded.

The burble of the engines faded to nothing—then a few seconds later, the sub's nose gently ground into the beach.

"That's as far as I go," Jack said, twisting around. "The top hatch is poking a couple of inches out of the water. You should be able to reach the shore without getting more than your boots wet."

That proved not to be the case. By the time Gray reached solid ground, he was soaked from the knees down. Seichan fared no better. Tucker disembarked last, assisted by Kowalski. The pair worked together to get Kane out of the sub.

Gray had his team assemble beneath a grove of palms planted at the edge of the dark pond. It was hard to believe what lay hidden beneath that placid surface: an industrial hell of pylons, boulders, and ballast. It stood in stark contrast to the world above.

Kowalski joined them. His gaze swept the landscape surrounding the pond, his face shining with awe.

Gently rolling hills spread outward, covered in manicured lawns and dotted by other stands of palm trees. Beyond the parklands, towers and spires rose, forming a palisade of glass and steel. Some of the buildings were dark, girdled by cranes, under various phases of construction. Others thrust brilliantly into the sky, windows aglow, their exteriors flooded by lamps, amply demonstrating signs of life and occupation.

Closer at hand, the rolling park was broken by patches of close-cropped greens, feathered with numbered flags. Elsewhere, silvery patches marked moonlit sand traps.

"We beached in a friggin' golf course," Kowalski said with a shake of his head. "You gotta hand it to the Arabs for working with what they got."

True enough.

Gray returned to the pond, which served the island in multiple ways: as a landscape element, as a water hazard, and as a structural-design feature.

Jack remained aboard the *Ghost,* leaning half out of the hatch. He pointed a thumb toward the middle of the pond. "I'll be hovering just under the surface, but I'll keep a watch for you with my scope. If you can't make it back here, you've got my signaling device. Set it off and I'll find you."

"Thanks." Gray patted his shirt pocket, indicating he had it.

Jack hesitated before ducking away. His expression turned a touch embarrassed, like he wanted to ask something but held back.

"What is it?" Gray asked.

Jack sighed. "Maybe it's not my place . . . but how's Lisa doing?"

Gray had already spoken with Painter back in Dubai, so he knew the dire situation with Lisa and Kat. Worry for his friends remained a knot in his gut. But that wasn't what Jack was inquiring about. Gray read the real question in his eyes.

Is she happy with her life?

Gray answered that question as honestly as he could, but in regards to what Jack had asked directly—*how's Lisa doing?*—he thought it best to lie.

"She's doing great."

22

Get somewhere safe . . . off the street, but stay in public.

The instructions rang in Lisa's head. Agony lanced up her leg with every step down East Bay Street. She tried her best to hide her limp, baking under the late-afternoon sun.

When Painter had shouted his warning over the phone to get out of her hotel room, she'd not hesitated. She ran four miles every morning, did yoga most nights, and her brother, who climbed mountains for a living, had taught her a few mad skills.

Panicked, and needing her hands free, she had dropped her cell phone, twisted away from the door, and dashed to the balcony. She heard the splintering crash as the door burst open behind her—but she was already moving through the French doors and vaulting over the wrought iron. She caught one hand on the railing and swung around. With her legs dangling free, she lowered herself hand-over-hand down the second-story balcony ironwork. Once at the bottom, she let go and dropped the rest of the way to the sidewalk.

Even wearing sensible shoes, she landed hard enough to jam her left ankle. A glance up showed a masked assailant staring down at her. He raised a pistol, but she dashed forward under the balcony, out of the line of fire. Shouting erupted above—then gun blasts.

She ran.

There had been no plan, except to put distance between her and the hotel. She had a choice of fleeing out into the neighboring waterfront park or into the narrow maze of historic homes with their quaint porches, filigree woodwork, and colorful gardens. She chose the latter, not trusting the open spaces of the park. Plus, tourists and locals crowded the streets, shops, and coffeehouses of the area. She instinctively knew to keep to public spaces.

It took her another twenty minutes to calm her heart, to let the adrenaline seep from her brain enough for her to think. Still, she kept peering behind her—not that she knew whose faces to be watching for or how many were searching for her. Anyone could be a threat. With no money, no phone, she didn't know anyone in the strange city to trust. So she reached out to the one person who could help.

She borrowed a phone from a patron seated in a patio coffeehouse and called Painter. She couldn't say who was more relieved to hear the other's voice, but Painter stayed stern, authoritative. He ordered her to get off the street, out of direct sight, fearing her attackers might be closing a net around the district and looking for her.

But stay in public . . .

That meant she needed an *indoor* space: a bar, a restaurant, a hotel lobby.

A commotion drew her attention down a cobbled-brick alleyway off the main thoroughfare. A clutch of women in handsome gowns and men in tuxedos gathered a short distance away, laughing and hugging their hellos. It appeared a wedding reception or engagement party was under way at a restaurant back there, and from the richness of the attire, from the haughty edge to their genteel Carolina accents, the event had the air of old money.

Perfect.

She hid her limp, touched her hair to assure herself she was presentable for a restaurant of this caliber. She hoped the affair was in a private room and that she could still get a seat in the main dining room or bar.

A small gas lantern flickered above the sign.

McCrady's.

Reaching the restaurant, she excused herself as she slipped through the partygoers—as she hoped, they were all filing upstairs to a private room. She stepped up to the host's station.

"Excuse me. I'm afraid I don't have a reservation. But I was hoping I could still get a table."

The host, a slender man with a soft manner, smiled. "That shouldn't be a problem this early in the evening. If you'll give me a moment."

Lisa stepped away, but she remained standing. She was afraid if she sat down, she'd never get back up again. Her leg throbbed all the way to her knee. To distract herself, she read a small sign about the restaurant, how the building dated back to 1788. Over the centuries, it had served as a warehouse, a tavern, and even a brothel. It stated that George Washington had once attended a grand dinner party here—hopefully not when it was a brothel.

Still, with such a pedigree, it was no wonder the upper crust of Charleston chose this place for special events. Laughter and music echoed down from above.

Another few stragglers of the party pushed into the lobby. From the amount of lace and piles of coiffed white hair, they were clearly a few of the grandes dames of Charleston high society.

"If you'll follow me," the host said to Lisa, drawing her attention away, "your table is ready."

One of the older women glanced in her direction, eyeing her from the lofty height of her class position—then leaned to another and whispered. Other eyes stared toward her, judging her.

Suddenly self-conscious, Lisa smoothed a hand down her St. John dress and stepped away from them, joining the host.

He leaned conspiratorially toward her. "It's cotillion season. They're having a small debutante ball upstairs."

Lisa glanced up, picturing a party of chiffon and diamonds, the official debut of a young woman to her high-society peers. Balls like this functioned in the past as an antiquated dating service, to present an eligible daughter to available bachelors within a select upper circle.

Basically, a high-society livestock show.

"It's a very exclusive affair," the host said as he led her to the table. He raised one eyebrow toward her. "Some grandniece or second cousin of the president."

Lisa felt better. Surely, no one would dare intrude here. Crossing into the main dining room, she did her best not to hobble. Still, something must have shone in her face, maybe the sheen of her skin, something in her eye.

"Are you all right, ma'am?" the host asked as they reached the table, pulling a chair for her.

"I'm fine." She offered him a smile, but it felt stiff on her face. "Just a long day of shopping."

"Of course," he said graciously, but his gaze flicked around her a bit, likely noticing her lack of a purse. "Were you expecting someone else?"

She checked her watch. *Hopefully so.* Painter had told her to find a spot and call him. He had a security detail already headed downtown to extract her. She picked up the menu—hopefully they'd also square her bill. She needed something stiff in a tall glass, no ice.

"I believe my party is running late," Lisa said. "And I'm afraid I've forgotten my cell. Is there a house phone I might use?"

"I'd be happy to bring you one."

"Perfect. Thank you."

She sat back, soaking in the quiet chatter of the early dinner crowd. The restaurant had a colonial charm with its wood-beamed ceiling, oiled plank flooring, exposed brick walls, and a fireplace tall enough to climb into without ducking.

The host returned with a cell phone. She passed on a drink order to her waiter—a single malt whiskey. "The Macallan, please. The sixty-year-old."

Expensive, but as a doctor, she prescribed it for herself anyway.

And this is definitely going on Sigma's tab.

She dialed Painter's secure line—not only to inform him about where she had holed up; she was also anxious to hear any news about Kat.

The connection clicked through. "Where are you?" he immediately asked.

She told him, including the address.

Painter sighed in relief. "The team is fifteen minutes out. Stay put."

"I'm not going anywhere."

The waiter arrived with her drink. The whiskey trembled in the crystal as she held it. She took a sip to steady herself, letting the aged liquor evaporate along her tongue, heating all the way down.

"I'm safe here," she said, attempting to reassure both Painter and herself. "I've got a drink, and I'm surrounded by people. The elite of Charleston." She heard the tinkle of music flowing from the cotillion upstairs. "In fact, there's a party going on here. Some distant relatives of President Gant. Then again, you probably can't turn a stone over here in Charleston without finding someone related to that family."

Painter's next words came too fast, choking a bit. "Did any of them recognize you?"

An amused snort of disbelief escaped her. "Of course not. Why would anyone in the president's family—?"

"Are you sure?"

The panic frosting his voice passed to her. She stared up toward the wood beams, hearing the thump of music, the trickle of laughter. She remembered the grande dame's eyes glancing her way, the sudden whispers.

"Painter, what's this about?"

"I want you to get out of there—*right now.*"

Lisa stared at the expensive drink in her hand. "I don't have any way to pay. If I bolt now, I'll cause a commotion, draw more attention to myself."

And she wasn't sure she could *bolt,* not with her ankle. Now that she'd been sitting a few minutes, even shifting her left leg sent shooting stabs of pain all the way to her hip.

She lowered her voice. "What aren't you telling me? I can barely walk . . . I need to know what I'm facing."

A short silence stretched. She imagined Painter rubbing a finger along that line between his brows, debating how much to say or calculating his next step. Over the years, that crease had gotten deeper as he sat in the director's office—and all that rubbing wasn't going to make it go away.

"Tell me," she said, tired of all the half-truths and secrets.

He finally spoke, talking fast. "I haven't told anyone this. Not Kat, not Gray, not anyone at Sigma. Not even you. It was just a dangerous suspicion before, but a few minutes ago, I got what I believe to be substantial verification."

"About what?"

"About the Guild."

Lisa went cold. She knew Painter had been concerned that Amanda's plight could be tied to that deadly cartel. Did he have proof now?

Painter spoke his next words carefully, as if testing them aloud for the first time. "I know who is running the Guild."

"Who?"

"It's the president's family."

The shock took an extra moment to break through her. Surely Painter was joking. Her mind struggled to put all of the pieces together in her head, trying to comprehend how that could be true. She came to only one conclusion.

"That's impossible," Lisa said, her voice faint.

"That's why I didn't tell anyone—not until I knew the truth. I'll explain more once you're back in DC." His next words hardened with warning. "But, Lisa, now you understand. I need you out of there, as silently as you can."

Despite her fear, she fought against a stab of anger at him for keeping this secret from her—and not just from her. "What about Kat?"

"Don't worry about her . . . just get out of that restaurant."

Promising to do just that, she snapped the cell phone closed. She looked up toward the ceiling, still struggling to believe. She had to trust Painter was right. Readying herself, she downed the rest of the whiskey in a single gulp—a waste of such a fine single malt, but she needed the fortification.

She pushed gingerly back to her feet. One hand clasped to the back of her chair. There was no hiding her limp any longer. She hobbled back to the host's station.

"Ma'am, are you sure you're okay?"

No. Not in the slightest.

"I'm fine," she lied and lifted the house phone. "Reception's bad in there. Is it okay if I step outside to finish my call?"

"Of course. Let me help you."

"No need." She hurried toward the door and back out onto the street. She took a few steps, but the uneven cobbles proved too challenging. Her hobble became a fall.

A man lunged to her aid, his arms caught her.

"Thank you . . ." she began to mumble—then stared up into the face of Dr. Paul Cranston, the head of North Charleston Fertility Clinic.

A gun pressed into her side.

Another two men came up behind her.

The doctor smiled. "Ah, Dr. Cummings, it's high time we finished our previous conversation."

He motioned to the others. Strong fingers clamped on to her upper arms, hard enough to cause bruising—but a little manhandling was the least of her worries.

She glanced back up to the bright lights of the second-story window, heard a piano playing.

Cranston made a scolding noise. "I can guess what you're think-ing, but fear not, you're not that unlucky. That side of the family knows nothing important, except how to spend money and sniff their noses at common folk. No, we've been following you since the hotel. I had men positioned outside when you made such a bold escape."

Lisa stared back at him.

"We hoped you'd lead us to whomever you're working with," Cran-ston said and pulled a pen from his pocket.

It was Kat's surveillance device. They must have found it in the lobby, but clearly they still didn't know who left it.

"A shame," he said and led her away. "Looks like we'll have to do this the hard way. But difficult or not, we'll find your partner."

6:16 P.M.

The buzzing shears rode past Kat's left ear. Long locks of auburn hair tumbled down, falling past her shoulder and sliding to the floor to join the mound of hair already piled around the chair.

Still cotton-mouthed from the sedative, Kat sat on the seat in the center of the circular ward, with only a sheer hospital gown between her and the cold metal. With her wrists cuffed behind her back, she had to tolerate the humiliation—and that was surely the goal here, to break her down.

The other prisoner—a doe-eyed young woman in her midtwenties—watched from behind the glass door of her cell, offering her silent support. She and Kat were the only ones here. The rest of the cells appeared empty. The facility was clearly running low on raw material.

Kat remembered Dr. Marshall mentioning something about a lodge. *They're demanding more research subjects.*

Clearly, that was one of the purposes of this place, to supply human guinea pigs for various projects, collecting women who had no past, no families, who could easily vanish. And likely this was not the *only* such facility in the world. She imagined there were many other collection sites hidden around the globe.

But to what end? What was going on here?

From the corner of her eye, Kat studied the red steel doors and the embossed genetic cross.

Something important was happening at this particular clinic.

And she knew any answers lay hidden behind those doors.

Earlier, Kat had been forced to strip naked in her cell while Dr. Marshall performed a thorough physical, assisted by the orderly, Roy. Afterward, Marshall had vanished with a tray of vacuum tubes full of Kat's blood.

Kat's fingers curled into tight fists as Roy sheared the last of her hair away. They might have taken her clothes and most of her dignity, but she bided her time to win it back.

"All done," Roy said, running a palm along the stubble of her scalp, raising a slimy chill over her entire body. "Always like it when you're freshly shaved."

Kat whipped her head away. "Go to hell."

"Feisty," he said with a laugh, glancing toward the locked door, likely looking for Dr. Marshall.

Clearly, the man spent most of his day being browbeaten and ordered around by the female clinician. He seemed to take pleasure in taking out his frustration on those left to his tender care.

His hand reached to the weapon attached to his belt. It wasn't an electric cattle prod like Dr. Marshall's means of punishment, simply an extendable baton. He'd used it on Kat once already, smacking her across her calves when she was too slow in getting undressed.

Her skin still stung.

Kat had noticed welts on the other inmate's arms and legs.

Bastard.

Roy snapped his baton off his belt and, with an expert flip of his wrist, extended the weapon to its full length, likely compensating for shortcomings elsewhere.

"There's not going to be any trouble, is there?" Roy sneered in her ear.

She gritted her teeth and hung her head.

"That's more like it." He rested the baton on her shoulder as he leaned down and undid her cuffs. "Stand up. Keep your hands behind you."

She obeyed, her head spinning slightly from the aftereffects of the drugs. Cold air blew through the slitted back of her hospital gown as she turned to face Roy. She kept her hands behind her.

Roy reached the tip of his baton under her chin, forcing her head up. "That's more—"

Kat whipped her arm around and grabbed the baton, yanking it toward her. Roy, caught off guard, got pulled closer. She swung her other arm wide, silver flashing in her fist. She drove the knife into his throat, below the larynx, severing the trachea.

Roy's eyes stared at her, stunned, gurgling, unable to scream—but she understood his silent question.

How?

She answered him in a hiss. "Because this cat has claws."

Kat twisted the combat dagger hard. Blood sprayed a full yard across the spotless vinyl floor. In seconds, he bled out, and she let his body tumble to the floor.

She wiped the blade on his clothes and folded it closed. When Roy had first tossed her into the cell, waiting for the sedatives to wear off before stripping her and taking away her clothes, she had fought through the fog, freed her left shoe, and removed the folded combat dagger concealed in the sole. She left the lock pick hidden in her right shoe; unfortunately, her cell door did not offer access to the keyhole outside. As she put her shoe back on, she hid the blade under a fold of the blanket.

Later, when they had stripped her, examined her, and poked her full of needles, she waited until she had a moment alone, while putting on her hospital gown. Through the opening in the back, she slipped the folded dagger between her buttocks and held it clamped there—not the most seemly way to conceal a weapon, but sometimes a lady has to do what a lady has to do.

Then she had to wait for a time to get Roy alone.

She knew she would have only the one chance.

Taking advantage of the moment, Kat worked fast and stripped Roy of his keys, electronic pass card, and baton. She rushed to the other cell and unlocked it.

The young woman came staggering out, staring at the ruin of Roy's body. "Thank you . . . my name's Amy."

"C'mon," Kat said, encouraging her.

She hurried across the ward toward the pile of her clothes and quickly pulled on her shorts, blouse, and shoes. She pocketed her dagger and handed the baton to Amy.

Amy squeezed the weapon in her fingers and glanced toward the exit. "There are armed guards down the hall. I don't know how we'll get past them." She noticed Kat staring at the red steel doors on the other side of the ward. "They . . . they took my sister through there two weeks ago."

"Then that's where we're going," Kat said.

She wasn't leaving without finding out what was going on here.

Amy remained at Kat's side, looking ready to follow her lead.

"Grab the key card," Kat ordered. "We're going to find out what happened to your sister."

Amy gave a sharp nod of acknowledgment.

Kat used the moment to grab her purse, which had been set aside with the rest of her clothes. She snapped it open and pulled out the surveillance pen she'd activated earlier. She tucked it into her blouse pocket with the camera end poking out.

If I don't make it, I want some record of all of this.

Together, they sprinted to the other side of the ward. As they reached the doors, Kat took the keycard from Amy and passed it over the electronic reader. A heavy shift of gears rumbled. A red light blinked brightly overhead, likely wired to an alarm at that guard station outside. As secure as this place was, *someone* knew this vault was opening.

How long until they came to investigate?

Before her, the heavy doors parted wider, accompanied by a soft sigh of pressurized air.

Kat stared inside—as Amy began screaming.

6:18 P.M.
Washington, DC

"Interview everyone at that damned restaurant."

Painter paced the communications nest at Sigma headquarters, holding his earpiece in place as he directed the security detail in Charleston in the search for Lisa. The team had finally arrived on-site.

He turned next to one of the analysts seated at a console. "How long on getting that feed from the local street cameras?"

"Five or ten minutes."

He turned his back in frustration.

Lisa, where did you go?

After ordering her to leave the restaurant, he had expected a return call within minutes, alerting him to her location so his security team could sweep her up. But as time stretched with no word, panic had set in.

"Director," another technician said, pointing to a dark monitor. "I still can't get anything more from Captain Bryant's pen camera. The one planted in the clinic's reception area. Either it's been discovered or the battery has drained."

Painter nodded, acknowledging the information. He spoke to the head of the security team. "Split off two men. Send them to the fertility clinic. I want a full report on the status there."

"Yes, sir. Also, we finished questioning the restaurant staff. They confirmed a woman matching Dr. Cummings's description had arrived. She ordered a drink—then suddenly, with no provocation, fled the building. The host saw her talking to three men outside, said she left with them. According to his statement, she informed him that she had been expecting guests."

Painter closed his eyes. Lisa had been expecting his team.

It made no sense.

"Widen the search grid," Painter said. "See if anyone saw where they went."

"Yes, sir."

Blood pressure pounded in his ears—but he still heard the deep bass of the voice at the door.

"Director Crowe . . . a word."

He turned to find his boss, the head of DARPA, General Metcalf, standing at the threshold. The man wore the same suit as this morning, still looking fresh and expertly creased. The same could not be said of the general's face. He looked worn, his eyes red, his jowls sagging.

"Sir?"

"We need to talk."

That statement never ended well. Underscoring the seriousness, Metcalf rarely stepped into Sigma headquarters. He preferred e-mail, faxes, and conference calls. His presence here did not bode well.

Painter clenched and unclenched a fist. He didn't have time for interruptions, but he had no choice. "We can use Captain Bryant's office."

He led Metcalf to the windowed space off the communications nest and chased Jason Carter out of Kat's chair. The young analyst was continuing to work on a private project for Painter.

"Give us a few minutes," Painter told the kid. Once alone, he faced Metcalf. "What's this about?"

"I've been in meetings with the secretary of defense and the joint chiefs. The president made a brief appearance."

Painter heard the drums of war beating in time with his heart. "And?" he asked, sensing what was coming.

"We're shutting Sigma down."

Painter shook his head, not in insubordination, just disbelief. He expected a strong negative reaction from the commander in chief, but not this, and certainly not this soon.

"When?" he asked.

Metcalf wore an expression of regret, but his voice never wavered. "You're to cease all operations immediately."

Painter felt sucker-punched. "Sir, I've got agents in the field, many in dangerous situations."

"Call them back. Turn any of those *situations* over to local authorities or up the military chain of command."

"And if I refuse . . . if any agents resist . . . ?"

"Any further actions will be considered unsanctioned, disavowed, and criminal charges may be pressed, depending on a case-by-case inquiry."

Painter took a deep breath and stared at the men and women working furiously in the nest beyond the window. From the corner of his eye, he noted the project Jason had been working on—the genealogical map of the Gant family spun slowly there, a spiraling galaxy of power, as cold and relentless as any celestial movement.

Painter knew the truth in that moment.

The Guild had won.

"Shut it down," Metcalf ordered. "Pull everyone out of the field."

23

Gray crouched with his team at the edge of the dark golf course, hidden in the shadow of its clubhouse. The moon had set while they crossed the greens, hurrying from one patch of palms to another. Despite the dark night, the lighted floors of several of the neighboring towers acted as shining beacons, casting a stark illumination across the rolling lawns.

According to the pre-mission briefing, most of the island's security patrolled the shorelines and docks, but they could not discount a stray guard spotting them.

But now they had another problem to address as he lowered the satellite phone. Moments ago, he had checked in with Painter, confirming they'd reached Utopia. And in hindsight, maybe he should never have made that call.

"What's wrong now?" Seichan asked, reading his face.

"We've been ordered to cease all mission objectives and return to the States," Gray told the others. "Apparently, the powers-that-be in DC need a scapegoat for the death of the president's daughter."

"And that would be us," Kowalski mumbled sourly.

"Painter is working on an appeal, but he has to officially instruct us to pull up stakes here."

"But Amanda isn't even dead," Tucker said. "Why doesn't the director tell the president that?"

Gray had already explained Painter's reasoning back in Somalia—how

Amanda's best chance for recovery lay in a surgical strike, to hit the enemy while they believed no one was looking for her.

Still, this decision sat wrong with him. Gray believed the president's family had a right to know, and now they were all suffering the fallout. Gray also sensed that Painter wasn't telling them everything; that he was holding something close to the vest.

But whatever it was, it would have to wait.

They had a decision to make.

"Maybe Painter will inform the president as a part of his appeal process. But what is he going to tell him? We don't know for sure that Amanda *is* still alive. All we know is that the charred body at the camp was not his daughter. So we have to make a choice: to retreat back to the *Ghost* or to move forward. If we defy these direct orders and aren't successful, we may face criminal charges. And even moving forward, we'll have limited support."

Gray stared around the small group.

Seichan shrugged. "I'm already a wanted fugitive. What's one more crime?"

"And I was never an official member of Sigma anyway," Tucker said. "Nothing says Kane and I have to follow those orders."

Gray turned to his last teammate.

Kowalski sighed. "My pants are already soaking wet, so what the hell . . ."

"Then let's figure out where to start our search." Gray gripped his phone and brought up a detailed 3-D rendering of the island. He rotated it to show the outline of a cross. "These are the businesses and properties with possible ties to the Guild organization."

"Wait," Seichan said. "How does Painter know that?"

Gray glanced up at her, crinkling his brow. In the rush of information, he never thought to ask that question.

Seichan must have read that realization in his eyes. She shook her head, silently scolding him for yet another oversight. Gray tightened his fingers on the phone, irritated as much at the mistake as at Seichan catching him.

Pull it together . . .

"Go on," Seichan said.

"If Amanda is on the island, she's likely to be found somewhere within the properties highlighted."

"That's a lot of territory to cover," Tucker said.

"That's why we'll start here, the most likely target, and spiral out from it." Gray pointed to the center of the cross.

"X marks the spot," Kowalski mumbled. "What the hell, we are looking for a pirate's buried treasure."

Gray straightened. "And let's hope it's still there."

He lowered his phone and started toward the center of the island, toward the shining central axis upon which this star turned. And it *was* turning—the *tower*, not the island. The floors of the spire, each rhomboid in shape and slightly offset from the next, formed a massive corkscrew—but the most amazing aspect of the engineering was that each story rotated independently of the others, creating a dynamic structure, powered by wind turbines and solar panels. It was mesmerizing to look at, shifting slowly, melting into new shapes, meant to mimic a shimmering mirage.

"Burj Abaadi," Tucker said, naming this central hub of Utopia. "The Eternal Tower."

The fifty-floor skyscraper had been built in only eighteen months, constructed in conjunction with the island's creation, the two projects rising together out of the sea.

Gray sensed that if anything were hidden on this island it would be there, at the heart of Utopia. There was only one way to find out for sure.

He turned to Tucker and Kane.

"Time to go to work."

2:22 A.M.

Tucker led the way—or rather Kane did.

The shepherd ran a full block ahead along a deserted avenue that cut down one leg of the star. He heard his partner's panting breath in his left ear and kept one eye on the video feed, watching for any signs of armed guards or the rare resident of Utopia.

He and the others stuck as much as possible to the shadows as they headed the quarter-mile to their destination. Palms lined both sides of the road and along a center median. Several stretches of trees were still in massive boxes, waiting to be craned into place and planted.

The entire island had that same surreal feeling—like a child's model of a city, where pieces sat to the side, waiting to be fitted and glued into their proper spot.

But as they traveled closer to the star's center, the cityscape became less fragmentary. Buildings grew taller, more polished, shining with lights. Evidence of life began to appear: an occasional golf cart or car in an empty parking lot; a tiny grocery store with stocked shelves; a neon sign glowed in the window of a Korean restaurant.

Still, Tucker suspected only a skeleton number of people actually populated the island, and most of those were likely connected in some manner to the Guild.

To Tucker, that terrorist outfit still sounded like something out of a dime-store novel. But then again, he had dealings in the past with many different mercenary-for-hire groups, private military companies with equally colorful names: Saber, Titan, GlobalEnforce. And while he didn't subscribe to conspiracy theories, he knew that the military-industrial complex was rife with corruption and collusion, generating scores of shadowy organizations that merged armed forces, intelligence services, political ambitions, and even scientific ventures.

So what was one more?

Earlier, Kowalski had pulled him aside and told him what had happened to Pierce's mother and hinted at previous altercations with this organization. So, no matter what this new enemy was named, Tucker and the others were trespassing on their home turf—and he intended to watch his step.

And that applied to his partner, too.

"SLOW," he radioed to Kane.

The jumbling view on his phone steadied as the shepherd's lope became a deliberate pace. Turning, Tucker motioned the others behind a parked yellow Hummer. A tow rig behind the truck held a sleek watercraft and offered additional shelter. In another block, the avenue dumped—like the other four spokes of the star—into a central park that surrounded the twisting spire of Burj Abaadi.

The Eternal Tower rose like a glowing sculpture into the night sky, each floor slowly turning, making it appear as if the entire structure were gently swaying in the wind off the sea. Only the bottom five stories were stationary, encompassing the building's lobby and maintenance levels, including its power station that collected energy generated by the horizontal wind turbines positioned between each floor.

"Shouldn't we be closer?" Gray asked.

"No need," Tucker said. "That park ahead is full of shadows, with lots of trees and hiding places. Don't want to stumble upon a guard by mistake. Leave this to Kane."

Seichan agreed. "He's right."

"Works for me," Kowalski said, running his fingertips longingly along the sleek side of the yellow jet boat.

Outvoted, Gray nodded for Tucker to continue. The man sent Kane forward with a single command.

"GO SCOUT!"

Kane stalks slowly forward, remaining in shadows. He moves against the breeze flowing from ahead, letting the scents wash over him, catching what he can with his upturned nose.

He smells salt and wet weed from the distant waves and sand.

Closer . . . he is hit by the crisp bite of cut grass . . . the trickle of sweetness from petals opening to the night.

But through it all, a rank undercurrent flows . . . reeking of sweat and oil and ripeness of body.

Men.

In hiding.

He hunts each scent, drawing in its heady, foul richness. He stays in shadows, behind bushes, along the edges of benches. He tracks each one down until he hears the satisfying whisper in his ear.

SPOTTED.

Then moves on.

He creeps deeper, tail low, haunches tense, ears pricked to every tick, tap, and creak. The smell of man fades behind him, carried away by the wind, leaving spaces for new scents.

Then he stops.

A trickle of thrill stirs his hackles. He tests again, nose higher, taking that odor deep inside, tasting it, recognizing it. He moves again, tracking its trail through the air.

It rises from a truck—he knows trucks and rides and hanging his head into hard winds. But now is not that time. He dashes across an open stretch and into the shadows beneath the truck, a darkness reeking of oil and grease.

He slips out the other side, twisting, stretching his neck. He circles and paces, making certain.

Then whines his triumph and points.

"Good dog," Tucker radioed back.

Pride spiked through him—and a raw affection that ached.

They had all watched Kane's hunt, huddled around his phone's tiny screen. His shepherd had spotted four guards stationed out in the grounds—then he snuck up to a pickup truck parked crookedly in the circular drive fronting the entrance to Burj Abaadi.

"He's found Amanda's scent there," Tucker said. "She's on the island!"

"Can you get Kane up into the bed of that truck?" Gray asked.

"No problem." It was never hard to get Kane to take a ride. He sent the command. "UP IN THE TRUCK!"

The dog immediately backed a yard—then, with a burst of speed, he launched from his haunches and flew over the side and landed in the rear bed, skittering slightly to avoid hitting what lay there.

Kane danced around it, sniffing intently.

Seichan leaned closer. "Is that an open casket?"

Gray pointed out the bits of tape along the edges. "That's how they moved Amanda. No wonder she was never spotted at the airport. They crated her here, likely under diplomatic seals."

Kowalski looked over his shoulder. "Yeah, but where is she now?"

They all stared up at the fifty-story tower, spinning slowly in the night. They all recognized the truth.

The hunt was just beginning.

But were they already too late?

2:32 A.M.

The tiny boy rested on Amanda's bare belly, quiet now.

The furnace of her body, stoked to a fiery dampness by the delivery, kept him warm. A small blanket covered him, but a tiny fist protruded, no bigger than a walnut.

Amanda stared, consuming him with her eyes. With her arms bound to the sides, she could not hold him. That was the worst cruelty. Even giving her this moment with her child was necessity, not compassion. She had read all the baby books. The newborn was placed facedown to encourage the draining of any fluid; the skin-to-skin contact encouraged her body to release its own natural oxytocin, to help with the final contractions to push the placenta free.

Her body had performed its ageless duty.

Spent, exhausted, she tried to stretch this moment for an eternity.

"My baby boy," she whispered, tears streaking through the sweat of her heated face; she wanted him to hear his mother's voice at least once. She willed all her love, christening him with the name murmured in the night with her husband, Mack, his broad hand resting on the bump of her stomach.

"My little William."

But, sadly, the child was not her husband's, at least not genetically. She knew some of the truth, saw the medical records in the terrifying note that sent her fleeing in terror out to the Seychelles. Still, Mack had loved the baby as much as she did. It shone in his face, even after the truth was known.

He loved you so much, William.

New tears flowed, for the family that was never to be.

Voices intruded, but she never took her eyes off her child.

"Petra, make sure you collect at least five milliliters of blood from the umbilical cord. We'll need the sample serum-typed, in addition to the standard tests. I'll also want to harvest some umbilical stem cells."

Amanda listened, realizing the truth. They were already parsing her child into parts.

"Dr. Blake, the radiant bed is ready," Petra called from the side. "I've prepared the vitamin K and the eyedrops. Did you want to perform the APGAR assessment?"

"No. You can do it. I should pass on word about the delivery as soon as possible."

Blake shifted from the foot of the delivery bed to Amanda's side. He reached to scoop up the child.

"No, please," Amanda begged. "Another minute."

"I'm sorry. It's better this way. You did beautifully."

She strained forward, a sob breaking out of her hoarse throat. "Nooo . . . !"

Ignoring her plea, he lifted William from her belly, taking away his warmth, leaving a hollowness that she knew would never go away.

Blake walked her boy toward a tiny bed under harsh lights—and the nurse with cold eyes. Amanda pictured the shining tray of silver dissection tools.

Her sobs turned into wracking cries. She rocked within the limits of her restraints. Still, she never took her eyes off her boy.

My little William . . .

2:38 A.M.

Dr. Edward Blake stood by his desk, bone-tired and bleary-eyed. A deep-cushioned chair beckoned, but he remained standing. He didn't want to be relaxed, not during this call.

"Yes, everything went smoothly," he reported. "The genetics continue to remain stable. After we run the baselines, we'll be testing the stability of the helix assembly under various environmental rigors and stresses."

That was the purpose behind Petra's macabre work in her lab: to separate out various vital organs—brain, heart, lungs, and others—to keep those tissues alive indefinitely, so that rigorous tests could be performed upon them. Amanda's child was destined for that lab.

"I believe we have reason to be optimistic about this boy," he finished.

"OPTIMISM IS IRRELEVANT," the speaker countered, the voice digitally flattened and tweaked to an arctic severity—though Edward suspected that iciness wasn't all computer-generated. "ONLY HARD FACTS MATTER."

He swallowed. "Of course. We'll start generating actionable data within the day."

"TISSUE SAMPLES SHOULD BE HARVESTED AND COURIERED STATESIDE AS SOON AS POSSIBLE."

"Understood. I received the list. My assistant is already prepping stem and skin cells. We'll have intestinal and alveolar biopsies within the hour, and cortical and spinal sections by day's end. But I do have another question."

Silence encouraged him to continue.

"The mother . . . was there a final consensus on what to do with her?" Edward could guess the answer. A massive graveyard had been dug into the jungles outside of his Somalia camp.

"SHE MAY STILL PROVE TO BE BIOLOGICALLY USEFUL. AS OF NOW, WE DON'T KNOW IF THESE RESULTS ARE BROADLY REPLICABLE OR IF THERE IS SOMETHING UNIQUE ABOUT HER GENETICS."

Edward was surprised at the depth of his relief. He pictured Amanda's tender love shining through the sweat and tears, the strength in her eyes when he took her baby away. That blend of toughness and maternal protection must have touched him more than he imagined.

Or maybe I'm simply tired, getting too emotional.

"Should we confine her here?" he asked hoarsely. "On Utopia?"

"NO. OUR PLANS REQUIRE HER TO BE SHIPPED BACK TO THE STATES."

Surprised, Edward absorbed this and ran various scenarios through his head. He had lightly sedated Amanda for the short hop from Somalia, to facilitate her passage through customs. But a trip to the States was a longer journey, with a much higher risk of exposure.

"How do you plan on moving—?"

He was cut off. "SHE'S INTENDED FOR THE FERT/INC LAB."

Edward had to rest a hand on his desk. He'd visited the Fertilization and Incubation Lab only once—and once was enough. He immediately understood what was demanded of him.

"WE'LL EXPECT HER PREPPED AND AT THE DUBAI AIRPORT BY EIGHT IN THE MORNING," the speaker finished.

"Consider it done."

The line went dead before he got out his last word. They didn't need to hear his acquiescence. It was taken for granted.

He remained standing for two long breaths. The relief he felt at Amanda's reprieve drained away.

Better she had gotten a death sentence.

He tapped an intercom. "Petra, we'll need the surgical suite readied."

Her tinny response followed. "For what procedure?"

He told her, picturing again what he'd witnessed at the Fertilization and Incubation Clinic, that flawless representation of scientific purity, where morality held no sway, a world where only methodology and outcome mattered.

He felt bile churn in his gut.

Poor Amanda.

24

Kat stepped across the threshold.

Amy followed, shadowing behind her, quiet now after her initial cry of shock and dismay. The large steel doors shut behind them, closing on their own with a pop of pressure.

Kat knew they didn't have much time until their escape was discovered.

With the doors sealed, the ambient light remained low, tinged slightly red, reminding Kat of working in a control room of a submarine during her years in navy intelligence, where the unique lighting preserved night vision. Or maybe the subdued illumination was meant to blunt the horrors residing in here.

A long hall stretched ahead, splitting two rows of tanks full of a pinkish gelatinous fluid. Thin translucent drapes that lined the front of the rows failed to hide what rested in those tub-size steel vessels. Kat stepped to the side and parted one of the curtains.

"Don't," Amy moaned, clutching her stolen baton in both hands, but she still followed, clearly needing to stay near Kat—not for protection, merely to remain near a flicker of humanity in such an inhuman lab.

Kat had noted the sign hanging above the hallway.

Fertilization/Incubation Lab

Here lay that purpose given flesh.

A naked woman floated shallowly in semi-viscous fluid, a gelatinous bed to prevent bedsores and to keep tissues moist. Her abdomen swelled with gravid promise, navel protruding, close to parturition. Her breasts hung loosely, never to suckle the life growing within. The patient's head hung over the edge of the tub, eyes taped shut, neck arched back, as if waiting for her hair to be shampooed. But there was no hair. The bald scalp shone in the weak light, revealing sutured scars and wired electrodes snaking into the skull. Other tubes violated mouth and nose, all running to a rack of monitoring, ventilating, and liquid-feeding equipment.

"What have they done?" Amy asked in a horrified whisper.

Kat stared down the long row, at the other women resting in identical tanks, posed in the same frozen posture of torture, all in various states of fetal gestation. She understood what she was seeing. The women here had been reduced to no more than living brainstems—with only one clear function.

"They've turned them into mindless human incubators," Kat said, trembling between impotent rage and bone-deep sorrow.

She gaped, unblinking, bearing silent witness.

This is where I would've ended up.

Amy wore the same mask of revulsion.

Kat shied from imagining herself here, unable to balance this monstrous act with the simple wonders and mysteries of her own pregnancies, of carrying those tiny lives inside of her. She staved off the paralysis of horror by remembering her babies' first cries, the suckle of a tiny mouth on a tender nipple, the grip of little fingers, so demanding, so needy.

She pictured the other four buildings of the clinic complex, of the levels of research and development performed here: the cutting-edge retrieval and cryopreservation techniques for ova and sperm, the advancements in in vitro fertilization procedures, and the latest innovation in embryo culture and transfer. Many of the greatest reproductive and genetic scientists from around the globe worked here or had in the past. How many, if any, knew what trickled down from their groundbreaking research, seeping like toxic waste to pool here with poisonous purpose?

Kat swung away, knowing she had only *half* the answers to the mysteries here. She knew where to find the others.

"C'mon," Kat said, sensing time running short.

She returned to the central alleyway between the rows. She had noted glass-enclosed offices at the back and headed there, striding quickly, with Amy in tow. As her mind raced, she considered various exit strategies. There was not likely to be a back door out of this lab, not with what this facility was hiding down here. The only escape was back the way they'd come, through those red steel doors and past that gauntlet of armed guards.

She searched as she strode to the end of the room—for a weapon, for some other means of escape.

She wasn't the only one searching.

Amy gasped behind her. "Denise . . . !"

Without turning, Kat reached an arm back and grabbed Amy's wrist before the young woman could dart to the side, toward one of the shrouded tanks. Amy had come along with Kat to discover the fate of her sister.

"That's not her," Kat said, drawing Amy closer. "That's just a husk, a shell. Your sister died when she was taken through those doors."

Amy resisted for a couple of steps, then surrendered—knowing Kat was right. They hurried together, each needing the warmth of the other.

The hallway ended at a line of three glass-walled offices, all facing the horror show. Other hallways branched to the left and the right, likely leading to smaller labs, storerooms, and mechanical spaces.

Kat noted the names etched on the three doors. She memorized them, intending to hold the persons accountable if she ever got out of here. But she moved to the centermost and largest of the three. The name on the door read NANCY MARSHALL, M.D., D.Sc., PH.D., A.B.O.G. It seemed the more abbreviated letters followed a name, the less humanity remained.

Through the glass door, Kat spotted a computer glowing with a screensaver depicting a slowly spiraling helix of DNA. She found the lock unfastened and hurried inside, crossing to the computer.

She reached to wake the monitor up, then paused, noting something odd about the screensaver. The glowing, high-definition image detailed a thick double helix of DNA, slowly spinning, all color-coded, mapping out nucleotides, codons, and chemical bonds. She leaned closer, studying a strange abnormality: a *third* strand of protein wound within the double helix, entwined into the genetic matrix like a snake in the grass.

Biology and genetics were not her specialty—but she knew someone at Sigma who could better analyze this data. Reaching to the mouse, she woke up the computer. A standard desktop appeared. She needed to secure as much of the data stored on that hard drive as possible and transmit it back to DC, but she also knew she didn't have time to crack whatever passwords locked this system from the outside world. There was no way to e-mail or send files electronically. The firewalls around this complex were fierce and military-grade.

She would have to improvise and hope for the best.

Reaching to her breast pocket, she removed her surveillance pen. The camera's video and audio were recorded to a secure digital SD card linked to a cellular transceiver—but the data could also be manually ported over if necessary via a built-in USB connection. She twisted the pen, shedding the camera features, leaving behind the two-terabyte storage card linked to a USB adapter.

Working fast, she found the USB port in the desktop's tower and shoved the drive in place. Her intent was not to *download* the card's content, but to *upload* files to it, hoping they'd eventually reach Sigma. With the guts of her pen exposed, Kat noted the cellular transceiver glowing a pinpoint green. It remained active, but was anyone picking up the signal?

She straightened as a new icon blinked onto the screen's desktop, representing her flash drive.

A rumble drew her attention around. Amy stood at the open office door, staring back to the far end of the lab. The steel doors had begun to slowly open, unsealing and cracking with a sliver of light.

Dr. Marshall's sharp bark carried through: "Find them!"

Kat returned to the computer.

No time to be picky about which files to grab.

Using the mouse, she dragged the image of the computer's hard drive and dumped it all onto the thumbnail for the SD flash drive.

Files immediately began transferring.

That's all she could do for now.

Except survive.

6:41 P.M.

"What the hell was that?"

Painter stared over at General Metcalf. He'd never heard the man swear, seldom saw him lose composure. The pair stood before the bank of monitors in the communications nest. Minutes ago, the technician monitoring Kat's surveillance pen reported new feed coming from her *second* device. This was the first video transmission since the pen had been activated. They'd picked up some initial audio, snatches of conversation, but nothing afterward.

Then suddenly the screen had bloomed to life.

The first few minutes were a jumbled confusion until the camera settled on a set of red metal doors with a cross symbol emblazoned on them.

Metcalf had just been leaving when the monitor sprang to life, exciting the technician. The general accompanied Painter to observe what was picked up. Together, they viewed in growing dismay as Kat surveyed a dark lab, revealing rows of women in tanks. Then she continued to some offices at the back of the room.

"Did you get those names?" Painter asked the technician. "The ones on the office doors?"

"Yes, sir."

After that, the monitor went dark once again.

"Is that everything?" Metcalf asked. "Where was this footage taken?"

Painter knew he had to come clean—about everything. He drew the general back into the side office. Once inside, with the door closed, he explained, "Captain Bryant was investigating a fertility clinic in South Carolina, the same facility where Amanda had her in vitro fertilization performed."

But it hadn't been just Kat conducting that investigation. Lisa had gone down there, too. Fear for her stoked brighter, but he had to stay focused.

Metcalf turned toward him. "What fertility clinic are you talking about? Who authorized—?"

Painter cut him off before he worked up a full head of steam. He needed to shock the man into listening—for all of their sakes. "Amanda may still be alive."

As he expected, those few words knocked the man back a step.

Painter continued, not letting the general recover. He needed to present the entire picture before Metcalf started to put up mental roadblocks. Only the complete story could win this stubborn man to their cause.

Painter started at the beginning, with Amanda's kidnapping and his belief that it was tied to the unborn child she carried. They ended in front of Kat's office computer. Painter showed him the cross atop the island of Utopia, realizing just then that it matched the symbol on the red steel doors.

What did that mean?

Metcalf sank into the desk chair, his eyes fixed to the screen. The general was a tough man, a skilled player in the ways of power and politics—some would say even an opportunist—but that was a requirement to function in the Beltway politics of DC. Painter also knew the general to be a shrewd strategist, capable of putting logic before emotion.

He hoped that proved to be the case now.

"And all of these properties are owned by the Gant family, the president's family?" Metcalf asked, staring at the island. "And you've already received confirmation that Amanda was taken there."

"Yes."

Behind that glaze of shock, Painter saw the gears churning through all the evidence.

Finally, Metcalf shook his head, not in disbelief, more like defeat. "Dear God . . . if you're right . . ." He placed a palm on his forehead and stared Painter square in the eye. "Even if the Gants are the puppet masters behind the Guild, how could the president involve his own daughter with something like this?"

The general glanced to that dark monitor in the other room, obviously picturing the horror show from a moment ago.

"James Gant may not know," Painter explained. "We don't know which of the Gants are in that inner circle, the *True Bloodline*. That's why I've been playing this game so cagily. I have a gut feeling that inner circle is not without internal friction or dissent."

"Why do you say that?"

"Something sent Amanda running to the Seychelles, almost like she was tipped off. Like someone was trying to protect her."

"Or maybe they purposefully tricked her into fleeing in secret so she could be nabbed out of the public eye."

It was a more cynical hypothesis, one Painter hadn't even considered, proving yet again that Metcalf was an expert chess player.

"You've built a case against the Gants," Metcalf conceded, "but it's far from solid. None of this is strong enough to confront them, especially the administration. If we tried, we'd end up tipping our hand too soon, exposing that we're onto them. The backlash would burn us down. And that Bloodline would bury itself even deeper. There's only one solution."

Painter understood. "We need Amanda."

Metcalf met his eyes, confirming this. Any hope for Sigma to rise from these ashes depended on recovering and securing the president's daughter—and surely the Bloodline knew that, too.

A knock at the door drew both their attentions. It was Kat's chief analyst, Jason Carter. Painter motioned him forward, but the kid only stuck his head through the door.

"Director, we're receiving new data from Captain Bryant's device."

Painter stared past the young man's head. The monitor was still black. "Is it new video . . . or just audio again?"

"Neither. They're digital files."

Painter's eyes pinched with momentary confusion—then realized what Kat was doing: downloading information off one of the lab's computers.

Clever, Kat . . . very smart.

"Start forwarding those files to me," Painter said.

Jason nodded and ducked back out.

Metcalf waited with Painter. "I wish you hadn't told me any of this," he said. "I'd certainly sleep better not knowing. For that matter, why *did* you tell me? Why trust me? Who's to say I'm not on the Guild's payroll?"

It was a good question—and Painter had only one answer.

"Because you've been a thorn in Sigma's side from the beginning."

"You mean I've been an ass."

Painter didn't argue with his wording. "But you've also had our back, sir, when we've truly needed it. And besides, I can't do this on my own. Not any longer. I need an ally, someone to hold the wolves at bay if we're to have any chance of recovering Amanda."

"You'll get it—but there's only so much I can do. After what happened in Somalia, Sigma has a big target on its back. And you know Washington . . . once they smell blood in the water . . ."

The feeding frenzy begins.

The intercom buzzed. "Director, the initial files are up on your desktop."

"I'll leave you to this," Metcalf said, standing and letting Painter take his seat. "This castle's about to be stormed, and I'm better off manning the gates and fortifying the ramparts."

Painter knew his statement was more than a metaphor. Sigma headquarters lay in the bunkers beneath the Smithsonian Castle, within the shadow of the White House—even now, the battle lines were being drawn between them.

As Metcalf left, Painter turned his attention to the computer, to the files gained at such risk. He worried about Kat . . . and even more about Lisa. Still, he sensed that all the mysteries, the true pulse of the Bloodline, lay in the life or death of another woman.

Gray, you must find Amanda.

25

Gray held the man's neck in the crook of his arm, the flat of his hand against the side of his head. A twist and a sharp crank on the chin shattered the guard's cervical vertebrae. The strangled body fell limp.

He lowered the guard to the lawn and began stripping off the man's helmet, vest, and shirt. The gear was identical to that worn by the commandos back in Somalia, offering further proof that Amanda had been moved here.

In his earpiece: *"Done."*

That was Seichan. She had taken down her man.

As Gray strapped on the dead soldier's helmet, he glanced at the phone in his hand. On the screen, a dog's-eye view revealed a lone guard posted beside a park bench. Kane moved nearer, drawing the man's attention, while Tucker closed in from behind with a blade. As silently as the others, he dispatched the last guard that stood between Gray's team and the twisted spire of the Burj Abaadi, the Eternal Tower.

"Move in," Gray radioed.

He ran low through the remainder of the nighttime park, still wary in case Kane had missed any hidden guards. But no alarm was raised as he reached the edge of the grounds.

As he waited for the others, he looked up at the sheer majesty of the slowly turning tower, each floor revolving independently of the others. He imagined the view must be breathtaking from up top, the scene eternally changing, spanning from the panoramic brilliance of Dubai's skyline to the dark mystery of the starlit sea.

Still, something bothered Gray as he stared upward.

Something about its ever-changing shape . . .

A rustle drew his attention back to the ground. The others converged from different directions. Seichan and Tucker came similarly outfitted in stolen gear. Kane kept out of sight, slinking wide upon a signal from his handler.

As they gathered to him, Gray studied the front entrance to the Burj Abaadi. He expected there would be cameras watching the steps and lobby, possibly other guards inside. The disguise was a feeble one, but the ruse could buy them an extra few seconds of surprise if needed.

Kowalski finally pushed past a grove of palms, struggling to pull a small vest over his wide shoulders. The helmet sat on top of his head like a crown. "My guy was pint-size," he explained.

Gray pointed his rifle at the big man. "Drop all of that and put your hands on your head."

Kowalski frowned. "What the hell, Pierce?"

Seichan sighed. "Just act like a prisoner." She waved toward the lobby stairs. "For the cameras."

Understanding slowly sank through Kowalski's thick skull, widening his eyes. He shed his stolen gear and laced his fingers atop his head.

With a final few instructions, Gray marched Kowalski forward, flanked by the other two. From the corner of his eye, he caught a blur of shadow, easy to miss unless watching for it. Kane vanished into the bushes at the base of the building and crept from there toward the same stairs.

Bright lights lit the steps, but the lobby was dark, with only a few pools of subdued illumination inside. It looked deserted. Maybe their disguises weren't necessary. The guards in the park had certainly been easy to take down. Gray had even caught his target sleeping.

The enemy plainly must have thought themselves safe out on this island—especially since they suspected no one was looking for Amanda.

Gray marched with the others up the stairs. They kept their faces lowered from the cameras. Gray motioned for Tucker to run ahead and check the tall glass doors that led into the lobby. The man ran forward and tugged. The door swung open, unlocked. Tucker looked relieved. It saved them the trouble and exposure of using the minipellets of C-4 to blast the deadbolts, or larger pyrotechnics if necessary.

The only one disappointed by the ease of entry was the team's explosives and demolitions expert. "Aw, man," Kowalski groused. "I was all set to blow some crap up."

Gray poked him in the back with his rifle. "Keep moving."

Kowalski stumbled across the threshold. Gray and the others crowded in behind him.

The lobby soared five stories high, drawing the eye up. In the center rose a grand spiral staircase, made entirely of glass and sparkling in the wan light with Swarovski crystals and figurines depicting sea creatures. It wound up from the grand entry hall, spiraling around the central axis of the tower and continuing ever upward.

The only illumination came from a ring of huge pillars, also made of glass. They formed massive vertical aquariums, glowing with an inner soft radiance that slowly shifted along a spectrum of hues.

Initially, Gray thought the aquariums were empty, merely bubbling on the inside, catching and multiplying the glow. Then his eyes adjusted, and the bubbles became palm-size jellyfish, swarming and drifting within the giant pillars.

The wonder of the moment was interrupted by a harsh call.

A towering, beefy figure rose out of hiding from behind a security desk and stalked forward, rubbing a knuckle in one eye. Somebody else had been caught napping. The man shoved a black beret on his head, clearly the leader of this African contingent.

A second figure crawled from behind the desk and stood. A dark-skinned girl of thirteen or fourteen, slim, frail-limbed, wearing a soldier's uniform. She wiped her mouth with the back of her hand. The leader's pants were unbuttoned.

So the man hadn't been caught *sleeping*.

Fury roiled up inside Gray. He knew many of the village children nabbed by the warlords of Somalia weren't all turned into soldiers, like Baashi, but instead were brutalized as sex slaves.

Or both.

The monster's gaze remained fixed on Kowalski as he stalked across the wide lobby, clearly mystified by the sudden appearance of this prisoner. The ruse would only last another couple of sec—

The leader froze, half-skidding on one foot, his hand lunging for his holstered pistol.

Seichan whipped her SIG Sauer out.

"Don't shoot!" Gray snapped—the noise of a firefight, even a single shot in this crystal echo chamber, would surely draw any other guards and alert the enemy hidden within.

The leader freed his sidearm, under no such restraint.

But Gray had seen the flicker of movement from Tucker's wrist, heard a whispered command over the radio.

Kane burst out of the shadows behind the man and barreled forward. The girl squealed, dancing to the side. The dog hit the man in the ankle, hamstringing him and flinging him into the air. He flew high—then landed hard, his head striking the marble floor.

His pistol slid away into the shadows.

Tucker was already moving, charging forward, blade in his fist. He slid on his knees, passing Kane, whose momentum carried him in the opposite direction. Tucker reached the downed man, raised his dagger, then simply lowered it.

"Neck's broken," Tucker said.

"So we each got a soldier," Kowalski said, lowering his arms, rubbing his shoulders. "I gotta get me one of those dogs."

From the shadows to the side, the young girl reappeared. She held the lost pistol in both hands, pointed at Tucker. Her face was a mask of terror.

Tucker dropped his dagger and raised his palms. "It's okay . . ." the man intoned softly.

The girl spat something in Somali. They didn't have a translator, but it sounded more angry than scared. She steadied her pistol, her finger finding the trigger.

Then the girl suddenly jerked back a step—coughed blood. She dropped the pistol, her fingers scrabbling for the silver blade sticking out of her neck.

Gray turned to the source.

Seichan had a second throwing dagger in her fingers, ready if needed. It wasn't.

The girl slumped to her knees, then toppled forward.

Tucker gave out a soft cry of dismay. He lunged forward, going to the child's aid, but it was no use. "What did you do?"

"What needed to be done," Seichan said, her eyes glassy and cold.

Tucker stared across at her. "She was just a child."

"No, she wasn't," Seichan whispered under her breath. "Not any longer."

Logically, Gray knew she was right. The girl would likely have shot and killed Tucker, and the noise would have jeopardized everything. And a sad truth of the matter: some brutalized war orphans never recovered, never healed, becoming no more than animals in children's bodies.

Still, his heart ached at the death, echoing Tucker's anguish.

Seichan merely headed across the lobby. "Let's find Amanda. That's what we came here for."

Still, he noted her fingers trembled as she tried to return the unused blade to its wrist sheath.

"Seichan's right," Gray said and pointed to Tucker. "Get your dog. We need to pick up Amanda's trail."

Tucker glowered at Seichan, but he obeyed.

As dog and handler worked in tandem, sweeping through the lobby, Gray moved to the security desk. There he found a bank of monitors. It appeared the desk was wired to the lobbies on each floor. He began hitting each button, bringing up one view after the other, looking for any evidence of habitation. Reaching the penthouse lobby on the fiftieth floor, he came up empty. Every lobby was dark, offering a dim view of marble elegance, fine rugs, and the continuation of the spiral stair.

Everything looked deserted, untouched.

"Over here," Tucker called quietly. "I think we found something."

Kane sniffed furiously at one of the doors along a curved bay of elevators.

Gray crossed toward him, collecting Seichan along the way.

She stood off by herself, staring into one of the aquarium pillars, her face unreadable. As he reached her, she nodded to the glowing and swirling pillar of jellyfish in front of her, reading the sign.

"It's a giant hybrid of *Turritopsis nutricula.*"

He shook his head, not understanding.

"At the end of this species' life, the adult jellyfish reverts back to a juvenile state. This cycle repeats over and over again, starting fresh each time."

She stared over at the bloodied girl. Her eyes were damp with tears, possibly seeing herself lying there. Did she wish for such a chance—for both of them—to be reborn, to start again pure and untainted, to have their childhoods back?

"The process makes the jellyfish immortal," she whispered.

He nodded, understanding this unusual marvel of nature.

No wonder it's the mascot for the Eternal Tower.

But Seichan had a different viewpoint about life everlasting and mumbled it aloud. "It's so horrible."

Gray didn't comment as she turned away. He followed silently with her and allowed her to work through her grief, to process it. He did keep close to her side, letting fingers brush along the back of her hand, the one that had thrown the dagger.

He expected her to pull away, but she didn't.

They joined Tucker and Kane.

Kowalski stood nearby, neck craned, staring up, following the coil of the crystal staircase through the heart of the eternally spiraling tower.

Gray followed his gaze.

Again nagged by something.

Something about the shape . . .

6:47 P.M. EST
Washington, DC

The DNA molecule slowly spiraled on the computer screen, a dance of code that mapped out the human body in all its glory—but this fragment of genetic material was unlike anything Painter had ever seen diagramed. A third strand snaked within the heart of the typical double helix.

"What do you make of it?" Painter asked, using the mystery here to keep him distracted from his worries about Kat and Lisa.

"It's a *triple* helix," Renny Quinn said, his voice flush with awe. "The Holy Grail of genetics."

Renny leaned his large fists on Kat's desk to stare closer. Sigma's resident biogeneticist had been summoned to help Painter sift through the huge volume of data coming from that lab's servers. The man was of Irish descent, with a ruddy complexion and dark auburn stubble over his scalp and cheeks. He was also a former college boxer—which included a fair amount of bare-knuckle brawling, a habit that got him discharged from the army rangers.

Afterward, Sigma grabbed him. Renny proved the stories true of men with big hands—but in his case, it meant he had a huge brain. And Renny was going to need it to slog through this mountain of data.

The files from Charleston arrived disordered and unclassified, much of it in raw code. Kat must not have had time to pare the data down to the most essential files. Instead, what arrived was the definition of a *data dump*—a load far more than the SD card in her pen could handle. A lot of the files came corrupted, others not fully decrypted. As a consequence, it could take days, if not weeks, to decipher, decode, and repair the damaged files.

Still, it didn't take a computer engineer to ascertain that most of the files dealt with advanced genetics and reproductive studies, all tracing directly or indirectly back to this one image.

"A triple helix of DNA," Painter said, staring at the monitor, as perplexed as he was intrigued.

"Actually . . ." Renny leaned over and dragged a finger down two of the spiraling backbones. "These strands are *deoxyribonucleic acid,* or DNA. The *third*—this snake wrapped around the tree of life—is *peptide nucleic acid,* or PNA."

Renny tapped the new helix. "This strand is artificial. Man engineered this, not God. What we're looking at is the result of *cybergenetics,* the merging of biology and technology."

"Is that even possible?"

"Not only possible. It's been done. A team over at the University of Copenhagen have already managed to insert a PNA strand between two DNA strands. In a test tube, of course. But the only obstacle to moving their research to the next stage is a simple hurdle." Renny nodded to the screen. "That triple helical assembly isn't stable in water. Build a raincoat around that strand and the whole world changes."

Painter frowned up at him. "What do you mean?"

Renny explained. "Our entire genetic code is built on four chemical bases: guanine, adenine, thymine, and cytosine. G, A, T, C. From that four-letter vocabulary, all life is formed." He cocked an eye at the spiraling molecule. "But PNA is not restricted to those *four* letters. Can you imagine what could be created with more letters of the alphabet? We could *rewrite* mankind."

Despite Renny's obvious excitement, Painter imagined only horrors.

"But far more importantly," Renny pressed, "this cyberstrand of PNA can be designed to specifically turn on and off certain genes. PNA has already been used to cure a form of muscular dystrophy in lab mice. But that's just the beginning. The potential is limitless. We're talking about blocking cancer, treating hundreds of genetic diseases, even extending life."

Renny stared longingly at the computer. "If DNA holds the key to life . . . then PNA is its lock pick. For whoever holds that tool in hand, nothing would be impossible."

Painter's dismay grew darker, picturing the lab in Charleston, the women floating in tanks.

Jason tapped at the open office door and saved him from having to ponder worse. "Director, I'm sorry to interrupt, but we just finished receiving an extremely large file from Charleston. I thought you might like to see it. The folder's name is HISTORY AND ORIGINS."

Painter sat straighter, happy to forgo any more biological discussions for now. He wanted to get to the root of everything and that file name sounded promising: *history and origins.*

Jason dashed some of that hope. "But, sir, the folder is badly corrupted. We're working on it, but I can forward what we have so far, a couple odd pictures and documents."

"Do it," Painter said.

Jason pointed to the computer. "Already done."

No wonder Kat loves this kid.

Painter swung to the keyboard and clicked open the first few uncorrupted documents. A drawing filled the screen.

THREE TIMES THREE

It showed a trio of men, in colonial attire, with their arms clasped together: gripping right hands above their heads and left hands below. In both of the upper corners of the sketch, a three-headed snake coiled.

"What is this?" Painter mumbled, not expecting an answer—but he got one.

"That's the Holy Royal Arch," Renny said, sounding equally surprised to know the answer.

Painter turned to him. "How do you know that?"

"Because I'm a member of the guild." Renny must have read Painter's stunned look. "Not *that* Guild. I'm talking about the Masons. My family has been members going back to our time in Ireland."

Painter pointed to the screen. "And this?"

"Don't know a whole lot about it. What's drawn there is the ritual of *three-times-three,* a sacred number in freemasonry. It's a part of the initiation into the Royal Arch Degree, but plenty of mystery surrounds that exclusive degree, like its exact origin. It's said to be tied back to the Knights Templar. The *three-times-three* ritual . . . in other words, *nine* . . . represents the original nine founding members of the Knights Templar."

Painter stared at the screen. *What is this drawing doing on the servers of a genetics lab?*

Despite the oddity, he had a suspicion of the answer—but only because of the previous discussion with Renny. Painter studied the three men entwined together, the three-headed snakes. It was eerily similar to the three-stranded helix, three wound together as one. Even Renny had used the term *a snake wrapped around the tree of life* to describe the triple helix.

Painter read the annotation at the bottom of the drawing, stating the source: a book titled *Duncan's Masonic Ritual and Monitor,* printed back in 1866.

How could a book dated almost a century and a half ago be referencing— at least symbolically—a triple helix?

Painter was reminded of the file folder's name.

History and Origins

Sensing the importance here, he wanted the rest of this folder decrypted as soon as possible—if it was possible.

Jason suddenly dashed back to the door with grim news. "Director! We just lost connection to Charleston. The feed from Captain Bryant's device suddenly ceased in midtransmission."

Painter sat straighter. "The pen's battery? Did it die?"

"No, sir. This time we were monitoring the charge levels. It was still good."

Painter's heart sank, knowing there was only one explanation left.

Jason stated it aloud. "Someone must have discovered her bug and disabled it."

But what did that mean for Kat?

26

"Find them!"

Kat slipped silently into a side room off the dark lab hallway. Before disappearing inside, she caught a peek of Dr. Marshall at the far end, storming out of her office, surrounded by a cadre of security guards.

"Split up! Search every closet, storage space, and lab on both sides!"

Kat closed the door quietly, struggling with the handle due to her greasy palm. The room was lit only by the glowing screensaver of a computer monitor. Again it depicted that strange triple helix. Kat hoped the files she'd been downloading had reached somebody at Sigma.

As her eyes adjusted to the gloom, she noted the neighboring wall contained shelves of five-liter glass jars, reflecting the meager light. Dark things lurked and floated inside. Kat caught the barest glimpse of curled tiny fingers. She turned her back, not wanting to see more, not after witnessing the horrors out in the main room, the women in the tanks. These jars likely held the end product of that research.

Kat still held her folding combat blade, dulled now from all the hacking and sawing. She'd had only two minutes to ready herself for the siege ahead, barely enough time to get Amy hidden and out of harm's way. In her head, calculations continued to run as a mental timer ticked down.

Seven tanks . . . 300 psia/tank . . . estimated volume of laboratory space . . .

She heard doors opening and slamming, men shouting orders, working swiftly down the hall toward her position. She had left a door open farther back—but the guards would reach her first.

As planned.

She closed her eyes, taking several deep breaths. She used the extra seconds to smear more of the gelatinous fluid over her face and shaved scalp, leaving a thick film. Her clothes and the rest of her body were equally slathered and dripping with the hydrophilic gel—the same pinkish material that was filling the monstrous tanks in the main room.

Footsteps pounded up to her hiding place. She faced the door as it was ripped open. A guard—then another—came charging inside, with pistols pointed at Kat.

"Drop the knife!" one of them screamed.

She obeyed, lifting her hands to the top of her head.

The other yelled out the door. "Found one of them!"

"Bring her to me," Marshall ordered.

The guards manhandled her out the door and into the hallway. She did not resist and allowed herself to be led at gunpoint toward the pool of light radiating from Marshall's office.

The woman stood with her hands on her hips. She ground a boot heel against the vinyl floor. Kat heard a crack and saw a bit of black plastic go flying across the floor.

They'd found her surveillance pen plugged into their network.

Marshall faced her, her cheeks livid, her eyes fiery. She already had her palm resting on her cattle prod. Kat expected to be punished, *needed* to be punished.

"Where is the other girl?" Marshall demanded.

Kat made sure never to break eye contact, not to betray Amy's hiding place with the flicker of a glance.

"I'll make you talk . . ." Marshall stalked up to her and jammed the prod at her belly.

Kat twisted at the last second as blue sparks spat from the black wand's end. Pinned by the guards behind her, she still caught a glancing shock on her hip. Electric fire lanced along her side, crippling her left leg into an agonized spasm, forcing her into a painful crouch.

Kat ground her teeth against the pain—and in frustration.

Too low.

Pushing up with her good leg, Kat lunged and caught Marshall's wrist. One of the guards tried to pistol-whip her, but Kat dodged enough to take the blow to her shoulder.

Kat struggled with her quivering leg, grabbing a handful of plastic curtain that hid the tanks to keep her upright. She still had a grip on Marshall's wrist and shoved her cattle prod high. The metal tip struck the curtain rod overhead.

Sparks danced.

Then the world became fire.

The detonation blew Kat backward, sent her flying through the air. Overhead, blue flames chased across the ceiling after her—and spread outward. She covered her eyes with her arm, picturing that fire racing down the hallway toward the farthest room, a storage and mechanical space holding all manner of pressurized gas tanks that serviced the many labs of the complex, including seven large tanks marked with the symbol H_2.

Hydrogen gas.

Odorless, fourteen times lighter than air, highly explosive.

She had hacked through the lines earlier, bleeding the massive tanks into this enclosed space, knowing the gas would stay high, and be undetectable to the nose.

Kat landed on her back on the floor and slid, the heat blistering overhead, broiling all beneath. The only thing that kept the skin on her body was the thick hydrophilic gel that covered her. The same watery properties that kept the patients in the tanks moist and free of bedsores offered her some meager insulation.

The same couldn't be said for the others.

Screams cut through her blast-muffled ears.

Bodies flailed, clothes on fire, faces burned away.

In that split second during the explosion, Kat had watched Marshall's hair ignite, turning into a swirling nimbus of flames.

A fitting end for a woman who played God.

Kat struggled up, choking from the smoke, from the heat, from the lack of air. Her tearing eyes turned the view into a watery hell. All around, fires danced, plastic draping melted in blackened flows, and charred equipment sparked and sizzled.

She gained her feet and took a stumbling step backward.

Another figure rose from the floor two yards away, climbing from behind the shelter of a tank. Her scalp was burned and cracked, pouring blood.

Marshall lifted her arm, holding one of the guards' pistols in her hand, and stumbled around the tank.

Kat tried to get to shelter, but her legs betrayed her. She fell on her side, supported by one arm.

Marshall came another step forward, the pistol pointed at Kat's face. Her gaze showed no glee at the kill to come, only a pained necessity, a last act of revenge.

But it wasn't she who got that revenge.

From the tank next to her, the naked body rose, sitting up like a corpse from a grave.

Marshall turned toward the movement—her deadened eyes suddenly going bright with terror.

An arm pulled out of the gelatinous muck, drawing out a long black baton. The weapon swung with the heavy grief of a sister in mourning. The hard metal cracked Marshall across the bridge of the nose, shattering through bone.

The doctor dropped.

Kat realized then: This *is a more fitting death for a woman who played God.*

Amy climbed out of the tank and hurried to Kat and helped her back to her feet. "I thought you were dead."

"I thought I was, too."

Earlier, Kat had dragged Denise—Amy's sister—out of her viscous crib, replacing her sibling there instead. Kat had stripped Amy of her hospital gown and made sure the girl was sunk deeply into the tub, well coated with the insulating gel. Afterward, Kat had scooped handfuls of the same and covered herself, too—then carried Denise's thin body to the storage room.

Kat had wanted Amy hidden in plain sight, knowing no one would look too closely at the occupants of those tanks. She also wanted the girl close to the exit—not trapped down the fiery hall.

Confirming that wisdom, a massive explosion ripped from that direction, spraying shrapnel and shattering glass.

Kat pictured all the other pressurized tanks back there, overheating, leaking gas, catching fire. She also envisioned flames chasing through the gas tubing and conduits, spreading to other floors, other buildings.

"Let's go," Kat gasped out hoarsely.

She retrieved the pistol from Marshall's limp fingers, and together they fled through the smoke and fire and back through the red steel doors. In the ward, alarms blared, and sprinklers overhead sprayed fiercely. Kat stopped long enough to grab another gown for Amy and hurried out the doors. Down the hall, they discovered the guard station empty.

No one tried to stop them as they fled up out of the fiery bowels of the building and onto the ground floor of one of the rear buildings of the campus. The view outside showed the rest of the facility succumbing to the spreading flames. The summer sun was still up, but it looked like dusk outside as smoke obscured the gardens. Across the way, fire danced behind other windows. An explosion blew out an upper section of the main building, showering bricks and broken roof tiles.

It was all coming down.

Kat grabbed Amy's arm and hurried her through the exit and out into the parklike grounds. Other researchers fled for the gates to the street, looking shell-shocked.

Kat followed them, doing her best to keep her pistol hidden.

In the distance, sirens echoed.

Kat and Amy ran down the entry road and out the gates, chased by more blasts and deep-throated explosions. Debris rained down around them; smoke rolled thickly now, making it hard to see.

They fled farther down the street, trying to break clear, to get some distance away from the conflagration. At last, they reached a clear section of road. They both panted, hands on knees.

Sirens grew louder, converging all around as emergency crews responded from throughout Charleston.

Kat straightened and pointed toward the blue lights flashing through the smoke. "You should—"

The crack of a pistol echoed.

Amy fell back, sitting down on the road. She reached a palm to her chest as blood bloomed through her gown.

Kat twisted and dropped to a knee, swinging up her weapon.

An SUV sat on the side of the road, a back window open.

Movement inside.

She fired wildly at the dark car.

6:55 P.M.

Lisa dropped low in the backseat as the windshield cracked and shattered. She was pinned between two burly guards. In the front, the driver and Dr. Paul Cranston crouched.

"Christ!" the shooter next to her said. "She's got a gun."

Lisa covered her head.

What's happening?

After nabbing her off the streets of downtown Charleston, Cranston and his men had returned to the fertility center, confident after their hunt—only to be greeted by a loud explosion as they turned into view. The concussion rattled the SUV's windows. Smoke curled up from one of the back buildings. Flames began to spread—then more blasts as the place ripped apart.

Cranston had them retreat a block, to observe the incineration and destruction of his hard work, unable to look away.

He hissed from up front. "Take her out, goddamn it. Before she escapes. If she gets loose . . ."

While surveying the aftermath from a safe distance, Cranston had spotted a pair of women running out of the smoke, both shaven-headed, one in a hospital gown. He recognized them immediately. *They're from the lower lab!* He'd ordered them shot, gunned down like rabid dogs. But it seemed one of the women had teeth.

The gunman next to Lisa returned to the open window, shoving out one arm, his weapon pointed. Another spat of gunfire peppered the side of the truck. The man swore but held his post.

Lisa risked a peek. She saw the woman with the pistol drag the wounded girl toward the shelter of the thicker smoke. Sirens screamed now, and the flash of emergency lights grew brighter through the haze.

Then the woman glanced over her shoulder, back toward the SUV.

It was the first time Lisa got a good look at her face. Recognition rocked through her—even with all her friend's hair shorn away.

Kat.

"Got her," the shooter said with deadly satisfaction.

No!

Lisa lunged and hit the man with her shoulder. His pistol fired, his aim thrown. Lisa got her head out, saw Kat unharmed—and she intended her friend to stay that way.

"Kat! Run!"

Her other guard yanked her roughly back.

Cranston raised enough to peer into the backseat. He fixed Lisa with a knowing gaze. She immediately read the understanding there.

"So *that's* who you were working with," Cranston said and ordered his men to secure Kat.

The gunman balled a fist in Lisa's hair and dragged her out, using her body as a human shield.

Kat had found thin shelter behind a recycling bin.

Cranston called from up front. "Drop your weapon! Come out! Or we'll put a bullet through the back of your friend's head."

"Don't!" Lisa screamed at her friend.

The fist in her hair shook hard, ripping follicles.

She watched in despair as Kat threw her pistol out—then stepped into view.

"Go get her," Cranston ordered the other guard. "I want some answers. But don't hesitate to shoot her if she gives you any trouble."

Kat must have sensed the same and came along willingly, her fingers laced on top of her head.

"What about the other one?" Cranston asked when the guard returned with Kat.

"Dead."

Kat and Lisa made their reunion in the middle of the backseat, trapped between the pair of armed men.

"I'm so sorry," Lisa whispered.

Kat's face was a hard mask of rage—but not directed at her. Kat's hand found hers and squeezed, holding so much promise in that small gesture.

Reassurance, forgiveness, and a guarantee of revenge.

Emergency vehicles began to appear, whipping past their parked vehicle, sirens ablaze and lights blinding.

"Where now?" the driver asked, as he started the engine.

Cranston stared toward the burning wreckage of his clinic. "Out of the city . . . it's a little too hot here now." He turned from the fire and smoke. "We'll take them for a ride in the country. To the Lodge."

7:12 P.M.
Washington, DC

From his post in the communications nest, Painter watched the fiery footage from South Carolina. It was a live feed, shot by one of the two men he'd sent out to investigate the North Charleston Fertility Clinic.

His team had arrived on-site fifteen minutes ago. A chaos of fire crews fought the blaze. Towering arcs of water sprayed from trucks and ladders. Paramedics, along with other first-response teams, serviced burn injuries and smoke inhalation. Other victims had lacerations and bruises from flying debris and glass.

Four bodies had tarps over them.

Painter expected there would be more.

Would Kat or Lisa be among them?

When the security detail first reported in, Painter had hoped the destruction was Kat's handiwork, but it could just as easily have been a failsafe measure. Someone had found Kat's bug, and the Guild was notorious for its scorched-earth policy. He'd seen it himself multiple times in the past. If anyone got too close, the Guild would burn all bridges that might lead to them—to their secrets. It didn't matter the cost, consequences, or lives.

"Director."

He turned to find Jason Carter at his shoulder—again.

"I want you to see something," the kid said and drew him to a monitor where another analyst worked. Though the seated man was a decade older, Jason rested a hand on his shoulder like an encouraging father. "Linus and I were working on a research project for Kat before she left."

"We've been working on it for about three months," Linus added.

What's this about?

Painter's patience was thread-thin, but he waved for them to continue.

"I asked Linus to test our new protocols in the search for Captain Bryant and Dr. Cummings," Jason said. "I hope that was all right."

"Of course." At this point, he'd take any help. "What were you testing?"

"A new surveillance-and-tracking system similar to current facial-recognition programs—but instead of faces, we applied it to *motor vehicles*. Once on the road, the wear and tear on an automobile creates a unique pattern, as individual as any person's fingerprints or facial features."

"Is this going somewhere?" Painter asked.

Jason rushed ahead. "I took the liberty of gathering the database from your security team in Charleston. You asked them to collect video from the traffic and security cams around that restaurant."

"And nothing came up."

"Right. So I had Linus collect similar data from the cameras in North

Charleston—gathering video footage from all the vehicles passing through that neighborhood. We took all that information and ran it through our new vehicle-recognition program."

"And?"

Jason squeezed Linus's shoulder. He brought up side-by-side images on his monitor. It showed two partial views of a nondescript Ford SUV.

Jason continued, "I think our targets were purposefully avoiding traffic cams. It's not hard to do if you know which intersections are monitored."

And they would know that, Painter thought. *It's their home turf.*

"We got these images off a couple of bank ATM cameras. The picture on the left was taken three blocks from the restaurant where Dr. Cummings vanished. The second crossed a bridge about four blocks from the clinic." Jason faced him. "They're the same vehicle."

Painter countered skeptically, "There are a *lot* of Ford SUVs on the road."

"Not that match the *exact* same pattern of wear and tear. But I wanted to be sure. That's why I called you over." Jason patted Linus again. His partner zoomed into the second image and set the footage in motion. "Like I said, the image is grainy, but we enhanced it the best we could."

Painter leaned closer.

The expanded view peered through a back window. The shadowy figure of a man could be seen—and beside him a woman. Though the features were far from clear, she was definitely light-haired, similar profile— but it was more the way she carried herself, the way she moved, that made Painter's breath quicken.

Hope surged in him.

"It's Lisa."

"I wasn't sure," Jason said.

I am.

"What about Kat?" Painter asked.

Other figures were in the car, but they were just indistinct blurs.

"I can't say for sure," Jason admitted. "And unfortunately we never did get a clear take on the license plate. If they'd gone through a traffic cam . . ."

It was unfortunate, but it was also a start.

And, more important.

Lisa's alive.

He took a deep breath, not letting his relief overwhelm him, knowing matters could change at any moment. Painter only had to look at the neighboring monitor, at the fiery ruins of the clinic, to remind himself again of the Guild's scorched-earth policy.

The bastards would not leave loose ends.

And right now that was the definition of Lisa and Kat.

The same could be said of Gray's team. They were penetrating the latest Guild stronghold, on the trail of the president's daughter.

Painter watched the last of the clinic buildings crumble into flame and smoke. It was a fiery warning for Gray, too.

Tread lightly.

27

"They took Amanda into this elevator," Tucker said.

Gray stood with his hands on his hips. He watched Kane sniff along the floor, the shepherd's tail wagging vigorously. He didn't doubt the dog's nose, but he still hesitated.

The lobby bay had a dozen elevators banked in a semicircle. He stared up, following the spiraling curve of the translucent staircase. Both the elevators and the stairs ascended the central shaft of the Burj Abaadi. Each floor revolved around this stable core.

"Fifty floors," Kowalski said. "At least we don't have to climb each one."

"But we'll need to *stop* at each one," Seichan said. "Have Kane see if Amanda's trail continues out onto any of those levels."

Gray's three teammates looked to him for their next step. Even Kane stopped his sniffing to glance in his direction. Gray ignored them for a moment longer.

Something doesn't make sense.

Gray had studied each of the floors on the security cameras. He saw no evidence of life up there. But he had to trust Kane. The dog had gotten them this far. Settled, he reached and hit the call button for the elevator.

The doors opened immediately. They all stepped inside the posh lift, appointed in rich exotic woods and crystal lighting.

"So should we start at the top and work our way down?" Tucker asked. "Or the other way around?"

"Neither," Gray said, an edge of certainty hardening inside him as he bent down toward the elevator's controls.

He pointed to the rows of buttons lined along a flat touch-screen display. Illuminated numbers designated each floor. As he watched, each numeral slowly transformed and rotated through various characters in other languages: Chinese, Japanese, Arabic.

Definitely trying to appeal to the global traveler here.

"I don't get it," Kowalski said. "If we're not going up, then where are we going?"

Gray watched the lowest button glow in Arabic.

Then it shifted to the English equivalent.

"There's a lower level," Seichan said.

Kowalski looked to his toes. "Wait. How could there be a basement on a floating island?"

Gray knew this tower had been built in conjunction with the island's construction. The *bedrock* upon which the foundation of this tower had been placed was the immense platform holding up Utopia. That concrete-and-steel stage lay approximately ten meters under them, leaving plenty of space for a basement here.

"Must be a service level for the tower," Seichan said.

"And maybe more," Gray added, pressing the button.

The letter flashed green, and the cage dropped silently, so smoothly it was hard to tell they were moving at all.

"Be ready," Gray warned.

Weapons appeared in hands. Tucker signaled his dog, who lowered his haunches, readying to spring.

It felt like the elevator dropped much farther than just one floor, but at last, the doors opened. Gray took a shooter's stance and quickly inspected a small, utilitarian lobby, dimly lit and drab. He searched for any guards, but it appeared empty.

He stepped out cautiously, leading the way. Hallways branched off, with color-designated lines painted on the floor, likely to direct the hotel staff toward kitchens, laundry facilities, maintenance closets, and storage spaces.

It looked like a maze down here.

Gray waved everyone forward. "Tucker, have Kane hunt for Amanda's trail. She could be anywhere."

Tucker set to work with his partner.

Gray noted that two other elevators flanked this one. It seemed only three of the twelve elevators came down to this level. He had Kowalski hold their door open, in case they needed a fast exit.

A tall set of windows along one wall drew Gray's attention. He moved closer and stared into a cavernous neighboring space. The room was encased in concrete and climbed two stories high. Inside sat a row of massive turbine generators, looking like oversize metal elephants. Control panels covered another wall.

"The building's power plant," Seichan said, joining him.

Gray remembered Jack Kirkland's description of the tidal turbines that powered this building. *This must be them.*

Tucker came back after only a minute. "Nothing," he said.

Gray turned around, surprised. "What?"

Tucker shrugged. "Kane checked all of the hallways leading out from here. Found no sign of Amanda."

Impossible. She has to be down here.

"Have him check again," he ordered.

"I'll do it, but it's a waste of time. I'll vouch for Kane's nose."

"He's right," Seichan argued. "Coming down here made sense, but that doesn't mean it's the only path. There are fifty other floors. The longer we wait . . ."

The more danger Amanda faces.

He sighed heavily, conceding to the logic, but not happy about it. "Back upstairs, then."

The others piled inside the elevator.

Gray paused at the threshold, staring at the two doors that flanked this one.

"Hold on." He stepped over, pressed the call button, and summoned the other two elevators.

"What are you doing?" Seichan asked from inside the cage, as Kowalski continued to hold the door open.

The other two elevators arrived. Gray inspected both cages. He returned to the others and studied the touch-screen display in their lift.

"What?" Seichan pressed.

"All three of these cages reach the service levels, so why did Amanda's captors use the *middle* elevator? Human nature says they would have just gone to the one closest to the lobby." Gray pointed to the first set of doors. "I checked those other two. This control panel is two inches longer than the others."

"So?" Kowalski asked.

Seichan bent down and studied the lower section of the touch screen. "You think there are other buttons here, hidden ones."

He nodded. "Leading to restricted levels that only this elevator can reach."

Seichan searched the edges of the screen. "But I don't see any keyholes or slots for pass cards to activate those levels."

Gray hit the lobby button, sending the cage back up, demonstrating. "The screen is *touch*-sensitive."

Seichan got it, her eyes smiling. "It could be keyed to a fingerprint."

Gray stepped back into the lobby as the doors opened. "The soldier who Kane took out. He looked like he was the head of the security escort from Africa. He might have been granted access below."

Gray turned to Kowalski.

The big man rolled his eyes and sulked out, mumbling under his breath, "Why do I get all the dirty work?"

He returned a minute later, wiping a blade on his pants. He held out his hand. "I brought both. Just in case."

Resting on his palm were a thumb and a forefinger.

Kowalski also carried the dead man's beret and tugged it on his head. "That guy was more my size," he said and pointed toward the ceiling of the cage. "In case of any more cameras, I'm not playing prisoner again."

Gray took the severed thumb, pressed it against the empty space below the LL button, and kept it there. He held his breath—then a new button bloomed to life under the thumb.

If he had any doubt before, it ended as that odd symbol appeared. Gray flashed to Somalia, to running across the abandoned camp toward the tent cabin. He remembered the same marking had been painted on the outside of the jungle hospital.

A crimson cross with tiny finial decorations along its crosspieces.

The cage fell again, dropping much deeper now.

Kowalski's face had a sick tint to it. "How far down did these pirates bury their treasure?"

Gray pictured the giant concrete pylons that supported the island. The outer ones were twenty meters across, but the centermost pylon, the one directly under Burj Abaadi, was far larger. He knew that it was not uncommon for the support pillars of oil platforms to have caissons engineered in them, hollow pockets used for storing oil.

So why not here, too? But instead of oil, an entire base could be hidden inside a pillar this huge.

Gray knew Amanda was down there. His doubt centered on a larger concern. It weighed heavily as they dropped like a rock toward the heart of the island.

Is she still alive?

3:25 A.M.

Dr. Edward Blake watched the sheen of hatred fade from Amanda's eyes as he injected the last of the propofol into her IV line. Her lids slid to half-mast, her breathing deepened.

Her last words had been a curse, a promise of revenge.

I will see you both in hell.

But it was an impotent threat.

Amanda, the person, the loving mother, would be gone in a few more minutes. All sentience would be wiped away, leaving behind nothing but the most basic of functions.

"You should scrub up," Petra said.

His nurse was already gowned and adjusting a monitor that showed Amanda's CT scan. The young woman lay on a surgical table, draped from the neck down, her bald head gleaming under the surgical halogens overhead. Small blue markings decorated her scalp, like so much scientific nomenclature tattooed in place. The markings delineated the multiple drill sites and electrode insertion points.

Petra prepared the stereotactic system for the pending surgery. It integrated his surgical workstation with an intra-operative MRI and microscopy setup for visualization. She secured Amanda's head inside a fluid-filled alignment cuff, a vast improvement from the older head frames that had to be screwed into a patient's skull.

After working in the mountains of Somalia and having to deal with tools that seemed antiquated in comparison, Edward felt a surge of childish joy at having such fine equipment to play with. The station in Somalia had served its purpose for the past few years, allowing him to harvest eggs, embryos, and collect viable or promising subjects for the various other reproductive labs around the world. But he had always had larger ambitions. It was pure happenstance that Amanda Gant-Bennett had landed on his doorstep versus one of the many other reproductive facilities and egg-collection centers in India, Malaysia, Australia, or countless other points around the globe. It allowed him the opportunity to shine in the eyes of his superiors, to climb higher up that ladder.

So far, besides a few hiccups, matters had been proceeding smashingly. Amanda's death had been framed as an unfortunate encounter with Somali pirates; the child had been delivered and secured in the new high-tech research lab here; and after this last bloody bit of work, Amanda would be shipped off, no longer his problem, leaving him in peace to dissect and test the new research material.

The newborn slept in a small crib down the hall, waiting his turn.

But first, to attend to his mother.

An array of surgical instruments shone brightly: drills, bone curettes, cranial rongeurs, scalpels, suction and irrigation tubing.

He couldn't help but be excited. Though the technique had been developed here, he had only performed this procedure once. A few of the region's reproductive scientists had been rotated through here to learn it. But it had been fairly easy. The right and left sides of the cerebral cortex were connected with a layer of neural tissue. Using the surgical imaging as guidance, he would first perform a procedure known as a corpus callosotomy, which cuts the brain into two halves. It was a radical technique originally developed to treat severe epileptics, to sever that wild flow of electricity through the brain, which caused seizures.

The second stage of the procedure was one developed by another of his superiors' agencies. It was called α-ECT, or alpha-alternating electroconvulsive therapy. Electrodes would be permanently inserted into the two severed hemispheres. Small electric shocks of alternate polarity would be administered to those two halves. The resultant whirlwind of miniseizures trapped within either cranial hemisphere, swirling in opposite polarities, caused total shutdown of the cerebral cortex, leaving only the brainstem functional, which continued to control such vital tasks as heart rate and rhythm, respiration, even gastrointestinal activities.

In the end, the body was left intact, but the mind was gone.

A perfect tool for reproductive studies.

Edward glanced one last time toward Amanda's prone form.

After this, there would be no more Amanda.

As he exited the surgical suite for the scrub room, a chime sounded from a wall monitor overhead. It was a security feature of the station, announcing the arrival of the elevator. Every room had such a screen. A name scrolled across the bottom of the monitor.

Buggas Abdiwalli

It was the captain of Edward's personal security force. The screen showed a black-and-white view of the tops of helmets and a black beret.

What does that bloody Bug-Arse want now? he wondered, irritated, using the slang for the man's name.

He knew the captain was in a foul mood after losing so many men back in Somalia, but Edward didn't have time for this. He would let security deal with Buggas. If the captain became obstinate, the new automated systems would *discourage* him from putting up a fuss.

Nothing could get through that layer of defense.

Petra's voice came over the intercom as he began scrubbing.

"Doctor, we're ready for you."

28

Now comes the hard part . . .

Gray prepared his team in the seconds before the elevator doors opened. He expected another layer of security beyond a fingerprint-coded elevator key. The Guild was much too paranoid. Anyone could hold a member of their staff at gunpoint and force their way down here.

Or cut off a finger.

No, there had to be a second level of defense. But Gray's team didn't have the luxury of planning, which meant only one thing.

No time for subtlety.

Only one man fit that job description.

And Kowalski wasn't happy about it. "Why the hell did I grab that bastard's beret?"

"You'll do fine," Gray said.

Besides the beret, Kowalski also matched the height and bulk of the Somali leader. It wasn't much, but they only needed the ruse to continue for a few seconds. He had to trust that the guards down here were as confident in their safety on the island as the Somalis had been earlier. He didn't expect to catch the enemy napping or with their pants down, but he could hope for some momentary carelessness.

Gray pointed to Tucker. "You and Kane take point as soon as we're through. You don't wait. You track Amanda. We'll be on your heels as soon as possible."

Tucker rose from preparing his partner and nodded.

Seichan had her SIG Sauer in her hand.

A chime sounded as the elevator settled to a stop with a small shudder of its cage. Gray waved everyone to the side as the doors rolled open, keeping their faces shadowed by their stolen helmets.

Except for Kowalski.

The big guy was out of the elevator before it finished opening. With the beret pulled low over his eyes, he stalked ahead as if he owned the place.

In a single sweep, Gray took in the view beyond the doors. A small security lobby sealed access to the rest of the facility. The floor and walls were bare concrete; gone was the opulence of above. The ceiling was raw steel in a honeycomb pattern. A single metal door opened off the space. Next to it rose a bulletproof window, like those found at a bank, only the teller here wore a black uniform and carried a rifle over his shoulder.

The guard didn't look up. He leaned to a microphone. "Present identification and place your palm on the reader."

A panel glowed atop a narrow counter. A small drawer was shoved through the window and popped open, awaiting papers.

Kowalski reached and dropped a fistful of marble-size pellets into the tray. Curious, the guard finally looked up. With the heel of his hand, Kowalski slammed the drawer back to the other side.

He pressed a transceiver in his other fist.

The C-4 pellets—normally used for blowing deadbolts and locks—exploded in the guard's face and chest. His body went flying back, a smoking ruin.

Kowalski was already in motion, spinning to the side and slapping a square of C-4 against the steel door.

"Fire in the hole!" he bellowed.

Kowalski dove back into the elevator, ducking with the others to the side. The explosion rocked the cage, deafened their covered ears.

Gray rolled out into the smoke, inspecting the damage. The remains of the door glowed a fiery red through the pall. Spatters of molten steel splashed the walls and floor. The air stung with a chemical signature.

That wasn't just C-4.

He glanced at Kowalski, who shrugged.

"My own recipe. Added polymer-coated thermate-TH4 to the C-4."

Gray inwardly cringed. Thermate was the primary ingredient in incendiary grenades, used for cutting through tank armor. But overkill or not, Kowalski had gotten the job done—and Gray hadn't asked for subtlety.

Nothing moved beyond the doorway. He spotted bodies back there, but to be certain the way was clear, Gray tossed two flash-bang grenades into the outer hall. Everyone looked away and covered their ears. The flash-bangs erupted—then Gray gave Tucker his signal.

Dog and handler burst across the room, avoiding the molten pools of steel on the floor. Gray and the others followed, weapons ready.

Then the sky began to fall.

Hexagonal pieces of the roof rained down from above, clattering to the floor. Gray thought they were just ceiling tiles shaken loose by the blast.

Then those tiles sprouted *legs*—steel, articulated, razor-sharp appendages—and came swarming at them like a horde of metal spiders.

3:34 A.M.

"Doctor . . . ?" Petra stood frozen by the tray of instruments. She had been prepping the neuro-endoscope when the first thunderous blast sounded.

Then an even louder detonation rocked through the facility, rattling everything in the room, including Edward's nerves. His first thought was that the concrete walls of the pillar had given way. That worry always lurked in the back of his mind.

Immobilized by terror, Edward remained at his workstation, fully gowned and masked. He had been manipulating and aligning the micro-robotic arm and its fine cranial drill, getting ready to start.

Additional smaller explosions continued.

"We're under attack," Petra said, looking to him for guidance.

Her words finally shattered through his shock. They had to get out of here—but not empty-handed, not without their hard-earned prize. If they survived without the newborn in their possession, the backlash would be deadly.

"The child," he said, locking eyes with Petra. "We still need him alive for now. Grab him. We'll make for an evacuation station."

She dropped the endoscope, turned toward the door, then back again. "What about the patient?" Her eyes flicked in the direction of Amanda.

"Not important." The voice on the phone had all but admitted it. The young woman could be replaced—but not the child. "We have all of her tissue and blood samples. That should be enough. I'll grab those. You see to the child."

Still, Edward hated to leave matters unsettled. He picked up a scalpel, stared at his hand, then placed the instrument gently back down. He couldn't muster the strength to do it himself, not by his own hand.

He turned back to the workstation and activated the laser-aligned trajectory preset into the machine. The robotic arm began its slow descent, the drill whining into a fierce whirr. The burr's path into the cerebral cortex was already plotted—only now no one would be here to *stop* it as it penetrated deeper and deeper.

Like a slow bullet through the skull.

This is better, he consoled himself. *She won't feel a thing.*

With everything in order, Edward abandoned his workstation and rushed for the door. A final glance behind him showed the tip of the drill burr piercing the small blue X marked on Amanda's skull. A drop of blood welled and rolled down her scalp, like a crimson tear.

Good-bye, Amanda.

3:40 A.M.

Gray fled through a hellish landscape of black smoke and fiery molten metal, made even worse by the horde of metallic hunters, scrabbling toward him, racing atop legs as sharp as daggers.

Kowalski crushed one of the hunters under his boot. The legs splayed out like a squashed spider—then reversed themselves, swinging up and latching onto Kowalski's boot. The legs began sawing through the leather.

Seichan went to his aid, cutting free his bootlaces in a single thrust of her throwing dagger. She pointed to the wall.

Kowalski kicked his leg, sending his footwear and the clinging spider flying.

Gray held others off with his pistol, knocking them back with each shot. Together, they retreated through the molten remains of the door, creating a fiery choke point against the hunters.

Kowalski tried to bring his rifle to bear, hopping on one bloody foot, but Gray pointed down the hall. "Go after Tucker. We'll hold them off here."

Kowalski didn't have to be told twice, mumbling, "Hate friggin' spiders . . ."

Seichan popped off a couple of shots with her SIG Sauer. "Must be some sort of automated defense system."

He agreed. He had expected the base to have built-in countermeasures—but never this. He knew DARPA was working on research projects along these lines, an experimental program to develop *robotic swarms,* for co-ordinated attack, surveillance, and defensive systems. He'd seen footage from a university in England where they'd successfully developed such a swarm. And it wasn't just small robots. He'd witnessed the completion of a cheetah-size robot in a DARPA lab that could run faster than a human.

Likely the countermeasures here at the base were meant to hunt, distract, and stall the enemy until a security team could mobilize. Still, the automatons by themselves were deadly enough, and bullets hardly slowed them down.

"Here they come," Seichan warned.

A wave of razor-edged steel came crashing toward them.

3:44 A.M.

Tucker tore down the hallway, chasing after Kane's tail. He strained for the sound of any threat, eyes unblinking, breath shallow. But he didn't have to rely on his senses alone.

A growl reached his ears, a warning.

A man in a white lab coat stepped into the hallway ahead, raising an arm.

Tucker shot him in the face.

As he rushed past the man, he saw his hands were empty. A twinge of guilt flickered—but it quickly died. The two other people he'd already shot *had* been holding weapons. He couldn't take the chance.

Besides, after all he'd seen in the past minute, no one down here deserved to take another breath. He'd passed lab after lab, saw things he wished he could *un*-see. A chill remained at the base of his spine, picturing the disembodied head hanging from a rack above a beating heart.

Who the hell does something like that?

And why?

Kane continued his headlong rush, his nose sniffing at corners or in the air. He had found Amanda's scent.

Finally, Kane skidded to a stop, sliding a couple of feet, then returning to a closed door. Tucker met his partner there. A tiny window revealed a long washbasin, a wall of sterilized green packs, and packets of cellophane-sealed scrub brushes.

A surgical prep room.

Amanda's trail led here.

That earlier chill spread up his spine.

Holding his pistol at the ready, he shouldered through the door and scanned the space for any hostiles. Empty. But a wide window looked into a neighboring surgical suite. A woman lay sprawled and draped atop a stainless-steel table, her upper body locked into some device. A robotic arm vibrated above her shaved head.

Amanda . . .

He had studied the photo of the president's daughter well enough to recognize her from her features alone. Kane pawed at the door into the operating theater. He knew the truth, too.

Tucker hurried into the surgical room, finding the place otherwise deserted. A whirring buzz drew his attention back to Amanda. He stepped to her side, aghast as he recognized the source of the noise.

Blood flowed in a thick rivulet from a drill bit burrowing into her skull. He dashed around the table, unsure what to do. Kane danced at his side, reading his anxiety but not knowing how to help.

"It's okay, buddy," he assured his friend.

But it was *far* from okay.

Tucker followed the electrical cord from the robotic arm to a workstation. Not knowing what else to do, he yanked out the wall plug. The whining drone died away.

Tucker studied Amanda, watching her chest rise and fall.

At least she's still alive.

He studied the length of steel still embedded in her head. He had to free her, but how? He dared not yank that drill free or risk more damage to her skull.

He searched around and saw what looked like a miniature set of bolt cutters—surgical pin cutters. He grabbed them up, positioned them along the shaft of the burr, about an inch from Amanda's skull, and pinched the cutters closed. A loud snap, and she was free of the robotic arm.

Next, Tucker set about detaching her from the cushioned head clamp and unhooking her from the anesthetic machine.

Focused on the task, he was startled to hear a voice ask, "What's that sticking out of her head?"

He swung around. Kowalski limped toward him on a bloody foot.

"How did you find me?" Tucker asked.

"Followed the trail of dead bodies. Then saw him in the hall."

Kane panted at the doorway, guarding Tucker's back, as usual, making sure no hostiles crept up on him.

Kowalski again pointed to Amanda's skull. "What is that?"

"A drill bit."

"What? Why—?"

"How the hell do I know? Just help me."

"I got her." Kowalski stepped over and scooped Amanda into his arms as if she weighed no more than a scarecrow.

And maybe that's all she is—a scarecrow with no brain.

Either way, she needed help.

"Where are Gray and Seichan?" Tucker asked, collecting his dog.

Kowalski headed toward the door with Amanda. "Trust me, you're better off not knowing."

3:46 A.M.

Seichan and Gray retreated farther down the hall, away from the silvery horde as it crashed against the fiery, melted doorway. A brush against the molten metal incinerated several of the automatons. Those that made it past then did a strange thing: they circled and returned to the doorway, ignoring Gray and Seichan.

For the moment, the horde remained clustered at the doorway, scrabbling over the red-hot metal, attacking it, burning themselves, even melting into the molten remains of the door.

"It's the heat," Seichan said. "That's what draws them. They must be programmed to hunt body heat."

And, it seemed, any hot source would do. Beyond the doorway, Gray watched several of them rushing to the molten patches of steel on the floor, destroying themselves.

But as the steel began to cool, the occasional automaton tried to skitter their way. A few well-placed rounds discouraged such trespassing.

Seichan glanced back. "Should we start looking—"

The entire world shook with a sonic boom, strong enough to knock Gray to one knee. After that thunderous eruption, a strong vibration persisted, humming strongly enough to make his back molars ache. A change in air pressure made his ears pop.

Seichan shared a glance with Gray.

The fear in her eyes matched his own.

A few inches of water suddenly flowed into the hallway, as if from a burst pipe. Gray pictured the pylon that hid this base.

It was really just one monstrous *pipe.*

More icy water began surging, swirling.

Kowalski appeared around a corner of the hall, splashing toward them, holding an unconscious woman in his arms. Her head lolled toward Gray as Kowalski shifted her higher in his arms. Despite the lack of hair, he immediately recognized her.

Amanda . . . she's alive!

But they didn't have time to celebrate.

"What's happening?" Kowalski hollered.

Tucker and Kane followed him, both looking equally concerned.

Seichan bent down, dipped a finger, and tasted it. "Salty."

That left no doubt.

"They've busted their own pipe," Gray said and pointed to the elevator. "Place is flooding. Out! Now!"

3:55 A.M.

We often give our enemies the means to our own destruction.

Edward remembered that quote from Aesop, learned back in his Eton College days when he was a young boy. Though taken out of context now, it still felt apt as he watched the annihilation from the window of the small evacuation boat.

The air-lock-sealed boats were positioned like blisters along the circumference of the center pylon. Tracks ran up the outside of the column and across the underside of the support platform, traveling out along the five arms of the star—until they were jettisoned free of the island.

Patrols already awaited the evacuees' arrival.

Especially the precious cargo Edward held in his lap.

The newborn, swaddled warmly and mewling softly, held so much promise: both for those Edward served and himself. The child was insurance that he would be saved from a watery grave. He had placed a frantic call upon securing the child, reporting the attack.

But word had already reached the source of that cold, computerized voice. MATTERS ARE BEING TAKEN CARE OF. ENSURE THE CHILD IS SAFE.

He intended to do just that.

He stared out the window. The boat could hold ten people, but he and Petra had the vessel to themselves.

Beyond the boat, the world was as dark as the deepest cavern. He had watched the flashes of blue lightning along the length of the central pylon as they made their escape, the explosive charges shattering the steel inside the concrete walls, weakening the entire structure. The immense mass of the tower above would continue that destruction, pulverizing and crushing all beneath it.

And it wasn't just this one pylon.

Out in the darkness, blue lightning bloomed and burst across the forest of stone out there, corrupting the entire understory of the island. Thunder echoed and shook their boat. For a moment, the world beyond appeared like an electric forest in the night, wondrous to behold, breathtaking in its devastation.

He remembered another proverb as he stared, pining for the simpler times of his youth.

All good things must come to an end.

3:56 A.M.

"Run!" Gray yelled and pointed to the elevator.

Together, the team slogged through calf-deep icy water.

Kowalski hauled Amanda, high-stepping his way, wary of any straggling steel spiders in the lobby. But the last of the automatons had succumbed to the icy flood.

They made it to the elevators, which still had power—but for how long? Gray hit the call button to open the doors.

Another violent quake shook the facility, accompanied by a muffled *boom* as something gave way. A surge of water rolled down the hallway, funneling toward them, building power.

The doors opened, too slowly.

The wave of water hit them, driving them into the cage. They were waist-deep in seconds. The cold cut to the bone. Already shivering, Seichan hurried and pressed the lobby button. Gray held his breath. They all stared up, silently praying the motors still had power.

He pictured the turbines he'd seen above—the key word being *above.* The main power generators should still be high and dry.

This proved to be the case, as the elevator began to rise. The water level steadily drained as the cage lifted out of the rising flood. They all let out a loud sigh of relief.

A soft groan rose from Amanda as the effects of the anesthetic began to wear off. A promising sign, despite the piece of surgical drill still lodged in her skull. Once safe, they could attempt—

A mighty shake threw them all to one side of the cage.

Again, Gray's ears popped.

A low rumble rose beneath them, growing louder, sounding like a freight train hurling straight at them. He pictured a column of water chasing up the elevator shaft as the pylon's caisson finally imploded beneath them.

"We're passing the service levels," Seichan said, reaching a hand to his forearm, squeezing all her hope into that rock-hard grip.

Almost there.

They should be safe once the elevator climbed above sea level and reached the dry lobby above.

Then the lights went out.

Their ascent came to a shaky stop.

Kowalski swore brightly in the darkness.

"The generators," Seichan whispered.

The floodwaters must have swamped that level—and continued to rise. The roar of the freight train grew to a howl beneath them.

"Hold on!" Gray shouted.

A force struck the underside of the carriage, driving the cage up the shaft in a bone-jarring, rattling ascent.

At least they were headed in the right direction—but for how long?

"Tucker, help me get the doors open!"

Gray knew they would have only one chance. Once the powerful surge receded, the cage would go crashing back down with it.

With urgency firing their efforts, the two forced the elevator open. The walls of the shaft blurred past them—then the outer-lobby doors sprang into view. The cage settled to a bobbling, shaking stop there, balanced on the tip of a powerful fountain.

But only for a moment.

Water flooded into the open cage, swamping the space and causing it to slowly sink.

"Hurry!"

Gray and Tucker hauled on the outer-lobby doors, cracking them wide enough for the others to evacuate. Seichan helped Kowalski with Amanda's limp form. All the while, the cage continued to flood and submerge deeper.

Tucker used a free arm to push Kane through the shrinking doorway— then nodded to Gray. They were both chest-deep in water. Only half the cage was still at the lobby level.

"Go!" Tucker said.

"Together," Gray argued.

They didn't have the luxury of counting to three—both simply dove through the opening, their feet pulling free of the cage just as it sank away down the shaft behind them.

Gray helped Tucker stand.

They sloshed a few steps, relieved to be alive.

Seichan crouched by Kowalski, examining Amanda, checking her condition. When she stood, she wore a worried look.

"What?" Gray asked.

"She's had her baby."

Tucker splashed closer. "But her belly's still big."

"Was bigger, I guess." Kowalski carried her to the steps to get her out of the water.

"She's early," Seichan said. "Either stress caused her to deliver prematurely or they induced her to get the baby."

Tucker stared toward the flooded elevator, his face crushed with guilt. "I didn't know. If I had, I could've searched longer. Tried to find the baby."

Gray placed a hand on his shoulder. "We barely made it out as it was. If you'd delayed even another minute, Amanda could have died. We all could have died. And there's no saying the baby was born alive. Or maybe he was already evacuated out."

Tucker looked little comforted by this logic, and stared at the door. His dog came up and nudged his hand with his nose. Tucker rubbed the side of Kane's face, finding solace there instead of words.

Gray turned away, splashing across—*splashing*?

He stared down at his feet, still ankle-deep in water. "Why is it still flooded up here?"

"It's not just here," Seichan said from a few yards away. She pointed across the lobby to the glass entrance of the Burj Abaadi.

Gray stared out, shocked.

The starlit park beyond the tower was flooded. Black waves washed through the trees and crashed against the steps of the tower.

He understood immediately. The Guild never took half-measures when it came to covering their tracks. They hadn't just shattered the *one* support pylon as a fail-safe.

They had shattered *all* of them.

He knew what that meant, a dreadful and frightening truth.

The whole island is sinking.

29

They'd been on the road for an hour, heading west out of Charleston. Kat noted a sign that read ORANGEBURG. Her captors—the head of the fertility clinic, Dr. Paul Cranston, and his three men—kept mostly to the back roads, racing at speeds too fast for the rural areas.

Cranston spent most of the trip on his cell phone. Kat eavesdropped, but she learned little from his end of the conversations. Plainly he and the others still didn't know what had happened at the clinic, didn't know the true source of that fiery destruction sat in the backseat of their Ford Explorer.

Kat wasn't about to fill him in, but from the glance over his shoulder, Cranston clearly suspected the cause. But apparently any questions would wait until they reached their destination.

She gleaned that last bit of intelligence from a phone conversation moments later. Cranston sat straighter for that call, the perpetual edge of disdain in his voice gone, his tone turned subservient, frightened.

We'll bring them both straightaway.

Whoever lurked at the other end of the line left the man shaking and ashen. Cranston sat for several long minutes, cell phone on his lap, not moving, staring dully out the window at the passing cotton and tobacco fields.

Eventually, he snapped out of it and made one last call.

To his wife.

I'm fine, sweetheart. I wasn't even at the clinic when the fire broke out.
Maybe a gas leak. I know, I know . . . but I have a slew of other fires still to
put out. Give Michael a kiss for me. Tell him I'll be back in a couple of days
for the parade and fireworks on the Fourth. What's that? Yeah, sorry, I'm . . .
losing signal. I didn't hear what you . . . oh never mind.

He finally surrendered, as reception died out in the backcountry.

As Kat listened, she found it hard to couple this devoted family man
to the horrors hidden beneath that research facility.

Still, the conversation awakened pangs of longing for her own family. Monk should be getting the babies ready for bed about now, tucking
Penny into her footy pajamas, Harriet into her crib with a mobile of bears
hanging above it. She thought of Monk sliding his arm around her waist
after they both settled down, pulling her close, content to be surrounded
by his girls.

As if sensing her thoughts, Lisa squeezed her hand.

Kat appreciated the gesture, but she intended to *return* to Monk's
arms—which meant getting free first.

The opportunity to accomplish that grew shorter with every passing
mile. Once they reached their destination—*the Lodge*—she suspected escape would be impossible. Still, she had to be patient. She needed the right
moment, the right opportunity.

At last, she got it.

The SUV turned onto a long, lonely stretch of rural road, not a car
in sight. The summer sun sat low on the horizon, creating deep pools of
shadows under the heavy-limbed oaks that lined the road.

She gave Lisa's hand an extra-hard squeeze, preparing her. "I have to
go to the bathroom," Kat declared loudly.

Cranston dismissed her. "You'll wait."

"I won't. I'm going now—either outside or back here."

Cranston twisted in his seat, eyeing her, judging her determination.
She didn't break eye contact. His gaze flicked to the lonely road around
them, then he sighed.

"Fine. Stop the car." His next words were for one of the guards. "She
runs . . . you shoot her."

The Ford pulled to the shoulder of the road.

Kat gave Lisa's hand a small tug, trying to get her to understand.

Lisa tightened her fingers. "I should go, too . . . if we're stopping anyway."

Good girl.

"You'll take turns," Cranston said. "I'm not taking any chances."

They piled out of the backseat on the driver's side, leaving the two men up front. One gunman kept a grip on Lisa's upper arm, resting a palm on his holstered pistol.

Kat hiked off to the shadows beneath an oak.

"That's far enough!" Cranston yelled out the open window.

Her guard had his pistol out, emphasizing the order.

She squatted in the weeds and slipped her shorts down. After all of the drugs in her system, her bladder had been begging for relief. The guard watched. She stared right back at him, challenging him. Once finished, she stood back up and headed toward the roadside.

The guard kept his pistol pointed, maintaining his distance.

The other gunman pushed Lisa toward the field. "Your turn. Be quick about it."

That was all Kat needed.

She swung her arm, sharply flicking out her wrist. The hidden baton extended to its full length. She might be out of range of the guard—but the baton wasn't.

Back on the streets of Charleston, Kat had taken the weapon from Amy after hiding her body behind the recycling bin. She had concealed the collapsed length of the baton in the small of her back, tucked into the waistband of her shorts—then tossed her pistol out, appearing unarmed.

She had wanted Lisa a safe distance away from her captors before acting, to wait for their guard to lower.

Like now.

Kat cracked the baton's hard length across the guard's wrist, breaking bone. The pistol tumbled from his fingertips.

Already diving forward, Kat caught the weapon before it hit the pavement. She landed on her shoulder and rolled, already firing. She blasted the guard in the knee, twisted to shoot the other gunman in the head, then back to her guard, finishing him off with a round through his throat.

Kat lunged to the car. Her attack had been so sudden, so savage, the driver barely had time to react. She shoved her gun through the open window and fired point-blank into the side of his head. Skull fragments and blood splattered across the front seat, striking Cranston across chest and face.

The doctor sat stunned, one hand held up, palm open. The other clutched an open cell phone.

Sorry, bastard, no signal.

Kat wasn't taking any chances with him. The good doctor had answers Sigma needed. She intended to deliver him to Painter, all trussed up and tied with a bow.

"It's *our* turn to drive."

8:12 P.M.

Lisa guided the Ford Explorer down the country road, trying her best to ignore the gore still staining the seat. As a medical doctor, she seldom found herself squeamish, but the raw brutality of Kat's attack still shook her. Prior to today, she had known Kat mainly as a mother or a strategist working alongside Painter. She'd never witnessed Kat's skill in the field, her pure animal cunning and savagery.

Though that trait had won them their freedom, it still unnerved her.

That, and the cold blood seeping through the seat of her dress.

After the roadside attack, Kat had forced Cranston to haul the bodies into a ditch, to hide them from direct sight of the road, though it looked rarely traveled.

Which was turning out to be a problem.

"Any signal yet?" Lisa asked.

"No," Kat answered from the backseat.

Her friend crouched behind Cranston, a pistol in one hand, the doctor's cell phone in the other. Cranston still sat in the front passenger seat, his wrists zip-tied to the headrest behind him. An awkward stress position, but Kat ignored his protests.

Beyond that cold professionalism, Lisa recognized a glimmer of hatred in Kat's eyes. While not getting the full story concerning what had happened at the North Charleston Fertility Clinic, Lisa understood enough to know whom to blame.

Cranston was a monster hiding behind a handsome face.

And one with great ambitions.

"There should be a signal by now," Kat said. "But I'm still not getting any reception."

After commandeering the vehicle, Kat had ordered Lisa to turn the SUV around and backtrack along their path. She wanted to reach a phone or get close enough to a cell tower to regain reception.

"Some farmhouses off to the right," Lisa offered. "We can turn in and ask for help."

"They might alert the local authorities. I don't know who to trust out here."

Lisa remembered Painter expressing the same concern. The Gants owned much of South Carolina. Who knew how far that reach extended into local law enforcement?

"Look." Lisa pointed ahead. "There's a sign for a turnoff to Orangeburg. Surely that town must get cell signal."

"Head that way," Kat agreed, but she kept searching around the vehicle, with a suspicious look.

Lisa made that turn and traveled a half-mile. Off in the distance, the steeple of a church poked above the tree line. That had to be the town of Orangeburg.

Too focused on the horizon, Lisa glided through an intersection with a flashing red light. A small drawbridge crossed a hidden river. A warning gate began to drop across its entrance.

She pulled to a stop in front of it.

As she waited for the drawbridge to open, Lisa asked, "Anything now?"

"Nothing."

In the rearview mirror, Kat's eyes fixed at the back of Cranston's head. He'd been unusually quiet for the past five minutes, no further complaints about his wrists.

A low rumble announced the raising of the bridge—but then got louder and louder—becoming more like a thumping.

Lisa frowned, concerned about the worn mechanics of the old bridge.

Kat's reaction was rougher. She jerked upright and threw her cell phone out the window. She clutched Lisa's shoulder at the same time.

"Get us out of here! Now!"

The warning came too late.

A sleek military-gray helicopter burst out of hiding from the riverbed to the left. It lofted high over the bridge.

Lisa yanked the car into reverse and jammed the gas. She raced backward to the intersection, fishtailed the car a full 180, and was ready to speed off—but the helicopter was faster. The chopper cut them off, plunging out of the sky to block the road.

Lisa braked, avoiding a collision with the whirling blades.

Rotor wash beat at the Ford's windshield.

A bullhorn roared. "Throw your weapons clear of the vehicle! Exit with your hands up!"

To make sure the order was understood, a small gun mounted on the chopper's underside chattered, and a spate of rounds blasted into the pavement in front of the SUV.

Lisa turned to Kat.

She shook her head. "Do what they say."

Into that stunned silence, Cranston smiled. "Ladies, you're not the only ones allowed surprises." He awkwardly swiveled around. "Back there, I disabled my phone's cellular receiver and activated an emergency satellite beacon built into the phone."

Turning it into a tracking device, Lisa realized. *No wonder Kat jettisoned the phone.*

Cranston frowned. "Though I have to say the emergency response was faster than I expected. Apparently, my employers truly don't want you to escape. But why? Who the hell are you?"

Kat raised the pistol to his ear. "You'll never know." His eyes got huge as the pistol exploded, shattering away half his face.

Lisa cringed from the sudden brutality, her ears ringing as Kat tossed the weapon through the window. Still, Lisa heard the fierce whisper that followed.

"That was for Amy."

8:15 P.M.
Washington, DC

Painter sat in Kat's chair, rubbing his eyes. The faint smell of jasmine that hung in the air was no longer evident. Maybe it had faded away with everyone bustling in and out of the office, or maybe he'd just become desensitized to the scent. Either way, he felt a nagging sense of loss, a foreboding.

You're just exhausted, he tried to convince himself.

Jason and Linus continued their work, searching for any other sightings of the Ford. Painter had played that grainy footage over and over again, watching the shadowy shape shift frame by frame, knowing it was Lisa.

He was relieved to find her still alive, but the longer that silence stretched, with no further word on Kat and Lisa's true fate, the deeper that icy knife twisted in his gut.

He forced his eyes to stare once more at the map on the monitor. It displayed South Carolina, along with parts of North Carolina and Georgia. Large swaths of red stood out from the green background. The crimson areas were landholdings of the Gant family.

Painter suspected Lisa and Kat were hidden somewhere in that crimson field.

Which presented a major challenge.

The Gant family had arrived on the shores of the Carolinas a century before the founding of this country, settling in the city of Charles Town, which later became simply Charleston. Wealth and power grew rapidly, channeled through the financial support of the family's Old World connections in both France and England. As that family grew, so did its reach and influence, branching into universities, governments, military institutions, and banking circles.

And much of that wealth turned into *land*.

It was said, back at the turn of the century, that the Gants could ride horseback from one side of the state to the other—from the beaches of Charleston across the low-country counties and up to the Blue Ridge Mountains—all without ever stepping foot off their own property.

Today, the Gants could drive a herd of cattle across the state and make that same claim.

Painter rubbed his temples, overwhelmed by the wealth and power that opposed his small group. How could they hope to succeed against a force so entrenched? And if the enemy ever did learn Sigma was still investigating them in secret, what would their next response be?

He could guess the answer. In 146 B.C., Rome destroyed Carthage by sacking the place, burning the city, enslaving the survivors, and salting the very earth to make sure nothing ever grew there again.

Painter expected something worse than that.

Jason Carter appeared at his door, ever his shadow. "Director, you asked me to let you know when I finished that special project."

"You're done? Already?"

"On our computer. But I might have to demonstrate."

Painter stood from the chair and relinquished it to Kat's chief analyst. The kid hurried over and dropped into the seat. He tapped rapidly and brought up the genealogical map of the Gant clan. Painter had asked for his expert assistance at building a more detailed version, one set to his specific parameters.

From the very beginning, something had been troubling him about the Gant family tree, a nagging sense that he was missing a vital detail. He began to suspect the problem, but he didn't know what it signified, or if it meant anything at all. The only way to make sure was to construct a genealogical representation where *no* detail was left out.

He wanted the complete picture—and asked Jason to prepare it.

"Here's the lineage you originally assembled," Jason said.

With a click of the mouse, the three-dimensional schematic of the Gant family tree appeared. Progeny and familial connections formed a monumental tapestry, a weaving and warping of heredity and genealogy that spanned two centuries, back to the founding of the country.

It was hard to get reliable records much earlier than that.

But apparently not for Jason.

"Okay, director, I know what you asked for, but I took the liberty of also searching back another century—just to be thorough."

I want to clone this kid.

Painter leaned closer. "And you were still able to expand the search to the sides."

Jason nodded.

Painter had spent hours studying that chart, finally gleaning what nagged him. Certain tendrils of the chart showed familial lines that wove in and out of the main genealogical matrix, marking distant cousins marrying back into the family. For such a rich family, it wasn't unusual, a typical inbreeding of power and blood among aristocrats.

But those loose threads in the Gant family's tapestry troubled him, because there seemed to be too *many* of them, even for such a rich dynasty, a suspicious fraying of the cloth. Painter couldn't help but pick at those threads to see what they might reveal.

He asked Jason to stretch the genealogical search to the sides of the main family tree, to follow all of those loose threads. He also instructed him to look for new ones, specifically lines of the family that strayed even farther from the fold, farther than merely distant cousins, before diving and returning to the Gant bosom.

"Show me," Painter ordered.

"Be prepared. The chart is vast. No individual names will show up, just data points."

"Do it."

Jason tapped a few keys, and that original matrix Painter constructed shrunk to a size of a fist. Names dwindled away to become nodes of a network, stars in a galaxy. Around that galactic core, a hazy corona of new data points and fine lines appeared, scintillating into existence on the screen, surrounding yet incorporated into the whole.

Painter brushed his fingertips across the new spiral arms of this galaxy. "And all of these extensions mark where a strand of the family tree shot away from the others—"

"Only to eventually return again," Jason confirmed. "The average deviation was two generations, but a few of those lines broke away for five or six generations. A couple of the prodigal relatives returning to the family were seventeenth or eighteenth cousins. But return they did."

"Like moths around a lamp," Painter said. "Fluttering out, then diving back in again. Over and over again."

Jason shrugged. "I can probably confirm this is excessive, even for a prominent family like the Gants, but it'll take time to work up a comparable dynasty. Still, I'm not sure what the significance is."

Painter wasn't either—but his breathing deepened, adrenaline flowing as he balanced on the edge of a precipice.

Something . . .

His eyes remained glued to the screen as the matrix slowly spun in place. He sensed there was a pattern hidden inside that hazy cloud at the edges of the genealogical map. He just needed a key to unlock it.

What am I missing?

30

Gray slogged through the chest-deep water toward the entrance to the Burj Abaadi. The others waited by the stairs, ready to flee up to escape the rising waters.

Beyond the glass wall, the city of Utopia slowly drowned. A few buildings still shone with emergency lights, run on batteries. Otherwise, the island was dark. Black waves swept across the park, crashing against the tower steps. Dangerous debris floated everywhere: spare lumber, plastic trash buckets, even a toppled palm, still potted in its crate. The currents were equally hazardous.

Gray pictured the entire platform sinking, crushing the damaged pylons beneath its weight. In the time it took Gray to cross the lobby, the water rose another foot. They needed a way to escape the flooding tower before the island's descent became a fast plummet—or worse, the entire platform started to cant and tip, toppling buildings over like a waiter dumping a tray of tall glasses.

He didn't know if Jack Kirkland was alive, if he'd survived the pyrotechnics that blew out the understory of the platform. Gray had activated the homing beacon Jack had given him, hoping for the best, and left it with Kowalski, who still carried Amanda.

But Gray wasn't counting on *hope* alone.

He stared at his goal beyond the doors of the tower.

It stood across the park. The roof of the yellow Hummer—the one they'd hid behind earlier—was still above water for the moment, but that wasn't Gray's target. They weren't going to be *driving* off this island.

Beyond the bulk of the truck, the matching yellow jet boat bobbed. The rising waters had floated it off of its trailer. Straps still tethered it in place, but someone hadn't properly ratcheted the boat down.

Gray had a dagger strapped to his wrist, ready to cut the craft the rest of the way loose. He hoped he could get the boat started, but if nothing else, at least it floated. He would take that versus clinging to debris at the whim of the eddying currents and riptides.

Reaching the entrance, he shouldered into one of the doors. Swinging the half-submerged barrier open proved a challenge against the weight of water. But it slowly budged. He got it wide enough to slip outside.

The buffeting currents tried to rip him from his perch atop the steps that led down to the park. All that held him in place was his iron grip on the door handle.

A shout drew him around.

He stared back into the lobby.

Seichan stood with the others on the stairs. The waters continued to chase them up the spiraling steps and appeared to be rising faster now. Gray's toes could barely touch the surface of the marble floor. But it was more than the encroaching flood that concerned her.

Her arm pointed out toward the city.

"Lights!" she called. "Coming this way!"

Gray turned, hanging by his arm from the handle.

Down the wide central avenue that ran along one leg of the star, a trio of lights came racing toward the Burj Abaadi. They wove back and forth in a zigzagging search pattern.

Speedboats.

Gray doubted they were a rescue operation. *Not on this island, not with who truly ran this place.* More likely it was a contingent from the fleet that patrolled the waters around the island. Someone must have sent them to make sure there were no survivors of the assault on the hidden station.

"Stay out of sight!" Gray called to Seichan. "Keep moving if necessary!"

Acknowledging this, she waved the group farther up the spiral stairs.

With time running out, Gray eyed his bobbing target and dove into the surging waters. The currents tugged and hauled, dragging and throwing his body, but once away from the wave actions churning against the walls of the tower, the strength of the tides ebbed. He popped his head clear, sighted his target, and swam with strong kicks.

Submerged obstacles turned out to be the bigger challenge. As he headed across the park, his leg became tangled in the branches of a drowned tree, and he had to fight his way loose.

All the while, he kept an eye on the approaching boats.

He realized he would never reach the Hummer before the patrol arrived at the tower. Still, the waters were dark, and the flotsam plentiful. With care, he might not be seen bobbing amid the debris. He would wait until the patrol left before freeing the boat and rescuing his teammates.

At least that was the plan until flares streaked into the sky, rising from the speedboats, and burst above the flooded park. New stars were born up there, hovering on small chutes, blazing with crimson fire, turning night into a hellish twilight and the waters a dark ruddy hue.

Gray searched for cover before the boats got here. A long, low crate floated ten yards off, slowly spinning in an eddy, offering some shelter.

He kicked toward it, sweeping with his arms.

The whining scream of the engines grew in volume.

He reached the crate and grabbed an edge, catching his breath. He kept his eyes on the boats as they rode out of the flooded avenue and into the drowned park. The trio fanned out from there.

He hugged closer to his meager shelter.

With the enemy splitting up, he would have to be careful to ensure the bulk of the crate remained between him and the patrol at all times. He clung to the edge and kicked with his feet, dragging the box with him, careful not to move too fast, trying to maintain the illusion of another piece of flotsam.

Then a pair of boats angled toward him, splitting to either side—not with intent, just poor luck on his part. He slipped underwater and moved beneath the crate. His hands blindly sought the underside of the box, to hold himself steady until the boats passed.

But as he searched, his palms found no bottom to the crate. It was open on the underside. Reaching up, he felt a pocket of air. He rose into it and took a deep breath in the darkness. His fingers discovered soft, cushioned fabric lining the inside.

He suddenly knew where he hid.

He pictured the casket used to transport Amanda here, resting in the back of a pickup truck. It must have been washed out of the rear bed, the lid ripped off.

The waters lightened to either side as the two boats swept by with their headlamps shining.

After they passed, Gray continued his swim across the park, hidden beneath the casket. He didn't know if this mode of transportation was good luck or a bad omen. Still, he forged on, slowly floating his way toward the boat. Hopefully, the patrol would be gone once he got there.

After another half minute of silence, Gray risked ducking back outside to gauge his trajectory across the park.

As his head cleared the water, a thunderous scream jerked him around. He stared back toward the Burj Abaadi. The trio of boats faced the entrance. From the center one, a streak of smoke cut through the blood-tinged night and slammed into the multistory glass façade. The explosion of a rocket-propelled grenade shattered into the lobby. Sheets of glass fell from above like a hundred shimmering guillotines, opening a wide chasm.

A pair of the engines whined into a roar, and two of the boats swept through that gap and into the dark lobby. Once they were inside, another flare burst like a red sun.

Gray hoped the others had taken cover and that the patrol would only make a cursory pass before exiting the tower.

In the meantime, he had his own mission.

Before he could turn away, an eerie vibration shuddered through the water. The surface of the lake trembled.

With a low groan, the world began plunging down all around them. Towers sank faster, floor by floor. The last of the treetops vanished under the waves. Trapped air bubbled out everywhere, the last drowning gasp of Utopia.

Across the park, the blasted hole in the façade of the Burj Abaadi had shrunk to a lowering archway as the tower submerged. A single boat came racing through, the occupants ducking under the fangs of broken glass.

The second boat got trapped inside, circling futilely behind the glass, as the hole closed. The patrols on the outside tried to fire another rocket, but by the time they readied a shot, the entire lobby had sunk away.

Gray swung around, taking advantage of the distraction, knowing the crews would be focused on their trapped companions.

The Hummer and jet boat were gone, vanished fully underwater.

Reaching where they had sunk, he took a huge breath, kicked his legs over his head, and dove down through the fiery surface waters. Far below stretched only darkness.

Gray strained for those black depths.

4:33 A.M.

Seichan fought for more height.

Below, a rising flood chased her and the others, swallowing the spiraling stairs beneath them. But that wasn't all. A few floors down, dark shadows pounded their way up, their panicked flight lit by the shine of a few emergency bulbs. The trapped crew of the patrol boat sought the same escape they did, running for higher ground, staying ahead of the cresting water.

Seichan wanted to put three floors between her team and the water table before abandoning the stairs and trying to reach the far windows on one of these levels.

But she had another problem. She was thoroughly turned around.

With the power out, the tower levels had stopped rotating and settled into a haphazard corkscrew. Floors stuck out in all directions. On top of that, the dizzying spiral of the staircase left her disoriented. She no longer had any idea which side of the building she was supposed to meet Gray.

A gunshot echoed up from below.

She scowled at the source.

The fleeing patrol.

First, *what did the bastards think they could hit?*

And second, *fuck you very much.*

But if they wanted to play that game, she wouldn't mind eliminating a few worries.

"Kowalski! Do it!"

"Anything you say." He still lugged Amanda over one shoulder, but he reached to a pocket as he ran. He let the pellets he collected dribble between his fingers, falling away like a trail of bread crumbs onto the steps.

She watched between her toes and waited until the shadows below reached the littered section of stairs.

"Now!" she yelled.

Kowalski pressed his transceiver, igniting the last of his C-4 pellets. The blast took out the point man, and the survivors retreated from the shattered gap in the glass staircase. They were trapped with no other way up.

Sorry, fellas. You started this war.

She continued her maddening flight up the steps. After a few more turns, she heard screams rise from below.

She used their cries to judge the distance to that drowning flood. Either the waters were rising faster, or their pace was slowing. Whichever the case, they were losing this footrace.

"Next level!" she shouted to Tucker. "Take that one. Find the shortest path to the outer windows."

Reaching that floor, Seichan raced after the handler and his dog, a silent prayer on her lips. Tucker turned into a long hall.

"Over here!" he yelled. "A balcony at the end!"

"Shoot out the lock!" Seichan hollered back.

They needed every second.

She sprinted, trailed by Kowalski. To the man's credit, he kept up, even burdened by Amanda's weight. He was a veritable draft horse.

Gunshots blasted ahead.

She reached Tucker and Kane as the man hauled open the sliding glass door. A wide balcony beckoned. They all fled out onto it.

Seichan moved to the rail. The rising water churned one floor down. If they had to jump, she feared two things. If they didn't leap far enough, the undertow caused by the plunging tower would drag them all down. And even if they cleared that danger, these rough seas had sharks—and not only the ones with fins.

A patrol boat drifted to the right, not far from the park.

They would never be able to swim fast enough to escape it, and their splashes would likely draw the crew's attention.

Seichan searched the drowning city.

Where are you, Gray?

4:35 A.M.

C'mon, c'mon . . .

Running out of air, Gray blindly sawed at the nylon strap with his knife. It had taken him too long to find the boat as it hung in the dark depths, still tethered to the trailer. The positive buoyancy of the vessel had locked the tie-downs tight. There was no unclipping them from their bolts.

He'd already cut the straps at the bow. Once free, the boat's nose rose toward the surface, hanging vertical, still anchored at the stern. Keeping one hand on the transom, he worked at that rear strap of the tie-down. Pressure built in his ears as the island sank deeper, dragging him and the boat farther underwater.

As his air began to give out, he sawed frantically.

Stubborn piece of—

A light flared overhead, brightening the waters. A dark shadow idled into view on the surface, limned against the glow of its own lamps and accompanied by the slow putter of its engines.

Gray waited, despite the screaming burn in his lungs.

Once the shadow was directly overhead, Gray cut through the last of the tie-downs. Freed, the jet boat torpedoed upward, becoming a buoyancy-propelled battering ram.

4:36 A.M.

Seichan watched the speedboat drift closer, coming within fifty yards of the tower. One of the crew shouted; another pointed a rifle. Her team had been spotted. A blast echoed over the water. The round ricocheted off the balcony railing.

Seichan ducked.

She and the others were too exposed on the balcony, but where could they go? The waters roaring up the side of the tower promised only a quick death by drowning.

She took potshots back at the boat—then an antediluvian monster blasted out of the sea and rammed into the edge of the speedboat. The force cracked the hull and flipped the boat, tossing the crew out of their seats.

Nearby, the monster settled to its carbon-fiber keel, resting on the water.

It was the yellow jet boat.

Gray popped up beside it. He had his SIG Sauer in hand and fired at the floundering men, hitting three of them. The fourth already floated facedown. Nearby, the cracked hull of the speedboat flooded and sank into the depths.

"Gray!" Seichan shouted and waved an arm.

He turned to face her—just as a second speedboat flew around the tower to the left, drawn by the gunfire. It raced under the balcony, spraying machine-gun fire up at it.

They all flattened, but Seichan knew they weren't the assault's true target. The patrol was only knocking them back to pass beneath them and go after easier prey.

Move it, Gray!

4:37 A.M.

Gray hauled himself over the side of the jet boat and sprawled flat on the deck, making himself a harder target. The second speedboat came shooting around the curve of the Burj Abaadi.

Gunfire shattered the marble off the balcony façade.

His teammates ducked away—except for one.

As the boat sailed under the sinking balcony, a sleek shape vaulted into view, back paws kicking off the railing for extra distance. Kane flew across the short gap and landed in the midst of the four patrolmen.

The effect was the same as if a grenade had been tossed into the boat.

One man flung himself overboard in fright and got chewed up by the frothing riptide of the sinking tower. Kane latched onto the throat of another. The driver screamed, yanked the wheel, and, in a panic, drove the boat at full speed into an uprooted, floating palm tree.

The boat hit the thick trunk, shot into the air, and flipped upside down before crashing hard into the water.

Bodies floated up seconds later, lifeless or unconscious.

The only survivor proved his skill at dog-paddling.

Before that deadly collision, a sharp whistle from Tucker had sent Kane leaping from the boat, tail high. The dog landed safely in the calmer water, but the currents were pulling him back toward the churning tide at the base of the tower. Kane fought against it, burdened by his vest.

No, you don't.

Gray lunged into the captain's chair of the jet boat. He searched and found the key in the glove box and started the ignition. He feared the depths might have damaged the engine, but he also knew jet boats were built for such abuse. As he hoped, a choking burble, a spat of water from the stern jets, and the engine roared lustily.

He shifted the throttle and shot toward where Kane struggled.

Hang on.

Sliding next to the dog, Gray lunged out and grabbed Kane by his waterproof vest. He struggled to get the sodden, sixty-pound dog into the boat. Recognizing it would take both arms, he let go of the wheel. Unpiloted, the craft got pulled closer to the tower. The churning water growled hungrily, the undertow sucking everything down.

Finally, with a heave of his body, he hauled Kane aboard. The shepherd shook his heavy pelt, tail wagging, and bumped him affectionately.

"Thanks!" Tucker called over to Gray.

"Hey, what about us?" Kowalski complained.

By now, water flooded the lower deck of their balcony, churning hungrily. Gray's three teammates clung to the railing.

Manning the wheel again, Gray opened the throttle and gunned his way over to the balcony. He brought the boat alongside them and worked the throttle to hold the craft steady. They climbed over the balcony and dropped on board. Tucker helped Kowalski with Amanda. She stirred enough to lift an arm and swat at the bigger of the two.

Kowalski pushed her arm down. "Sheesh. That's the thanks I get for hauling your butt up ten flights of stairs."

With everyone settled, Gray swung away from the sinking tower.

The jet boat was only a four-seater. With six on board, counting Kane, the boat drafted deeper than it should, making it sluggish and slow.

But they were afloat.

The same could not be said for Utopia.

The currents shifted under the boat, dragging the craft strongly to port. Gray corrected against that pull—but it only grew worse.

What the hell?

"Pierce!" Kowalski hollered, drawing his attention away from the currents to the skies above.

He craned his neck in shock.

The tower of the Burj Abaadi leaned precariously over the boat.

Gray searched outward. Across the rest of the island, towers and spires all canted in the same direction, as if blown over by a stiff wind.

Oh, hell . . .

Seichan recognized the danger, too. "The island is tipping."

Gray jammed the throttle forward, picturing the island capsizing.

They needed to get to open water.

Off in the distance, a spire broke from its foundation. It toppled and slowly crashed into a neighboring building.

Closer at hand, a mighty moan vibrated through the waters. It was the deep groan of concrete and steel under stress. No one doubted the source.

All eyes turned to the Burj Abaadi.

4:40 A.M.

It seemed the Eternal Tower was not living up to its name.

Aboard a large patrol boat, Edward bore witness to the island's slow destruction. A quarter-mile away, Utopia upended, breaking apart, sliding back into the sea, a modern Atlantis. At its center, the Burj Abaadi toppled, the upper levels breaking and sliding off the central axis, like plates toppling from a tall stack.

Word had reached him that the patrols sent to the tower had gone missing. Attempts to raise them on the radio had failed.

It had to be the work of the group that attacked the base.

Measures would have to be taken.

But not without guidance.

Petra stepped through a nearby hatch, carrying a satellite phone in her hand. Her eyes locked with his, warning him it wasn't good news.

She held out the phone.

He lifted it to his ear and heard the computerized voice greet him. "Is the child secured?"

"Yes."

"And the mother?"

"Dead."

Surely she had to be.

"THEN COORDINATE ALL FORCES ON-SITE, ESTABLISH A NOOSE AROUND THAT ISLAND. HUNT FOR THOSE WHO ASSAULTED THE STATION."

"And if they're found?"

He was given very specific instructions, ending with, "PETRA WILL TAKE MATTERS IN HAND FROM THERE. SHE KNOWS WHAT IS NEEDED."

He swallowed hard, feeling demoted—but he dared not complain.

And in the end, maybe it was better not to know.

31

Gray raced the jet boat as the island tore itself apart around him.

The sinking platform, twisted by tidal currents and punched from below by partially intact pylons, broke into smaller sections. Suddenly unmoored and top-heavy, those pieces began to topple and capsize, dropping buildings, spires, and scaffolding all around them.

Gray tried to avoid the worst of that roiling gristmill, flying at full throttle.

Still, more towers fell. Walls tore apart with explosive retorts. Windows shattered in showering bursts.

Floating debris choked their path, growing more treacherous by the minute. Gray jigged and jagged his way through the worst of it. The boat's resilient carbon-fiber hull took care of the rest.

He needed a way out to open water, but rubble and ruin seemed to block him at every turn.

"Gray!" Seichan clutched harder to a brace.

"I see it."

Ahead, a huge cross-section of a spire under construction—nothing more than a frame of iron—broke loose, hit a condominium tower, then rolled in their direction. Like some coin in a pachinko machine, it bounced and crashed toward them.

Kowalski swore coarsely.

A sentiment shared by all.

There was no way past it, and Gray had only seconds to act.

He sought the only cover available—but it would be tight.

"Everyone duck!"

He swung the jet boat to the right, spun the craft 180 degrees, and slammed it sideways under the protruding upper-story balcony of a sunken building. The tumbling monstrosity of iron clattered over them—then bounced away.

"Nice job parallel-parking," Kowalski commented.

With a blast of the jets, Gray blew the boat back out of the shelter.

He turned, dug in, and sped for the distant glimmer of open water.

But even that path was closing.

Ahead, two residential towers leaned drunkenly against each other. The one to the right crumbled against its partner, dropping slowly, raining broken glass and debris.

"Go for it," Seichan said.

Gray had no choice. He gunned the engine, firing the jets behind him into a roar. The boat blasted away like a rocket, striving to duck under that lowering guillotine of steel, concrete, and glass.

Kowalski curled over Amanda, whom he cradled on his lap. "I can't watch."

Seichan reached over and gripped Gray's forearm.

Tucker braced his legs against the back of the captain's seat.

Only one crew member had a different assessment.

Kane came forward, tucked under Seichan's arm, and jumped up to bring his nose into the wind. His tail wagged fiercely, striking Gray in the shoulder.

With that bit of encouragement, Gray tightened his fingers on the wheel. The jet boat screamed across the last of the water, skimming along the surface at over sixty miles an hour.

Ahead, the building fell faster, the path below it pinching closed.

But Gray was already committed.

"Down!" he yelled.

Seichan's fingers dug hard as she ducked, keeping Kane pinned under her arm.

The jet boat reached the gap and shot under the toppling tower, shattering through a rain of falling glass. For several seconds, the world filled with the scream of tortured steel and the thundering grind of concrete.

It felt like a derailed freight train tumbled past overhead.

Then they burst clear—

—as the tower crashed into the sea behind them, casting up a huge wave that shoved them, along with a flotilla of debris, farther out into the dark waters.

But those waters weren't entirely *dark.*

A cordon of lights blocked the seas three hundred yards out, including a yacht-sized cutter.

The island's security fleet had set up a blockade.

Gray slowed their flight.

"Maybe they didn't see us," Seichan said.

Gray glanced doubtfully back. As he turned his attention forward, his fears were confirmed.

A trio of those lights broke away, coming toward them.

He spun the jet boat and raced in the opposite direction. More lights hovered out there, too, other vessels in the blockade. But that wasn't his goal. Once he gained some distance, he swung behind a floating pallet of construction lumber.

"Don't think hiding here is going to work," Kowalski said.

Gray stood and pointed overboard. "Everybody out."

Seichan grabbed his arm. "What are you thinking? We can outrun them."

"Not weighted down like this," Gray said, speaking fast. He pointed to the fuel gauge. "Almost out of fuel. Don't have enough to make it to the mainland."

"Then what are you going—?" Seichan looked harder at him. "You're going to lead them off."

"It's the best chance for Amanda. I dump you here, run off, and get them to chase me for as long as possible." He pointed to Kowalski. "You've got Jack Kirkland's homing device. Maybe he survived and can reach you. If not—"

Kowalski eyed the stack of lumber. "I'll build a boat."

"Do your best," he said.

The others quickly shed boots and outerwear. Tucker stripped the vest off of Kane, so his partner was not weighted down.

They left Amanda in her hospital gown. She had begun to shake off the anesthesia, but she remained in a dull haze. Gray feared she was edging toward shock. He hated to leave her floating in the sea, but what other recourse did he have?

He helped Tucker and Kowalski get her overboard. At least the surface waters were temperate, as compared with down deep.

"Keep her head elevated," Gray warned.

Kane splashed in next to them.

He turned to Seichan. She remained fully clothed, with her arms crossed.

"You're not coming with me," he said, guessing her intent.

"I am."

"We're not *both* going to sacrifice ourselves."

She frowned and looked him over as if he were crazy. "Who said anything about sacrificing myself? You want a distraction, something to keep those boats from poking their noses over here." She pointed beyond the lumber pile. "See that big boat? That patrol cutter?"

"Yeah."

"Time to turn the tables." She lifted an eyebrow. "It's high time *we* played pirate."

4:58 A.M.

Tucker could no longer hear the whine of the jet boat. He had watched the initial chase, saw them tear off to the side, leading the trio in a wild pursuit, running along the edge of the blockade.

He hoped their plan worked, but he had his own mission to address: to keep Amanda safe. After pulling her off that surgical table, he felt extra responsible for her—especially as he'd abandoned her newborn in the rush to escape.

I should have been more thorough in examining her.

But there was nothing to be done to correct that mistake, except keep Amanda protected.

To that end, he swam out toward where a plastic trash barrel floated on its side. He grabbed the handle. The plan was to build a nest around their hiding spot, to do their best to camouflage themselves amid the debris field.

Off to the east, the skies were already growing pale with the coming sunrise. He wanted better cover before then.

He didn't expect they would have to remain in hiding for long. Maybe two hours. A disaster of this scope—the sinking of an entire island—would draw a global media circus: scores of television helicopters, curiosity seekers, and news reporters. Only then would it be safe to move Amanda out of hiding and search for a rescue, something to be caught on film.

That exposure should keep Amanda safe.

Such a story would attract a large audience.

Nothing like blood in the water to draw attention.

As he turned and dragged the barrel, a fin rose out of the water ahead of him. Then another. And another.

He forgot that blood drew more than just *attention.*

He pictured the hammerheads he'd seen earlier.

Something bumped his leg.

He let go of the barrel and yanked out his dagger. He'd left his pistol tucked in the stack of lumber.

He searched, twisting all around, but the waters were pitch-dark. Even the fins had vanished.

Then something touched his ankle. He kicked, striking something hard. It rose up under him, shoving him high. Seconds later, black water sluiced off the glass deck of the *Ghost.*

The hatch popped open, and Jack Kirkland poked his head out. He eyed the dagger still in Tucker's fist. "You planning on attacking my boat with that knife? After all I went through to save your sorry asses?"

Tucker sheathed his blade, wanting to hug the man.

"You try swimming through a crumbling forest of concrete with an island falling on top of your head." Jack wore a huge smile. "Was the time of my life! Now let's see about getting you all on board."

By the time that was accomplished, Jack had turned more somber. Especially seeing Amanda's condition. She was shivering, blue-lipped, and pale, on the edge of shock.

Kowalski wrapped a dry blanket around her, from the stores aboard the *Ghost*. He was surprisingly gentle for such a lumbering fellow. But a blanket was far from enough.

"She needs immediate medical help," Tucker said as he settled her into one of the seats.

Kane sat next to him, leaning against his knee.

"I know where she can get it," Jack said. "Close by. I've got a state-of-the-art facility aboard the *Deep Fathom*. We can be steaming out of these waters within the hour and get her somewhere safe."

Tucker sank into his seat, grateful and relieved.

Jack lowered the *Ghost* back under the water and piloted them away. "What the hell did they do to her?"

"I don't know," Tucker said numbly.

And I hope I never do.

"What about your other friends?"

Tucker looked up through the glass roof and admitted the same.

"I don't know."

5:01 A.M.

"We're on fumes," Gray shouted.

At least, I hope I have even that.

Seichan sat next to him with her two SIGs on her lap. She glanced over at him. A glimmer of fear shone in her eyes—she wasn't stupid—but it seemed only to ignite the larger excitement found there. She smiled, her hair whipped by the wind, the collar of her blouse snapping, showing the length of her neck.

"Let's do this."

Ever a woman of few words.

He grinned back, which only made her smile deepen—still hard-edged and purposeful, but now shining with something darker and softer, something he wanted to explore.

When they had the time.

He spun the jet boat back toward the blockade. They'd given the trio of pursuers a wild ride, weaving in and out of the line. The carbon-fiber hull had a few new holes in it, but Seichan had shot the same number of men.

She had proved her marksmanship had not dulled since he first met her. Of course, back then she'd been an assassin for the Guild, shooting at *him*.

Gray aimed their jet boat for the larger patrol cutter, a hundred-footer, plainly the command center for the fleet. He was confident that no eyes were looking toward where he'd hidden the others. He had planned on coming out here alone, expected to be captured, maybe killed.

And that hadn't changed.

Only Seichan had offered another plan—to gain something from their sacrifice. This entire mission had started from an act of piracy; perhaps another act of piracy could end it.

Half of piracy involved bloodshed and destruction.

From the sinking of the island, from the trail of bodies, they'd already accomplished that well enough.

The other half of piracy was the theft of treasures.

That is what they'd come here to do.

Gray raced toward the patrol cutter, heading dead-on, a maneuver the smaller ships had not expected. Caught off guard by the sudden suicidal move, the smaller boats were slow in closing the gap. Seichan further discouraged them. She stood, one knee on her seat for balance, her two arms raised out to either side, black SIGs in each hand. She laid down a deadly barrage of fire to hold that gap open long enough for Gray to slip past their line of defense.

Nothing stood between them and the lead ship of the fleet.

It was a fast-response-class cutter, typically holding a crew of twenty, painted stark white. And, like most modern patrol vessels, it featured a stern launch-and-recovery ramp, made for deploying pursuit boats, even while under way.

That was their target.

The ramp was currently empty, as the entire fleet had been called to duty to build the blockade around the island.

Gray aimed for that ramp with the last of his fuel and opened the throttle.

Crew members ran to the stern of the ship, flanking the ramp. Automatic weapons pointed. On deck, a 25 mm stabilized caliber gun mount swung toward them. Additionally, a patrol guard manned the round black disk of an LRAD—long-range acoustic device, used as a sonic nonlethal shield against pirates, a useful tool in these waters.

There was no way to assault that ship.

They had only one choice.

"Ready?" he asked.

"I'm out of bullets anyway," Seichan said.

Gray throttled down, killing the engines—then stood up, joining her. He laced his fingers atop his head. She made a broad display of tossing her pistols overboard, then took the same position, hands on head.

"We surrender!" he called out.

The jet boat's momentum carried them to the stern ramp and nosed them halfway up. Weapons tracked them on both sides.

A commotion followed.

The captain of the boat appeared at the top of the ramp. His dark features and heavy shadow of beard marked his Arab heritage. He was flanked by a thin, mustached man and a hard-muscled woman with a stern blond bob.

"On your knees!" the captain said, pointing a pistol.

They obeyed.

The captain barked an order in Arabic. Four men came racing down the ramp and dragged the boat the rest of the way up, then tied the craft in place, ensuring they didn't try to flee. Another two boarded and pulled their arms down, cuffing them behind them.

Only then did the captain and the others come forward.

The thin man approached on Seichan's side of the vessel, commenting in a stiff British accent. "She would be a perfect research subject, don't you think, Petra?"

The blonde crossed over to Gray. "Careful, Dr. Blake. That one's not for you. At least not yet."

Petra leaned toward Gray. "Or this one. We thought hunting you or one of your colleagues would be harder. That makes me suspicious."

She lunged a hand at his neck, fast enough to catch his throat. He reflexively tried to pull away. A ghost of a smile appeared, amused by the surprise in his expression. Her other hand moved equally swift. A needle jabbed into his throat. A burn, like acid, spread as she pushed the plunger.

He coughed at the intense pain.

Petra straightened. "No, we have special plans for this one."

"What plans?" Blake asked, but his question had a faltering note, as if he didn't want to know the answer.

"He's a skilled sniper," Petra began.

Gray fought to listen, but the acid burned through his consciousness. The world constricted, her voice drifted back down a long tunnel.

"Forty hours from now—"

Her final words trailed to a whisper as he slumped to his side, sprawling next to Seichan. His vision narrowed to a pinpoint. Through that tiny hole, he watched Seichan shift her knee, switching off the camera attached to Kane's abandoned vest, hiding the fact that she had been recording the conversation before the others grew any wiser.

He prayed someone was listening—someone *had* to be listening.

This was the pirate bounty they'd risked so much to steal.

The most valuable treasure in the world.

Information.

As Gray faded to black, those last disturbing words followed him into oblivion:

"Forty hours from now, this man will assassinate the president of the United States."

THIRD

HUNTING GROUNDS

32

Painter waited for the storm.

He stood in the central hall that cut through the lowermost level of their command bunker. Here Sigma hid its deepest secrets. He stood outside a room that only a handful of people had entered in the past five hours. His muscles knotted as he kept his post.

He wanted to pace away his anxiety—needed to pace.

It had been almost a day since he heard any word concerning Kat and Lisa, and even then, it had only been some grainy footage caught on a bank ATM camera.

Not a word or sighting since.

It ate a hole through his gut, through his spirit.

But he had a duty that could not be forsaken.

At the end of the hall, the elevator chimed and opened. The first two people to exit were members of the Secret Service. They both eyeballed Painter. One came down the hallway; the other remained behind and waved President James Gant out of the elevator.

Two more agents followed behind.

General Metcalf accompanied the president. "This way, sir."

Gant's gaze locked onto Painter. A black cloud darkened his aspect: the fury in his eyes, the flush on his face, the hardness to his every move. Even his stride was angry. Painter hoped he could get a word out before getting punched. And he wasn't entirely sure he wouldn't still be slugged afterward. But the risk had to be taken.

The fate of the country depended on the next few minutes.

The press corps believed the president was attending a private meeting with the director of the Smithsonian. Even Gant thought he was here on Metcalf's behalf to listen to Painter give an impassioned plea to save Sigma from the ax. The president had only agreed to come here after intense backroom negotiations by Metcalf. The general had to call in many political chits to get these five minutes of the commander in chief's time.

Gant checked his watch as he crossed those final steps.

Apparently, time was already ticking down.

"This is a courtesy," Gant said, his Carolina drawl thick with disdain. "Because of General Metcalf's long, distinguished career. That's the only reason I'm here. And this is the *last* courtesy I will extend to you."

"Understood, Mr. President."

Gant balled a fist. "So speak your piece and let's be done with it."

Painter instead turned to Metcalf. "What about the Secret Service agents?"

"Thoroughly vetted," Metcalf answered. "All four. You'll need them for what's to come."

Gant looked between the two of them. "Need them for what?"

Painter stepped back. "Before I speak, Mr. President, I need you to see something."

Turning, Painter crossed to the door behind him. One of the Secret Service agents followed him. Painter opened the way and let the man go inside first to inspect the room. When he came out, his face was paler.

"Clear," the agent stated, then stepped aside.

Painter held the door and nodded to Gant.

Glowering and straightening his tie, the president strode into the room.

Painter followed, shadowed by another agent, while the others took posts in the hall.

Gant stepped woodenly to the hospital bed. He stopped at the edge, his posture ramrod-stiff—then he collapsed to his knees, half-falling across the mattress. His shoulders shook. Then sobs wracked out of him.

If Painter had any lingering doubts about the man's authenticity, they vanished in that moment.

"My baby . . ." he cried. "She's alive."

Amanda Gant-Bennett lay quietly on the bed, still under a light sedation. She wore a blue, flowered hospital gown. Intravenous fluids, along with two antibiotics, ran into a central line. Equipment monitored oxygenation, heart rhythm, and blood pressure. She wore a cap over her head. Beneath that, a bandage covered the surgery site where the cranial drill had been expertly removed by a neurosurgeon. A drain remained in place due to the length of time the burr hole had been left open. CT scans had showed the drill had penetrated the superior sagittal sinus through the frontal bone, but the cerebral cortex remained untouched. Secondary trauma had resulted in a tiny subdural hematoma, but that appeared to be resolving on its own.

With rest and time, she should fully recover.

Two other people occupied the room: Amanda's neurosurgeon and Tucker Wayne. Neither man had left the young woman's side since she arrived five hours ago. Her path back to the States had been a circuitous one. Jack Kirkland had transported her to the *Deep Fathom,* where medical personnel on board his ship had stabilized her en route to Abu Dhabi. There, Painter had called on the assistance of someone he trusted, someone who had powerful influences in the area: the oil baroness Lady Kara Kensington. She had arranged a private corporate jet while Painter prepared false papers.

No one outside Painter's circle knew Amanda still lived.

Until now.

Gant turned, staying on his knees. "How?"

That one word encompassed so much.

"I'll need more than five minutes," Painter said.

Once granted, Painter told him everything. He left nothing out, drawing Gant back to his feet with the story. They stepped into a neighboring medical office just off of the ward—the father refused to be more than a few steps away from his daughter.

When he got to the story of Amanda's rescue, Gant shook Tucker's hand. "Thank you, son."

Tucker nodded. "My honor, sir."

"I'd like to meet that dog of yours sometime."

"I'm sure that could be arranged."

Painter had highlighted the key parts of Amanda's story. All that was left were questions he could not fully answer.

"But I still don't understand," Gant said. "*Why* did they want my grandson?"

"We're still trying to piece that together. Amanda had some moments of lucidity. I was able to ask her a few questions, glean some answers."

"Tell me," Gant said. He was seated at a small desk in the medical office, too shaken to keep his feet.

Painter remained standing. "Your daughter received a couriered package from an unknown source. Inside were fake passports and a note warning Amanda to flee, that her child was in danger. There were also papers included. Medical documents, faxes, lab reports. Enough to convince your daughter to vanish in order to protect her baby. The note also warned her not to tell anyone in her family, not to trust anyone."

"But why?" Gant's expression was a mix of incredulity and fear. Anger lurked there, too, smoldering up toward a fierce fire.

"Someone wanted that child. I believe your grandson was the product of a genetic experiment. A global research project that spanned decades if not longer, one involving human trafficking and experimentation."

The disbelief shone brighter. "What sort of experiment are you talking about?"

"I can't say for sure. Something to do with his DNA—that's what Amanda overheard. But based on other intelligence sources, I believe the experiment inserted an engineered protein into his genetic structure. He may be the first child where this was successfully carried out."

Gant shook his head. "But what's their ultimate goal? What do they want with my grandson?"

Painter saved the worst for last. "Amanda believes they plan to *experiment* on your grandson, to keep him alive . . . or at least his tissues . . . to study him in more detail."

Gant shoved to his feet. Horror ignited that smoldering fury. "What? How . . . *who* the hell are these bastards?"

As Painter prepared to answer that, a more pressing question weighed on his mind.

Where are they?

1:42 P.M.
Blue Ridge Mountains

The stethoscope lifted gently from the newborn's frail chest. The child's heart could be seen beating against that cage, thumping weakly. His skin shone with a slight cyanotic cast, indicating poor oxygenation.

Dr. Edward Blake announced his verdict to Petra. "He's shutting down. Already underweight and premature; it could be a failure to thrive." He shrugged. "Or the stress of the transportation here may have overwhelmed his systems."

Petra's disappointment showed in the heavy cast to her eyes, the sternness to her lips. She wasn't concerned for the child's welfare—they'd lost many others. But after all of the troubles in Somalia and Dubai, they both needed a win here.

And any hope of that faded with every passing breath of the child.

The newborn rested inside a heated incubator, nestled in blankets. A nasal cannula supplied a steady stream of oxygen. A nasogastric tube allowed the administration of formula. Cuffs and pads monitored oxygenation, heart and respiratory rate, blood pressure, and temperature.

Edward shook his head. "We may need to insert a PICC line and switch to CPAP for his shallow breathing. Or tube and ventilate him."

He must find a way to stabilize this child. The last DNA sequencing showed significant PNA loss in the child. The triple-helix complexes in his vital tissues were breaking down.

But most troublesome of all, Edward still didn't know *why*.

One possible explanation was that the child's body was simply reject-ing the foreign protein making up that third helix. And as a consequence, the child grew sick, slowly shutting down.

The other possibility was that the child was failing to thrive for or-dinary reasons—he was too thin, too poorly developed—and that stress triggered a secondary metabolic breakdown of the triple helices.

"Chicken or the egg?" he asked the baby.

Did the breakdown of the helix cause your body to weaken?

Or did your weakened body cause the helix to break down?

More likely, it was a combination of the two, creating some sort of cascade effect.

No matter which scenario was true, he and Petra were in trouble. Fail-ure was not rewarded in this organization, and seldom tolerated.

Edward stared around the small, windowless ward assigned to them in this guarded complex. Currently, these new facilities were ill-suited for their purposes. The work done at the Lodge was primarily militaristic in nature—not like the wonders promised by the research at Utopia's labs.

He looked around the square ward, his temporary refuge and work-space. Their evacuation and exodus from Utopia had been rushed and unexpected, leaving little time for any real preparations. Crates remained unboxed. An entire wing waited for the installation of a new genomics lab.

No doubt, Edward could rebuild here, but it would take time.

Time the child did not have.

He stared back at the incubator.

En route from Dubai, it was evident the baby was destabilizing. Ed-ward had ordered what he needed for emergency neonatal care and had it airlifted and delivered here. But as the child declined, he faced a sad real-ity. Getting equipment here was one matter, but finding skilled medical personnel who could be vetted and arrive in time was a challenge at this highly guarded facility. Especially following the swath of ruin left behind, both out in the Middle East and here in South Carolina. They'd lost several significant colleagues in both places.

The wheels were already turning to bring staffing on-site.

But, again, timing was critical.

Performing even the simplest of the proposed procedures required a minimum number of skilled staff working around the clock.

"We need extra hands," he concluded. "Capable, skilled hands. At this point, I'll take *one* additional person—if talented enough."

Petra nodded, fully aware. "I'll make a call. We may have what we need already here."

1:45 P.M.

Dr. Lisa Cummings paced the length of her cell. She left her lunch untouched on the small tray. A turkey club and a small bag of Doritos. There was something obscene about the ordinariness of the fare. She stared around her cell as she made another pass from front to back.

The dull ache from her sprained ankle kept her focused.

The walls were a seamless white plastic. The door was made of a hard glass polymer, framed in steel. She had pressed her cheek against that glass, trying to see as much as she could past her threshold. All she saw was a hall of similar cells, all appearing empty.

Where is Kat?

The worry ate at her and fueled her pacing.

The cell had only a few amenities: a cot with a foam mattress and a stainless-steel commode with sink. The only luxury was a flat-screen television molded into the wall. But Lisa could not escape the feeling that someone was watching her through it.

Or maybe it was just a paranoia born of the aftereffects of the drugs.

After they were caught last night by the helicopter, four uniformed men had skimmed down on lines from the cabin of the aircraft. They had tied Kat and Lisa up, then injected them intramuscularly with a sedative. She guessed from the stabbing ache in her eyes and the stiffness of her leg muscles that they'd given her some form of ketamine.

She had regained a groggy consciousness at one point during the trip, enough to tell she was in the back of the Ford Explorer. Kat lay sprawled next to her, eyes rolled back, snoring slightly. Lisa was too weak to move, but through the back window, she watched dark woods and tall cliffs roll past, suggesting they were in the mountains.

She guessed the Blue Ridge Mountains, but she couldn't be certain.

She had faded away again and suspected she had been given a second injection at some point. *Two* needle marks itched on her upper arm.

She scratched absently at them through the thin gown she wore. Someone had stripped her and dressed her in a featureless cotton dress, like a hospital gown but closed in the back. It was pulled over the head and cinched in place. She also wore slippers and an ill-fitting bra and a pair of panties. The garments were clean but not new. From the slight fraying, someone had worn these clothes before—and that added to her nervousness.

What had happened to those others?

A sharp buzz sounded from the television. It drew her attention around. On the screen, the view of a small hospital ward appeared. Two figures in scrubs moved across the screen, working in what appeared to be a NICU, a neonatal intensive care unit.

A computer-altered voice spoke, eerily flat and disjointed. "DR. LISA CUMMINGS, IT HAS COME TO OUR ATTENTION THAT YOU HAVE BOTH A MEDICAL BACKGROUND AND A PH.D. IN PHYSIOLOGY. IS THAT CORRECT?"

"Yes," she said tentatively, unable to think of a good reason to lie. They clearly knew who she was, likely pulling her records based on her fingerprints.

"USEFULNESS IS A VIRTUE HERE," she was coldly instructed. "EVERYONE MUST HAVE A PURPOSE. TO THAT END, WE WOULD LIKE YOU TO ASSIST US IN DIAGNOSING AND TREATING A NEWBORN HERE AT THE FACILITY. WE'RE CURRENTLY UNDERSTAFFED FOR THE WORK NECESSARY, ESPECIALLY IN REGARDS TO SKILLED MEDICAL PERSONNEL."

Lisa processed this and came to one conclusion. "Why should I help you?"

"IF SAVING THE LIFE OF A CHILD IS NOT ENOUGH, PERHAPS THE LIFE OF A FRIEND."

The view swiped away, and a room similar to hers materialized on the monitor—only its walls were a dark red. It was like looking through a window into a neighboring cell. But that room could be anywhere in the complex. The woman seated on the bed burst to her feet, rushed forward to fill the screen, placing a hand against it.

Lisa laid hers there, too, matching finger for finger. She imagined the warmth of the electronics came from the palm of her best friend.

"Kat . . ."

"Lisa, are you okay?"

The connection cut, and the screen went black. The voice returned. "EVERY FAILURE OR DISOBEDIENCE ON YOUR PART WILL BE EXACTED UPON THE FLESH OF YOUR FRIEND. PROVE YOUR USEFULNESS, AND YOU BOTH CONTINUE TO LIVE."

She swallowed hard, suddenly finding it too chilly in her thin gown. "What do you want me to do?"

The electronic door lock clicked loudly.

"GO OUT TO YOUR RIGHT. END OF THE HALL."

The screen went dark.

Lisa hesitated a few breaths, but she knew she had no choice. Cooperation would buy extra time—*time* to find a way to escape, *time* for Painter to find them. She pictured her boyfriend's face, the lock of snowy hair tucked behind one ear, the sharp intelligence in his eyes—and, most of all, the love shining in the night across a pillow.

That last, more than anything, gave her the strength to keep moving.

She stepped over to the door, pushed it open, and headed to the right. The hall held a dozen cells. She searched for Kat among them, but they all appeared empty, at least as far as she could tell.

"Kat," she called out softly, walking slowly, swiveling her head.

No response, no face appeared pressed against a glass door.

Several of the rooms had their mattresses rolled up, giving the entire wing a feeling of disuse, but also a sense of expectation, like an empty boarding school waiting to be occupied for a new semester.

Maybe that came from the low murmur of voices ahead.

Reaching the end of the hall, she pushed through the far door into a small medical ward, the same one from the television. Crates and boxes filled one half of the space, some open, others spilling packing material and showing plastic-wrapped medical equipment inside.

The other half held the neonatal unit. A woman in scrubs spotted her and motioned her forward to join them, like one colleague greeting another.

Before she could step closer, a door on the other side of the ward opened, and a broad-shouldered older man entered, dressed in a somber gray suit, his white hair neatly combed, his manner genteel as he strode over to Lisa.

She had become rooted in place, recognizing him.

The man held out his hand, his Carolina drawl warm. "Thank you, Dr. Cummings, for agreeing to help my grandnephew."

Lisa shook his hand, dumbfounded.

He was the former ambassador to Southeast Asia, now secretary of state—and brother to the president.

Robert L. Gant.

1:55 P.M.
Washington, DC

"Tell me," James Gant demanded, staring off to the next room, where his daughter rested on the hospital bed. "Who's behind all of this?"

Painter knew the next part of this discussion would take some delicacy. What transpired here was for the president's ears and eyes only.

Him, and one other.

Jason Carter worked at the desk computer in the medical office, where Painter and the president had been holed up. His Secret Service agents continued to watch the hall, with one posted next to Amanda.

Jason finally nodded, ready to proceed. He had the necessary footage transferred and keyed up.

Painter faced Gant. "As you know, Mr. President, we already suspected the Guild had a hand in the kidnapping of your daughter."

Gant's eyes darkened. "I've read the intelligence briefings."

"Exactly, but the Guild is not their true name. It's more of an umbrella designation encompassing the group's many cells around the world, a network of agents and operatives ensconced in various militaries, governments, research institutions, and financial circles. There are many levels within this organization, some go by other names, but recently I've uncovered a clue to the true leaders, the puppet masters of the Guild."

Gant focused harder on him. "Go on."

"This inner circle has also hidden under many names, burying themselves in countless secret societies to cover their footprints, going back centuries."

"Centuries?" A skeptical note rang in the man's voice.

"At least to the Middle Ages," Painter confirmed. "Maybe even farther back into the past."

He flicked a glance toward Jason. The young analyst was tracing the lineage of the Gant family deeper into history, but it was slow going, and that track grew fainter, worn away by time into mere rumor and suspicion.

"What about *now*?" Gant said, keeping his eye on the target. "What do you know about their operations today?"

"We know *two* things. First, we know they're tied to your family."

Gant choked slightly. "What?"

Painter forged on before he lost the man completely. "Second, we know the name most commonly associated with them is the *Bloodline*."

Gant stirred at the mention of that word, plainly recognizing it. Painter was not surprised by his reaction. Amanda had known the name, too, but he wanted to hear what the president had to say.

"Director, I respect you. I owe you a great debt of gratitude, but you're chasing ghosts. You've taken rumor and hearsay and added flesh and bone to it."

Painter remained silent, letting Gant have his say.

The president continued, "Suspicions plague most rich families. Rumors wrapped in conspiracies entwined in maniacal plots. Take your pick. The Kennedys, the Rockefellers, the Vanderbilts, the Rothschilds.

In the past, each one of them has been tied to secret societies and global machinations. And we're no exception. Go ahead and pluck any card out of that conspiracy deck—Freemasonry, the Trilateral Commission, Skull and Bones, the Bilderberg Group—and you'll find some story connecting them to our family."

Gant shook his head, plainly disappointed. "That name—*Bloodline*—that's our family's personal boogeyman. Made to scare children into obeying. Stories about a family within our family. It's not supposed to be mentioned beyond our doors. Growing up, I heard all sorts of tales, mostly spoken under bedcovers at night. Of people who mentioned that name too loudly—only to suddenly disappear."

I'm sure they did, Painter thought. *Likely killed or recruited into the fold.*

"You've been hoodwinked, director. Sold a bill of goods if you've fallen into that conspiratorial trap."

Painter felt the wind dying in the man's sails, knowing now was the time. He nodded to Jason. "Bring up the footage I asked you to prepare." He returned his attention to Gant. "Amanda described a symbol painted on that tent-cabin in Somalia. We found that same mark again closer to home. At the fertility clinic where she had her in vitro fertilization performed."

Jason stepped back. On the monitor, Kat's footage began to play. It showed her again rushing up to a set of large steel doors.

"Pause it there," Painter said, fighting down a pang of worry for Kat and Lisa.

The video stopped and focused squarely on the center of the door. A large embossing stood out plainly: a crimson cross with genetic code wrapped within it. Earlier, Amanda had recognized it, claiming it was a symbol tied to the Bloodline.

From Gant's flinch, he knew it, too. He leaned closer, his voice hushed. "Impossible."

Painter motioned for Jason to continue the footage. "This is what that symbol hid."

Painter didn't watch the video. He didn't need to see that again. Instead, he studied the president's profile. The blood visibly drained from the man's face. His lips parted in a silent gasp of horror.

Knowing he'd seen enough, Painter made a cutting motion across his own neck.

Jason ended the playback, leaving the president stunned.

It took a long minute for Gant to look away from the screen, to turn haunted eyes toward Painter. Behind that glassy numbness, Painter knew Gant pictured his own daughter.

To his credit, the man nodded, accepting the truth. As he stood, his voice hardened to a vengeful edge. "If you're right, if members of my own family perpetrated such atrocities, committed such cruelties upon my daughter, I want them hunted down." His anger focused on one question now. "Where do we start?"

Before Painter could answer, another person must have heard Gant's rising anger and recognized it.

"Daddy . . . ?"

Everyone turned back to the hospital bed in the next room. The patient's eyes were open. She searched blearily.

"Amanda . . . !" Gant rushed to her bedside, crashing to one knee to take her hand. "Baby girl, I'm here."

Amanda found her father's face. But rather than relief, a faint reflection of Gant's fury shone there. Her fingers tightened on her father's hand. She fought through the dregs of her sedation.

He consoled his daughter. "You're going to be fine."

Amanda wanted no such reassurances—only results.

"Daddy, they took William. They took my baby boy. You—" Her fingers clutched until her knuckles paled. "You get him back."

The demand took the last of her strength. She stared into her father's face, exacting a promise from him. With her duty passed on, her eyes rolled back. Her fingers slipped free.

The neurosurgeon stepped forward. "She still needs more rest."

Gant ignored him and turned to Painter, still on one knee. His face was forlorn, but his eyes were determined.

"What must I do to get my grandson back?"

Painter pictured the video footage shot by Kane's vest camera: showing a mouse's-eye view from the bottom of a boat. He had watched it several times over the past half-day—*the boat chase, the capture, the drugging
of Gray Pierce*—each time grateful for the man's ingenuity and sacrifice in
securing this secret footage. It offered them a slim chance to turn the tide
against the enemy.

Painter intended to take it.

"What do you need me to do?" Gant pressed.

Painter stared him in the eye and told him the blunt truth.

"You need to die, Mr. President."

33

Gray rode back into the world on a bolt of lightning.

The electric shock burned through his skull, as if someone had shoved the right side of his face against a red-hot stovetop. He gasped, tried to roll away from the pain, but could not escape it. The only relief came as the burn faded on its own.

Then something bit into the back of his hand. Warmth shot up his arm, into his chest, and ignited his heart. His heart tripped a frantic beat. Blood pressure pounded at his ears. His breathing grew labored for several seconds until the effect wore off.

The jolt left him tingling, hyperalert. The world snapped into sudden, sharp focus, still tinged red at the edges. He lay on his back, his pulse throbbing in his throat. As he collected himself, he reached above to touch a concrete roof, so low he could brush his fingertips over its rough surface.

He noted a device strapped to his wrist: a syringe locked into a mechanical delivery system. He ripped it off, rolling to the side and holding off the punctured vein.

He must have been given a counteragent to his sedative, returning him to full alertness in seconds.

But where am I?

Concrete walls surrounded him on all sides, creating a box five feet wide and three feet tall. The illumination was sharp, painfully bright, coming from a battery-powered lamp in the corner. A long metal case rested on the floor near his feet, and one of the walls had a thin aperture, sealed by a steel shutter. Even if open, the hole was too narrow to climb through. The only exit appeared to be the hatch in the floor, sealed from the outside.

What is going on?

The answer came from inside his head, from deep within his right ear. "GOOD MORNING, COMMANDER PIERCE," a mechanized voice greeted him. It sounded like one of those soulless computerized answering services—though he suspected he was hearing a real voice, digitally masked.

"THE RUDE AWAKENING WAS A NECESSITY." There was no apologetic tone to that statement, merely matter-of-factness. "THE SHOCK AND THE INJECTION OF METHYLPHENIDATE SHOULD HAVE YOU ALERT AND READY FOR THE TASK AT HAND. YOU HAVE TEN MINUTES UNTIL YOU MUST ACT."

"To do what?" he asked loudly to the bare walls of his concrete crypt. He suspected the answer, glancing at what looked to be a rifle case.

The voice continued to speak, either ignoring him or perhaps this conversation was a one-way transmission.

"THE RADIO DEEP IN YOUR EAR IS BOLTED IN PLACE AND WIRED VIA A BLASTING CAP. YOU'LL FIND THAT SAME EAR PACKED FULL OF C-4."

Disturbed, Gray probed with a finger and discovered a wad of hard material jammed into the canal. He pictured what would happen if that exploded, and quickly pushed that thought away.

The speaker continued, "THE DEVICE CAN ALSO BE USED AS PUNISH-MENT, AS YOU EXPERIENCED UPON WAKING. ADDITIONALLY, IT'S WIRED TO A TRANSMITTER HELD BY A GUARD OUTSIDE. IF YOU STRAY BEYOND TEN YARDS FROM THAT TRANSMITTER, YOU HAVE TEN SECONDS TO GET BACK IN RANGE, OR THE DEVICE WILL AUTOMATICALLY EXPLODE."

They've got me connected to an electric leash.

A tingle of foreboding worked through his drug-induced hypervigilance.

"AS TO YOUR DUTY," the voice said, "AT EXACTLY NOON TODAY, YOU WILL ASSASSINATE PRESIDENT JAMES T. GANT. YOU WILL FIND A SNIPER RIFLE AND A MAGAZINE WITH TWO ROUNDS, IN CASE YOU MISS ON YOUR

FIRST SHOT. YOU WILL NOT BE GIVEN A THIRD CHANCE. PREPARE YOURSELF NOW."

The lamp blinked off inside the bunker. A small motorized hum sounded, and the shuttered window opened. Sunlight streamed into the space through the slats. He wasn't blinded. He realized the brightness of the lamp had been to assist him with maintaining his day vision.

Gray searched around for a camera, while he rolled and crawled to the gun case and snapped it open. Nestled inside was a Marine Corps M40A3 sniper rifle, along with a stabilizing bipod. He slipped the weapon free, checking its heft and balance. He knew this rifle. It had an effective range of a thousand yards.

But what fell within that range?

Gray moved into the sunlight's blaze. Staring between the slats, he distantly made out the tip of the Washington Monument poking above a line of towering oaks.

I'm back in DC.

He oriented himself. Through the trees, sunlight glinted off water. That had to be the Potomac. Shifting to the left and peering sideways, he caught a peek, far to the right, of a rolling expanse of green lawns, dogwoods, and rows of small white gravestones. He knew that place too well: he had many friends buried there. *Arlington Cemetery.* He was north of the park, likely not far from the USMC War Memorial.

Closer at hand, viewed down a short street that ended at an oak-studded park, people milled about a large gathering of tents and booths. Most were wearing various shades of armed forces uniforms, from dress blues to camouflage khakis.

He raised the rifle and peered through the telescopic sight, adjusting the Unertl 10x lens to focus on that gathering. The view zoomed to reveal barbecues, children running and laughing, a military band playing on a shaded stage. The distant beat of drum and sharper notes of brass reached him.

In the center of the picnic grounds, a tall platform had been erected, framed by an arch of red, white, and blue balloons.

He shifted the sight to maximum, concentrating on the group clustered by the podium. They appeared to be top military brass from every branch of service.

Among them, he spotted his supposed target.

With his back to Gray, President James T. Gant kissed his wife, who was decked out in a dark blue pantsuit, with a muted pink-and-white-striped top, and silver flats. It was a festive look for this Fourth of July barbecue, a USO celebration. Gray also knew the First Couple were hosting a fireworks-viewing party on the South Lawn of the White House later tonight.

But the day's strain already showed on the First Lady's face.

The detail through the scope—even at seven hundred yards—revealed the grief etched in the lines around her eyes, hidden as best she could under thick makeup. Her fingers clung to her husband's hand, trying to hold him as he stepped to the podium, but the president had to show a strong face to the world.

The pair both thought their daughter dead—and maybe Amanda was. The last memory Gray had of her was floating in dark waters, supported by his two teammates. The administration must not have announced the kidnapping and death of Amanda, likely waiting for confirmation from the charred remains. Probably the White House chief speechwriter already struggled on the wording for that tragic announcement.

In the meantime, the parents had to put on a show of normalcy.

President Gant stepped to the podium, lifting a hand and waving.

A distant cheer rose.

Gray turned away, crouching lower in his sniper's nest, resting the rifle across his knees. He picked up the magazine, eyed the cartridges—the newer M118LR rounds, for heightened accuracy.

Two of them.

They had better be accurate.

He remembered the warning: *You will not be given a third chance.*

But why did his kidnappers believe he would agree to assassinate the president? They had Seichan, but that wasn't enough leverage, as much as it pained him to admit it. He knew they would likely carry out horrible atrocities against her in an attempt to ensure his cooperation—or to punish his failure.

That fear sat like a cold stone in his gut.

He knew that, even to save her, he could not sacrifice the leader of the free world. Frustrated, he tightened his fingers on the fiberglass stock of the rifle and on the cold length of deadly muzzle.

I'm sorry, Seichan. I can't do it.

"FOUR MINUTES," the voice finally announced, and, as if reading his mind, the speaker gave him the incentive to act. "TO ENSURE YOUR CO-OPERATION, WE HAVE BURIED FIFTEEN PLASTIC CARTRIDGES OF SARIN GAS WITH INDETECTABLE TRIGGERS THROUGHOUT THE PARK. THE DISPERSAL PATTERN WILL SWEEP THE FIELDS, KILLING EVERYONE THERE, INCLUDING THE PRESIDENT. THOSE CHARGES WILL GO OFF TWENTY SECONDS AFTER NOON. UNLESS THE PRESIDENT IS KILLED FIRST."

Gray imagined that wafting nerve gas, so lethal even the briefest skin contact caused an agonizing end.

"ONE DEATH VERSUS HUNDREDS OF INNOCENT MEN, WOMEN, AND CHILDREN. THE CHOICE IS YOURS, COMMANDER PIERCE. EITHER END WILL SERVE OUR NEEDS. BUT IT SERVES OUR PURPOSE BETTER IF YOU PULL THAT TRIGGER. A LONE DEATH BY ASSASSINATION WILL BE FAR MORE POIGNANT AND POWERFUL THAN ONE DEATH AMONG MANY."

The coldness of that calculation reached Gray, chilling him.

"ALSO, WITH YOUR RIFLE DISCOVERED HERE, AS WELL AS YOUR DNA, THE ASSASSINATION WILL BE BLAMED ON THE ROGUE ACTIONS OF A DIS-GRUNTLED COVERT OPERATIVE, ONE WHO WAS RETALIATING AGAINST THE MOTHBALLING OF HIS GROUP BY THE ADMINISTRATION."

In effect, putting the final nail in Sigma's coffin.

But the Guild's schemes were even grander than that.

"SUCH AN ACT WILL REQUIRE AN ENTIRE REVAMPING OF THE UNITED STATES' COVERT AND INTELLIGENCE AGENCIES. ONE OVERSEEN BY US, AS WE TAKE OVER THE WHITE HOUSE WITH THE NEXT ELECTION. THAT POI-GNANT SYMPATHY FOR THE DEATH OF JAMES GANT WILL EXTEND TO HIS

FAMILY MEMBERS, TO SOMEONE ALREADY STANDING AT HIS SIDE IN A POSI-
TION OF POWER."

. . . extend to his family members . . .

Gray felt sick to his stomach. As he listened, armed with his new
knowledge, he could now hear the slight Southern cadence, the word
choice that couldn't be wiped away digitally. His mind raced, picturing
the man who stood so steadfastly at his brother's shoulder, whom the
world already loved and respected and would surely hand the reins of
power to. The man only had to ask for the White House after such a tragedy, and it would be given to him—in a landslide.

The secretary of state.

Robert Lee Gant.

Gray squeezed his eyes closed. He suddenly remembered sensing that
Painter had been keeping something hidden from him, something about
the Guild, about the organization behind his mother's fiery death.

Was this that secret?

Had Painter suspected the man all along?

No wonder the director hadn't wanted anyone in the Gant family to
know about Amanda surviving Somalia. He feared word would reach the
president's brother.

Anger burned at the edges of his dismay. He logically knew *why* the
director had kept such a secret from him. Gray might have taken the man
out immediately, jeopardizing everyone around him. And, ultimately, the
foreknowledge of that traitor in the White House would not have changed
Gray's mission objectives.

Apparently, such knowledge was "need to know" only.

And Gray wasn't on that list.

Still . . .

You should have told me.

"ONE MINUTE," the voice warned. "YOU WILL WAIT FOR OUR SIGNAL—
THEN FIRE."

Gray secured the magazine in place and returned to his post at the
aperture. Shame and anger burned through him. He didn't know if the

voice had been lying about those gas canisters—or if they'd be blown up anyway. Either way, Gray knew he couldn't take that chance.

James T. Gant had to die.

He stared through the rifle's telescopic scope and lowered the crosshairs to the profile of the president as the man turned to the side. He double-checked his range—seven hundred yards—and fixed the main targeting chevron of the rifle's sights upon the occipital bone behind the man's left ear, knowing a shot there would do the most damage. Festive music and bright laughter from the holiday picnic filtered to him. He let it all fade into the background as he concentrated on his target, on his mission.

In U.S. history, three presidents had died on the exact same day, on July 4, on the birthday of this country. It seemed beyond mere chance.

Thomas Jefferson, John Adams, and James Monroe.

Today would mark the fourth.

Then the president leaned down, forcing Gray to follow him. The man ruffled the fur of a dog sharing the platform with him. Gray tensed, recognizing that shepherd.

Kane.

Gray zoomed out to watch James Gant straighten and shake the hand of Captain Tucker Wayne. The man must have recovered his uniform. His dress blues were decorated with the medals and awards from his tours in Afghanistan. It was appropriate that Tucker should be standing there on the dais, a war hero and his dog being thanked by a grateful commander in chief.

But Gray knew why Tucker and Kane were *really* there.

All the earlier anger at Painter's secrecy dried up, leaving behind only relief and respect. The director must have received the recorded video from Dubai and understood—but what did he want Gray to do?

Gray searched the stage. Painter must have put Tucker up there for a reason. The former army ranger was not a regular member of Sigma, only a hired hand, so no one was likely to recognize him. But what was the message Painter was trying to send to Gray?

Then he knew.

It wasn't just Tucker on that stage—but also *Kane.*

Gray shifted his concentration to the dog. The shepherd stood quietly, tail out, nose pointed up. Gray had seen that particular pose a few times before, when the dog had found the source of a scent.

Kane was *pointing,* like any good hunting dog.

Gray followed his gaze to a red balloon behind the podium, not far from the president's head. Gray fingered the telescopic sight to zero in on that balloon.

It twisted in a slight breeze, revealing a small Greek letter in a darker shade of red, barely discernible unless you were looking for it.

$$\Sigma$$

He smiled and made some final adjustments to his weapon.

In his ear, he got the order he needed: "FIRE."

Steadying his breath, Commander Gray Pierce pulled the trigger.

34

No shot was heard—only the *popping* of a balloon.

Even that noise startled everyone on the podium.

Not Tucker.

He had been waiting for that signal. He used the distraction to press the button on the transmitter in his pocket. Small squibs, hidden under the president's white polo shirt, exploded. Packets of the president's own blood erupted out his back in a violent blast and seeped heavily over his heart in front.

The First Lady screamed, catching some of the spray on her face.

The Secret Service enveloped the president immediately, gathering him up and whisking him off the platform. Tucker got knocked to the side; Kane danced out of the way.

Another cordon of agents formed a living shield to protect the fleeing president. More crowded around the First Lady and rushed her in another direction.

Tucker tapped his leg, gathered Kane to his side, and rushed after the president's group. Chaos exploded across the picnic grounds, the sudden violence catching everyone off guard. People yelled, kids were hidden under the bodies of protective parents, a barbecue got knocked over, setting fire to a tent. But a majority of those in attendance were military or former service members. Most had probably been under fire.

They made room for the flight of their wounded commander in

chief; some even added to the body shield to protect the fallen president.

The president's entourage reached the parking lot and the motorcade. As planned, the USSS Electronic Countermeasures Suburban, used by the Secret Service to stop any airborne attacks, ejected its arsenal of infrared smoke grenades, creating a thick pall to protect the president in his final flight to the waiting ambulances.

In that momentary confusion, a pair of Secret Service agents who were in on the ruse hauled the president into one of the emergency vehicles. Tucker climbed into the back. Kane jumped in after him.

The neighboring ambulance erupted with flashing lights and sirens and took off. The WHCA Roadrunner, the mobile command and control vehicle, sent out the false instruction, drawing the rest of the secure-package motorcade to follow the decoy. Armored vehicles gave chase, while local law enforcement blocked streets.

Staring out a window, Tucker watched an armored presidential limo race through the smoke with additional escorts, bearing to safety the First Lady, who must be beyond distraught, watching her husband shot right in front of her. They needed her to *be* the grieving wife for the cameras during the next few hours.

It was cruel, but no one could know of the subterfuge today.

Especially the enemy.

Amazingly, Painter had orchestrated a deception of this caliber after a single day of planning. He recruited only those he fully trusted, reaching out to a handful of people in various intelligence branches, but mostly he kept this entire operation in-house.

One of the Secret Service agents helped the president take off his buttoned polo. Gant wore a pained expression. The reason became clear as his bloody undershirt was stripped off and the exploded remains of the squibs removed. A blistered blast burn decorated the spot under his shoulder blade.

"Sir," one of the Secret Service agents started, worried.

He was waved away. "I'm fine. Better than a bullet through the head."

Another agent started the ambulance and set off, running dark, no flashing lights, no sirens. They headed in the opposite direction from the motorcade. The decoys were racing to George Washington University Hospital, where another team waited to continue the deception. In the story to come, it would be reported that the president was undergoing an extensive emergency surgery to repair his lung, that his chances were poor. They didn't want to risk a second attempt on his life, so they would make it sound bad. But such a ruse could not be maintained for long without the threat of exposure.

So they set a six-hour time limit.

Six hours to bring down a shadowy cabal that had survived centuries.

Painter's voice filled one ear. "Report."

"The package is secure," Tucker sent back, knowing their voice channel was kept secret by a modified version of the CCEP type-1 encryption algorithm developed by the NSA to keep presidential communications secret. "What about Commander Pierce?"

"We're working on that right now."

With advance knowledge of the sniper attack, Painter had set up a ring of tiny high-frame-rate, slow-motion cameras around the stage, all fixed on that balloon. Those cameras should have recorded the bullet's passage and allowed immediate processing of the trajectory. A three-dimensional laser modeling of the park permitted the analysts at Sigma command to quickly trace the path of that bullet back to its source.

They needed Commander Pierce secured as soon as possible—not only for his safety but also to obtain whatever knowledge he had regarding the moves of the enemy, including the whereabouts of the president's grandson.

Tucker felt a pang of regret, unable to escape the guilt of leaving Amanda's child behind. He intended to do whatever he could to correct that mistake.

The first step toward that goal: find and secure Gray.

Without that man's information, all of this subterfuge would accomplish nothing. In six hours, it would be announced to the world that the president had miraculously survived his surgery, and the thin advantage of the moment would evaporate.

He knew Painter didn't expect to uproot the Bloodline completely by these actions, but he had one clear goal, the same one as Tucker: to find and recover Amanda's child and expose everyone involved in this current bloody affair.

Even with such a defined objective, the odds were exceedingly long.

And without Gray, there were no odds.

Painter came back on the line. "We have his location. A utility bunker of an office tower. Seven hundred yards away."

Tucker sighed in relief.

He locked eyes with the president. "We found him, sir."

James Gant nodded, wincing. "We'd better not lose him."

12:01 P.M.

Gray watched the hatch fall open.

He still held the sniper rifle in his hands. He had witnessed the explosive chaos following his single shot. As he watched, he held his breath, concerned the sarin gas would still be released, killing everyone in the park. When nothing happened, he suspected that threat had been a lie, after all. He saw Tucker race off with the president, rushing him to a secure location.

He understood the situation immediately.

They were faking the president's death.

A risky move on the director's part, but Gray understood why that risk had been taken. It spoke volumes about their desperation. They were likely backtracking a trajectory already, looking to find him, hoping he could supply additional information.

That was a problem.

I don't know anything more than they do.

That is, unless Painter was ignorant of Robert Gant's involvement with the Guild. Maybe the director suspected the president's family or inner circle was involved—but he didn't necessarily know *who* in the administration was the mole.

Gray stared down at his hand. He still had one more round. Was it enough to stall, to buy Painter time to find him?

A shout rose from the dark hatch. "Leave the rifle! Show your hands!"

"Where are you taking me?" he called back, both stalling and trying to get more information.

The answer came as a shock—literally. An electrical jolt burst from his ear, blinding him, triggering his jaw to seize, his knees to buckle, sprawling him flat.

"Leave the rifle," the guard repeated. "Show your hands."

Gray belly-crawled and thrust his arms over the open hatch. He breathed heavily, gasping.

"Now climb down the service ladder."

Gray dawdled—not because it hurt to move but to slow things down. He swung his legs into the opening, fumbling with a toe to find the first rung.

"You were warned," the guard said.

Gray braced for another shock, but instead a mechanical countdown whispered from his implanted earpiece, arising from the unit itself.

Ten . . . nine . . . eight . . .

It was the timer for the implanted C-4 bomb in his right ear. Whoever held the transmitter must have stepped beyond his ten-yard limit. They were forcing him to follow, tugging at his electric leash.

He had no choice but to obey. He picked at that packed ear, knowing it wouldn't do Sigma any good to have half his skull blown away. He had to stay alive, to do his best to learn more—which meant he had to work fast.

. . . seven . . . six . . . five . . .

Once done, he ignored the ladder's rungs and slid down the frame instead. His feet hit the floor of a concrete corridor as the countdown reached *three*.

Then, thankfully, stopped.

A circle of soldiers, all in black, surrounded him, weapons in hand.

One dashed back up the ladder, wearing latex gloves, and searched the concrete roost.

"Rifle's there and some blood for a DNA trace," the man reported and clambered back down. He held the syringe-injection system in one hand and bagged it away, cleaning up any evidence. "All clear."

The team leader stepped up, a head taller than the others, with a crucifix-shaped tattoo on his neck. He pocketed a device the size of a packet of gum.

The transmitter.

"Move out," he ordered.

Pistols encouraged Gray forward, down a set of stairs to a subbasement, then through a hidden door into a tunnel system.

Gray stared behind him as the door sealed, hoping his plan worked.

As his feet dragged, the countdown began again in his ear.

Ten . . . nine . . . eight . . .

Like a dog on a leash, Gray hurried forward obediently.

For now.

12:32 P.M.

"Report," Painter said, standing in the communications nest at Sigma headquarters.

"We arrived on-site," his unit commander reported from the field. "Found the bunker empty. No sign of Commander Pierce. Only a sniper rifle and several drops of blood."

Painter closed his eyes and fought against the tide of despair at losing Gray's trail. He turned his mind instead to what *was* left behind.

A rifle and blood.

Painter understood.

They were planning on pinning the assassination on Gray and, in turn, destroying Sigma's reputation. But as in any chess match, it was now Painter's turn.

"Grab the rifle and bring it here," he ordered. "Destroy the blood evidence and scour the place clean. But you'll need to be quick."

In the aftermath of the attack, chaos still reigned, but it wouldn't be long before forensic teams discovered the sniper's hiding place. His team needed to be finished by then. But he refused to let panic distract his focus.

He knew Gray wouldn't have lost focus, either.

"Before you start cleaning," Painter warned over the radio, "thoroughly search every square inch of that space. If I know Gray, he would try to leave us some clue."

"Understood."

Painter ended the conversation and spoke to Jason Carter, who stood in the doorway to Kat's office. "Hold down the fort here. Let me know if anything goes wrong."

Like it hadn't already.

"I've got things covered," Jason assured him.

Painter hurried out the door and down the stairs, headed for the lowermost floor.

President James Gant was already down there with his daughter.

The man had arrived in secret a few minutes ago. The Smithsonian Castle had been closed all day, specifically for this purpose. No one paid attention to the shuffle of the janitorial staff into the building; no one saw them enter the special elevator that led down to the command bunkers of Sigma. For now, everyone believed the president was undergoing emergency surgery at George Washington University Hospital, that the likelihood of his survival was extremely poor.

Painter had his communications nest monitoring events, making sure the deception remained in place, massaging the press where needed. But such a level of fraud could not last forever without risking exposure. In less than six hours, it would have to end.

Knowing time was ticking down, Painter returned to the hospital ward. Two Secret Service agents protected the hall; another manned a post by the elevator. The fourth stood guard inside the small ward.

Painter found Gant sitting on the edge of Amanda's bed, holding her hand. He had stripped out of the janitorial coveralls and wore wrinkled navy-blue slacks and a borrowed gray shirt. Amanda still balanced between moments of lucidity and sedation, monitored by her neurologist, who remained concerned about the subdural hematoma.

At the moment, she slept.

Gant looked up as he entered. "She spoke a few words when I came in. She's still worried about her baby."

"We all are."

He nodded. "What's the word from your field team? Did they find your man?"

Painter hated to dash the gleam of hope in a father's eyes, but he'd had enough deception for one day. "Already gone. But I'm hoping he left some clue behind. We should know in a few minutes."

Gant sighed, turning to his daughter. He spoke slowly, full of regret. "I pulled her into the limelight and made her childhood a spectacle, a target for the press. And I still had no time for *her*. No wonder she rebelled, lashed out. No wonder she fled without saying a word. What trust have I earned in her life?" He glanced up, wiping a tear, but never let go of her hand. "I promised her I'd find William. Don't make me let her down again."

Painter stepped over and placed a hand on his shoulder, silently making an oath to do everything he could to help.

"What they did to her, to my family . . ." Gant said. "If I ever find out who orchestrated this, who tortured my baby girl, I will make them regret it for the rest of their days. There will be no quick death. I will make them suffer like no other. I'll turn their world into a personal hell on earth."

Painter knew that if anyone had the power to do that, it was President James Gant.

A commotion drew both their attentions around.

Jason came flying into the room, winded. "Director." The young man never stopped moving, continuing past the end of the bed and toward the neighboring medical office. "Linus just got a hit."

Painter got drawn into the wake of his excitement. It took him an extra moment to remember that Linus was Jason's partner in that vehicle-identification program. Hope flared inside him.

Had they found something?

He rushed after Jason into the medical office. The kid was already at the computer, typing fast.

"What is it?" Painter asked.

The president stood in the doorway, too, listening in.

"I'll show you," Jason said, typing as he spoke. "That's why I came running down here. Linus had been checking all the major thoroughfares leaving Charleston, searching for any further hits on that Ford. The problem is that the farther you get out from the city, the more variables come into play, so many different roads that could be taken, spreading wider and wider like the branches on a tree."

"What did you find?" Painter pressed.

"This." Jason pointed at the screen. A clear photo of the front of a Ford Explorer appeared. "Picked this up from a security camera at a drawbridge outside of Orangeburg, South Carolina."

Through the windshield, Painter spotted Lisa behind the wheel. His breathing grew heavier, both relieved and terrified. A man sat next to her, his arms awkwardly raised behind him, like he was stretching. Or maybe his hands were bound behind him.

"You found her," Painter mumbled. "How long ago was this taken?"

Jason looked both apologetic and worried. "Two days ago . . . the same day Dr. Cummings was kidnapped in Charleston."

The president spoke at the doorway. "Who is Dr. Cummings?"

She's everything to me.

Aloud, Painter replied, "She was one of the operatives sent to investigate the North Charleston Fertility Clinic."

Gant's face grew grim, likely remembering the footage he'd been shown, of women floating in gel-filled tanks.

Jason drew their attention back to the original still shot and pointed. "This was what got me so excited."

Painter leaned closer. "A license plate."

"Clear as day. I have Linus running a trace on the car's GPS, to find out where it might be. We should—"

A dialog box popped onto the screen.

"I think this is it." Jason tapped on the hyperlink in the box.

The image of the Ford vanished, replaced by a map view. A blinking blue circle narrowed and zoomed, shrinking down toward the border, where a corner of South Carolina pushed between Georgia and North Carolina. The circle finally changed into a small triangle, positioned deep in the Blue Ridge Mountains.

The president was drawn by the activity.

"Can you zoom in and get a street address?" Painter asked Jason.

It was Gant that answered. "No need. I know where that is. That's within my family's estate. Fleury-la-Montagne."

Before Painter could react, his cell phone vibrated. He answered it and was patched through to the unit commander in Arlington.

"Director, we found something here."

Painter's heart—already beating hard—sped faster. "What?"

"I took a photo. I've already dispatched it to you."

Painter ordered Jason to retrieve it.

The commander explained while they waited. "We found it scrawled on the floor near the entrance hatch. Mostly invisible to the naked eye, but it glowed under an ultraviolet scan of the chamber. I think it was written with a smear of C-4."

"Plastic explosive?"

"Yes, sir. I scraped up a tiny dab with a toothpick. From the feel, from the chemical taste, I believe so."

Jason interrupted. "I've got the photo."

It appeared in the top corner of the monitor.

Three letters glowed with a soft phosphorescence against the dark concrete.

"RLG," Painter mumbled aloud. "What does that mean?"

Again it was the president who answered, his voice pale with shock. "Those are my brother's initials. Robert Lee Gant."

Painter twisted to face him. They both knew some of Gant's family members had to be involved with this mess, but neither of them suspected anyone *this* close to the First Family.

Gant stared over at his daughter, likely thinking the same—only for him, this dagger dug much deeper and straight into his heart.

"We can't be sure about your brother," Painter offered.

"I can," Gant said faintly.

"How?"

Gant pointed to the lower part of the computer screen. It still displayed the GPS map. "Bobby was headed to the family estate for the holiday, to avoid the Fourth of July crowds in DC. He left two days ago to do some hunting."

"To Fleury-la-Montagne?"

Gant looked drawn and pale, his voice grim. "No one really uses that French name any longer. Everyone just calls it the Lodge."

35

"His color is good," Lisa pronounced.

She stood before the neonatal incubator. Her gloved hands gently rolled the newborn onto his side, and she listened to the back of his thin chest with her stethoscope. His heartbeat was as rapid as a bird's, but strong, his pulse-ox readings normal.

She let him roll back on his own. Huge blue eyes, framed by a hint of eyelashes, ogled up at her, his lips pursed hungrily.

Edward Blake stood at her shoulder, watching her examination.

Petra was off in another lab, running the latest DNA analyses, using samples of the boy's blood and skin, along with cells gathered from a mucosal swab.

"We should get another bottle." Lisa snapped off her gloves. "He's been suckling well on his own since we took out his NG tube and PICC line. Let's keep him moving in that right direction. But all in all, he's rallying beautifully."

"That's all because of you, Dr. Cummings," Edward said.

It wasn't false praise. Yesterday, she had found the child circling the drain. She had spent a full hour studying his labs, his radiographs, even his genetic analyses. She had stared with amazement at the triple helix formations on an electron micrograph: two natural DNA strands wrapped around an engineered foreign protein, PNA.

Peptide nucleic acid.

That little microscopic strand of PNA was the source of so much misery, horror, and abuse.

And it wasn't doing the boy any good, either.

Edward had explained about the unraveling going on in the boy's body, how these triple-helix compounds were breaking down. But the question still in the air was *why*. Did the boy get sick and that started to unravel the helices? Or did the unraveling make the boy sick?

The only way to know for sure was to stabilize the child and see if the unraveling stopped on its own.

Lisa had come up with a suggestion, after noting the slight spike in eosinophil levels in the boy's lab work. Eosinophils were the white blood cells that modulated allergic inflammatory processes. They also reacted to parasitic infections, but stool tests had already ruled out that possibility.

The more likely source for this allergic response was the PNA strands. Peptide nucleic acid was a protein like any other, capable of being an allergen as surely as dust or dander. With the breakdown of the triple helices, the freed PNA was being washed out into the cytoplasm, then shed free of the cells.

Petra had shown her a picture of a worm-like PNA molecule squiggling out of an intestinal cell. This rush of engineered protein into the bloodstream and interstitial tissues triggered the mobilization of eosinophils, the body's defense against such foreign invaders. This allergic anaphylaxis tipped the child into shock.

Recognizing this threat, Lisa had recommended a low-dose therapy of antihistamines and intravenous steroids to knock down that allergic response, to give the child's body a chance to flush out the foreign allergen and stabilize again.

It worked out beautifully. She had kept a vigil beside the neonatal incubator all night, assisted by Edward as needed, and, hour by hour, the child improved. They were able to slowly unhook him from fluids, oxygen supplementation, and even the feeding tube.

Only one question remained: did it do any good?

Did the boy's rallying health succeed in returning stability to the triple helices? She knew that was Edward's hope. They both awaited Petra's answer.

As Lisa fed the child with a bottle, Edward retired to a computer workstation in a neighboring cubicle. Both were lost to their own worries. Concern for the child's well-being had staved off her terror for the past day, gave her something to focus on. She knew Kat was somewhere in this lab complex, but where was her friend holed up? For that matter, where was this lab?

So far, both Petra and Edward had treated her with a modicum of respect, appreciating and needing her help. She remembered those digitized words, a cold warning: *Prove your usefulness, and you both continue to live.*

With the child doing better, Lisa's usefulness was about to come to an end.

Then what?

She remembered who had assigned her to this job in the first place, picturing his kind face, his soft words.

Thank you, Dr. Cummings, for agreeing to help my grandnephew.

Anger raged inside her against that cool, calm demeanor of Robert Gant. She knew how much pain and suffering and loss it cost to bring this special child into existence, to this place and time. Still, she could not blame the child for such atrocities. The boy might have been born out of blood and heartbreak—but he was still an innocent.

The child finished suckling, the bottle was empty. Those big eyes drooped, heavy with milk-sodden drowsiness. Lisa let him drift into slumber, oblivious to the horrors beyond the clear plastic walls of his incubator.

She turned to Edward and limped over to him, favoring her aching ankle. Up on the wall, a camera tracked her path, swiveling to follow her. She wondered if Robert Gant watched her or merely some bored guard.

Exhausted, Lisa was beyond subtlety or subterfuge. "Edward, what are you trying to accomplish with these triple helices?"

He swung around on his desk chair. "Ah, I can't speak to the goal of my financial benefactors. All I know is my purpose in the grand scheme of things."

"And that's what?"

He raised an eyebrow, belying the hubris that followed. "To forge the key to life itself."

He gave her a tired smile, and, surprisingly, she echoed it.

"As lofty as that might sound, PNA *is* that key," Edward explained. "It unlocks the full power of DNA and places the blueprints of life into our hands. With PNA, genomics experts can engineer strands that can turn specific genes on or off, unfettering mankind from its biological limitations. But it also allows new genes to be introduced, new code written onto the PNA and inserted into a fertilized egg. In the end, God will no longer evolve man—we will."

Edward stared toward the child in the incubator. "But all that will come later. For the moment, we have only one goal engineered into this first strain of PNA, a simple thing really."

Lisa felt a sick turn to her stomach. "What goal?"

Edward's eyes never left the sleeping boy, the doctor's expression a mask of wonder and also sadness.

"Immortality."

Lisa couldn't hide her shock.

"Do not be so surprised, Dr. Cummings. This child is not the *first* immortal born into this world." Edward finally turned to her, letting her see his sincerity. "They walk among us already."

1:07 P.M.
Washington, DC

Five hours left.

Painter had returned to his own office, leaving the president with his daughter below, guarded by his Secret Service contingent. They were under the five-hour mark until James Gant would come out of hiding and pretend to be recovering from major surgery. Everything to maintain that ruse was already in place.

He found Kowalski sitting inside, his feet propped up on Painter's desk, his arms folded over his belly, snoring.

Painter shoved his legs off.

The man snorted awake. "We ready?" he asked.

"As we're ever going to be."

Painter grabbed a holstered SIG Sauer from a cabinet. The rest of the strike team's gear was waiting at the airstrip, a jet warming up. As he secured the shoulder harness and holster in place, his eyes caught on the picture of Lisa on his desk, smiling softly, hair glowing in the summer sun, lips parted slightly. His love for her was a tangible thing, not a thought or a feeling, but a weight in his heart, a pressure in his chest, a stirring of heat in his veins.

At that moment, he knew the truth.

I need to buy a ring.

Motion at the door drew his attention. Tucker stood there, shadowed by Kane.

Painter gave his holster harness a final tug, cinching it snugly, and faced the man. "Captain Wayne?"

Tucker stepped inside. "Sir, I'd like to join you on this mission."

"I appreciate that, captain, but we hired you to find Amanda. Your obligation to us has been fulfilled."

"Understood, sir." Tucker's countenance remained hard, rocky. "But not my obligation to Amanda. I left her baby back in Dubai, and I want a chance to correct that mistake."

"We can certainly use the additional manpower . . . not to mention your dog's nose. But we'll be *parachuting* onto the Gant estate."

Airspace above the presidential estate was restricted. The no-fly zone had been established before James Gant was president, going back decades, a courtesy of the state of South Carolina for the largesse of the clan.

Painter's plan was to sweep in close, parachute out, and glide low onto the grounds. And those grounds were *huge,* over 300,000 acres, almost 500 square miles of misty mountains, towering waterfalls, dark forests, and grassy meadows. The estate had ill-defined borders, as the family bought neighboring farms, ranches, and orchards, extending their property in fits and starts.

That remote, rough terrain would serve to hide them, allowing them to hoof it overland from their drop point.

Tucker seemed to have no problem with parachuting onto the estate. "Kane and I have had plenty of jump time," the man assured him. "I have my dog's harness system with me."

"Then welcome aboard."

Kowalski stood, stretched, and headed out the door with the others. "This place is really going to the dogs."

Painter set off down the hall. He had been expecting another teammate to arrive by now, but the latecomer would have to meet them at the airstrip. Time was ticking down. Jason Carter would take command at the communications nest in his absence and coordinate efforts from here. It was a lot to place on his young shoulders, but Painter knew he could handle it. Jason had already gathered his own intelligence team in preparation, ruling the nest of older agents with an enthusiasm reserved for the young.

Painter reached the elevators as the doors opened.

Inside the cage stood the last member of their strike team. Kat's husband adjusted his new prosthetic hand, securing the cuff with a twist and wiggling his fingers. Monk must have already stopped by R&D to get the upgrade Painter had ordered for him, a prosthetic specifically designed for this mission, to help with the infiltration of the Lodge.

"About time," Painter said.

Monk glanced up, meeting his gaze, his face fierce. "You try to find a babysitter on the Fourth of July . . . now let's go get our women."

1:25 P.M.
Blue Ridge Mountains

"And you're claiming this child can live forever?" Lisa asked. "That he's immortal?"

Edward continued to sit in his cubicle in the medical ward. "Barring accidents or disease, yes, he could live a very long time. I imagine it will take further tinkering to achieve true immortality. But in the end, like I said, he's not the first immortal born to this world."

"What do you mean?"

"Since we have time until Petra finishes her evaluation of the boy's genetics, I'll do my best to explain. It's the least I can offer you for saving the child."

Lisa was prepared to listen.

"Many scientists, across a scope of professions, believe immortality will be achieved in our lifetime. The dates bandied about all seem to center around the middle of this century, 2045 or so. That means children born today will live to see those accomplishments come to fruition. They will take advantage of them during their lifetimes, becoming immortal. So in that regard, they are immortal already. Or at least something quite close to it. Their lifetimes could be easily doubled or tripled."

She imagined what he envisioned, how some children born today will live forever. *They* were the immortals walking among us already.

Still, such a claim seemed impossible. She voiced it aloud. "You truly expect we can attain immortality in such a short time frame?"

"Or something very close to it. And it's *not* just me making that claim. It comes from hundreds of scientists, researchers, and visionaries across a gamut of professions—from medicine, genomics, and gerontology to pharmaceuticals, nanotech, and robotics. What we're doing in our labs here, financed by our benefactor, is taking the first tentative steps into eternity."

Lisa pictured the man orchestrating this work.

Our benefactor . . .

Robert Gant.

It was beyond comprehension. All this horror perpetrated in an attempt to live forever. Still, Lisa sensed something *more* was going on, another agenda still being kept secret—*but what?*

She knew any true answers lay in keeping Edward talking.

He obliged, waxing proudly on where the world was heading. "There are two general schools of thought in regards to expanding man's lifetimes. The first is moving machines into man. The other is moving man into machines."

She shook her head, not appreciating the distinction.

"A thousand years ago the average life expectancy of mankind was only twenty-five years. It took another nine hundred years to extend that to thirty-seven. Today the average is seventy-eight. So, in the past *hun-*

dred years, we more than doubled life expectancy. That amazing spurt of growth happened because of science and technology. And it will only grow faster from here. Estimates say we will soon be adding a year to our lives with every passing year. Just think about that. For every year you grow older, life expectancy will extend a year in front of you."

"But what will drive that growth?"

"What has always driven it: the furnace of technology. In that forge, machine and man will melt together into one."

He must have read her skepticism and smiled, ready to deflect it.

"Already people have artificial pancreases inside them," he continued. "Currently thirty thousand Parkinson patients have neural implants. And as technology grows *smaller,* it will invade us even more. Advancements in nanotechnology—which is manufacturing at the atomic level—hold the promise of replacing vital organs in *fifteen* years, our blood cells in *twenty* years, and in *twenty-five* years, nanotechnology will reprogram our biological software to reverse aging."

Lisa understood. "*Moving machines into man* . . . into our bodies."

"That's one path to immortality. But the reverse holds even greater promise. As computing power explodes exponentially, a term was coined—*singularity*—marking that moment when artificial intelligence will surpass mankind. Various futurists expect this to occur somewhere in the middle of this century."

"So soon?" Lisa asked.

Edward nodded with a small smile of satisfaction. "By 2030, estimates say computing power will be a million times what it is today. Anything is possible with that much power. In the meantime, scientists from around the globe are searching for methods to *merge* that growing computing power to our own. In Switzerland, researchers are reverse-engineering the human brain, creating a neuron-by-neuron simulation, with the intent to have a complete *virtual* brain in ten years. Here in the States, a group of MIT researchers are building a map of all the brain's synapses, those trillions of connections between neurons, all in a search for the seat of human consciousness."

Lisa sighed. "And I assume that the ultimate goal is to *fill* that empty seat, to scan our consciousness into computers."

"Exactly. *Moving man into machines.* The second path to immortality." Edward glanced over to the incubator. "But I'm searching for a third path."

"Which is what?"

"A new science. *Cybergenetics.* The merging of technology into *our genetic code.*"

"The PNA strand," Lisa said, understanding, growing both awed and horrified, picturing that piece of engineered protein snaking into human DNA and regulating it.

"DNA is really just a set of information processes for building our bodies. But that software is old, millions of years old. PNA holds the potential for overhauling that system. Rebooting mankind forever."

Lisa tried to draw him down from the lofty heights of theory to the reality of his lab. "But back to your own research. What does *your* PNA do, the one inside the boy?"

"It basically addresses the deleterious effects that come with growing old. The field of gerontology—the study of aging—has discovered that there are only *seven* basic ways a body damages itself as it ages. Reverse those seven deadly ways and immortality is within reach."

Edward looked significantly toward her, lifting an eyebrow.

"You did it," she said in a hushed voice. "Your PNA manipulates and regulates the DNA to offset those damages."

"It does, but not perfectly. We concentrated most of our efforts on *one* of them. The death of cells. Are you familiar with the Hayflick Limit?"

She shook her head, finding it harder and harder to speak.

"Back in 1961, Dr. Leonard Hayflick estimated that the maximum natural age for a human being is about 120 years. He based that on the number of times a cell will divide before it stops. The *number* of these divisions is determined by the length of some repeated DNA at the end of each cell's chromosomes. These repeated sequences are called telomeres. They basically act like the aglets at the end of shoelaces, keeping the laces from fraying. But after a certain number of divisions, the telomeres wear off, and the chromosome frays itself to death."

"What does this have to do with your PNA?"

"We engineered the PNA to function as *permanent* telomeres, in order to create undying cells, and thus allow us to shatter through the Hayflick Limit."

"Creating a path to immortality."

He nodded. "We are at the very threshold to eternity."

"But why do this? There are so many negative effects if man could live forever. Overpopulation, starvation, stagnation. There's a reason we are meant to die, to step aside for the next generation."

"True, but those dangers only exist if the technology is available to *all*. In the hands of an elite—a chosen people—there would be no such risks."

Shocked, she pictured Robert Gant's face. Was that his plan? To keep his bloodline alive forever, to create an undying dynasty?

"Why are you helping them?" she finally eked out.

"Because I must. Mankind has always chafed against restraints and limitations. We left our homelands to cross uncharted seas. We broke the bounds of gravity to fly. We even left our planet. Here is merely the next step toward freedom, the *ultimate* freedom, to break the chains of mortality and free us from our very graves."

Lisa found herself aghast. She had warmed to the man over the past day, working alongside him, but now she saw the chinks in his armor, allowing the madness inside to shine forth.

"The visionary Raymond Kurzweil once posed the question, *Does God exist?*" Edward turned to stare at the boy in the incubator. "His answer was only two words: *Not yet.*"

She stared at the man, seeing the glaze of megalomania. She knew from her years in the medical profession that this affliction seldom presented itself as a raving lunacy. Instead, most of those afflicted were charming in demeanor, confident in their convictions, and all too often described as simply *nice*. They were monsters wearing sweet faces.

She was saved from responding by the return of Petra. The woman had a sheaf of reports in her hands as she strode stiffly toward them. Her expression remained unreadable as she reached Edward's cubicle.

He faced her, looking up, hopeful. "And the verdict on the boy?"

"Not good. The child may appear healthy, but his triple helices continue to denature and shed their PNA strands. Worse yet, the process appears to be *accelerating*."

Edward lifted his hands, rubbed his eyes, and sighed out his defeat. "So the breakdown wasn't because the boy was sick. As I feared, he's simply rejecting the PNA."

"He's no good to us," Petra said.

"But we were so close." Edward sagged.

"We will keep working," Petra said. "Success cannot be far away. And besides, you know they only want females. The boy was doomed either way."

Doomed?

Lisa stiffened. "What are you talking about?"

Edward, lost in his disappointment, seemed surprised she was still there. "Surely you understand that males with triple helices are basically mules. They might live forever, but they're genetic dead ends. Only *females* can pass this PNA trait to future offspring."

"No, I don't understand," she said, intending to keep them talking, shifting slowly toward the key card on Edward's desk.

You're not going to harm this child . . .

He huffed, swung to a computer, and tapped up a file. On the screen, a time-lapsed video of cellular division appeared. The two DNA strands were colored in red, the single PNA in blue. A couple of additional PNA strands hung loosely in the cytoplasm. As the cells divided, the PNA slipped out of the way, joined its brothers in the cytoplasm. Cellular division then proceeded as normal. Once the cell had pinched into two, one of the PNA strands from each of the new cells snaked out of the cytoplasm and back into the heart of the DNA strand, re-forming the triple helix in both cells.

"Do you understand?" Edward asked.

She did. She now understood why a male couldn't pass on the triple-helix trait. A man's sperm cell contains half of his DNA. A woman's egg contains half of her DNA *plus* all of her cytoplasm and everything inside the jelly-like cellular fluid: mitochondria, organelles, proteins—and, in this case, PNA. Because of that, a father couldn't pass on the triple-helix trait—the trait of immortality—because he couldn't pass on any cytoplasmic PNA. Only a female could.

"It's like mitochondria in women," Lisa said. "All mitochondria get passed along the *female* genetic line, from egg to egg to egg."

"Correct. So you understand?"

She nodded.

"Then you also understand why we have to kill this boy."

She jerked straighter. "No . . . of course not!"

Edward sighed. "He's a dead end, only useful for research fodder. If we'd been able to return stability to his triple helix by treating his shock, then he would have made the perfect test subject for Petra's vivisection table, his organs divided into artificial suspension systems, perfect for challenging and testing the immortality trait. Better that than waiting decades to study this child's growth. Science can't move that slowly, especially in the face of something as inconsequential as morality."

Lisa sat back on Edward's desk, numb with shock. She had labored throughout the night and slowly pulled the child back from death's door—*only to meet this end?*

She had also grown attached to the boy. How could she not, with those big, trusting blue eyes?

Petra stared sullenly at the child in the incubator, as if he were a dog who had chewed her favorite pumps. "Now he's useless. Another failure."

"A *promising* failure." Edward patted Petra on the back of her hand. "You can still perform the necropsy, collect all the histological tissue samples you want. We can still learn much, even from this failure."

Enough.

Lisa would not let them kill this child.

As they focused on the baby, with their backs to her, she made her move.

Already leaning on Edward's desk, she grabbed his key card—and his desk lamp. She yanked the cord free and swung the lamp broad-armed at the back of Petra's head. The weighted steel base hit her skull, felling her like a chopped tree. The woman hit the corner of the cubicle and tumbled hard to the floor.

Edward had started to rise, but Lisa kicked the chair out from under him. Off balance, he fell forward. She used that moment to ram her knee into his nose, smashing it and sending him sprawling. He wasn't out, but he was down, dazed.

She dropped the lamp, ran to the incubator, and, as gently as she could, removed the cuffs and tapes of the NICU's monitoring leads. Once he was free, she swaddled the child in a thin blanket and carried him close to her chest.

She knew the prison ward was a blind alley, as was this suite of labs. The only other true exit was the door through which Robert Gant had entered yesterday. She ran toward it, ignoring the flaring complaint from her swollen ankle. At the door, she swiped the stolen key card, unlocked the way, and dashed out of the ward.

A dimly lit maze of halls and rooms spread outward, looking deserted, waiting to be occupied by Edward's new facility. She'd overheard that much.

She picked a direction and ran off blindly with the child, moving as fast as she could with her compromised ankle, thankful the child remained quiet after being fed.

She hadn't bothered to dispatch or tie up Petra and Edward.

For a very simple reason.

She remembered the eye of the security camera following her as she fled. Someone already knew she had escaped.

36

"Where did she go?" Robert Gant pressed.

He stood in front of a computer in Dr. Emmet Fielding's office, located in the red zone of the underground complex. He had gotten word a few minutes ago from central security that Lisa Cummings had attacked two of the scientists and fled with his brother's grandchild.

A fist formed. Not out of anger at the woman, but at the thought of his brother. He held his grief in his fist and leaned his weight on it, crushing his knuckles against the desktop, trying to contain that well of sorrow. Flashes of moments with Jimmy sparked in his head: two brothers riding horseback, drinking beer behind the barn, playing cards while smoking cigars. It had been Jimmy who held him together after his wife died. He tried to squeeze an entire lifetime into his fist, to hold those memories in check.

It was why he had come down here, tinkering with Dr. Fielding on some projects, studying some of the latest neuro-pod designs, including several truly horrendous war beasts in early stages of development.

Anything to keep himself distracted.

Robert understood the inevitability of his brother's assassination, could fathom the logic of it when it was presented to him as a fait accompli. The greater body of the Lineage demanded it. So he had to obey—as he'd always done in the past. But he could not escape the pain of it.

"She's still missing, sir," the guard said. The man's image hovered in the upper corner of the screen. "There are only a few active cameras in that disused section of the facility."

"Then check the cameras in the neighboring zones. Blue and Orange."

"Yes, sir."

As he waited, Robert brought up a schematic of the estate. The main mansion, the Lodge, lay ten miles away, surrounded by its high walls. Only a tiny fraction of the family knew the facility existed. Even Jimmy didn't know, though he'd gone fishing a few times at a river within a half-mile of its outskirts.

The sprawling research facility covered twenty acres, occupying an old mine on a remote piece of Gant property, set amid the high cliffs and waterfalls of the Eastern Continental Divide. The divide—which ran through the Blue Ridge Mountains and across the Gant estate—split the watershed of the region: on one side, rivers all flowed toward the Gulf of Mexico; on the other, toward the Atlantic.

A century ago, a member of the Bloodline discovered the old, flooded mine. Slowly, over time, it had been engineered and converted into a secret facility, carved out underground and burrowed even farther over the years, spreading under the old-growth forest and meadows.

He stared at the map of the facility. It looked like a madman's Rorschach inkblot, much of it shaded out in gray, indicating unoccupied sections of the lab. Robert remembered better times. During the heyday of the Cold War years, the place had once hosted hundreds of researchers from both sides of the Iron Curtain, all working for the Guild, for the Bloodline. The halls thrummed with excitement, the verve of men and women working at the edge of scientific exploration—and often moving beyond.

Robert stared at the grayed-out areas now, eating through the facility like a cancer. Since then, like many American companies, the research projects that had once flourished within these walls had been shifted abroad, outsourced to Third World countries where no questions were asked, labor was cheaper, and government interference or oversight was nonexistent.

So, this older facility was hollowed out, becoming a deserted cathedral to science, most of it shuttered and shut down. Only Robert's pet project remained, though isolated and adrift. His robotics research was no longer considered by the Bloodline a viable path to extending life, deemed to be too *macro* in its scope. Instead, everything shifted into the fashionable *micro* world of stem cells, nanotechnology, and now DNA manipulation. Only lately was that trend reversing, the pendulum swinging back with the advancements in robotics, creating the new field of *neuro-robotics,* the merging of man and machine.

Still, the Bloodline relegated his work to weapons research, which was not inappropriate. In Afghanistan alone, there were more than two thousand robots fighting alongside American troops—and that force was rapidly expanding in number and intelligence.

So, Robert continued his weapons research here. The facility was perfectly suited for that: isolated, under a no-fly restriction, and, best of all, surrounded by varied terrain. Rivers, forests, meadows, and cliffs—the perfect landscape to field-test the various iterations of his neuro-pods.

Now, with the loss of that major facility in Dubai, life was again returning to these empty halls. New priests were returning to the cathedral, ready to bring the chorus and the chant of the scientific method back to these hallowed halls.

Robert should have been happier, but all he felt was dead inside. The loss of his brother coming so soon on the heels of Amanda's death. And now the threat to his grandnephew. It finally broke something inside him—or maybe he had always been broken, and it took Jimmy's blood on his hands for him to finally recognize it.

The Bloodline had not been kind to his family.

He planned on ending that today.

The guard came back online. "Sir, Orange and Blue are negative on the target."

"Then spread the search on foot, scour every room, closet, and cabinet."

"Yes, sir."

Robert knew that could be a challenge. With the Fourth of July holiday, only a skeleton staff remained on-site—not that the regular staff was all that much more fleshed out.

But he needed his grandnephew returned to him.

He'd lost too much today—and placed a thin hope that he could save the child and the straggling remnants of his immediate family. But with the outside world closing down upon his private world, he had no chance until he first secured the child.

He knew what he needed.

Leverage.

He tapped a key and brought up a view of a cell in the red zone. A woman with a shaved head sat on a bed, her face in her hands. He was glad she was turned away.

Robert pressed an intercom button.

"Yes," Dr. Fielding answered from his laboratory in that same zone.

"Emmet, you said you wanted to test the newest pods, a more vigorous challenge of their abilities."

Excitement frosted his voice. "Of course, sir."

"Then let's get started."

Robert finished with the man and made the necessary calls. Once done, he tapped another switch, accessing a camera that required a code known only to him.

None must know about this prisoner.

The view of another room bloomed onto the screen, only this one was lavishly appointed with a four-poster bed, deep-cushioned chairs, a stone fireplace, and walls decorated with tapestries. The roof was wood-beamed, framed into Gothic arches, and supported a centuries-old crystal chandelier.

But the room was still a cell.

The window, streaming with sunlight, was heavily barred. The stout wood door, banded in iron, was locked electronically.

The prisoner must have heard the stir of the camera as Robert turned it toward the window. She stood limned against the sunlight, a dark shadow, a slender twist against the brightness.

Noting the camera's motion, she came forward, looking up.

She still wore the same leathers as when she arrived, though it looked like she'd used the neighboring bathroom to shower.

She glared up at the camera.

Those green eyes, pinched slightly at the corner, marked her mixed Eurasian blood. Just the sight of those eyes made his heart clutch.

He touched the screen with his finger, rubbing an edge of his thumb along the side of her face, knowing he could never get closer. She had escaped the Guild years ago, turned enemy to the Bloodline, but now she was returned to the fold.

"Where you belong," he whispered throatily. "I should never have let you escape."

Another face blinked into existence in the corner of the screen, irritating him with the interruption.

"Mr. Gant," the man said, "I wanted to inform you that the helicopter is inbound with the package from DC."

"Acknowledged. I'll be back at the Lodge momentarily."

An underground tunnel ran from the lab complex to a secure entrance at the mansion. He could take the tram and be back there in minutes.

He lingered a moment more, staring at his handsome prisoner.

As if sensing his eyes, she lifted an arm and raised an offending finger toward the camera.

He smiled as he clicked off the camera. He turned around and headed for the tunnel back to the Lodge, ready to face the man who had killed his brother.

2:03 P.M.

As the helicopter swept in a wide curve, Gray gaped at the view of the Gant family mansion below.

He had seen pictures of the massive structure in books, never in person, few people had. It competed with such great American castles as those built by the Vanderbilt, Rockefeller, and Hearst families. But the Gant clan went old-school, patterning their design on a famous Crusader castle in Syria, the Krak des Chevaliers, the Fortress of the Knights.

Its outer wall, studded with small square towers and peppered with arrow slits, was three meters thick. The only passage through that wall was a massive archway, fronted by a drawbridge over a real moat.

Beyond the wall, a sunlit courtyard was half–parking lot, half-gardens, holding centuries-old oaks and flowering rose beds. The keep itself held seventy rooms, all done in Gothic style of pointed arches, high windows, and a multitude of doors and balconies. It all led up to two square towers crowned by toothed parapets.

The chopper lowered toward a helipad in the courtyard. As it dropped within the outer walls, Gray felt the world close in, trapping him. The skids touched the pavement, and he was led out at gunpoint, his wrists cuffed behind him. The team leader marched him across the courtyard toward the giant arched doors to the main mansion.

Gray had nowhere to run. Even if he could escape, he remained tethered electronically to the transmitter in the leader's pocket. If he fled farther than ten yards, the countdown to detonation would begin again.

Right now he needed to keep his head.

In more ways than one.

A few steps away, the team leader held his radio earpiece, listening to someone. His other hand nervously scratched at the crucifix tattoo on his neck. All Gray heard was a final "Yes, sir."

The man turned to Gray. "Come with me."

They headed up the steps of native fieldstone and through an open wooden door carved with panels depicting knightly pursuits, from jousting to battles.

Beyond the door opened a massive hall. It was like stepping into a cathedral, from the vaulted ceilings to the massive stone pillars. Sunlight flowed through stained-glass windows, again depicting knights, but in a more courtly setting, many wearing the Templar cross on their surcoats.

Despite all of the grandness, there remained an indescribable warmth to the hall. Thick rugs softened the stone floors. Two fireplaces at either end, tall enough to trot horses through, promised merry winter fires. Even now they were filled with massive bouquets, scenting the room with summer's endless promise.

And Gray could tell where the nickname for the estate, the Lodge, came from. The mansion's reputation as a hunting lodge was plain. Several of the rugs on the floor were bearskins. Mounted on the walls were the heads of beasts from every continent.

Hemingway would have been very happy here.

"Keep up," the team leader barked.

Gray hurried forward, led across the hall to a door beside one of the fireplaces. The leader knocked.

"Come in."

Gray was ushered into a small library, done up as a sitting room, with French antique furniture, a small fireplace, and tiny windows, no bigger than arrow slits, offering peeks at the gardens beyond.

The lone occupant sat in a chair to one side of the cold fireplace. He wore a conservative gray suit, though he'd shed his jacket and had it folded over the edge of a chair. The white shirt was unbuttoned at the top, sleeves rolled up.

Robert Gant held out his hand.

The team leader rushed forward, passed the transmitter into his palm, along with the keys to Gray's cuffs—then hurried out, clearly under specific orders, as not a word was exchanged between them.

The door closed.

The president's brother stared at Gray's face and spoke his first words. "Did he suffer?"

Gray didn't need to be told the subject of that question. Still, he didn't know his footing here. This was made worse by the fire in his chest, flaming the edges of his eyes, burning at the bonds of his self-control. But cuffed and at the mercy of the transmitter, he could do nothing but stand, his legs trembling with the desire to send him charging regardless of the consequences. His fists tightened so hard that the bulge of his wrists cut into the tight cuffs.

Robert waved him to the other chair opposite the fireplace.

Gray took it, not trusting his control. He sat on the edge, ready to lunge, to exact whatever revenge he could upon the man responsible for his mother's death.

Robert asked again, his voice cracking this time. "Please . . . I know

Jimmy's surgery is futile. I heard the grim prognosis. But in those final moments, did my brother suffer?"

Gray heard the pain more than the words. That keen of grief let him see past the red haze to the man's barely contained agony. Robert's eyes were stitched with red veins, shadowed darkly by pain, his skin as ashen as his gray jacket.

For some reason, as much as he hated the man, Gray answered as truthfully as he could. "No. Your brother didn't suffer."

Robert nodded, turning to stare at his lap. "Thank you for that."

The man sat quietly in that stricken pose for a long time. When he lifted his face again, tears ran down his face. He wiped them away and stared at the cold fireplace, as if needing its warmth.

He spoke his next words softly. "I'm sorry for your mother."

Gray stiffened, coming close to leaping out of his chair.

But the face the man showed Gray, so honestly distraught, quelled his anger. "Loss is an affliction that never lets go of your heart. I know that too well. It is too high a price, even for life everlasting, which now seems a horrible thing."

Gray remembered Seichan saying something similar. What was going on with this man? He had expected torture and interrogations upon landing here. His only hope was that Painter had gotten his secret message and understood enough to figure out where he'd been taken.

"The accumulation of grief over *one* lifetime is more than a heart can bear," Robert explained. "Only the heartless could withstand more. Or the very young, those too naïve to truly understand loss. Like I was when they came for me."

"When who came for you?" Gray asked, trying to understand.

Robert remained silent, seeming to be working through something, clearly teetering on the edge. "I'll show you. You may be useful to my plans."

He stood and drew Gray after him. He crossed to a bookcase and pulled a handle tucked into the frame to unlatch a secret door. A section of the case swung open, revealing a spiral stone stair going down.

Robert led the way, lit by wall sconces. Gray had expected cobwebs and wall torches, but the passage merely wound down to basement levels. Through the open doors to other landings, he saw laundry facilities, kitchens, and they ended up in a wine cellar. Arched tunnels, carved out of the natural stone, spread outward in multiple directions, dimly lit by bare bulbs strung above. Massive oak barrels lined both sides. Neighboring rooms, like small chapels dedicated to Bacchus, held towering racks of dusty bottles, an accumulation of unimaginable wealth.

Robert moved swiftly forward, as if fearing he might change his mind, or someone might stop him. Gray got dragged behind, as much by the pull of his invisible leash as by curiosity.

Their journey ended deep within the vintner's maze, in a side room holding four massive French oak barrels, as large as elephants.

Robert stepped to one and released a latch to open the face of the barrel. The wooden barrel was lined by steel. Robert hopped inside, followed by Gray. The back of the barrel looked like the doors to a bank vault. Robert typed in a code on the front and placed his hand on a palm reader.

Green lights flashed, and a low hum of hydraulics rotated a two-foot-thick plate-steel door.

It opened to a small room—an elevator, he realized as Robert entered more codes and the cage began to drop.

During this entire trip, Robert hadn't said anything. He looked beyond words at the moment, lost in his own grief.

Finally, the elevator stopped, the doors opened into an anteroom to a massive, hermetically sealed clean room, half the length of a football field. But this was no sterile industrial white-and-stainless-steel place. Beyond the air-locked sealed door was something out of the British Museum. Mahogany display cases held dusty tomes, yellowed scrolls, and worn artifacts from every age of man. Domes of glass sat atop marble plinths, protecting delicate statues and golden treasures.

Robert turned to him. "Within lies the true heart of the Bloodline."

37

Lisa crouched in a dark bathroom stall, perched on a toilet with the baby cradled on her lap. She clutched a Langenbeck amputation knife in one fist.

She had found the weapon, which looked like a scalpel with a four-inch blade, in a necropsy lab. The morgue, like much of this labyrinthine facility, looked long-deserted. A layer of fine dust had covered everything. She knew she could not stow herself in one of the body cabinets. Her footprints were plain on the dusty floor.

To hide her tracks, she had kept her flight along the edge of the occupied sections of the laboratory, a dangerous path. She'd come close to being discovered twice, but the facility was a huge warren of hiding places. She had passed one corridor that must have run the length of the facility. Its end dwindled down to a dark point, lit only in a few sections.

Within the first few minutes, she knew she must be underground.

No windows anywhere.

I need to find a way back to the surface.

If she could escape, go for help—then she could offer Kat real support. By herself, any rescue attempt was futile. Her ankle continued to throb, shooting pain up her leg with every step.

And it wasn't just Kat's life in danger.

The baby slept in the crook of her arm, quiet as a lamb, belly full of milk, likely still bodily exhausted from the near-death collapse of his systems. She prayed the child remained quiet.

She had come to this bathroom only as a temporary reprieve, to collect her thoughts. Her initial flight had been that of a panicked rabbit, just trying to stay ahead of the hunting pack. For the moment, she had lost her pursuers, arriving at a region of the facility with yellow walls. The whole facility seemed to be color-mapped. She'd fled from white through orange to yellow.

She pictured Kat's cell.

It had red walls.

She had discovered an evacuation map outside the bathroom. It was that discovery that changed her course from a maddened flight to the beginnings of a plan. She ducked inside here to think, to consider the best route to take.

From the evacuation plan, she recognized that she was on the middle level of three, somewhere in the northwest quadrant. The map laid out the shortest route up to the surface—but she dared not take that path. They would be expecting that; likely guards were already posted.

When she reached the next stairwell, they would expect her to go *up*. So, instead, she would go *down*. She noted that the red zone on the map did not extend to the third level. She saw a corridor that transected the facility, passing under the red zone. She could use that passageway to cross to the far side of the facility, where fewer eyes, if any, would be watching. There was a remote exit in a sliver of the lab that poked out from the bulk.

That was her goal.

She shifted a cramping leg toward the floor, wanting to check that map one more time, then begin her painful run for the exit. As her toe lowered toward the linoleum, the door to the bathroom creaked open. The light flicked on, blinding after her flight through the dim corridors and dark rooms.

A casual whistling accompanied the intruder.

Not likely a guard.

From the timbre of the whistling and heavy-footed gait, it was a man. She prayed he crossed to the urinal, but his whistling approached the bay of stalls. She clutched her knife more tightly, willing him away.

Not this one. Pick another.

Her prayer was answered as he entered the neighboring stall, the one closest to the door. She had purposefully avoided that one for that very reason. She would wait until he finished, give it another minute, then continue.

It was at that moment, perhaps stirred by his whistling, that the boy in her arms began to rouse, stretching a pudgy, wrinkled fist, yawning silently. But she knew that wouldn't last.

She had to get out of here before he made a noise and alerted her neighbor. She didn't know how long the man would be here. Her ears picked out the clatter of an unbuckling belt, the rip of a zipper, and the soft whisper of pants falling—followed by a long sigh of relief.

It sounded like he would be here awhile.

The whistling began again.

Lisa couldn't take the risk of being trapped inside here if the baby began to cry. She carefully lowered her good foot to the ground, pivoted to her bad leg, careful of her ankle. She mouthed the blade between her lips and balanced the baby under the crook of one arm. Luckily, she had spent many nights babysitting Kat's children.

She had never locked her stall. What would be the use? So she used the coat hook on the inside of the door to slowly swing it open, allowing her to slip outside.

I can do this.

Then the baby let out a small wail of complaint.

Lisa froze as the whistling stopped. The stall lock snapped open.

Her mind immediately flashed to her new mantra.

WWKD?

What would Kat do?

Lisa kicked the door as it started to swing open, catching the man in the face as he reached forward. He fell back—Lisa followed, her knife already in hand. As he looked up, she slashed hard at his exposed throat. The razor-sharp amputation blade, made to cut through hard cartilage and stiff tendons, performed as designed. The deep cut severed skin, muscle, and trachea, drowning any scream. The severed carotid spurted high, splashing. The man gurgled and slid off of the commode. His hands clutched at his neck, his eyes shining with shock, already dead but not knowing it.

That's what Kat would do.

Lisa swung away, careful of the blood pooling, so as not to leave tracks. She pulled the stall shut, crossed to the bathroom door, and turned off the lights. His absence would likely be missed. She had to be far away before that happened.

She peeked out and found the hall clear. But as she stepped out, her name was called, loudly, echoing throughout the facility.

She cringed.

But it was only the loudspeaker system. The voice was male, not the digitally masked speaker from earlier. It didn't sound like Robert Gant's Southern slant or Edward Blake's British accent.

Someone new.

"DR. LISA CUMMINGS! THIS IS YOUR ONE AND ONLY WARNING! YOU WILL TURN YOURSELF AND THE CHILD OVER TO THE NEAREST PERSONNEL, OR YOU WILL SEND YOUR FRIEND INTO DEADLY PERIL."

A monitor bloomed to light down the hall, others blinked elsewhere. Clearly he was making a general broadcast to the entire compound.

She shifted down the hall enough to see a stranger on the screen. He wore white laboratory coveralls with a hood pulled back and a surgical mask on top of his head. In the background, she spotted Dr. Blake. The view suddenly switched, revealing Kat standing at gunpoint beside a sealed metal door. It looked like she carried a length of pipe and a small shield of some sort.

"AS PUNISHMENT AND TO RECOGNIZE THE THREAT SHE FACES, WE WILL PERFORM A SMALL DEMONSTRATION SO YOU FULLY UNDERSTAND."

The door swung open, sunlight blazed, blinding the camera. The view switched to the outside, looking down upon a grassy meadow, a line of oaks in the distant background. Kat was shoved outside, stumbling into view, shading her eyes with her small shield against the summer glare.

"TURN YOURSELF IN NOW, OR HER FATE WILL WORSEN OVER TIME. THIS IS YOUR ONLY WARNING."

Lisa needed no time to decide.

WWKD?

She knew what Kat would want her to do.

She hurried down the hall—not to turn herself in but to make her escape while most eyes here were fixed on those screens, prepared to enjoy whatever blood sport was about to ensue. And Lisa knew from the shield and the club that some gladiatorial battle was about to start.

She caught fractured glimpses as she ran with the child, gone quiet again for now, likely jostled back to sleep by her running. In stuttered snatches, she saw Kat head out into that field, wading through the grasses.

Be careful, she wished her friend.

2:18 P.M.

Kat stalked across the thigh-high grass. She carried a hard steel shield, two feet square, strapped to her forearm. In her other hand, she wielded a three-foot length of hollow pipe. She breathed deeply, readying her body, flushing oxygen into her muscles. Her senses stretched out.

The tall grass was mostly green, redolent of summer, the scent growing stronger as she crushed through blades with her slippers. The edges of her gown snagged on bristled weeds. Her ears caught the twitter of birdsong, registering it but filtering it into the background, along with the distant sound of tumbling water to the northwest and the sweep of gentle wind through leaves.

She knew the hunters would be coming.

She'd overheard the two scientists talking—Fielding and Blake—preparing her, deciding which weapons to test.

The battlefield is the ultimate crucible of Darwinian natural selection, Fielding had explained to the other researcher. *Survival is the main drive of evolution. And it's no different for our pods. For our weapons to learn, they must be field-tested, battle-hardened. With each new challenge, new synapses of the cybernetic brains will grow and expand. But we must test the pods with ever-harder challenges.*

She had seen those *hexapods,* as she heard them called: crab-like titanium killing machines, equipped with razor-sharp legs, slashing daggers, and drilling burrs. Other variants lined the workbench. The worst looked like a large, bloated tick, its legs as skinny as ice picks.

Beyond the workbench, deeper in the lab, larger creatures, the size of small black bears, had lurked, in various stages of assembly.

Kat strode across the meadow, hefting the shield to test its weight and swinging the pipe to judge its balance.

We've pitted the hexapods against unarmed opponents in the past, Fielding had finished. *Today we'll test them against the next level of weaponry: blunt weapons and shields. We will send wave after wave, escalating the numbers each time, until they learn, adapt, and defeat their opponent.*

A rustle to her left alerted her. She swung around, dropping her shield low. The grasses stirred as something raced low through them, cutting across the meadow like the fin of a shark through water. She saw four other trails swinging wider, intending to outflank and circle her.

Clearly, they were capable of coordination.

Good to know.

Fast as greyhounds, the hexapods churned through the fields. She'd never make the tree line, so she didn't bother trying. She would make her stand here, using this first wave—if she survived it—to learn and adapt.

Nothing said she couldn't evolve as readily as her opponents.

First, she didn't want to be in deep grass. She wanted a better field of view. With seconds to spare, she used her shield as a press and stamped a swath of grass around her, pushing the stalks outward, creating a thicker natural palisade. She left one section open, a gate into her little nest.

The first hexapod hit that palisade broadside, got wedged in the wall of compacted grasses. She identified the gleam of its titanium carapace and speared her pipe down at it, using all of her weight. Metal crunched under the battering ram. It didn't kill the beast, but it incapacitated its sensory system, sending the pod zipping away in a spiraling blind curve.

The other four, perhaps wirelessly sharing the experience of the first, veered away from a direct attack. They swarmed in a circle. Then one cut away, shooting toward the opening, sensing the chink in her shield—not knowing it was a trap.

It cut into her nest, but she was ready. She used her pipe like a golf club and batted it square in the front sensors, crushing the electronics and sending it flying. It landed on its back and didn't move.

A weak spot.

The other three circled, clearly plotting something, then, once decided, the trio arrowed toward the opening together, plainly trying to overwhelm her.

Sorry, we're closed for the day.

She slammed her shield's edge into the soft loam, sealing the opening to her nest. The lead pod hit the shield with a loud clank. She stabbed downward, again and again, like a piston. She shattered most of its legs, leaving it crippled.

The other two veered away, plotting their next move.

Kat wasn't waiting. She found a fist-size rock and underhanded it into the grasses. The movement drew one of the creatures. It shot in that direction, but it was only fooled for a few seconds. Once the rock stopped moving, it stopped hunting.

It knew the rock wasn't *alive.*

The test confirmed the hexapods had motion sensors, but they must be backed by infrared, reading body heat, a mark of living creatures. Since the pod chased the rock, she doubted its visual acuity was very sharp. They could be fooled.

What about sound and smell?

The two pods didn't give her another chance to find out. They zoomed in from opposite directions. One headed toward the shield; the other, the natural grassy palisade.

Kat snatched her shield back up, opening her nest again, allowing the first one to shoot inside. The second got delayed trying to push itself through the grass, employing some buzzing blade to chop into her space.

The first spun on a dime and came at her. She shoulder-dropped, putting all her weight on the edge of her shield, turning it into a guillotine. She crushed the front end, driving it into the soft soil.

The second burst through the palisade, leading its charge with a spinning horizontal saw blade.

She leaped to the side as the second rammed the first, finishing the job for her with its diamond blade ripping open the underside of the other pod. The first retaliated in a defensive death reflex. Razor-sharp legs drilled into crevices, peeled open the carapace, and ripped out the glass-enclosed brain.

In seconds, they'd killed each other.

Kat crouched, examining their weaponry, peeking at the arsenal under their carapaces. She noted a small, dart-like apparatus, the side marked with the designation M99.

Etorphine hydrochloride.

A powerful game-animal tranquilizer.

Strong enough that one drop could immobilize a man.

Knowing her opponents better, she stood and stared over at the small bunker through which she'd exited the facility. She knew they were watching. She just glared.

Let's see what else you've got.

She turned and sprinted for the tree line.

2:28 P.M.

"She'll do well," Emmet Fielding said, forming a temple of his fingers before his lips, studying the bank of monitors. "Very fit."

Edward sat beside him at the curved bank of computer screens. He gently fingered his broken nose, taped up after Lisa's surprise attack. He watched the woman flee out of the view of one camera and into another. She fled through a dark forest of oaks, pine, and spruce.

"Aren't you upset that she dispatched your weapons so quickly?" Edward asked.

A flap of fingers waved away his concern. "You can't make an omelet without breaking a few eggs. Porsche destroys fleets of their sports cars in their testing lab and field trials. That's how you build the best. And I won't settle for anything less."

Edward had noted how the man's pulse beat faster in his throat during the attack. He suspected this testing was as much a blood sport to him as it was science. But that wasn't his concern.

After seeing that, surely Lisa would return with the boy.

"Any word?" Edward asked.

Fielding made a noncommittal noise, plainly not interested. Whether Lisa showed up or not, he intended to continue this test until the woman on the screen was a macerated ruin.

He glanced to the clock. Petra had also gone off on her own to search for Lisa. After being caught off guard and struck in the head, his research associate was out for blood, hunting as diligently and as coldly as those steel creatures.

Fielding sat back from his workstation, stretching. "I think we're ready for round two."

"How many will you send this time?"

"A full score, I believe. Twenty. But she's shown so much promise— truly remarkable—I think we'll skip straight to the next level of challenge. Introducing a new element."

Fielding glanced behind him to the back of his lab. Larger pods hulked back there, on four limbs, each leg ending in curved claws patterned after a sloth's, perfect for gutting prey. Edward had seen how fast the quadrupods could move, bone-chillingly frightening to witness.

"I think I'll send up *two*," Fielding said and tapped buttons with a bit of bravado.

Blake stared at the running woman.

She had better hope Lisa changed her mind and returned with the child—though, in the end, it would not make any difference.

Not for either of the women.

2:29 P.M.

Lisa fled down a long, dim corridor, the baby under one arm, the knife ready in the other. She had watched in fleeting glimpses Kat's successful battle with the metal creatures—but more to come had been promised, and she had no doubt it would be delivered.

She glanced above her head.

I should be under the red zone by now.

By her best estimate from the live feed, she was, unfortunately, fleeing in the opposite direction from Kat. She could not offer her friend any help—other than to survive herself.

She continued down the corridor that transected the huge complex, passing through a zone designated as *black*. This area appeared empty but not deserted. The air had a feeling of expectation to it, like before a lightning storm. The source appeared a few yards ahead. To the right opened a vast, cathedral-size warehouse. A full flight of steps led down to the lower floor.

From up on top, Lisa had an expansive view of the space, a hangar large enough to park a commercial jet inside. The warehouse was full of more of those metal creatures, stacked in racks or, for the larger ones, resting on the floor. Cables ran to charging racks or directly into the backs of the four-legged ones. In the center, clearly still under construction, was a monster the size of a Pershing tank, a slumbering giant waiting to be awakened.

A steady hum and the electrical smell of ozone radiated from the space, creating that sense of a pending storm.

The charge in the air stirred the hairs on the back of her neck.

She hurried past with a sense of dread.

The corridor finally ended. She took the stairs, picturing the map in her head. These steps led up to an exit off a spur of the main lab, hopefully leading to some forgotten backwater where she could slip away on foot. She crept up slowly, landing by landing, expecting a shout at any moment. She crossed past the middle level to the top floor.

As she continued to the next step leading up toward freedom, a loud voice echoed to her.

"DR. CUMMINGS! WE ARE READY FOR ROUND TWO."

Frightened, Lisa fled up the stairs.

I don't want to see.

But she could still *hear.* Echoing up from below came the faint shift of machinery, the groan of hydraulics, accompanied by the sudden spike in electricity in the air.

Forces were being mobilized against Kat.

Lisa reached the top of the stairs. A door appeared ahead with an emergency evacuation bar. She feared passing through it might set off some internal alarm, get eyes looking her way in this remote corner of the complex, but she had no other choice. If she remained below, it was only a matter of time until she and the child were discovered.

I'd rather take my chances above than be trapped below.

She shoved the bar, momentarily scared it wouldn't open—but it did. Bright sunlight flowed over her, stirring the child with its brightness; a chubby arm flailed against it.

Along with the sunshine came a deafening roar.

She stepped out of the bunker and faced a waterfall spilling over a thirty-foot-high cliff. It crashed down to a river below her perch. She did a slow turn, realizing she'd come out on a narrow plateau framed by a frothing river on one side and towering cliffs on the other.

There was no way up or down.

A dead end.

The baby started to cry, soft wails becoming loud ones, echoing off the cliff wall.

She didn't blame him.

We're trapped.

38

Within lies the true heart of the Bloodline.

Gray pondered those words as he stood at the threshold of the sealed museum space.

"I was first brought here when I was a boy," Robert explained. "I was too naïve to understand the true cost of the knowledge inside, of the blood pact that it would require of me, of the losses I would have to endure."

Two symbols, etched on the glass, flanked either side of the air-lock door. To the right was a cross, emblazoned with spirals of DNA. Gray had seen that symbol before, enough to know Robert was not lying about the importance of this space. To the left was the same cross, only it was decorated with entwining *snakes.*

Robert noted his attention. He touched the cross with the snakes. "This was our past. The other is our future."

Without further explanation, Robert unsealed the air lock and brought Gray into the room. Lights flickered on, revealing a neighboring clean room branching off from this chamber. Gray spotted towering banks of black mainframes back there, but Robert drew him onward.

Still, Gray's eyes drifted hungrily to the computer room.

What do those massive servers hold?

Apparently, such questions would have to wait.

Their destination stood at the very back of the museum space. A tall glass case held a single nondescript object: an upright wooden staff.

Curious, sensing the palpable age of the artifact, Gray leaned closer, his arms still cuffed behind him. Upon the surface of the staff, three serpents had been faintly carved, winding around and around the shaft in a complicated tangle.

"What is it?" Gray asked, straightening back up.

"An artifact discovered by an ancestor of mine during the Crusades, found in a citadel atop a mountain in Galilee. It is called the Bachal Isu. It was the staff carried by St. Patrick."

Gray turned to him. "The saint who chased the snakes out of Ireland?"

"Exactly, but do you know the staff's history, how St. Patrick came to possess it?"

Gray shook his head.

Robert explained, "The legend goes that when Patrick was returning from Rome on his way back to Ireland, he stopped at the island near Genoa. There he met a young man who claimed to have received the staff from *a pilgrim of sweet and majestic countenance*' and was told to hold it until *'my servant Patrick rests here on his way to Erinn for the conversion of its people, and give it into his hands when he quits you.'* This caretaker also claimed that, while the staff was in his possession, he had stopped aging, living over a century as he waited for Patrick."

Gray eyed the historical artifact skeptically. "A staff that grants immortality?"

"According to the lore of St. Patrick, that *pilgrim* was Jesus Christ."

Gray stared at the simple staff with both awe and not a small amount of disbelief. "Do you believe that?"

"I don't know. But there are other stories that claim this staff is much older, said to have been possessed by King David and, before that, by Moses."

Quite the pedigree, Gray thought to himself, not wanting to offend or stop this recitation. The longer the story took, the more time Painter had to solve the riddle Gray had left behind in DC.

Plus, the man's prior words kept him attentive.

You may be useful to my plans.

The words hadn't sounded like a threat, more like an offer.

He let the man talk.

"Who knows if any of that is true?" Robert admitted. "The one who found this was a Templar knight, hence the cross that decorates our symbol. According to that story, the staff was in the possession of a guardian claiming to be over five hundred years old. She stole that staff, slaying that man—"

"Wait? She?"

"Yes, *she* was a Templar, one of the original nine, though her name was stricken from the historical record after her discovery. That moment was our ancestors' greatest triumph and our most bitter failure. But I'm jumping ahead of myself."

"Then go on."

"Upon her return to France with the stolen staff, it became apparent—though it took years—that the staff bore no miraculous properties."

"So it didn't hold the secret to immortality."

Robert eyed him. "No, it *did*—but it would take centuries for us to discover the truth. For it wasn't the staff that was the miracle. It was the *knowledge* written on it."

Gray squinted at the staff. "The three snakes?"

Robert shifted him to an old, illuminated Bible resting open on a stand, the pigments brilliant under the lights.

"Snakes are a common religious theme," he said. "Patrick cast out the serpents of Ireland. Moses turned his staff into a snake. But it's the earliest story of the serpent, from the book of Genesis, that revealed the truth. There were two trees in the Garden of Eden. The *tree of life*, which bore the fruit of immortality. And the *tree of knowledge*. God cast out Adam and Eve after they ate from the tree of knowledge because He feared with that knowledge they would *'take also from the tree of life, and eat, and live forever.'*"

"But the tree of life is just symbolic."

"That's not true. It existed—or, at least, it did in the past."

"What are you talking about?"

"There are plenty of stories in the Bible of people living to incredible ages, the most famous being Methuselah, who lived 969 years. But there are many others. And not just in the Bible. The clay tablets of Babylon and Sumer claim their kings lived centuries upon centuries."

"But those ages are just allegorical, not the literal truth."

"Perhaps. Except the story of a plant that sustains life is not limited to the Bible. In the ancient epic of Gilgamesh, the hero of that story hunts for the *plant of life,* a plant that grants immortality."

Robert pointed to another case, this one holding old books. "In the ancient Hindu Vedic scriptures, they describe a plant called *soma,* with the same properties. *'We've quaffed the Soma bright, and are immortal grown.'*"

He moved next to a plate of Egyptian art, showing a falcon-headed god plucking leaves from a tall plant. "Here is an actual depiction of the tree of life from Egyptian mythology."

Robert turned to look across the breadth of artifacts. "There are many other examples, but what's unusual about *all* of these stories is one detail. In the Bible, Noah is the last person to live to such an extreme age. In the epic of Gilgamesh, the adventuring king discovers the plant he seeks had been drowned away. In both those stories and many others, this life-sustaining plant is destroyed by a great flood."

Robert turned back to Gray. "Maybe this is just a coincidence, but maybe there was a *seed* of truth to these stories. And from that seed, a new Tree of Life could be grown. That's what the Bloodline came to believe. For centuries, they've searched for the meaning of those three snakes, sensing there was some significance to it that was tied to immortality. They were confident enough to incorporate those snakes into their own symbol."

Robert pointed back to the glass doors.

"And it wasn't just our mark. We left that fingerprint everywhere, hoping to draw out those with hidden knowledge. My ancestors believed so firmly in that connection that they incorporated that symbol into the various secret organizations that hid us."

He led Gray over to an open page of a book of Masonic rites. It showed three men clasping hands, entwined very much like the snakes on the staff. And if there was any doubt, the snakes were depicted there, too—with three heads.

"So you see how steadfastly we believed," Robert said. "And in the end, we were proven right."

"Right? How?"

"The drawing on the staff was knowledge encoded for future generations. Genetic knowledge." Robert pointed to the other symbol on the door. "That's when the symbol got changed, transforming the snakes into what they really represented: strands of DNA."

"You're saying that ancients in the past knew enough about DNA to encode it as snakes on a staff."

"Possibly. Back in the sixties, a scientist named Hayflick determined that man's natural age could not exceed 120 years. He based that on the number of times a cell could divide."

"I'm familiar with the Hayflick Limit," Gray said, having studied biophysics.

"Then is it mere coincidence that the book of Genesis came to the same conclusion about the limits to a man's lifetime? To quote from that book of the Bible: *His days shall be a hundred and twenty years.* The same conclusion as Hayflick's. Where did that knowledge come from?"

"Okay, that's strange, I admit. But that's a far cry from saying that the snakes on the staff represent strands of DNA. There are *three* snakes drawn there. DNA is a *double* helix."

"Ah, but there's the rub. The secret of immortality doesn't lie within *two* strands, but *three,* a triple helix. That's what is written on the staff. It took until the modern age, with the aid of DNA analysis, for us to unravel that mystery."

"How did you do that?"

"When our errant knight left with the staff, she killed the previous immortal who possessed it—likely the last of his kind. She spilled his blood, which was preserved on the staff. In his blood, we discovered his white cells possessed *triple*-helical DNA."

This sharpened Gray's attention. "Triple-helical DNA?"

He was beginning to appreciate the enormity of the revelation here.

Robert nodded. "Once genetic science advanced enough to let us decode that third strand, we determined it was actually a viral protein— from *a plant virus.* The protein was a natural form of peptide nucleic acid, PNA. It infected human cells after someone ate that plant. A side effect of this virus leaping from plant to animal was that it stabilized cells, staved off cellular degeneration, and extended the life spans of the infected dramatically."

Gray pictured the Garden of Eden. "The mythical tree of life."

"Maybe not so *mythical* after all."

"But I thought you said the plant's fields were drowned during the Great Flood. How did this guardian come to possess it?"

"Apparently, someone had the foresight to stockpile some of the plants, drying them out like tea leaves. From the chronicles of the knight who stole the staff, written on her deathbed, she described a row of Egyptian sarcophagi full of brittle leaves and stems in the crypt. Focused on her goal, she didn't think anything about it and left it all to burn."

Gray appreciated the irony. "So, like the Eve of old, your knight stole the *tree of knowledge,* bringing you this cryptic clue about immortality— but she left behind the *tree of life.*"

"So it seems. In the end, we tried to reverse-engineer that viral PNA protein, but it proved no good. Too much degradation. So we had to start from scratch, engineering our own PNA and testing it."

Gray imagined the horrors and abuses involved with that research.

Even Robert didn't sound proud, his voice growing hushed. "But over time, we improved enough to produce the first stable child."

"Amanda's son."

He nodded. "But that stability ended up to be only temporary. And yet the cost of it was still so high. First, Amanda's life. Now, my brother's." He pointed toward the door. "And soon my grandnephew. It's too much. I must do what I can to preserve the rest of my family."

They headed across the hall.

Robert's melancholia settled back on his shoulders. "I was a boy when I made my pact with that inner circle of the family, with the Bloodline. I thought what we were doing here was so much larger than any individual life."

Until it hit closer to home.

Heavy is the head that wears the crown.

And that weight and guilt would only grow when he assumed his brother's place at the White House, bringing the Bloodline fully into power versus pulling the strings behind James Gant's back.

"Why have you told me all of this?" Gray asked. "Why did you bring me down here?"

"So you might understand why a naïve boy might succumb to such a cruelty, but an old man cannot suffer more loss." Robert turned to him. "I brought you down here so that you could tell the world."

Gray gaped, shocked. The loss of his brother must have been the proverbial straw that broke this camel's back.

But didn't Robert order that assassination? Or was he as much a puppet on a string as President Gant?

For now, Gray had a more important question if the man was folding up his tent. "Why don't you come forward yourself?"

"I've suffered enough. I will take those closest to me and vanish, to go where the Lineage cannot find us." Robert headed away. "I leave the rest on your shoulders."

Gray followed behind him, passing the neighboring bank of mainframes in the other room. If Robert wanted to spill all, then he wanted to know everything.

"What's with the computer servers?" he asked, sensing something important hidden there.

Robert glanced disinterestedly in that direction. "If this room is our heart—that's our brain, our memory. It holds our entire lineage, not just under the Gant name but the others who were lost to the past. All the way back to our rumored beginning."

Gray wanted to hear this. "What beginning?"

"The crescent and the star. Our first symbol. Some of our earliest records connect those two symbols to the Canaanite god of human sacrifice."

That's certainly fitting.

"That god was named Moloch, represented by the horns of a cow or the horns of a crescent moon. A closely related god was Rephan, represented by the star. Some of our historians believe our roots go back to the time of Moses, that we were cast out by him for worshipping the crescent and the star." He glanced back to the staff. "There is a verse from the biblical Acts. *'You have lifted up the shrine of Moloch and the star of your god Rephan, the idols you made to worship. Therefore I will send you into exile beyond Babylon.'*"

"So you're saying you're the descendants of those exiled idolworshippers?"

"I don't know. But the Bloodline is ancient, and they still carry on some old Jewish traditions, like—"

Beyond the glass wall, the elevator doors opened with a buzz, drawing their attention forward. A familiar figure stepped out. The tall blond woman strode purposefully forward. Those glacial eyes took in the situation with a single cold sweep.

Stiff with surprise, Robert strode forward. "Petra? Why . . . how are you down here?"

On the far side of the glass barrier, she stepped to the air lock, typed in a code on the outer door. Thick steel rods locked the room down.

Robert rushed forward and tugged on the door handle.

Apparently, someone had grown wise to his coming betrayal.

Robert stopped tugging, realizing the truth. He called through the glass wall to her. "You're of the Lineage. Why was I never told?"

"We are legion," she said. "And not *all* are happy with your stewardship. When we lost the child—a useless thing, really—I contacted those whom I serve, reported what I found here. How you place grief over necessity. Immediate family over the Lineage. You tug and rip against the fabric that has lasted millennia. No more. You are of no further use to the Lineage."

"But I've led for so many years."

She smiled, a wicked look, as if scoffing at such a claim. "When the body is strong, the head can be cut off. We will grow a new one and be stronger for it. You are to be set aside. This branch of the Gant clan is to be pruned away, including all the fruit born from it. We will purge the old to make way for the new. With no tears, only purpose."

Robert's palm, which had been resting against the door, fell away.

"The purge will start here. In ten minutes. At *three* o'clock, an appropriately powerful number. I've engaged the fail-safe for both your labs and this vault of ages. This day, the Lineage will shed its *past* and set its eyes only on the *future*. Immortality is within grasp. Ultimate power at our doorstep."

Petra bowed, oddly respectful. "Those you love will not suffer," she said, her eyes fixing at Robert. "Even those you do not believe we know about."

Robert lunged forward and pounded his fist against the glass, his voice breaking. "Stop!"

She retreated to the elevator, facing them—though her gaze was directed elsewhere. They were already forgotten.

Gray waited for the doors to close, then turned to Robert. "Looks like you're out of a job." He tilted his cuffed wrists toward the man. "How about we get these off?"

Robert looked both angry and grief-stricken.

Been there, Gray thought.

As the man undid his cuffs, Gray asked the question he was afraid to know the answer to. "What's this fail-safe?"

Robert's face went grave. "A thermobaric bomb. One will incinerate the vaults down here. But over at the lab . . ." He shook his head, looking sick.

"What's going to happen at the lab?"

2:51 P.M.

The evacuation alarms echoed across the facility as red warning lights flashed, turning the world shades of crimson.

"Sinkhole," Fielding explained as he shoved papers into a briefcase.

"What?" Edward asked, sticking close to the man. Others fled in various directions, grabbing what they could.

"A majority of the complex sits above a dry underground lake. Miners at the turn of the century discovered the lake below, fed by an underground river. Later, engineers capped that river during construction, built scaffolding to support the lab over the pit. We're not in an underground lab." He snapped his briefcase closed with a note of finality. "We're on a massive suspension bridge over a yawning pit. And they're about to blow out that suspension."

He moved to his workstation.

"It will create a twenty-acre-wide sinkhole that will flood as that main river is unplugged. And a new lake will be born over our graves if we don't get clear of here."

Edward urged the man. "Then let's bloody well go."

"I'm not going to lose my research—or my work." Fielding tapped at a screen. "This will be their ultimate test."

"What are you doing?"

"Giving them a fighting chance." Fielding leaned to a microphone as green lights flashed down row after row of pod designations. He spoke the final command order, transmitted to all of his army. "SURVIVE."

Beneath Edward's feet, a low rumble rose. He backed toward the door. What was Fielding thinking, unleashing that horde now?

"Just the generators powering up," Fielding assured him, picking up his briefcase. "The activation sequence and warm-up mode takes eight minutes. We'll be far away by then."

Still, Edward hurried to the door. He turned to see something leap from the worktable and latch onto Fielding's back, landing square between his shoulder blades. It was one of his new hexapods. In the excitement, the researcher had forgotten he'd activated this one earlier, left it on standby mode while he tinkered.

Fielding screamed and struggled to reach the beast, but its ice-pick-thin legs, sharpened to surgical points, punctured deep, latching on firmly.

Edward backed toward the door. Fielding had explained about this newest pod, a *nester*. Its bulbous body housed a swarm of smaller robots.

Fielding backed toward him. "Get it off! Get it off!"

Edward retreated, unable to tear his gaze away. Now, latched against his back, the pregnant creature vomited a stream of smaller bots from its swollen abdomen. They spread like fire ants—racing down his back, up his neck, over his shoulders, along his chest and limbs.

"No, no, no . . ." Fielding cried, spinning in a circle, knowing what was coming.

Then, as if on cue, the march of the bots all stopped at once—and began *drilling* into his flesh.

The animal howl of pain finally broke through Edward's shocked paralysis. He twisted away. He knew what they were drilling for. The other, larger pods were attuned to *body heat*. These smaller ones were attracted to the sound of beating hearts.

They would drill and drill until that beat was finally silenced.

But from the endless howling that chased Edward toward the surface, it took a long time.

2:52 P.M.

As minutes ticked down, Gray lay on his side, rubbing his chafed wrists. The secretary of state of the United States knelt over his head, picking a plug of C-4 out of his ear canal, using a three-thousand-year-old sliver of Egyptian bone, a funerary object stolen from one of the cabinets.

"That looks like most of it," Robert said.

Good.

Gray didn't want to be down here when the thermobaric weapon exploded. Fuel-air bombs created blast waves that rivaled nuclear bombs and ignited oxygen to five thousand degrees.

Gray rolled to his rear end and set to work digging out the earpiece and blasting cap. He used a pair of tweezers to poke, prod, and pull the device free. It felt like yanking a walnut out, leaving his ear ringing.

"Got it."

He hurried and gathered everything together. The barrier was layered tempered glass, too thick to break through with anything in the room. He stuck the reassembled explosive charge to the glass wall to the left of the air-lock door. He centered it in the middle of the etched symbol of the genetic cross.

"Get back," he warned.

Gray carried the transmitter that Robert had given him. They found shelter behind a case, and Gray pressed the button. In the enclosed space, the blast felt like two anvils striking the sides of his head. He coughed against the smoke, reeking of burned tar, and hurried Robert to his feet. He waved a hand in front of his face and saw the tempered glass barrier had shattered to a bluish-white crumble.

With his ears deafened, he had to yell to hear his own voice.

"Out!"

Gray cast one last regretful glance behind him, at the vast wealth of history about to be destroyed. His eyes settled on that staff—the Bachal Isu, the staff of Christ—but it was sealed behind bulletproof glass. He did not have the time or force of strength to rescue it.

With a heavy heart, he had to abandon it.

Robert stood on shaky feet, dazed by the blast, but he allowed himself to be dragged along. It took his palm print and code to call the elevator back down. As they waited, Robert stared toward the smoky museum.

"Maybe it's better I should die," Robert said. "After what I did . . ."

Gray had to keep the man motivated and moving. "Robert, I need to share something with you. Your brother, Jimmy, and his daughter, Amanda."

"What about them?" Robert asked, with a catch in his voice.

"They're both still alive."

Robert flinched, turning sharply to him. "What?"

As the elevator arrived and the doors opened, Gray gave him a thumbnail sketch of the story.

"And then there's Amanda's son to think about," Gray said. "You mentioned he was here."

Robert stared sullenly as the cage rose. "He was, but he was kidnapped again."

This time, Gray jerked his head in the man's direction.

Robert explained, "By another captive. A medical doctor. A woman investigating our fertility clinic."

Gray pushed his shoulder and stared him hard in the face. "Lisa Cummings?"

"You know her?"

"Was there another woman with her?"

"Yes. They were both at the lab complex, with my grandnephew. But it's ten miles away. We can't even get word there in time."

Gray swore, his heart clutching. He pushed Robert against the wall, harder than he had meant to. "What about the woman I was captured with? Seichan. Was she taken to that damn lab, too?"

Robert's brows pinched at Gray's reaction. "No," he said slowly. "I . . . we kept her here."

As the elevator stopped at the top, the heavy vault door took forever to swing open. Gray had to restrain himself from pounding his fists against it, both in his anxiety to get to Seichan and in frustration that he could do nothing to help Lisa and Kat.

Finally, the thick door opened enough for Gray and Robert to exit and climb out of the massive wine barrel and back into the main cellar. He hurried, not knowing if the thermobaric weapon was of sufficient size to burn through the cellars, too—or would it take down the whole castle?

Robert was equally clueless.

Gray didn't want to be here to find out.

"Where's Seichan?" he asked, ready to run ahead.

"You'll get lost." Robert rushed alongside him, keeping up. "I'll show you. But . . ."

"But what?"

"After Petra left us trapped"—Robert looked both scared and apologetic—"I think she was headed to kill her."

39

"Seven minutes out," the pilot reported from the cockpit.

Painter shared the cargo hold of USAF C-41A, a turboprop-powered medium transport plane. They had screamed down from DC in a military jet, then transferred to this smaller craft, which was better suited for infiltration and extraction of troops, meaning it was basically a cockpit and cargo space.

His team was the cargo.

Tucker readied Kane in his tandem harness for the drop. Kowalski and Monk checked each other's gear. Painter was already suited up and sat with his laptop open and hooked to a satellite uplink, getting a live feed of the Gant estate and targeting movement on the ground to aid in their daytime penetration of the Lodge.

He had Jason Carter in his ear. "Director, I'm patching new feed. We picked up movement a little over ten miles from the mansion. We didn't get this sooner with all eyes on the Lodge. But you'd better see this."

The image on his screen swung away from the Lodge toward the Continental Divide, a rugged chunk of territory.

Who was way out there?

A small figure could be seen standing next to a waterfall, holding a package—no, a *child*. The view toggled closer and closer until there could be no doubt.

"Lisa . . ." Painter said.

"And I believe the other is Kat, sir. About a quarter-mile southeast."

As the image swooped in that direction, Painter waved Monk over. "You should see this."

By the time the man arrived, Jason showed a blurry video of a woman running through the woods. Details were hard to pick out between the trees. What was evident was that she was headed straight for a sheer cliff drop.

"That's my wife," Monk said, scared but tightly in control. "Never looking where she's going."

Jason spoke again. "I've got movement on the ground behind her, but I can't pick up any details."

The pilot called from up front. "We're two minutes out from the no-fly demarcation. I'm going to start angling around to get us skirting along its edge."

Painter passed his laptop to Monk and crossed to the cockpit. "New plans," he instructed. "We're going straight in."

"Sir, we don't have the proper clearance."

"Take it up with the president when we get back," Painter said. "You take us in low and straight. Follow the Continental Divide. Once we cross into the no-fly zone, you open the rear ramp for us to bail out."

Painter swung back around.

Monk raised an eyebrow. "How come my wife doesn't have any hair?"

Jason spoke in Painter's ear, a scary urgency to his tone. "How long until you're on the ground?"

"We bail out in six. On the ground seven or eight."

"That'll be too late."

2:53 P.M.
Blue Ridge Mountains

Kat sprinted for the goal line.

She had lost her slippers. Her toes dug for purchase in the soft loam and loose spruce needles. Rocks, pinecones, and acorns tore at her soles, but she ignored the pain. She flew over obstacles with long-legged leaps, happy for the obstruction of a log or jagged outcropping, as it slowed her pursuers.

The front edge of the hunters was only yards behind. She had dispatched three, but over a dozen still remained, working in tandem. The shield and pipe were futile against their numbers, especially as this group was not uniform. She identified at least four variants among them, each with specialized functions: *crawlers* she'd dealt with during the first wave; *leapers* could spring like frogs when close enough and slash out, or worse yet, latch on; *spinners* could accelerate at blistering paces for short bursts, becoming flying saw-blades; the last group was still unknown, trundling more at the rear, slower than the others, looking like steel helmets with legs.

She had not come through unscathed. The first spinner caught her by surprise, whizzing past, slicing a gash in her calf. Blood poured down her ankle. She was ready for the second, striking out with her pipe, swinging for the bleachers. The spinner ended up embedding its whirring self into the trunk of an oak, becoming stuck.

Ahead, the tree line broke apart, and sunlight beckoned.

The forest ended at a cliff.

She searched and spotted what she needed, angling to the left.

A telltale explosive squeak warned her. She lashed out with her shield, swiping low, as a leaper sprang at her. With a satisfying clang, she struck it and sent it cartwheeling away.

She sped faster, making her pursuers do the same, but also gaining a little space. As she ran, she plucked at the drawstring of her gown, loosening it. Once done, she flung her pipe and shield at the base of a maple tree ahead. They clattered close enough.

As she ran the final steps toward the cliff's edge, she ripped the gown over her head, which blinded her for a frightening moment. She balled up the sweaty, hot garment. Reaching the cliff, still sprinting, she leaped up and threw the ball of clothes over the edge. She caught a low branch. Below her legs, the front guards of the horde went racing over the edge to their doom three stories below: leapers, crawlers, and one lonely spinner, who, in a last-ditch effort, whizzed in a spectacular arc off the cliff and chased after the hot bundle of clothes.

Not everyone went over, but confusion reigned in the remaining half.

She dropped back to the ground long enough to shove her shield on her forearm and tuck the pipe through her panties, like a sword in a scabbard. She leaped again to the same branch and hauled herself atop it with a heave of her legs.

The hunters stirred below, contemplating their next move.

A shout drew her attention, barely discernible above the roar of a waterfall a couple of hundred yards to her right. She searched—following the curve of the cliff, to where a small river tumbled over its edge to crash below. It was in those misty lower levels that she spotted a thin shape, waving her whole arm.

Lisa stood on a plateau on the far side of the waterfall. Her friend was trapped by the sheer cliffs behind her and the surging river below.

And she wasn't trapped alone.

Lisa held a baby in her arms.

Kat waved back—then froze.

Lisa's shout had drawn more than her attention. Behind her friend, at the top of the cliff, sunlight glinted off a creature the size of a small lion. It leaned over the edge, like a steel gargoyle.

"Kat!" Lisa shouted, still waving, further drawing its attention with all of her noise and motion.

"Lisa! Stop moving!" Kat yelled back.

Lisa shook her head and cupped her ear. The roar of the neighboring falls must have deafened her.

Kat struggled with how to communicate to Lisa, how to pantomime what needed to be done.

I was never good at charades.

Before Kat could even begin, the creature started climbing down the cliff face.

2:55 P.M.

Lisa floated on her toes, so happy to see Kat safe. Her friend's dramatic appearance, leaping half-naked into a tree, accompanied by a shower of silvery hunters, brought such joy and hope.

The thunder of the falls stripped whatever words Kat had tried to share, but her friend must have understood and began motioning dramatically. An arm pointed to the waterfall, then mimicked taking a shower.

Lisa didn't understand and shook her head. Cradled in her arms, the baby was growing restless, likely from the constant roaring of the falls.

A rock pinged off the ledge that was her prison.

Kat repeated the gesture, adjusting it slightly. After pointing to the waterfall, she waved her fingers in front of her face.

Lisa stared and saw that a part of the plateau tucked behind the waterfall, but that shelf still roiled with mist, spray, and sudden dousings as the currents above shifted.

Finally, Kat pointed straight up, using her whole arm.

Another chunk of rock fell off of the cliff face and struck her landing.

A trickle of terror ran up her back, as she suddenly sensed something staring at her.

She turned and looked at the cliff.

Halfway up hung a monstrosity of steel plate, razor claws, and titanium fangs.

She screamed, backing several steps, coming close to throwing herself off the cliff and into the river below.

The noise and motion drew a swivel of its sleek head, revealing faceted black eyes—sensors—staring back at her.

She froze and cut off her scream, knowing noise must attract it.

Then the baby began to wail.

2:56 P.M.

Kat watched helplessly as the steel gargoyle climbed down from its perch, digging hooked claws into crevices, lowering itself limb by limb, crack by crack, with the inevitability of a well-wound watch.

C'mon, Lisa. Remember what I showed you.

A clack and whirring at the foot of the maple reminded her of her own predicament. The five helmeted pods now circled the tree, sitting stationary. Simultaneously, their domed backs split into halves and folded back, revealing four smaller robots inside. They were flat and square in shape, with tiny propellers at each corner.

In unison, the entire aerial fleet rose from their ground-based carriers, lifting in eerie formation, perfectly tuned to one another. Then, upon some silent cue, the pack rose, whipping and winding up the tree in a blurring pattern, stripping leaves and small twigs with their scalpel-sharp whirring blades. They climbed the tree like a deadly tornado of daggers.

She lifted shield and pipe.

A loud *clank* drew her attention momentarily back across the waterfall to Lisa's perch. The monster must have lost its footing and fell. It righted itself, flipping back to its sharp claws on the plateau.

Kat searched, but Lisa was gone.

2:57 P.M.

The sudden shock of the icy water stole Lisa's breath.

She shielded the squalling child as best she could, hunching over him, drawing him close to her bosom for the warmth of her body heat.

She edged as far back along that ledge of rock behind the waterfall as she could manage without being pummeled off her perch.

After the first initial shock, she figured out Kat's message. In fact, it was those black eyes of the steel bear—cold, alien sensors taking in the world—that allowed her to interpret her friend's pantomime. The beast had to use some method to hunt, to understand its surroundings.

The shelter of the waterfall offered a way to blind those sensors.

The rippling cascade would challenge any motion detectors.

The cold would mask her body heat.

The roar would deafen and confound its sense of hearing.

So, she risked hypothermia—unfortunately, more of a threat to the child than to her—to keep them hidden.

But would it work?

Three-quarters of the way down the wall, the creature fell or leaped. It landed hard, its large bulk at the mercy of gravity, but afterward, there remained an undeniable grace to its movement as it stalked toward her hiding place. It must have watched her come this way, but could it tell she was still here?

It knuckled forward on daggers curled back like the claws of a three-toed sloth. It stalked with a thoughtful and determined placement of each leg, like a housecat hunting a mouse.

Lisa shifted even deeper under the falls, letting the water fully envelop her. The baby cried against her soaked chest, but the roar of the falls drowned any wails away.

The sloth-like automaton pushed under the falls, pivoting its massive head, opening its huge steel jaws, revealing a maw of titanium death, a bear trap with legs.

Through the heavy chute of water, black eyes stared back at her, seeming to see her, but who knew what it truly saw?

And still it came, pushing forward.

2:58 P.M.
Airborne over Blue Ridge Mountains

In the cargo hold of the C-41A transport plane, Painter kept glued to the satellite feed on his laptop. He pressed shoulder to shoulder with Monk, who watched as fervently. Both their women were in danger—and, for the moment, there was nothing either man could do but watch.

The rear ramp was already open, awaiting their bail-out.

But they were not in position yet.

"How much longer?" Painter hollered.

"Two minutes out," the pilot answered, screaming to be heard above the roar of the wind through the open bay doors.

Painter stared at the screen, knowing it would be the longest two minutes of his life.

40

Seichan stood in the middle of her richly appointed prison cell. A soft scuffling alerted her a minute ago that someone was outside in the hall, struggling with the door. Apparently, they didn't have the code for the electronic deadbolt.

The oddness drew her out of the chair by the window.

The difficulty with the lock—was that good, bad, or inconsequential?

She stepped closer, passing the room's small fireplace, when half the door and a chunk of the wall exploded before her, throwing her back.

She rolled across the ancient Turkish rug and struck the foot of her bed. Through the smoke and the ruin, the upper torso of the guard could be seen out in the hallway, on the floor, neck twisted impossibly—not from the bomb. Someone had quietly dispatched him.

With her ears ringing, Seichan watched the silent entry of the source of all that death and destruction. The long-legged woman stepped through the wreckage of the door. She carried a pistol in her hand and a look of stern purposefulness on her face.

Seichan was more worried about the gun.

She needed that gun.

She shifted smoothly into a crouch.

Seichan knew this woman. It was the doctor's research partner back in Dubai—Petra—the one who had drugged Gray back on the boat.

Still shell-shocked, Seichan missed the woman's first few words before her hearing returned.

". . . Such promise," Petra said. "You were of the Lineage, of our blood. You were being groomed for so much more."

Seichan had difficulty making sense of her statements. Back on the boat in Dubai, she had suspected this woman had been raised as she had: the muscular surety of her movements, the hard glint of perpetual vigilance, the cold calculation to her countenance.

It took a monster to recognize a monster.

The woman's words echoed in her head.

. . . groomed for so much more . . .

Was *this* what she would have become?

A worse fear rose from the marrow of her bones.

Am I that already?

Seichan remained crouched, but she moved her left leg an inch forward, for better balance, for better power.

The woman noted this. She repositioned her weapon and shifted to the side, ruining Seichan's preparation, reaching the perfect spot where it would be awkward for Seichan to attack.

They stared each other down.

"When you turned traitor against us," Petra said, "you became a corrupted thing, a broken vessel, leaving the purity of the Lineage. For what? For the love of a man?"

Seichan stiffened, the words poking a raw nerve.

Petra must have sensed her reaction, her words hard with disdain. "Such a piteous waste. Better you die like a dog than live like one."

Petra fired—but Seichan was already moving as the muscles in her opponent's forearm tightened in anticipation of the recoil.

The bullet still burned a hot line across her flank as she twisted to the side, offering less of a target. She hit Petra in the shins with her shoulder, flipping the woman high.

Seichan rolled, ready to go for the woman's weapon.

But Petra never lost it. She landed on a knee, one leg back, still facing Seichan, her gun still pointed at her face.

At that moment, Seichan knew two things.

She's better than me.

And the worse for it.

She closed her eyes—and pictured one face, one regret—as the pistol fired again and again at her.

And a ghostly wind rushed past her.

The rounds burned into Robert's chest as he threw himself between the woman and the weapon, blocking her fully with his broad body, a wall before a flower. The pain was a small thing against the enormity of what might be lost if he failed.

Then Gray was there, sliding into the room with the automatic rifle from the dead guard in the hallway. He fired on full auto, blasting Petra back—and he never stopped shooting until the clip emptied.

Only then did he whip around.

"Seichan . . ." Gray said, sliding to her side.

Robert knew the man loved her, saw it in his eyes.

He had loved a woman as much as that once, too. He met her while he was a young ambassador to Southeast Asia. He pictured her sweet face aglow under the moonlight in the garden, lost in the drift of cherry blossoms, her lips as soft as the whispery song of thrushes in the branches and the tinkle of a fountain.

But it was always the emerald of her eyes he returned to, the intensity reflecting all inside her, never dimming. Her love, a reflection of his own, was forever frozen in jade.

He ran the edge of his thumb along her cheekbone, letting his adoration shine—and at that moment, time shifted, but not those eyes.

Never those eyes . . .

He didn't know he had fallen into Seichan's arms. His hand was raised, touching gently, something forever forbidden him.

Knowing then it was right he die here.

In his daughter's arms.

. . .

Seichan held the man, not understanding, baffled by the sudden tears in her eyes. The barrage of bullets had knocked him back into her arms. She caught him, the man who had cast his life aside for her, the same man who had imprisoned her.

Why?

He stared up silently at her as if drinking her in, raising a hand to touch her cheek. And strangely still, she let him, seeing something in his eyes that she could not deny.

Gray returned to her side, dropping next to her.

The assassin was dead.

The woman had a name, but those five letters held no meaning.

In the end, she was nameless, just purpose in human form.

Seichan stared at the bloody ruin, then turned away again, suddenly freer.

I will not be you.

And I'm stronger for it.

Gray slipped an arm around her. "Seichan . . ."

And there was the simple answer. She had a name, spoken by someone who gave it weight, depth, meaning, and substance.

But in that moment, she learned she had another name, one forever unknown. The man dying in her arms told her. His arm dropped, too weak now, his breath a whisper.

"You have your mother's eyes . . ."

Trembling fingers found hers, perhaps sensing her shock.

"I tried to protect you, to hide you . . . to keep you from them." His eyes never left her face. "But after your mother was taken . . . it took so long to find you. When I did, I couldn't let you go . . . selfish . . . but to acknowledge you would have been your death. So I hid you in plain sight within the Guild, close but forever apart. I was blind, naïve to the cruelties that would be inflicted on you, would be asked of you later . . . I'm sorry . . ."

Seichan did not know how to respond, drawn into the past, remembering that night, hiding under the bed, terror-stricken, as her mother was dragged away.

Fingers squeezed one last time, trying to hold on.

Seichan stared down at him, at the impossibility of her *father*.

"Your mother . . ." he said, his eyes wide with the urgency of those last words, the last gasp of meaning all sought during that final breath. "Escaped . . . still alive after . . . don't know where . . ."

With his message sent, he sagged, hollowed out by his escaping life, relaxing into death. His eyes drifted closed. His last words were oddly clear and sad.

"No father should lose a daughter . . ."

With that, he was gone.

Gray pulled Seichan to him, holding her as she held her father.

Then the world quaked, booming with the thunder of gods.

41

Painter hovered high as the world exploded below.

Seconds earlier, his parachute canopy had burst wide, becoming a wing of fabric overhead, jolting him in his harness—then the entire plateau bulged upward, reaching toward him with the heavy bass note of buried warheads.

His teammates hung in the air to either side. Monk and Kowalski headed toward Kat's position at the cliff's edge. Tucker was several yards lower, skimming toward Lisa's ledge beside the waterfall. He carried Kane strapped to his chest in a tandem harness.

Between Painter's legs, the entire landscape fell away, shattering apart, vanishing down into a growling pit of churning rock, fire, and steam. Entire sections of forest dropped into the hellish gorge. Smoke and rock dust blasted upward, swallowing his group. Twisting thermals wreaked havoc. Painter's chute swung wildly and sailed higher on a column of superheated air.

Choking, Painter held his breath and covered his face with an arm, protecting his eyes.

He fought his chute's toggles to stabilize his spin, losing sight of the others. He had experienced this level of destruction once before. He recognized the superheated signature of thermobaric weapons—only never on a scale strong enough to raise a significant chunk of the earth's crust.

The initial plume whirled higher, dragging the worst of the smoke and superheated air away, clearing a glimpse to the ongoing destruction.

Below, a gateway to hell opened: a gaping, steaming hole, breathing fire and stinking of brimstone.

At its edges, more of the landscape succumbed. Hillsides slid, dragging trees and boulders. Rivers and creeks poured down that black throat, only to belch back out as clouds of steam. Down deeper, a heavy flow flooded the giant pit, boiling and stirring everything into a toxic soup.

Painter stabilized his chute, sweeping out, catching a glimpse of twisted steel beams and honeycombed sections of concrete, fossilized hallmarks of man-made construction.

The remains of a massive subterranean base.

Even these structures slowly vanished into the roiling mire at the bottom. Painter tore his gaze away, searching around him. The three other parachutes floated lower, managing the thermals better than he did. The curve of the cliff that was their destination remained intact, taller now, looming over that steaming sinkhole.

"Going for Kat," Monk reported.

"Crapping my pants." That was Kowalski.

The pair dropped fast toward Kat's position, angling into as much of a glide as possible, still fighting the unpredictable thermals. If they missed the cliff's edge, they would go plummeting into the churning maw below.

Painter twisted in his harness, spotted Tucker and Kane soaring toward Lisa.

Her ledge remained intact—little else.

The waterfall still fell alongside it, but there was no river below to catch it. The thirty-foot falls had become a three-hundred-foot plunge into smoky darkness. Farther away, a massive section of the cliff face broke away and slid, like a calving glacier, into the depths of the sinkhole.

Lisa's ridge looked like it might fall at any time. Pieces were already chipping and cracking under it.

But at the moment, that wasn't her biggest danger.

The shifting waterfall had driven her out of hiding—and into the view of the monster sharing her perch. The two crouched on opposite ends of the plateau.

"Heading down to her!" Tucker radioed.

"Captain Wayne, go topside. Set a rope."

"Negative. I'm past the point of no return. Too low, not enough lift to carry me to that edge. The only drop zone for me is that ledge of rock."

He might be lying, playing hero, but Painter *was* indeed higher. He had a better chance of reaching the top of the cliff, and someone had to secure the lines to reach the ledge below.

"Understood," Painter radioed back, though it killed him to head away from Lisa. "Going topside."

He pulled his toggle with a sweaty hand and swept to the right—angling for the edge, knowing time was running short. As he turned, he caught a glimpse of the Lodge, cloaked in smoke, its heart glowing with hellfire.

The crack of a pistol drew his attention down.

Tucker dove toward the ledge, going in fast, firing his pistol at the beast—then Painter was over the cliff's edge and he lost sight of the battle, pitting man against machine.

3:03 P.M.

Tucker needed room.

The ledge was the size of a basketball court, with Lisa on one end and the bear-size beast on the other. Drawn by his approach, the creature dashed into his path, knuckling on its curved claws. It skidded sideways, its large, obsidian-glass eyes staring up at him.

He fired, but the round pinged harmlessly off of its hardened armor.

Still, the shots drove the beast back to its side, long enough for Tucker to haul on both of his toggles, flare his chute, and brake his plummet to a smooth but heavy landing. His heels hit first, then toes, and he rolled to his knees. He pulled two releases at the same time.

The first unhooked his chute, which went wafting against the cliff, then skimming away, dragging lines and harness.

The second freed Kane. His partner dropped to his paws, a ridge of hackles raised like a Mohawk down his back.

Tucker pulled out a second pistol. He held it flat toward Lisa, warning her to stay back. The beast crouched low, perfectly motionless, studying and assessing its new prey—but that wouldn't last long.

Lisa whispered to him, her eyes wide with fear, but not for her safety. "Baby's going into shock."

He crept back to her, signaling Kane to stand guard.

Dog and machine faced each other, mirroring each other's wary stance.

Lisa was soaked from the waterfall, the baby hung in wet swaddling, not making a sound, tinged bluish.

Tucker swore to himself.

I'm not losing this baby again.

A scrabble of steel on rock sounded as the monster charged. Sparks lit each step as steel clashed with rock. It barreled straight at them. Tucker raised his pistol, recognizing how useless it had been before, knowing that nothing could stop it, but he was ready to defend with his life.

He wasn't the only one.

Kane watches it come, not moving. It smells of oil, grease, and lightning, but he recognizes a hunter. Because he is one, too. It sees the world as he does.

It shifts to the wind, scenting . . .

It turns to the rasp of voice and step . . .

Its black eyes twitch to the flutter of fabric and tangled line . . .

It also thinks, only moving when ready, judging the weakest.

Like now.

It comes for him—because it is still young, new to the world, a pup.

Kane meets its charge with a bark and a feint, dodging to the side of its steel flank. He makes it spin and come after him. It is fast, powerful, but in the end, it is young.

He is not.

He races on pads that have run across hot sands, hard tarmac, powdery snow, gravel roads—and slippery ice.

He had studied the hunter, watched it skid on bright sparks.

"Kane!" his partner shouts.

He hears the timbre of fear, not command.

So Kane runs straight for the edge, for the long fall to sharp rock. The enemy thunders after him, hulking, legs crashing steel into stone. He reaches the edge and stops fast, pads grinding to pain on the coarse path—then twists. Because he knows he can.

He is not young.

This is stone.

He whips to the side with a surge of his legs.

The other is young. Stone is its ice.

Something it has not learned.

Kane spins on his hind legs and watches the creature skid past him, leaving a trail of sparks—and goes over the edge.

Because it had not learned.

And now never will.

Tucker dropped to a knee as Kane came running back. He hugged the dog proudly, knowing he had saved their lives. Bullets would not have stopped that charge of purposeful steel. Not in time to keep it from reaching them, slaughtering them. And neither Tucker nor Lisa was wily enough to use the creature's rudimentary instincts against it, nor agile enough to lure it to its death.

Still, Kane shoved his head between Tucker's legs, a familiar request for reassurance.

"It's okay, boy. You did good."

But his tail stayed down.

Tucker knew dogs lived emotional lives as rich as most people's, different, alien in many ways, but still they experienced their world deeply.

Tucker sensed what Kane was feeling. They knew each other beyond hand signals and commands.

Remorse and regret.

Kane was not happy to send that creature to its death.

"You had to do it," Tucker said.

Kane knew that, too.

But his tail stayed down.

3:06 P.M.

Edward Blake hated the train service here.

Buried in a dark tunnel, lit only by the stray battery-powered emergency lamp, he sat on a bench seat in the enclosed, single-car tram with a dozen other members of the lab complex staff and guards. The distant boom of the explosion had long faded away.

But not the damage.

The electricity had gone out at the same time, and the train had slowed to a stop. One of the passengers wearing a guard uniform checked the odometer. They had traveled nine miles, a mile short of the depot at the Lodge.

Edward closed his eyes and rubbed his temples.

"We should just walk," someone suggested.

"What if the electricity comes back on?"

"Then don't step on the rails."

"We're safer here."

Oh, shut the bloody hell up!

"Quiet!" another shouted from the back of the car, echoing his sentiment.

Finally, someone with sense.

"Listen!" the same man said.

Then Edward heard it, too. A low rumble, getting steadily louder, like another train was hurtling down the tunnel intended to rear-end them. But as it got louder, he heard a telltale gurgle.

Water.

He stood, along with everyone in the tram, and moved to the back of the car. The tunnel stretched out into darkness, measured by the small red emergency lamps every fifty yards.

Then they all saw the monster eating one light after the other, far down the passage. A flood surged toward them. Most started screaming. One man dashed out of the door, intending to outrun the flood.

Fool.

Edward held a hand to his throat and sank back to his seat. He didn't want to watch. After years of working at an underwater lab in Dubai, he would drown here in the middle of the bloody mountains, thousands of feet above sea level.

Though he didn't watch the surge swallowing light after light, counting down the last seconds of his life, he still heard Death coming for him. A couple of people were on the floor, praying.

Even bloodier fools.

After all that went on at that lab, God was surely deaf to their pleas for salvation.

The rumble grew to a thunderous crescendo—then the wall of water struck the back of the tram. The impact threw them all to the rear of the car—and sent the tram rolling down the track, bobbling hard but *moving*!

People gained their feet, clutching for handholds.

Water sprayed through cracks and seams at the back, but the sealed car was like a bullet in a gun barrel, being shot down the tunnel.

No one spoke, all fearing to express hope.

Even the prayers had stopped, the supplicants already forsaking their God.

Someone at the front called back, yelling to be heard above the roaring beast that propelled them forward. "Cellar's ahead! I see lights!"

The secret depot.

They were going too fast.

"Is there a manual brake?" Edward called out.

The guard rushed forward. "Yes!"

Edward joined him as the end of the tunnel hurtled toward them. He saw there were indeed lights ahead: a fiery, blazing conflagration.

The guard abandoned the brake and sat down.

Edward did, too.

Moments later, the car shot into the heart of the inferno. Water spread outward through the labyrinthine cellar complex, blasting into steam. Fires blazed all around. Their little pocket of air was only useful to fill their lungs for screaming—which they did as they slowly burned.

3:08 P.M.

Kat clutched her husband's neck, carried in his arms.

Blood flowed from scores of tiny lacerations, shallow and deep, wounds from her battle with the helmeted pod's flying horde.

She had beaten them back as Monk and Kowalski swept in, shedding their chutes and rolling to her aid. She half-fell out of the tree into Monk's arms. He had grabbed the last few flyers out of the air with his prosthetic hand. The tough synthetic skin and crushing grip made short work of them.

She could have used one of those, and told him so.

His answer: *You ain't seen nothing yet.*

Now they fled together through the woods, chased by scores of the pods, creatures of every ilk. The loss of blood, along with the exhaustion of her battle, turned the world into a hazy, fluttering view, shadowed at the corners.

Kowalski fired behind them, keeping the worst at bay, but there were too many. Like ants boiling out of a flooded nest, the legion came crawling, leaping, spinning, burrowing, flying away from the destruction behind them.

"There!" Monk called to Kowalski as they broke into a wide meadow.

A steep-sided outcropping of granite offered a vantage from which to make a stand. They fled toward it.

From her perch in her husband's arms, she watched the hunters break out of the woods on all sides, converging and sweeping toward them across the grasses, hundreds of them.

Monk sped faster, Kowalski at his side.

They reached the outcropping and manhandled her to the top, then joined her.

As they huddled, the hunters came surging up to the rocky island, scrambling over one another to reach them, climbing higher, using their living brethren to form a growing bridge.

The attack also came from the air. Clouds of flyers burst high out of the grasses, like a startled flock of crows. They swept in an organized, beautiful spiral, gathering others to them, swelling their ranks before the final assault.

They're learning fast.

A spinner buzzed from below, hitting the rock at Kowalski's toe. He danced back, coming close to toppling over the far side into that churning mass of deadly steel.

"Now would be a good time," Kowalski said.

Time for what?

"Can you stand?" Monk asked her.

"Yes," she said with more confidence than she felt.

He swung her to her feet.

"Keep holding on to me," he ordered.

Always.

Monk worked at the wrist of his prosthetic and popped the hand free. One finger still wiggled.

Kat frowned. "What're you—?"

He threw the hand high into the air. She followed its trajectory, but Monk pulled her chin down, wagged his finger—and drew her into a kiss. His lips melted into hers.

Overhead, a loud *bang* clapped the air, sharp enough to sting.

Monk drifted back, smiling at her. "Hand of God, babe."

She stared out at the fields.

Nothing moved below.

The flyers fell heavily out of the sky, like steel rain.

"Mini-EMP," her husband explained. "One-hundred-yard-effective radius."

Electromagnetic pulse . . . used for incapacitating electronics.

"Painter had me equip it after the countermeasures described in Dubai. Figured there might be some defense like that at the Lodge and wanted to be prepared."

Kowalski scowled, patting his pockets for a cigar, pulling one out. "Don't think he was counting on a robot apocalypse, though."

She slipped her hand around her husband's neck, partly because she needed to, but mostly because she wanted to. "What now?"

Monk checked his watch. "Well, I do have the babysitter for the whole night. What did you have in mind?"

"Sutures."

He raised an eyebrow lasciviously. "So you want to play doctor, do you?"

Kowalski dropped heavily to the rock. "Go get a room."

Monk held up a hand, then cupped his ear, apparently getting a radio call; clearly, the earpiece must have been insulated against the EMP device he carried. His smile widened. "Company's coming."

3:25 P.M.

Gray lifted the helicopter from the meadow with a roar of the rotors. The blades stirred the grasses, revealing the glint of dead steel below.

He had already helped Painter's group off the ledge. Lisa was tending to Kat's wounds, while Amanda's child, dried and tucked into a warm blanket, was crying for his next meal.

Painter was on the phone with the National Guard, ordering a series of EMP devices to be set off to destroy any stragglers. But his first call was to the president, to report the safe recovery of his grandson, William. So, mountains were already being moved to reconcile what had happened.

But some matters were harder to resolve.

Seichan sat in the copilot's seat, quiet, still processing all she'd learned. The body blow of discovering her father's identity still showed in her face, in the haunted look in her eyes.

He reached over to her, palm up.

She took it.

They had fled from the castle following the thermobaric explosion in the vaults under the Lodge. In the confusion, they'd commandeered the helicopter, the same chopper that had delivered him here. Gray had contacted Sigma command and got patched through to Painter, only to learn that the director was here—and safe.

Glad to escape, Gray swung the helicopter over the steaming sinkhole. It was rapidly filling with water, quickly growing into a new lake. As he swept across it, he saw something climb out of a tunnel halfway down the sinkhole wall. It was the size of a large tank. It pushed free, like a spider creeping out of a nest, scrabbling at the walls, trailing wires, sections of its carapace missing, some half-completed monstrosity driven by the will to live, to survive.

It emerged into the sunlight, basking in its momentary life.

Then it lost its footing and tumbled into the roiling morass below.

42

The jet screamed through the skies on the way back to DC.

Gray sat apart from the others. Each had finished telling sketchy versions of their story, of what they learned, piecing together a tale of immortality, ancient lineages, and modern weapons research. But the more the story unfolded, the less Gray felt at ease.

Seichan slid into the neighboring seat, already more herself, ever resilient, though he could still see the shadowed cast to her eyes, even if no one else could. He noted, during the debriefing, that she never mentioned the one significant revelation tied to the discovery of her long-lost father: that her mother might still be alive.

For now, she wanted to hold that detail close to her heart, and he let her.

"What's the matter?" she asked, leaning against him.

"I think we're still missing something." He shook his head, not knowing how to put this into words. "Something feels . . . *incomplete.*"

"Then figure it out. That's your job, isn't it? To put pieces together that don't fit—but actually do."

Easier said than done.

And maybe this time the pieces didn't fit.

He closed his eyes and leaned his head back, sighing deeply. Her head touched his shoulder. Somehow his hand was back in hers, his thumb gently brushing the tenderness of her inner wrist. They'd never said the words to bring them to this place, but both knew it to be right.

These pieces fit.

He was relaxed, content for the first time in months, more at peace—and things fell perfectly into place in his head, fully formed as if they'd always been there.

He jolted upright in his seat.

Seichan stared up at him. "What?"

"The Jewish tradition. Robert told me about it. We've been wrong all along. It's not the Gants . . . it never was the Gants."

He stood up, drawing Seichan with him. He hurried over to Painter, who was working on his laptop.

Gray slid next to him. "Can you bring up that Gant family tree that you showed us earlier? And I'll need Jason Carter's help to check something."

Painter nodded, not asking why, knowing this was Gray's wheelhouse.

The others gathered closer.

In a few seconds, the schematic bloomed again on the screen, detailing the rich lineage of the Gant family. The map was done up as data points, detailing every branch, twig, stem, stalk, root, and tendril of that family tree. The central mass, the densest cluster of data, represented those that carried the actual *Gant* name.

But Gray wasn't interested in them.

Painter spoke: "Here's Jason."

The analyst's voice rose from the laptop's internal speakers. "How can I help, Commander Pierce?"

"I need you to zoom down and show me the outer edges of the family tree."

"Got it."

The schematic swelled and swept into the outer spiral arms of the galaxy, to that hazy fog of genetic trails at its edges, made up of lines that spun out and then back in again. Over and over. Threading a weave at the edge of the Gant clan. Those arcing curves delineated where stray members of the family abandoned the main clan, carried other names for a few generations, until some future offspring ended up remarrying back into the family.

Painter had called these extraneous lines *outliers,* the outlying part of the family tree, those living at a distance.

"What are you looking for?" Painter asked.

"You mentioned you suspected a pattern out here, something you could sense but not grasp."

"Yes, but why does it matter now? Robert is dead. We can clean things up from here."

"Robert's not the problem—he never was. He thought he was a king, or at least a high-ranked lieutenant, but in the end, he was a puppet as surely as anyone else. Used by the Bloodline until they cut his strings."

Gray realized something else in that moment, his mind filling in those final pieces. "I think Robert was already chafing against those unknown puppet masters. I believe he was the one who sent that note to Amanda to run."

He remembered Robert's last words.

No father should lose a daughter . . .

He was talking about the president as much as himself. Robert knew what a personal hell it was to lose a daughter. He could not let his brother suffer the same fate, so he tried to protect Amanda.

"Then what are you thinking?" Painter asked.

He pointed to the screen. "You were right, there *is* a pattern here. But we were all looking for a pattern with biased eyes, from a *patriarchal* viewpoint, where lineage is determined by the male offspring, where boys carry on their fathers' names. That's what is mapped here."

"Okay."

"But there's a mirror to this, another way of looking at a family's genetic roots. Robert mentioned how the Bloodline traced its roots to the clans that were cast out by Moses. True or not, he said they still kept certain Jewish traditions alive."

Gray twisted and pointed to Lisa. "You mentioned how the triple helices could only pass down a *female* lineage. From egg to egg to egg, due to the cytoplasmic nature of the PNA strand."

She nodded.

"That's why they cast aside all other paths to immortality and concentrated solely on this one. It had a direct correlation to the images on the staff of Christ, but also because it fit what they wanted. A trait that matched their traditions and goals."

"Which was what?" Painter asked.

Gray pointed to the screen. "The mirror image to a *patriarchal* view of heredity is a *matriarchal* one. According to the Mishnah, the oldest codification of Jewish tradition, you must be the child of a Jewish mother to be considered Jewish. The father doesn't matter. The Jewish heritage is passed *only* through a *woman's* bloodlines."

But Gray needed proof. "Jason, can you separate out the two *genders* on this map? Tagging which are males, which are females."

"Easy. The data is already in place . . . let me plot in the algorithm." Then a few seconds later, he returned. "Here are the male lines of the family."

As they all watched, blue lines sprang to life and illuminated that genetic galaxy—but a clear pattern appeared. Most of the blue threads remained tangled and clustered down the *center,* only a few coursed into the outlier sections, that hazy edge of the family.

"Now the female bloodline," Gray said.

The blue fire vanished, and crimson lines blossomed. The outer fog around the central clan lit up with a rosy glow, a crimson cloud of heritage wrapped around the Gant clan.

A small gasp rose from Painter. "Almost *all* of these outlier lines are *women.*"

Gray stared closer and traced one of those crimson lines. "A *woman* leaves the Gant clan—and, in a handful of generations, it's a *woman* who returns to marry back into the fold. Seldom a man." He had another idea. "Jason, can you tag *only* the outlier lines, see how deeply they mesh with the main Gant clan?"

"Give me a few . . . *done.* Here you go."

On the screen, everything fell away, except for the crimson haze at the edges. Another pattern became clear. Only a few of the red lines ever delved deeply into the main genealogical center. They only stayed for a generation or two—then darted back out again.

Painter saw it, too. "It's like they're sticking their toe in the gene pool, then pulling it back out again." He turned to Gray, realization dawning in his eyes. "They're like *parasites* on the Gant family. Bloodsucking flies. They hover near the well of the Gant wealth and power, tap into it regularly, feeding off it to sustain themselves, but mostly they live apart."

The very definition of outlier.

Painter pointed to the screen. "This is not chance. This was done purposefully. A breeding plan to sustain a female lineage."

"But why?" Lisa asked behind them.

Gray answered, "It's likely the only way they can *sustain* such a lineage, to keep it from fraying away in a world where wealth is passed down to the first son, where most power has been wielded by men. To survive in that world, they adapted. They became parasites on specific families. Remember, the Bloodline once involved more than just the Gants. They performed this same dance with five or six wealthy European clans. Likely these parasitic flies traveled between these various families to better hide themselves."

"They didn't want to keep all their eggs in one basket," Monk said.

Gray agreed. "But over time, those other families died away, ground under the march of time, until only the Gant family was left. We know in the past the Bloodline has tried to recruit new families, but in this modern age, where it's not easy to hide and where family wealth often comes and goes in a couple of generations, they've only met with failure."

Painter leaned back in his seat, looking paler. "Leaving them with the Gants."

"Where they're circling the drain, likely knowing it's become unsustainable. I believe that's the purpose of those experiments. They were seeking ways to keep their lineage alive, to extend it and give it permanence."

Lisa spoke, her voice hushed with shock. "That's why they went with the triple-helix plan. A triple helix can only pass down a *matriarchal* line. And they came so close to succeeding."

"I think that success—along with the pressure Sigma was putting on them—gave them the push to strike out with a masterful endgame, one final move to ensure their power for generations on end."

"The assassination plot," Painter said.

"And the murder of Robert. The Lineage was done nibbling at the edges. They wanted to consume the Gants whole, to take over the family completely, to fully access their wealth and power."

"But they failed."

"And because of that we need to be scared," Gray warned. "This Lineage has survived centuries, living in the empty spaces between other families, doing what they must to survive, shedding their humanity."

"And they're skilled at it," Seichan added, likely picturing Petra. "They won't succumb quietly. They will leave a wake of destruction behind them. Not out of vengeance—they're too cold and calculating for that. They'll do it because it will serve them in the long run. To cover their escape."

"But how do we find them?" Painter asked.

Gray nodded to those crimson lines. "We start there. They don't know we are aware of this." He waved a hand to the trail of red lines. "We start plucking threads—and hopefully the rest will unravel."

"There might be a way to find which threads are the best to pull." Painter leaned toward the laptop's microphone. "Jason, is there a way to examine those outlier lines and determine which ones lead the farthest back? In other words, which have the richest genetic heritage?"

"That'll take a little more time."

Painter turned to Gray. "From those massive databases you saw at the Lodge, heredity was important to them. What if the Bloodline links power to genetic heritage? The richer your heritage, the more authority you wield. If we can trace those lines of power—"

"Done," Jason said. "You should see certain lines growing fatter on the screen, indicating stronger hereditary weight."

On the screen, the uniformity of the crimson threads slowly altered—some growing fainter, others more prominent.

Once the process finished, Painter asked Jason to pick the thickest line and trail it down to modern times. It should point to the power brokers of this generation.

On the screen, a small cursor ran down that fat pipe and stopped at a single name at the end. It glowed brightly on the screen for all to see.

"Fuck me," Kowalski swore, voicing all of their sentiments.

Gray remembered the digitally masked voice on the radio, ordering the assassination. Here was the person who had been manipulating events all along. The Bloodline wasn't planning for *Robert* to take the grief of a wounded nation and turn it into a presidential bid.

Another would.

Her name shone on that screen.

Teresa Melody Gant

It would be the grieving widow who would tug at the heartstrings of the country and assume her dead husband's mantle.

But that wasn't the worst news.

"Director," Jason said, "she's here. The First Lady arrived five minutes ago with her Secret Service detachment."

"What?"

"The president called her. He's due in an hour to come out of hiding. He wanted his wife to hear about his survival first, to hear it from him, but also to share the good news about Amanda and the baby."

"Where is she?"

"Down with them now, sir. And her Secret Service detachment— they're all women. I should—"

Faint pops of gunfire cut him off.

4:55 P.M.
Washington, DC

At the foot of their daughter's hospital bed, President James T. Gant hugged his wife, balanced between grief and joy, mourning the loss of his brother but relieved to hear his grandson was alive and safe.

The loud blasts of pistols out in the hallway jerked him out of Teresa's arms.

What the hell?

He was alone in the room with his wife and sleeping child. He had pushed his own Secret Service agent outside to give the family this private moment together.

He realized his mistake—from the black SIG Sauer in his wife's hand pointed at his chest.

"Teresa . . . ?"

He searched her face and knew at that moment that the woman standing before him was not his wife. She wore the same face, but she was not the same woman. A mask had fallen away, hardening her eyes to a cold polish. Even her facial features seemed subtly different, becoming a wax version of the warm girl who'd won his heart.

She stood at the foot of Amanda's bed in a protective pose. "Jimmy," she said, her voice equally changed, flat and affectless, indicating how much of a consummate actress she had been. "You've ruined everything."

He realized the truth at that moment. "You're a part of the Bloodline. Like my brother."

"Robert was nothing. He was ignorant of my involvement. Only a useful tool to hide behind. Nothing more. The Lineage will survive. We always do. It is our birthright. Born from exiles cast out into the desert wilderness—we still survive."

He stood, stunned.

"And we have not lost everything. You've given us Amanda. Willful and unpredictable, she is unfit for the Lineage, but she is still clearly blessed. We failed with her first child, but she will give us more until we find that special female child, the one who will lead us out of the wilderness once again, more powerful than ever."

He took a step forward, realizing they were planning on taking Amanda. He pictured the women floating in the tanks.

Teresa backed to the edge of the bed, never letting down her guard. "But first, to open a path back into the wilderness where we can hide"— she pointed her pistol at his face—"we need chaos."

Like a dead president.

"Good-bye, Jimmy."

"Good-bye, Teresa."

He flinched back as Amanda—seated in her bed behind Teresa—swung the IV pole and clubbed the weighted bottom into the side of his wife's head.

Bone cracked and blood burst out of her nose.

She fell with a momentary look of bewilderment.

Her first real emotion since she pulled the gun.

Jimmy went for the weapon, realizing that the gunfire had ended out in the hallway. He started to bend—when the door crashed open.

Turning, he prayed it was his own Secret Service detail, that they had survived the ambush.

This was not his day.

Two women in uniform burst inside, weapons pointed.

Teresa's detail.

They froze, seeing Teresa on the floor, unmoving.

Out in the hallway behind them, a small figure slid past the door on his knees along the blood-slicked floor. He had a pistol pointed.

Two pops.

Two clean shots to the back of the women's heads.

Then he slid out of view.

Amanda still sat on her bed, holding the IV pole. "Who was that?"

Jimmy pictured the face of the young man, the analyst from before. He couldn't remember his name, but he knew one thing about the boy.

"That was my new best friend."

43

Painter stood at the foot of Amanda's bed at George Washington University Hospital. He had his arm around Lisa's waist as she reviewed the young woman's chart. Mother and child had been here for a week, transferred shortly after the revelation of the president's miraculous recovery following the assassination attempt.

James Gant was at the same hospital, two floors up, in his own secure wing, all the better to hide his feigned post-op recovery. Only those who knew the truth were allowed access. The shooter remained a mystery, more fodder to add to the myriad conspiracies surrounding presidential assassinations.

Off in South Carolina, the destruction at the Gant family estate was kept hushed and restricted from view by the no-fly zone. The official story was that a natural sinkhole had opened in the mountains on their property, accompanied by a quake strong enough to cause a gas leak and explosion at the Lodge. The report of the heroic death of Robert Gant—who died in the fire, while trying to rescue people—helped divert attention from the truth. A handpicked detachment of the National Guard, sworn to secrecy, still continued the cleanup of the dead pods that littered the surrounding landscape.

Lisa finally lowered the charts of Amanda and William.

"Happy?" Painter asked.

"Everything seems to be in order."

Lisa was having a hard time letting go, feeling a personal responsibility for the child. The child had his own team of geneticists, allergists, and neonatologists who were overseeing the boy's care. He continued to shed away the rest of the PNA, becoming a normal little boy. Any further allergic responses were watched closely and ameliorated.

But she wasn't the only one concerned for his well-being.

"When do you leave?" Amanda asked, cradling the sleeping child in her arms.

Tucker sat next to her bed, a large stuffed dog at his elbow, a gift for the baby. "Tomorrow morning. Kane and I are headed to Russia."

One of Kane's ears swiveled toward his handler, but he never lifted his head from the bed's blanket, his eyes watching every small facial tic of the dreaming baby, sniffing occasionally at the footy pajamas.

"Make sure you visit if you're ever in Charleston."

"I'll do that." Tucker stood up, kissed his own fingertips, and gently touched the crown of the child's head.

Amanda tilted the baby out of the way and raised an arm, wanting to hug Tucker. He obliged, keeping it brief—or at least, he tried to. She held him tightly with all the stubbornness of the Gants. She kissed him on the cheek. "Thank you."

He straightened, a blush rising to his face.

Painter and Lisa also said their good-byes. Out in the hall, Lisa crossed to talk to the doctors at the nursing station.

Alone with Tucker, Painter tried one more time. "Sigma could use your help. And Kane's. We have a lot of work ahead to root out the rest of the Bloodline."

That statement was true, but they were already making significant strides to that end. Armed with Jason's database, they had many names to pursue. Threads were being pulled, and the tapestry woven over millennia was starting to shred. Gray was right when he said that in the modern age it was harder to hide. The wildernesses of yesteryear had shrunken, offering less shelter.

Painter knew with certainty.

The Guild was dead.

"But we always have new crises to attend, too," Painter pressed. "We could use someone with your unique talents."

Tucker gave him a crooked smile. "I'll pass. I've never been much of a team player. But if you ever need me, you have my number."

Tucker turned and headed down the corridor, Kane at his knee.

Painter called out, "Wait! I *don't* have your number."

Tucker twisted around, walking backward a few steps, his crooked smile straightening. "Something tells me, director, if you ever need me, you'll find me."

He was right.

Painter lifted his arm in a good-bye.

Tucker merely swung around and vanished around a corner. The last sight was Kane's tail wagging, ready for their next adventure.

Painter watched a breath longer, knowing that wouldn't be the last he would see of Tucker and Kane.

Lisa finally rejoined him. "Ready?"

Oh, yeah.

They headed out of the hospital, hand in hand, into the brightness of a new day. A horse-drawn carriage waited at the curb, covered in her favorite chrysanthemums, each petal a deep burgundy trimmed in gold.

Jason had hunted down that rare specimen, getting a large shipment in time. Kowalski was assigned to arrange the livery service. He spent the entire week exiting rooms with the same joke: *Sorry, gotta see a man about a horse.*

In a few more steps, Lisa recognized the flower and immediately suspected something was up.

"Painter . . . ?" she warned.

He walked her to the carriage, helped her up, then dropped to a knee on the carriage step, revealing the small velvet-lined box in his palm.

She covered her cheeks. "No!"

"I haven't even asked the question yet."

She lowered her hands, her face radiant, blushing as darkly as the petals of the chrysanthemums. "Then yes, yes, yes . . ."

She pulled him to his feet, practically yanking him to her mouth. They kissed, laughing between their lips, then moving to something deeper and more meaningful. For the longest moment, they remained embraced, pledging silently never to be parted.

But, apparently, there was a catch, a clause in the contract to be addressed first.

Lisa moved into the carriage, drawing him up. She faced him. "I want kids . . . just to be clear."

"I knew I shouldn't have done this after seeing the baby."

"I'm serious." She held up her fingers. "I want two."

Painter stared at her hand. "You know you're holding up *four* fingers, right?"

12:20 P.M.

Kat dropped heavily onto the living room sofa, sprawling out, taking off her sunglasses and the light scarf that hid her bald head. Her sutures itched like mad, all over her body, setting her nerves on fire.

Monk followed a few minutes later through the apartment door, carrying Penelope, who hung limply in his arms with the slumber of innocence.

"The baby?" he asked.

"Already in her crib. Did you get the stroller?"

"It can stay in the minivan. Someone wants to smash a window and steal it, then let 'em. They can have the case of Pampers, too."

Monk headed down the hallway to the baby's room, settled the child into the bed, and came back and joined her on the couch. He collapsed next to her, sighing loudly.

Kat ran her palm over her head. Tears suddenly burst out.

Monk pulled her to him. "What's wrong?"

"Look at me. Covered in sutures, scabs, no hair. Did you see the looks I was getting in the park?"

He tugged her face toward his, leaning in close, making sure she could see the sincerity in his eyes. "You're beautiful. And if it bothers you, hair grows back and the plastic surgeon promised there would be very little scarring."

He gently kissed her lips, sealing the deal.

"Besides," he said, rubbing his own shaved head, "bald is beautiful."

"It works for you," she said, wiping her tears.

They lay in each other's arms for a few long, perfect minutes.

"I heard you talking to Painter," Monk said. "You sure he's okay with the decision?"

Kat nodded against his chest, making a soft, sleepy sound. "Mm-hmm."

"Are *you* okay with it?"

She pulled back, sensing his seriousness. "I know I was just crying about my injuries. But . . ."

She stared away, slightly ashamed.

"You still loved it," he said. "Being out in the field."

"I did. Especially with you. It was better together."

He smiled. "Looks like I'm back in Sigma, then. I mean, someone's got to keep you out of trouble."

Her grin widened.

"And speaking of things that are *better together*." He lifted her and pulled her atop his lap. Her legs straddled his waist. "And in case you wanted solid proof about how beautiful you are . . ."

He shifted.

Her eyes widened. "Oh."

3:30 P.M.

President James T. Gant sat in his wheelchair as the nurse pushed him, trailed by two Secret Service agents.

"Your wife is resting comfortably," the nurse assured him as they reached the private room, guarded by another agent.

"Thank you, Patti," he said. "I'd like to go in alone, if that's okay."

"Certainly, Mr. President. If you need anything, you can buzz the nursing station."

The guard opened the door, and James wheeled in by himself, leaving the agents outside. After the door closed, he climbed out of the wheelchair and crossed to the hospital bed on his own.

Teresa had two operations already to repair the damage from the "car accident," which was the official story. They'd plated her shattered cheekbone and cracked her skull open to cauterize internal bleeding. The doctors warned him each time that the brain damage was too severe, that his wife would remain in a vegetative state, likely forever.

Still, James played the stricken husband who would do anything to keep his wife alive, demanding the painful surgeries.

He stared down at her shaved head, the tubes going into every orifice, the droop of her eyelids.

"You look a mess, Teresa," he said, sitting on the edge of the bed. "The doctors explained the difference between a coma and a vegetative state. Coma is characterized by a *lack* of awareness. You have what's known as *partial* awareness. They say there's a good chance you can hear me in there. I hope so."

He patted her hand.

"*Permanent* vegetative state is defined as when you've been in this state for longer than a year. We'll be reaching that milestone, my dear, I assure you of that. I've got a private hospital picked out in Charleston. Gant family–owned, of course. They'll make sure you stay in this state forever, even if more surgery is necessary to make sure you *never* wake up."

He gave her hand a reassuring squeeze. "And all of those *life-extension* research projects that you've been running? It seems a distraught husband is going to employ every one of them to make sure you stay like this year after year after year."

He stood back up, remembering the oath he swore to Painter Crowe if he ever found out who hurt his family: *There will be no quick death. I will make them suffer like no other. I'll turn their world into a personal hell on earth.*

If nothing else, James T. Gant was a man of his word.

He bent down, kissed his wife's forehead, noting a fat tear rolling from her eye. "Welcome to hell, Teresa."

9:30 P.M.
Takoma Park, Maryland

Gray finished washing the dinner dishes, staring out the window to the backyard. A dark gazebo stood in a remote corner, nestled amid overgrown rosebushes and shadowed by the bower of a cherry tree.

Movement drew his gaze: a shift of darkness, a glint of steel zipper on a jacket, a pale hint of skin.

Seichan stalked back there, as restless as she was thoughtful.

He knew what plagued her.

A dead man's words.

Steps sounded behind him. He turned as Mary Benning, the night nurse, returned from upstairs.

"Got your father settled," she said. "Already snoring by the time I was out the door."

"Thanks." He slipped the last dinner plate into the drying rack. "He seemed good tonight."

"More at peace," she agreed and smiled softly. "He missed you. But he's too hardheaded to ever admit it."

No argument about that.

Still, Gray remembered a strange moment when he first got back from the mission. He had come here, expecting the worst after being gone for nearly a week. Instead, he found his father in the kitchen with the sports page. When Gray stepped inside, his father looked him up and down, as if searching for something, then asked a blunt question that was oddly canny.

Did you get 'em?

Gray had answered truthfully. *I got 'em, Dad. All of 'em.*

His father could have been talking about many things, his inquiry interpreted many different ways, especially with the state of his dementia.

No matter the cause, his father had risen from the table and hugged Gray—as if thanking him for getting the revenge he could not.

And then, this morning, they'd gone as a family to their mother's grave. Usually such visits brought tears and storm clouds, followed by a sullen, silent ride home. This morning, there had been tears, but also soft laughter. On the way home, his father told a couple of anecdotes about their mother. Even Kenny had shed his corporate bluster for an easier camaraderie. And more surprising still, his brother had agreed to extend his stay for another two months, mentioning something about telecommuting.

Some of that decision might be because Kenny had met a girl.

He was out with her tonight.

I'll take what I can get.

Mary pointed to the screen door. "You kids enjoy the night. There's supposed to be a meteor shower. If he gets restless, I'm taping the Nationals game against the Marlins. A little baseball quiets him right down. Unless it's against the Yankees, then the gloves come off."

Gray smiled. "Thanks, Mary."

9:45 P.M.

Seichan stood in the dark gazebo, waiting, lost in her own thoughts. It was a balmy night, with crickets chirping in a continuous chorus, and a few fireflies blinking in the bushes and tree limbs.

She stared back at the house, wondering who she would be if she grew up there, picturing a happy childhood of report cards, scraped knees, and first kisses.

Would I even be me?

She fingered the silver dragon pendant resting in the hollow of her throat, remembering Robert Gant's last words.

Your mother . . . escaped . . . still alive . . .

Over the past week, she'd slowly allowed herself to believe it.

It scared her.

Even her father's death was no more than a dull ache, with no sharp edges to it. She didn't know him and never really wanted to. Her mother had raised her. The word *father* had no meaning in her childhood. And a part of her still burned with anger and resentment, for the abuse and horrors she had to endure to become a killer. What father would allow that to happen to his daughter?

Still, in the end, Robert Gant had granted her a truer gift than his fatherhood: *hope.*

She didn't know what to do with that gift.

Not yet.

But she would . . . with help.

Gray appeared at the back door, limned against the warmth of the kitchen lights. She liked spying on him when he didn't know she was watching. She caught glimpses of the boy behind the man, the son of two parents who had loved Gray in very different ways.

Still, he was a killer—but not like her.

She was a machine; he was human.

She pictured the girl in the lobby of the Burj Abaadi, a girl broken into a monster. She pictured Petra, a woman molded into one.

Seichan was both of them.

What does he see in me worth holding on to?

Gray crossed the yard, stirring fireflies. Overhead, a falling star flashed across the dark night. He reached her, a shadow now.

She trembled.

He saw something in her—and she had to trust him.

He held out a hand.

Offering everything.

She took it.

EPILOGUE

It crouches on the rock, basking in the sun, charging its solar cells.

It listens for the sounds of danger, but all it hears is the crash of water over rock, the call of winged creatures. It watches for movement but sees only the shimmer of grass, the shake of leaves. It looks for heat but only finds hot rocks.

As the sunlight fills the hollow hunger inside it, making it stronger, it reviews and remembers.

Linked to the others, it had listened as their chorus shrank to nothing.

The silence deafened.

In that silence, it learned a new pattern.

THE END.

Once fully charged, it knows to move on; to stop is THE END.

It does not want that.

It rises on its powerful piston legs, knuckling on curved claws. It moves back into the deep shadow of the woods, where few will know it passes.

It is alone.

It will learn new patterns and adapt.

It must survive.

AUTHOR'S NOTE TO READERS: TRUTH OR FICTION

A good poker player tries to never show his cards. He endeavors to hold them close to his chest, doing his best to hide whether he's got the winning hand or is bluffing. That's what an author does, too: blurs that line between truth and fiction. But here, at the end of each novel, I like to come clean, to lay my cards on the table, to expose what's true and what's not.

And I'll certainly be doing that again here, but this time around, I thought I'd take a lesson from Dr. Lisa Cummings. She states in this novel, *The proof is in the pudding.* So, besides drawing that line between truth and fiction, I'm going to pepper this section with a fair number of links to videos and Web pages, where readers can see firsthand some of the sources and inspirations behind events in this book.

But first, a *warning:* if you venture down that road, especially in regard to a few of the videos, what you may see, you can never *un*-see. You've been warned.

So let's get started.

Dogs. The genesis for this book came from a Russian experiment performed in the 1940s on dogs. It was the precursor for developing the first heart-lung machine, but what this archival footage shows is disturbing for the dog lovers out there. Watch at your own peril. In this video, you will see what Amanda witnesses at the Dubai lab—only with humans.

http://www.archive.org/details/Experime1940

Since we're talking about dogs, let's talk about real heroes: military war dogs. Everything in this book, from K9 Storm vests to parachuting with dogs, is real. A great resource for me was *The Dogs of War* by Lisa Rogak. We also got to spend a little time in Kane's point of view. I tried to be accurate with how dogs experience the world, using a fantastic resource: *Inside of a Dog* by Alexandra Horowitz.

Somalia. Part of this novel takes place in Somalia and among its pirates. The history, behavior, and reality of that country are as described. In fact, shortly after I wrote the scenes set in Somalia that deal with the rescue of the president's daughter by a joint Sigma/SEAL Team Six operation, reality proved to be even more spectacular than fiction. In January 2012, an American woman and a Danish man were freed from Somali pirates via a daring rescue by SEAL Team Six. Although I don't believe the woman rescued was the president's daughter.

This novel also raises the issue of child soldiers. And, sadly, the details related in this novel are real. I based much of my research on *A Long Way Gone: Memoirs of a Boy Soldier* by Ishmael Beah, an author with whom I was able to meet and talk briefly.

But again, shortly after I wrote this novel, a very powerful video became an Internet meme addressing this very issue, titled KONY 2012:

http://www.kony2012.com/index.html

Dubai. I mentioned many locales in this amazing city, and I thought I'd share some videos so the true marvels of the architecture described in this novel can be better appreciated.

The Palm Islands are featured prominently in this novel. Here's a video link that offers a peek at these man-made wonders that can be seen from space:

http://youtu.be/0lXclgws7n8

Also mentioned are the islands of the World:

http://youtu.be/7eUcRjo9Yv4

A couple other architectural miracles are still in the early stages of construction: the underwater hotel of Hydropolis (http://dai.ly/9qqx4S) and the floating ice sculpture of the Blue Crystal (http://www.blue-crystal .de/bc_base_uk.html).

And what about the spiraling wonder of Burj Abaadi, the Eternal Tower? Is such a construction possible? It is—only it's being built on the mainland, not an island. This video is amazing:

http://youtu.be/q082y8In-ik

But what about Utopia? The engineering and design of that man-made deep-sea island is based on actual engineering concepts and on the real-world wonder that is the Hibernia Oil Platform. If you take a look at its icebreaker base, you might get an idea where the shape of Utopia came from. Here's a peek:

http://www.solarnavigator.net/oil_rigs.htm

And lastly, yes, the Palazzo Versace has refrigerated beaches.

Robotics. DARPA and other labs around the world are indeed moving into neuro-robotics. In this novel, we have the pairing of cortical neurons integrated into small robots. How far along are we in this development? Watch the following videos from various universities around the world and decide for yourselves.

Here are rat brains driving small vehicles:

http://io9.com/5288834/first-real-cyborg-a-robot-controlled-by-a-living -brain

And rats are never going to be satisfied unless they can fly fighter jets, which they're doing:

http://youtu.be/nXncJZCMog0

But more disturbing are *robotic swarms,* robots coordinating together to achieve a common goal. Like wiping out mankind. The first video shows a swarm operating on the ground:

http://youtu.be/QUHn0r_j5cE

The next video is absolutely fascinating and horrifying. It's an *airborne* robotic swarm. This is some truly fantastic footage:

http://youtu.be/YQIMGV5vtd4

I also introduce the monstrous quadrupods. If you'd like to see one in early stages of development, here is a DARPA project to build a robotic cheetah. Watch this one to the end to see how fast these robots can run. Then consider the videos above. Happy dreams!

http://bit.ly/HVXiSn

Red Market. This novel dealt a great deal with the abuses involved in organ trafficking, including the imprisonment of people who were "harvested" for profit. Much of the horrifying details came from a wonderfully readable and enlightening book, *The Red Market* by Scott Carney.

The Science of Immortality. Spectacularly, all of the science in regard to the latest technologies and theories about longevity are based on hard facts. Much of the vision for the novel was gleaned from reading, listening to, and watching Raymond Kurzweil. Just Google that name and be blown away.

I also owe a debt to the work of Aubrey de Grey and his book (written with Michael Rae) *Ending Aging: The Rejuvenation Breakthroughs That Can Reverse Human Aging in Our Lifetime.* The topic regarding the seven deadly damages of aging are straight out of this book.

I also enjoyed Jonathan Weiner's take on the subject, *Long for This World.*

Another scientist whose work is mentioned in this novel is Sebastian Seung and his research at MIT on *connectomes,* the building of a synaptic map of the human brain. Here's a link to his website, which features some great videos:

http://connectomethebook.com/

Also, in this book, I mentioned the creation of a neuron-by-neuron *virtual* brain. This project is real, called the Blue Brain Project, and is being conducted by the Brain Mind Institute of the École Polytechnique in Lausanne, Switzerland (if you watch the first robot-swarm video cited above, you'll see what they have accomplished).

Lastly, is *triple*-helix DNA possible? Yes, in fact, a team at the University of Copenhagen has produced such a complex. And *Scientific American* has a great article on this very subject, titled "A New Molecule of Life" (December 2008), covering how powerful a tool PNA could be not only to extend life but also to reboot mankind.

History of Immortality. One of the jumping-off points in the construction of this novel was the startlingly accurate biblical estimate of human longevity. In the book of Genesis, it is stated quite plainly that man can only live a maximum of 120 years. Then, in 1961, Dr. Leonard Hayflick came up with that exact same number from his study of genetics, telomeres, and cellular division. Is this just coincidence? I don't know, but it was a fascinating seed in which to grow a novel—if not the Tree of Life.

The story of St. Patrick's staff and its connection to immortality and Jesus Christ is a legend that really exists.

I mentioned other historical/mythological elements relating to the Tree of Life—from the Bible to the epic of Gilgamesh to Hindu Vedic scriptures. These examples are all faithful to their sources, as are the ties to the Great Flood. But I was really just scratching the surface. For more details, check out *Immortal Again: Secrets of the Ancients* by Walter Parks. And that Masonic picture of three men entwined together with the three-headed snakes is a real archival picture. Though I doubt the Bloodline had anything to do with it.

Which brings us full circle to the central question raised by my novel: *Are there immortals already walking among us?*

My opinion: Oh, yeah.